KT-549-813

Maureen Child writes for the Mills & Boon Desire line and can't imagine a better job. A seven-time finalist for the prestigious Romance Writers of America *RITA*® Award, Maureen is the author of more than one hundred romance novels. Her books regularly appear on bestseller lists and have won several awards, including a Prism Award, a National Readers' Choice Award, a Colorado Romance Writers Award of Excellence and a Golden Quill Award. She is a native Californian but has recently moved to the mountains of Utah.

Yahrah St. John became a writer at the age of twelve when she wrote her first novella after secretly reading a Mills & Boon romance. Throughout her teens, she penned a total of twenty novellas. Her love of the craft continued into adulthood. She's the proud author of thirty-nine books with Mills & Boon as well as her own indie works. When she's not at home crafting one of her spicy romances with compelling heroes and feisty heroines with a dash of family drama, she is gourmet cooking or travelling the globe seeking out her next adventure. For more info, visit www.yahrahstjohn.com or find her on Facebook, Instagram, Twitter, BookBub or Goodreads.

Also by Maureen Child

Red Hot Rancher
Jet Set Confessions
Temptation at Christmas
Six Nights of Seduction

Dynasties: The Carey Centre

The Ex Upstairs
Ways to Win an Ex

Also by Yahrah St. John

The Stewart Heirs

At the CEO's Pleasure
His Marriage Demand
Red Carpet Redemption
Secrets of a Fake Fiancée

Locketts of Tuxedo Park

Consequences of Passion
Blind Date with the Spare Heir

Discover more at millsandboon.co.uk

THE WRONG MR RIGHT

MAUREEN CHILD

HOLIDAY PLAYBOOK

YAHRAH ST. JOHN

MILLS & BOON

All rights reserved including the right of reproduction in whole or in part in any form. This edition is published by arrangement with Harlequin Books S.A.

This is a work of fiction. Names, characters, places, locations and incidents are purely fictional and bear no relationship to any real life individuals, living or dead, or to any actual places, business establishments, locations, events or incidents. Any resemblance is entirely coincidental.

This book is sold subject to the condition that it shall not, by way of trade or otherwise, be lent, resold, hired out or otherwise circulated without the prior consent of the publisher in any form of binding or cover other than that in which it is published and without a similar condition including this condition being imposed on the subsequent purchaser.

® and ™ are trademarks owned and used by the trademark owner and/or its licensee. Trademarks marked with ® are registered with the United Kingdom Patent Office and/or the Office for Harmonisation in the Internal Market and in other countries.

First Published in Great Britain 2021
by Mills & Boon, an imprint of HarperCollins*Publishers* Ltd
1 London Bridge Street, London, SE1 9GF

www.harpercollins.co.uk

HarperCollins*Publishers*
1st Floor, Watermarque Building,
Ringsend Road, Dublin 4, Ireland

The Wrong Mr Right © 2021 Maureen Child
Holiday Playbook © 2021 Yahrah Yisrael

ISBN: 978-0-263-28311-2

1121

MIX
Paper from
responsible sources
FSC™ C007454

This book is produced from independently certified FSC™ paper to ensure responsible forest management.

For more information visit: www.harpercollins.co.uk/green

Printed and Bound in Spain using 100% Renewable electricity
at CPI Black Print, Barcelona

THE WRONG MR RIGHT

MAUREEN CHILD

To the family and friends who circle the wagons when tragedy strikes. Whoever and wherever you are, know that sometimes a single phone call can help someone hang on.

One

Bennett Carey was a man on the edge.

And his mother was about to push him over.

“Mom,” he said, straining for the patience he was not known for, “I don’t need you to redecorate my house.”

Candace Carey sat opposite his desk and waved one hand at him. The sun caught the huge diamond on her wedding ring and sent flashes of light across his face.

“I’d hardly call it a house, Bennett,” she said, and glanced around. “And certainly not a *home.*” She shook her head. “Your office here at the company has more personality than that house. You’ve lived there five years and it still looks as though it’s a rental. Or vacant.”

Scowling at her, he muttered, “Not nearly vacant enough at the moment.”

Ever since his parents had begun what their children were referring to as “the Retirement Wars,” there was no telling what Candace would do next. And apparently, Bennett told himself, even in his office at the Carey Corporation headquarters, he wouldn't be safe from his mother's interference. He'd actually offered his assistant, David, a raise—if he could keep Bennett's mother out of his office. David declined.

Bennett couldn't even blame the man. Their father, Martin Carey, had promised his wife that he would retire, take the trips the two of them had always planned to make. But, Bennett told himself, Martin was incapable of walking away from the family corporation. Oh, his dad had meant to retire—he simply couldn't bring himself to turn his back on the family company. Though Bennett was the CEO now, Martin made sure that his son ran *nothing* without his input. So to show her husband how it felt to be deserted in favor of work, Candace had left her husband of nearly forty years and moved in with *Bennett*.

"The walls are beige, Bennett."

"I like beige."

"No one likes beige," his mother countered, lifting her chin, signaling her willingness to do battle. "It's a non-color. Only slightly better than white." She shivered a little. "You need color in your life, Bennett. In more ways than on the walls of your house. You're in serious danger of becoming just like your father. Before you know it, you'll be devoting your life to this blasted company and letting everything else turn to dust around you."

Standing to face her, he argued that point. "I'm not. I have a life. Hell, I was just up at my cabin in Big Bear."

He'd run there, actually, in an attempt to get away from the family currently driving him nuts. It was supposed to have been a week of peace and quiet. He'd lasted two days. Who the hell could live without the sounds of the city? Without a decent internet connection? Without *concrete?* There was far too much nature at the cabin.

"You haven't had a single woman over in the two weeks I've been living with you."

His jaw dropped and his eyes went wide. "Of course I haven't. You're my *mother.*" When your mom was living in your house, it wasn't exactly conducive to having a one-night stand with a willing female. Hell, unless he could get his mother to move the hell out, he'd probably die a monk.

He couldn't believe they were even having this conversation. Suddenly the damned peace and quiet at the cabin looked more appealing.

"And being your mother," she said, "I'm well aware of how important a good sexual relationship is to a healthy life."

He held up both hands and shook his head. "Stop. I beg you. Just…stop."

She gave an inelegant snort. "I had no idea you were such a prude, Bennett."

"I am not a prude," he ground out, and gave himself a mental pat on the back for not shouting at the woman he'd loved his whole life. "But I'm not discussing sex with my mother."

"Your sisters don't have a problem talking with me about this."

"Yeah," he muttered. "I'm not talking about their sex lives, either." They were his sisters. He didn't want to know.

"Well, I think—"

Bennett's phone rang at just that moment and he could

only silently thank whatever gods were taking pity on him. He reached for the desk phone and barked, "Yes?"

As he listened to his assistant, Bennett held up one hand to stop his mother from talking. All he could think was, he'd been grateful to the gods too quickly.

"How bad is it?" he asked.

"Bad enough, sir," David answered. "The fire department's on-site."

"Fine. I'm going there now." He hung up, reached for his suit jacket and swung it on, then buttoned it. "Sorry Mom, we'll have to continue this discussion later." Or never.

She reacted to his expression and curt tone. "First, tell me what's happened."

"There's been a fire. At The Carey."

She gasped. "Is anyone hurt?"

"I don't know yet." He stalked across the room and tossed back over his shoulder, "I'll let you know when I do."

It took him a little less than a half hour to make the drive from Irvine, California, to Laguna, where their five-star restaurant had stood on the cliff's edge for decades.

The restaurant was a rustic, yet elegant place, built with lots of cedar, weathered from the ocean air and with miles of glass to take advantage of the view. A wide, covered front porch offered navy blue cushioned chairs for waiting crowds. The building itself sat on Pacific Coast Highway, but far enough back from the street that there was room for a dozen stone planters filled with bright splashes of colorful flowers. The parking lot was off to the left and at the back of the restaurant, a wide, slate patio offered seating on the cliffs with an unbeatable view of the Pacific.

At the moment though, there were three fire trucks, a couple of police squad cars and paramedics—which worried Bennet. He hoped to hell all of the employees had gotten out safely. He parked his BMW a block away because of the emergency vehicles and hurried through the mob of people gaping at the huge hole in the restaurant's shake roof and the smoke lifting into the air and twisting in the wind streaming in off the ocean.

Bennett loosened his tie and unbuttoned his shirt collar. He felt like even the air was heavy and sitting in his throat, wrapping itself around the knot already lodged there. There was water everywhere and the stench of burning wood and plastic and God knew what else. Even the ocean wind couldn't dissipate it enough to keep Bennett from tasting it with every breath. *A damn mess*, he thought. And heartbreaking along with it.

"Mr. Carey."

He turned to face a fireman in his late forties. The man's face was soot streaked and his uniform jacket wet with water and chemicals. "One of your employees pointed you out. I'm Captain Hill."

"Is everyone safe?" Bennett's first question. He could think about the rest of this situation once he was assured no one had been hurt.

"Yeah." The man looked toward the restaurant. "Only ones in there at the time were the chefs, and they got out fast. Made the call to us and waited outside."

"That's good." And a huge relief. Buildings could be fixed; lives lost were irreplaceable. "How did it start?"

Captain Hill pulled off his helmet and ran one hand

through his hair. Idly, Bennett wondered how the man's hair was so wet while he was wearing a helmet.

"The inspector will be on-site later today and make the official call. But I can tell you it looked electrical to me. Bad wiring. How old is the building?"

Bennett sighed. "About sixty years." His own fault, Bennett told himself. He should have taken care of this when he became CEO of the company. But with everything else going on, and his father constantly sticking his nose in, who had had the time? He should have made the time. Damn it, being in charge meant making sure *everything* was as it should be.

"Is it all right if I go in? Take a look around?"

Hill frowned a bit, but then said, "It's safe. Dirty and wet, but safe. Just be careful. A few of my men are still inside, so if you need something, ask."

"Right. I will. Thanks." Bennett made his way to the restaurant, stepping over hoses, through puddles and around the firemen currently putting away their equipment.

Once inside, he took a long look around and sighed. It wasn't just the damage from the fire that would have to be dealt with. The efforts to put out that fire had destroyed furniture, walls and floors, as well. This was a nightmare.

"Perfect." He had been in the restaurant just two nights before with Jack Colton, his sister Serena's fiancé. That night, the place had looked as it always had. Elegant, but somehow comfortable at the same time. Pale walls, the color of adobe were adorned with heavy dark beams and wide windows, flanked by brass lamps that looked as if they were made at the turn of the century. Every table was covered with white tablecloths and would normally boast brass vases holding seasonal flowers. The silverware was heavy, the crystal was hand carved, the service was impeccable and the food was unmatched anywhere.

Now, he thought, it looked as though a war had been fought in the middle of the dining room. And, he supposed it had. The war had been won, thank God, but there was another battle yet to come. The traditions in this place tugged at him even as he realized that it would all change now.

And it seemed that lately, he was surrounded by change. His sisters shifting things around. His brother, Justin, making himself scarce—avoiding the family. His mother, for God's sake, moving in with him. And his father refusing to let go and making Bennett's life far more complicated than it had to be.

Looking at The Carey, he accepted the damage as he would one more boulder dropped onto his shoulders.

He stepped past the sinuous, winding bar toward the swinging door into the kitchen and couldn't swallow another sigh. "Yeah, we won't be serving dinner anytime soon." Which posed a problem well beyond the mess he was staring at.

Now that he knew his employees were safe, Bennett could focus on the issue that was staring him in the face. He had a formal dinner planned here at the restaurant in four weeks. Invitations had gone out. Media announcements had been made. It was too late to change the venue and damned if he'd cancel it. So that left him one choice only.

Taking out his cell phone, Bennett hit the speed dial and waited until his assistant answered. "David. Get the best contractor in the county on the phone. I need them working on the restaurant ASAP."

"Yes, sir."

Bennett hung up a moment later and continued toward the kitchen, kicking trash out of his way as he went. The whole place was a wreck, he thought, gaze scanning the damage done by the men and women who had saved the building. It wasn't just the kitchen that would need to be restored.

The floor—hundred-year-old oak planks—would have to be sanded and refinished. The bar was smoke-stained as well as waterlogged, and the bar mirror had been shattered along with most of the liquor bottles. The heavy walnut tables had been tipped over and just a cursory glance showed him that some of them needed repairs, too. Not to mention the chairs.

He opened the notepad on his phone and started a list. From flooring to liquor to walls and furniture, Bennett muttered curses under his breath with every addition. Still, making that list gave him something to focus on. Lists, if used properly, he thought, could solve any problem. They were the way Bennett kept his world from spinning out of control.

He pushed through the swinging door and his first glance at the kitchen made him groan aloud. "Four weeks. Four lousy weeks until this has to be a working, top-grade kitchen."

"Yeah, I don't see that happening."

Bennett looked left and watched his head chef, John Henry Mitchell walk toward him. African American, he was six foot five, with short, black curly hair and sharp brown eyes. He was built like an NFL lineman and was a damn artist in a kitchen.

"John Henry." Bennett held out his hand and the other man shook it. "Relieved you made it out safely."

"So am I." The big man's voice rolled around the room with the sonorous roar of thunder. "I had two of the sous-chefs in here, prepping for tonight."

"They're okay?" Bennett asked, even though he'd already been assured that everyone had made it out.

"They're a little rattled, but they'll do." John Henry shook his head and stared at the far wall. "It started there," he said, pointing at a section of burned-out wall. "I didn't notice right away. Probably would have if I hadn't been in the refrigerator, going over supplies."

"Not your fault."

"Oh, I know that," he said, turning to look at Bennett again. "It was the wiring, Bennett. Firemen said it just erupted and from there, spread like hellfire. Ran right up the wall and across the ceiling." His gaze followed his words and so did Bennett's. "From there, it went into the attic and the roof. This old cedar and the shake roof...just fed the flames and, well, you know the rest." He shrugged massive shoulders. "I got the boys out of here, called the fire department, then stood outside and watched."

"Yeah." Bennett kicked a piece of charred wood and listened to it skitter across the floor. The stainless steel prep counters were filthy and pooled with dirty water. "Thanks for getting that call in so quickly."

"This is a hell of a thing, Bennett."

"It damn sure is."

A couple of minutes of silence stretched out as both men surveyed the damage. "What're you going to do about the formal dinner? It's just four weeks out."

"I know," Bennett muttered. "I've got my assistant calling a contractor now."

John Henry laughed and it sounded like a landslide. "It's coming onto summer, Bennett. Every contractor in Orange County is going to be busy—putting in pools and patios and God knows what else. I've got my own guy starting a retaining wall in my backyard on Monday."

"I'll find one," he said, and it sounded like a vow even to himself. "If I have to offer bonuses or double pay, I'll do it."

"Well, that should take care of it," John Henry mused.

"You bet it will," Bennett said, shooting his friend a hard look. "Money motivates better than anything I know. I'll get the damn contractor. The dinner's still on, John Henry. You keep refining the menu. Steaks of course—"

"Of course."

The Carey restaurant offered the best steaks in California, hands down. And that was *one* tradition that wasn't about to change.

"You handle the rest of the menu," Bennett said, waving one hand.

John Henry laughed a little. "Yeah, I figured to do that. I would never leave that up to you."

Wryly, Bennet smiled. "Good call." He took a deep breath and scowled at the stench of smoke and burned wood. Then he looked around the destruction again before fixing his gaze on his old friend. "So do you need anything?"

"No. I'm good."

"We'll pay salaries whether the crew is working or not until the restaurant's up and running again."

John Henry gave him a small smile. “I already told everyone you would.”

Bennett’s eyebrows lifted. “That sure of yourself?”

“That sure of you, Bennett.” He pushed both hands into the pockets of his khaki slacks. “I’ve never known you to *not* care about your employees.”

Embarrassed, uncomfortable, Bennett brushed that aside. It wasn’t like he deserved a reward or something. It was just the right thing to do. Still, he made a mental note to begin a new list with everything their employees might need to hold on until the restaurant reopened. “No reason for you to stick around, John Henry. Go on home. I’ll let you know when the work starts here.”

“Good,” the other man said, “I’ve got a few ideas for some improvements.”

“I’ll bet you do,” Bennett mused.

Laughing again, John Henry said, “Hey, as long as we’re rebuilding, we might as well make those changes I’ve been ragging you about for the last five years. For example, higher counters so a man doesn’t have to bend in half to work…”

“Fine. Make a list.”

John Henry laughed again and slapped Bennett on the back. “How many lists have you started already today?”

“Two,” he admitted with a shake of his head. “And more to come no doubt.”

Bennett knew he was going to give John Henry whatever the hell he wanted as far as the kitchen went. The man was the best damn chef in California. Keeping him happy meant no other restaurant would be able to steal him away. “When I talk plans with the contractor, you’ll be in on it.”

John Henry nodded, and when the old friends looked at each other, they both laughed.

Bennett sighed and said, smiling, "Yeah, you knew you'd be in on that conversation. Have your list ready, and I'll let you know as soon as I find the contractor."

John Henry grinned. "Better get on that. Four weeks is not a lot of time."

A few days later, Bennett was at the end of his patience. That cliff he'd been clinging to a few days ago suddenly looked comfortable compared to where he was at the moment. He hated to admit it, but John Henry had been right.

Bennett's assistant had called every well-known contractor in Orange County and from each one had gotten a resounding no. Hell, Bennett had even asked a few friends to call in favors and nothing had worked. Not even the promise of a boatload of money. What was the world coming to when *money* didn't solve problems?

Every big outfit was busy as hell, thanks to summer looming ever closer. And Bennett was in a serious bind. His restaurant had to be restored, and the only way that would happen is if he took a chance on a small company with several good online reviews.

Which was why he was here, at The Carey, meeting with a woman who didn't look big enough to swing a hammer. He watched that woman now as she moved through the restaurant, checking out the damage. She was tiny. Just a little over five feet, but she was impressive.

She had a small, compact body with curves he shouldn't be noticing. Her hair was short, too, with black spikes and curls framing a face that was heart shaped, with a full mouth, high cheekbones and green eyes that were bright and shining with eagerness. She wasn't at all what he'd been expecting.

Hannah Yates of Yates Construction.

His gaze locked onto her as she moved around the room, and he scowled a little as he realized that he was having to fight to concentrate on the situation. Hannah Yates was too distracting—which he did not need at the moment. What he needed was a damn good contractor. Instead, he was watching a sexy pixie.

According to her, it had been her father Harry's company until she took it over three years before. She'd shown up with references, pictures of the other jobs she'd completed, both before and after, and she hadn't stopped talking since she'd walked in the door. Even now, she was talking to herself as she roamed the wreckage, shaking her head.

From what he could tell, she seemed to know her business. He just wasn't sure a small company would be enough to get the job done in the time he required.

She was busily making notes on the tablet she carried, and occasionally, she took out a measuring tape and ran it across a burned-out surface. It wasn't easy for Bennett, but he kept quiet and let her concentrate. She reached across the bar with that measuring tape and he absolutely did not notice how her jeans cupped her butt. Hannah Yates was his last hope of getting the restaurant back up and running in time.

"How soon do you need this done?" she asked, tossing him a glance over her shoulder.

"Four weeks."

"Hah!" She grinned, shook her head as if she were

talking to a nutcase and went back to muttering to herself.

Shrugging out of her dark green hoodie stamped with Yates Construction across the back, she tossed it onto an overturned table leg. Then she shook her head and pushed one small hand through that short, black hair. Something stirred inside him and he fought it down.

He was out of options. Bennett had tried everything. This woman and her small company were his only hope. It wouldn't be easy to trust her with this job, but he didn't have much choice here, either. And that was hard to take for a man used to being in charge. It was a hell of a thing, he thought, to be forced to put his trust in a woman who looked like a sexy elf.

Two

Four weeks. Hannah Yates smothered another laugh and told herself he'd been kidding.

His gaze followed her as she moved through what had once been the most exclusive restaurant in Laguna. God knew she wasn't a stranger to scenes like this, but she could at least take a second to think it was a shame. Heck, she'd never had the chance to eat here—who could afford it? And now she was finally inside, seeing it at its absolute worst.

She had the distinct feeling she was seeing Bennett Carey at his worst, too. He didn't look happy to be dealing with her, but if he wanted to save his restaurant, he'd have to get over that.

Just look at him, she thought. Standing amid the rubble, looking like a model for *GQ* or something. Somehow, he'd even managed to keep the shine on his Italian shoes in spite of the rubble and grime around them. When she turned to check another measurement, Hannah actually *felt* him watching her.

She knew he was actively wondering if she could do the job he needed. Because she was short and cute, men tended to underestimate her. Well, it wasn't the first time she'd had to prove herself. She could do it again.

Just because he was, without a doubt, the most gorgeous man she'd ever seen, didn't mean she could take her eyes off the *real* prize.

Which was the possibility of landing this job.

She wasn't looking for a man, and if she were, she wouldn't be looking at Bennett Carey. He was way out of her league, and she knew it. Didn't hurt to look, she supposed, but *touching* was definitely off the table. Hell, she'd been burned before by dating a wealthy man and had no intention of ever making that mistake again.

But working for him, that was something else.

She picked her way through the detritus left behind by the fire and the men and women who'd put out the flames. The oak floors were scarred and even scorched in a few places. They'd need to be sanded, repaired and stained again. Tables needed to be reinforced, and that gorgeous bar needed exactly what the floors did.

No, she'd never been here before, so she only had hearsay to know it had been a showplace. All she had to do now was convince Bennett Carey that she and her crew could make it a showplace again.

This restaurant was a landmark in Laguna, and if she were the one to bring it back to life… That would put her company on the map. So to speak.

For a moment, Hannah let her mind wander to just how much The Carey project could impact her future.

Her dad, Harry, had built a small, but honest company with a good reputation. When she took over from him three years before, she'd built on what he'd given her, and already, their reputation was growing, spreading—which was the only reason Bennett Carey was interviewing her in the first place. Well, that, and he didn't have a lot of choices right now.

She knew as well as he did that every big company in the county was already booked for summer jobs that were starting now. So his choices were few and that gave *her* the upper hand here. He needed her and Yates Construction.

Even more than she needed this job.

All she had to do was play the situation well.

Finishing up her notes, Hannah walked to where Bennett Carey waited and stopped right in front of him. "You've got some serious damage here."

"Yes," he said wryly, "I'm aware."

Ignoring that, she glanced at her tablet, scrolled through the notes, then looked up at him. "All I'm saying is, it's a big job."

"Are you incapable of handling it?"

"Hardly." Hannah tapped one finger at the logo on the left breast of her red T-shirt. "This says Yates Construction. That means I construct."

He took a breath and released it on a sigh. "My question was more in the line of wondering if your company was big enough to handle the job."

She stiffened, lifted her chin and straightened up to her full five-foot-four height. "My company can handle *any* job. I gave you references. Call any of them you like."

"I talked to a couple of them while you were making notes."

"Well, you don't waste any time, do you?"

"There's no time to waste," he pointed out. "And I checked you out before I set up this meeting. You get excellent reviews, but none of your jobs have been this size."

True. Yates Construction had a good reputation, but most of the jobs they did were residential or small businesses. She was proud of every one of them. But The Carey restaurant was something else. Something *more.* Which was why she wanted this job so badly. Working for the Carey family would give her entry into the world of big money and bored people looking for a way to spend it.

"If you put them all together they are."

"My point is—"

"I know what your point is," Hannah interrupted. "My crew can do it."

He didn't look convinced, she thought, but he hadn't said no, either. And men like him—wealthy, powerful—never had a problem saying no, which told her just how much he needed her company. He didn't look happy about that, either. Honestly, with his stern features and dark blue eyes, he looked like the world's most gorgeous statue. And she half wondered if he looked as good naked as he did in that impeccable suit he was wearing.

Beside the point, Hannah.

Refocusing, she said, "I've got more *before* and *after* pictures of our completed jobs here on my tablet if you want to see them."

She called them up and Bennett quietly swiped through them. Hannah knew the pictures were impressive because she'd taken them. She'd been on-site for every one of those jobs and knew just how good her crew was. His scowl deepened as if he really hated having to admit she was as good as she claimed to be.

A minute or so later, he handed the tablet back to her.

"I'll need the work completed in four weeks," he said again.

Hannah looked up at Bennett Carey and exploded in laughter. He hadn't been kidding. Honestly, she should have tried to hold it in, because she really wanted this job. But on the other hand, the man was standing in a fire-ravaged restaurant wearing a suit that probably cost more than her truck and issuing ridiculous orders like a king.

"Something funny?" He gave her a look meant to intimidate.

It didn't.

"Oh yes, that was very funny. Seriously, I thought you were kidding when you said that before. Four weeks. To fix all of *this*?" She held up one hand and told herself to get a grip. She was a professional, after all. "Sorry. I probably shouldn't have laughed, but honestly, look around, Mr. Carey. Four weeks?"

He did give the destruction another long look before shifting his gaze back to her. "I've got a very important formal dinner scheduled to be held here in four weeks. There's no postponing. There's no moving it to another venue. I want it here."

"And I want to be five foot ten," she muttered. One of his eyebrows arched, but she continued. "I understand, but you must know that it's practically impossible for anyone to get this job done in the time required."

"So I've been told," he said through gritted teeth. "Repeatedly."

"And yet here we are." He frowned, and she wondered if that was a permanent expression.

"Impossible or not, I need this done."

"Does anyone ever actually get away with saying no to you?"

His lips twitched briefly, and she thought he might be even more gorgeous with a real smile. Though she doubted she'd see one.

"I don't like the word *no*," he admitted.

"Huh. Neither do I. So we have that in common." He didn't speak, but she didn't need him to. Probably better if he didn't. He was clearly used to giving orders, and she was never very good at taking them. Hannah took another look around the inside of the restaurant and did some mental calculations.

If she said no, he'd only try someone else. If she said yes, it could either be the best thing she'd ever done or an exercise in futility. But oh, she wanted to say yes.

Hannah took a breath. Every one of the bigger, more well-known companies he'd undoubtedly spoken to had told him not only that they were already booked, but that expecting the job to be done so quickly was ridiculous. Well, she was hardly the biggest contractor in Orange County. But even if she said so herself, she was the best.

"Okay, so other contractors have told you the same thing."

"Yes." He ground out that single word. "Along with the fact that they're completely booked for the next two months."

"So, you really need me and my crew," she said. She wasn't his first choice but if she pulled this off, she'd be everyone else's first choice from there on out. Yates Construction was a damn good firm and once she'd proven that fact to Bennett Carey, they'd be on their way.

"Basically," he said.

"We can do it, but I can't promise you four weeks," she said, meeting his gaze squarely.

"If you can't deliver in four weeks, I can't use you."

"I'm all you've got," she pointed out. Well, judging by his expression, King Carey didn't like hearing *that*. Whether he liked it or not though, they both knew it was true. Without Yates Construction, he was simply out of luck.

He looked around again, as if reminding himself just how bad the situation was. Then he looked back at her. "How long would you need?"

Now it was her turn to meet his gaze. She didn't need to look around the room again; she'd seen all she needed to. "In a perfect world, eight weeks."

"Last time I checked, the world is far from perfect," he pointed out.

"True. So, say six weeks." He didn't look happy, but then he probably never did. Still, she wanted this job. "If I did it in four weeks, I'd have to pay overtime to my crew every day. We'd be putting in a lot of late hours."

"So it is possible."

She grinned. He might be grumpy but he was quick. "Figured you'd pick up on that. Sure, it's possible, if you don't mind working your crew…and yourself, to death."

"Four weeks of overtime doesn't sound so bad."

"Not bad," she agreed, nodding. "But expensive. It would significantly impact my estimate on the repairs."

"I'm not worried about that."

Good to know. Another reminder of just how different they were, she decided. Hannah couldn't imagine not worrying about what something cost.

He scrubbed one hand across the back of his neck and Hannah could almost feel tension vibrating off the man. It took a long minute or two, but finally, he said, "I'll handle the overtime for your crew."

"Yeah," she said with a short laugh. "I know."

He glanced around the room, then met her gaze again. "What you don't know is, if you finish the job in four weeks there's a bonus in it for you, as well."

Everything inside her went on alert, but she didn't show it. There was never any telling what an über-rich person might do. His idea of bonus and hers might be light-years apart anyway. Probably were. Still, she had to ask. "What kind of bonus?"

He scowled, and she knew he wasn't happy about the situation.

"Fifty thousand. Over the cost of the job itself."

Hannah's jaw wanted to drop but she managed to regain control before she let him see what that offer meant to her. Silently, she gave herself a mental pat on the back for keeping her excitement from him. Wouldn't do to let him see just how badly she wanted this job and that bonus.

Still, her heartbeat galloped, and Hannah could have sworn she saw stars. *Fifty thousand dollars* as a bonus? Over and above what she would have charged him for the job—including overtime—anyway? In a split second, she saw what that kind of money could do for her and the company.

She could pay off loans on new equipment, settle every bill hanging over her head and she could give her crew the kind of bonus that they all deserved. While she was thinking, relishing the kind of monumental change that amount of money could make, Bennett spoke again.

Apparently, he thought she was going to refuse him, because he blurted, "Fine. A hundred thousand."

She nearly staggered and, this time, didn't bother to hide her shock. "Are you out of your mind?"

One of his eyebrows winged up. "You're not interested?"

"Well, of course I'm interested," Hannah snapped, forgetting all about her silent vow to be polite to the man. "I'm not an idiot."

"So it's something else," he said. "Do you need more as an incentive?"

"No," she countered, though she was tempted to see just how high he would go. "But I think you need a therapist."

He choked out what might have been a strangled laugh. It was hard to tell, but then, he didn't look like the kind of man who did a lot of laughing. He was probably just out of practice.

"Is it a deal or not?"

She didn't answer that right away. She had to do some fast thinking, figuring, mentally shifting her crew around from other jobs to accommodate this one. And even while she did it, she knew she would take the job. She needed it. Not just for the ridiculous bonus but because the cachet of working on The Carey would be a jumping-off point into all sorts of first-class renovations, restorations… Seriously, the mind boggled at the opportunity that would be just waiting for her to grab it.

Yet again, she didn't want him to know how eager she really was for this job. The only reason he was talking to her at all was that all of the bigger companies were booked. So let him wonder if she was going to turn him down, as well. Besides, it was going to take a second or two for her to find her voice again.

A hundred-thousand-dollar bonus. Yeah, she needed a second.

"Four weeks," she muttered, taking another look around.

"Not a day more," he told her.

"We'll be pulling a lot of late nights to get it done in time."

"Already agreed to the overtime," he said simply.

"Yeah, you did." Imagine having a client *not* bitch about paying overtime.

"Then there's the bonus," he added, like an adult holding out a candy bar to a sulky child.

She looked up at him. He was really tall. His dark blond hair was just a little rumpled, and she thought that he'd probably been running his hands through it. And oddly enough, she liked knowing that nerves and worry could affect him, too. His eyes were the same shade as a sapphire and glittered just as brightly. She really was thinking way too much about how gorgeous he was, but honestly, she'd have had to be blind not to notice.

"A hundred thousand dollars," she repeated. Nope, didn't get any easier to say—much less believe.

"That's what I said."

Clearly the rich were *really* different. How desperate was he, to toss that much money around? Bad for him, potentially good for her. He didn't seem dangerous, and it was his money, after all. She already knew rich people were eccentric. Of course poor people were just called crazy, but that had nothing to do with anything.

Narrowing her gaze on him, she said, “This dinner must be really important to you.”

“It is.”

“I’ll have to shuffle some of my current jobs around to make this work.”

“You’ll be rewarded,” he reminded her.

“There is that,” she mused, still trying to keep from letting him see what this meant to her.

“So,” he said impatiently, “is it a deal or not?”

She held out one hand. “It’s a deal.”

His big hand completely enveloped hers, and the heat his touch engendered swept through her entire body. There was a sizzle in her blood, and just for a second, her mind actually blurred. And Hannah had to wonder if, bonus or not, she’d made a mistake in dealing with Bennett Carey.

To settle herself, she pulled her hand free of his grip and started talking again.

“You’re sure you’re okay with the overtime,” she said, gauging his reaction. “My crew will be putting in a lot of extra hours.”

His jaw tightened briefly, but he gave her a sharp nod. “I told you I’m fine with it. As long as my schedule isn’t interrupted, we have a deal.”

Shaking her head a little, Hannah muttered under her breath.

“What was that?”

She really needed to just *think* these things. “I said, maybe you should be interrupted more often. You seem wound a little tight.”

“Thank you for your observation,” he said stiffly. “I’ll keep it in mind.” He checked what looked like a solid gold watch. “When you begin work, my head chef, John

Henry Mitchell, will be contacting you on some specific changes he wants to the kitchen."

He'd surprised her again. He didn't seem like the kind of man to release even a tiny bit of power to someone else. "Wow. You're giving over decisions to your chef?"

"I don't cook."

"Yeah. I guessed that." He probably had a personal chef at home, too. "I'll need the key."

"Yeah. I guessed that." Her lips twitched when he threw her words back at her.

He handed the key over. Hannah's fist curled around it, and she held on tightly to her future.

With one last glance around at the rubble that had once been a kitchen, he said, "I'll leave you to get started."

When he walked out of the restaurant, Hannah had the distinct feeling she should have saluted.

At the family meeting that afternoon, Bennett sat back quietly, observing the Careys—siblings and parents—and only half listened to the conversations flying around the room. Idly, his gaze shifted to the floor-to-ceiling windows. Tinted to keep the sunlight quietly at bay, they still provided a view of a deep blue sky and several other chrome-and-glass buildings clustered together in the office park.

There was a blue smudge in the distance that was the ocean, and closer, was the constant traffic on the 405 freeway. Here, high above the city and the noise, the silence could be deafening—unless you were in a Carey family meeting. Maybe, he told himself, that was why their youngest brother, Justin, managed to avoid these meetings regularly.

Another irritation for Bennett. He didn't know what Justin was up to, and he didn't like being in the dark. One day soon, he and his little brother were going to have a long talk.

During a pause in the incessant chatter, Bennett caught everyone's attention by announcing, "I've hired a contractor to make the repairs on The Carey."

Instantly of course, the questions started flying.

"Who?" his sister Amanda asked.

"Hannah Yates of Yates Construction," he answered.

"A woman," Serena said, smiling and nodding. "Good for you, Bennett."

"I didn't hire her because she was a woman."

"You probably didn't notice," Amanda muttered.

Serena snorted.

Bennett frowned, because whether his sisters would believe it or not, he'd noticed *everything* about Hannah Yates. From those amazing green eyes, to the curves packed neatly into such a tiny frame and the way she moved, all grace and confidence.

"Yates Construction?" His father, Martin, wrinkled his brow. "Never heard of them."

"And you know all of the construction companies in Orange County, do you?" His mother Candace's voice was so sweet it could have caused cavities, but the sting was still there.

"No," Martin said, "but I—"

"I'm sure Bennett's taken care of checking credentials and references."

"Thanks, Mom," he said tightly. He half expected her to give him a smiley face sticker. "Yes, I did."

He glanced at the dim sunlight pouring through the windows again. He knew that outside, there was a lush greenbelt that lay like a ribbon uncoiled to fall where it may. And right at the moment, Bennett wished he were there. In the quiet.

"How long has this Hannah Yates been doing construction work?" Amanda asked.

Bennett looked at her. "Apparently all her life, but she took over her father's company three years ago." He managed to slide a quick look his father's way. After all, Bennett had taken over the Carey Company and yet, Martin Carey refused to hand over the reins entirely. Seemed to him that Martin could learn a thing or two from Hannah's father.

"Can't be easy for her," Amanda said, "running her own company in that field."

"Mandy's right." Serena spoke up and fiddled with her brand-new emerald engagement ring while she did. "She must be good at what she does. I imagine she faces all sorts of problems while trying to build a company in what is generally considered a man's territory."

"Yeah," Bennett grumbled. "I'm not looking to lead the feminist charge. I just need a contractor and Hannah Yates says she can do it."

"And you're taking her word for it?" His father again, and Bennett bit his tongue to keep from saying what he'd like to say.

Martin was supposed to have retired months ago. But the old man was clinging to the Carey Corporation as he would to a slippery edge on the side of a mountain. His fingers couldn't be pried off. While he could understand his father's reluctance to let go, Bennett had trained for this job his whole life. He was capable and eager to take over the reins of the family legacy.

Bennett was the CEO but Martin made sure he kept his hand in well… Everything.

"Believe it or not, Dad, I researched her. She has a good reputation and her former clients can't say enough positive things about her."

"And that's good enough for you?"

Patience, he reminded himself. Bennett loved his family, and it was only that love that helped him hold on to what little patience he had. God knew it wasn't his strong suit. He'd always believed in charging ahead, going after what you wanted, letting no one and nothing slow you down. So holding back for his father's sake was costing him.

"Like Mom said, like I just told you, I checked her out. And it's not like we've got a lot of options, Dad." He shrugged and shook his head. "Every one of the big, well-known contractors around is already booked for the summer."

"So we're settling," Martin said, with a huff of disapproval.

Bennett looked at his sisters for support. Serena winced. Amanda hid a smile behind her hand. No help there.

"If you had retired as you were supposed to," Candace said, capturing the attention of everyone in the room, "we'd be on a Caribbean cruise right now and you wouldn't know anything about this."

Martin scowled. "But I do know."

"Yes, exactly. You do. Why? Because you won't leave this company as you promised you would," Candace said, and turned away from him.

"Aw, Candy…"

Bennett rubbed the bridge of his nose. The Retirement Wars continued. Seriously, between his parents, the company, the fire at The Carey and his missing brother, Bennett felt the ledge under his feet crumbling. And that didn't even take into account his sisters, their new fiancés and their ability to poke at him.

"The pictures of her work are really amazing," Amanda tossed in, and Bennet wanted to kiss his sister for the surprising show of support.

"It is," Serena tossed in as she took the tablet from Amanda. "I especially love the renovations done to the kitchens. Since that's exactly what we need done, I think that's a good sign."

"Someone's kitchen in their house is a whole different thing from a professional kitchen in a damn near legendary restaurant," Martin grumbled. No one commented.

"She can have it done in time for the party?" Candace asked, still ignoring her husband.

"It'll cost overtime, but yes." Bennett kept talking to avoid hearing his father's opinion.

"You're paying overtime?"

Apparently, he couldn't avoid his father's opinion. The old man's face was florid, and Bennett could practically see his blood pressure rise. Probably wouldn't be a good idea to mention a one-hundred-thousand-dollar bonus.

Looking into his father's eyes, Bennett said, "I'm paying whatever I have to, to get the job done."

"As a CEO should," Candace said with a knowing glare at her husband.

"Fine." Martin sat back, glowering at his son. "I just hope you know what you're doing."

Bennett remembered the heat he'd felt when he'd shaken Hannah Yates's hand. That fast, electrical jolt of something… Interesting. Something he hadn't expected and didn't have time for.

As he thought back to the sexy pixie laughing up at him, Bennett heard himself say, "Yeah. So do I."

Three

At her father's house a couple hours later, Hannah sat on a dining room chair with her head between her knees, breathing deeply. Her head still felt a little light and her mind was spinning with possibilities.

Absently, she stared down at the wide oak floorboards and focused on a single knot in the wood that looked like a wide eye staring back at her. Her heart was racing, her mouth was dry and she was pretty sure her right eye was twitching.

"You okay, peach?" Her father's voice as he patted her back hard enough to dislodge whatever he thought might be stuck in her throat.

"Ow, Dad," she said, "I'm not choking. I'm okay. Really. I think."

"All right, then." Hank stepped around in front of her.

Hannah could see the scarred toes of his work boots. "If you're okay, you want to say all of that again?"

She mumbled while still trying to take deep, even breaths.

"For God's sake, girl, sit up and say that again. *Slowly.*"

When Hannah was sure she wouldn't pass out or start hyperventilating, she sat up, planted her hands on her knees and looked up at her dad. "Bennett Carey's paying all overtime with no bitching—well almost none. *And* he's giving us a one-hundred-*thousand*-dollar bonus if we complete the repairs on time."

Now it was Hank's turn to look a little pale. He reached out one hand until he found the back of the chair next to his daughter and then dropped into it. He frowned, scrubbed one hand across his gray grizzled jaw, swallowed hard, then asked, "Is he sane?"

She choked out a laugh. Funny that Hank had said what she'd been wondering.

"I don't know. I don't think so." She thought back on their conversation and could only come up with, "At least, he didn't seem dangerous. I just think he needs this job done fast. And he doesn't seem like the kind of man who's used to having people say no to him."

"More than one kind of danger," Hank muttered.

True. She remembered Bennett Carey and his eyes and his mouth when he talked or scowled or both and the buzz of something interesting that had happened the moment she'd shaken his hand. And yes, there was more than one kind of danger. But for this chance, this opportunity, she was willing to risk it.

"Dad." Her gaze locked onto his as she spelled out

her motivation one word at a time. “I’m not interested in that kind of danger. Already been burned, remember?”

“Oh, I remember,” Hank told her, his gaze searching hers. “I want to make sure you do.”

“Hard to forget.” She’d dated a rich client once. He’d been smooth and slick and had sent her flowers for no reason at all. He’d swept her off her feet and into an engagement that had nearly cost her everything. She’d trusted too easily, believed too deeply and eventually fell way too far. She wouldn’t be making the mistake of falling for another rich guy, no matter how tempting he was.

“I just don’t want to see you get tangled up in something hard again, Hannah.”

“I’m not tangled,” she argued, refusing to remember that buzz of interest. “I’m taking a job. For the money. For the bonus. Dad,” she said softly. “One. Hundred. Thousand. Dollars.”

He still looked concerned. “To get an eight-week job done in four weeks.”

“Well yeah,” Hannah muttered with a shrug. “There’s that.”

And truth be told, she was a little worried about it, hence the hyperventilating. Yes, she’d assured King Carey that her crew could do it, but she knew it wasn’t going to be easy. Still, with carte blanche for overtime and that amazing bonus—maybe King Carey really was crazy—she would find a way to pull it off.

Hank Yates propped one elbow on the dining table that had been sitting in the same spot in the same house for the last thirty years. It was maple, and looked as if it had been through a war and come out the victor. A little battered, a little scarred, but through it all, still polished once a week and still standing.

And that, Hannah thought, was something you could say about the whole house. A quick look around at the rose-colored walls with the cream crown molding; the gleaming, if scarred oak floors; the burgundy couch and chairs; and the black recliner that was Hank's personal heaven.

And Hank himself, for that matter. She looked at her father and saw the man who had been her hero and role model all of her life.

Hank was five foot eight and still muscular from his years of working construction. His face was weathered from spending his life in the sun, but the wrinkles around his eyes and mouth were from smiling. Not much got her father down, and she knew that he had a spine of steel.

Hank's wife, Hannah's mother, had walked out on the family when Hannah was only three. The woman had decided that being a wife and mother was stifling her need for happiness. So she walked out, divorced Hank a year later, and she'd never been seen again.

That was fine with Hannah. Sure, when she was twelve or thirteen, she'd wanted a mom to talk to about periods and boys and everything else a growing girl needed to know. Her friend's mother had helped her through a few questions, and she was still grateful for it. But Hank had stepped in, too. If he'd been embarrassed, Hannah hadn't seen it.

He was just there. A rock. As he'd always been. He was the one stable point in Hannah's universe. Always there. Always steady. Always ready to stand behind her when she needed him. He'd been both mother and father to Hannah all her life and she couldn't love him more.

Hank had raised her on construction sites and his

crew had been her very protective uncles. They'd taught her carpentry, plumbing, roofing, electrical—everything she might need to run her own crew. As she was now, and had been since taking over Yates Construction. Some of the guys were still working with her, and even Hank got tired of fishing every day and would show up at a job just to keep his hand in.

She'd need him to give a hand on this job.

"Have you talked to Steve?" Hank finally asked.

Her foreman. "No. I wanted to tell you first. Ask you what you thought about it."

He laughed shortly. "You're asking me *after* you made the decision."

True. "Well…okay, yes."

"Like when you bought that old truck, drove it home and the engine fell out on the driveway?" He smiled as he said it, and Hannah laughed.

"I was seventeen," she reminded him, and didn't bother to point out that once she and her dad had worked on that truck, she drove it for five years.

"Doesn't seem much has changed," Hank mused.

"I suppose not," she agreed. "But Dad, how could I turn that down? Once we complete the job, we can pay off the last of that loan and still have enough left over to buy new equipment and—"

Hank held up one hand and shook his head. "I get it. I do. And I want what you want."

"Thanks, Dad—"

"*But*," he added with a smile, "that said, I don't want you working yourself to death just for a bonus. Just to get rid of that loan."

Hannah leaned forward and laid one hand on Hank's

arm. "It's not just that. Paying off past mistakes, Dad. We get this done for King Carey—"

He snorted. *"King Carey?"*

She shrugged as she remembered that aloof look on Bennett Carey's features and how he'd given the impression that he was expecting her to genuflect. Not to mention his impatience, the take-charge attitude and the nearly imperious attitude.

"That's what I was calling him in my mind," she admitted. "He's bossy. Sort of…aristocratic, I guess. Anyway. If we get this job done for the Carey family—" she paused, took a breath and sighed at the possibilities "—we'd have them on our résumé. We'd get the bigger jobs in the county. We could take Yates Construction right to the top."

He watched her for a long minute. "But no pressure?"

She laughed, gave his arm a squeeze. "Exactly. I'm going to call Steve in a minute and tell him to get the crew together." She sat back and started thinking. She'd been over every inch of the destruction in The Carey, but she needed to walk it again, now that she had the go-ahead to work the project.

"It's an old building," she mused aloud, "and we know, because of the fire, the wiring was a problem in the kitchen." Tapping one finger against her chin. "We'll have Marco Benzi come in and check the rest of the wiring in the building."

Marco was the best electrician she knew. He and his guys could cut into the walls in select spots to make sure the wiring in the rest of the building wouldn't be an issue.

"Good plan."

She grinned. "The ceiling's got to come down and

the damage in the attic fixed. The roof's in pretty good shape—except for the burned-out portion—"

"Naturally."

Another fast grin. "Tiny and Carol can take care of ripping out the ruined roof beams and shingles while the rest of us do the demo on the kitchen. Most of the counters have got to go, so we'll pull all of them and rebuild uniformly. Some of the white oak floorboards are scarred up and a couple are charred where burning pieces of the ceiling dropped onto them. We'll have to sand and refinish and to make sure it matches the rest of the room, we'll just sand down the whole kitchen."

"Makes sense. Devin Colier is the man there."

"True." She paused and looked around. "I should have my tablet. Or paper. Write all this down."

Hank laughed shortly. "You'll remember. Always did have a sharp mind."

"You're my favorite human," Hannah said, grinning. "You're right. I'll remember." She always used Devin when she needed floors repaired or refinished. The man was a genius, and when he retired, she was going to be heartbroken.

In four weeks, Hannah would be able to prove to Bennett Carey just how good she was at her job.

"And," she said with a wince, "I'm going to need you, Dad. I know you've got that fishing trip planned with Tom Jetter, but—"

He waved that off. "It'll wait. Tom and I can both come in and help."

Tom had worked for Yates Construction for thirty years, so having him on board for this job would be a huge help, too.

"That'd be great."

Hank gave her a pat, stood up and walked to the kitchen. She followed and gave a quick look around.

Sage green walls, forest green cabinets and white quartz countertops. She and her father had redone the kitchen just two years before, and she still loved it.

The old Craftsman-style house in Long Beach, California, had been Hannah's classroom. Over the years, her father had taught her plumbing, carpentry, masonry—when they laid the stone patio in the backyard—and every other thing a contractor needed to know.

She'd built a four-poster bed for herself at sixteen and at seventeen had renovated an old closet into a half bath powder room.

Hannah knew every square inch of this house and though she lived in her own place now, this would always be home.

Hank poured some coffee and she automatically asked, "How many cups have you had?"

He rolled his eyes and took a deliberate, satisfying sip. "Who's the parent here?"

Her eyebrows arched. "Sometimes I wonder."

"You're a funny girl." Hank sat at the kitchen table and pushed out another chair with a shove of his foot. "Call Steve, let him know what's going on, then we'll make your list and start lining up supplies."

"Okay," she agreed, and dropped onto the chair. As she hit speed dial for her foreman, she gave her father a long look. "But I'm keeping an eye on you. The doctor said no more than three cups of coffee a day."

Hank snorted. "What does he know?"

Hannah sighed and waited for Steve to pick up. Her father's ulcer worried her, but if she could get him to give up his two pots of coffee a day, that would help.

Beyond the everyday worries was Bennett Carey. She couldn't share this with her dad, of course. He would instantly be concerned about her making the same mistake all over again, which she wouldn't. She wasn't looking to date Bennett Carey—although, as she thought of him again—with his piercing blue eyes and tall, gorgeous body—she wouldn't mind seeing him naked.

"Steve!" Her voice lifted and her excitement bubbled through. Thank God, talking to her foreman would take her mind off the man she should *not* be thinking about. "We've got a job and wait until you hear."

At home that afternoon, Bennett closeted himself in his office. The better to avoid his mother. She had a couple of her friends downstairs, looking through design books, God help him.

Desperate, he picked up the phone. When his sister answered, he said, "Damn it, Amanda, you have to help me!"

"Who is this?"

He glared at the phone. "Not funny."

"Sure it is," she said, laughing.

Bennett's grip tightened on his phone. "I don't see anything funny about this."

"That's because you have no sense of humor."

"Thanks. Thanks very much." Why had he considered for even a second that she would be on his side? Both she and Serena were enjoying his misery far too much to help him out of it.

"Mom and her pals are looking at paint samples and upholstery and… Damn it, stop laughing." Irritated beyond measure, Bennett walked to the wall of windows, then opened the French doors and stepped out onto the balcony to take in the ocean view. Here in Dana Point, the sea looked wild and seemed to stretch on forever. Ordinarily, that view calmed him down. Today it barely touched the tension coiled inside.

First a pixie with attitude giving him grief over rebuilding The Carey, and now his own mother making his home life a nightmare.

"Okay, now I'm feeling sorry for you," she admitted, "although your house could do with *something.*"

"You haven't seen my house in five years."

"Yes, thanks so much for inviting me so often."

"Not what I'm talking about."

"Fine," she said, then asked, "Have you changed anything?"

"Of course not."

"And my point is made."

"*My* point is going unanswered. You and Henry have a giant house in Irvine. You could take Mom."

"I could, but I'm not going to," she said. "I love Mom, but she's obsessed with wedding plans. I don't need her on-site doing it."

"And you think I do?"

"You're not making wedding plans."

"That's not helpful."

"As helpful as you're going to get," she said.

"And *this* is why I will not be making wedding plans. Ever." Scowling out at the sea, he added, "Your species enjoy making mine miserable."

"Don't know what you're missing. You should talk to Henry," Amanda said, practically cooing. "He'll tell you how…happy he is."

Bennett closed his eyes, took a deep breath and said,

"Please don't make me want to hurl. I don't need to know these things about my sisters."

"Your loss."

"Thank God."

"Bennett," she said on a sigh, "once she and Dad make up, your problems are over."

Sure, that was just right around the corner. His mother was settling in. Hell, she was *nesting*. In his house. "And have you seen signs of that happening?"

"Well, no…"

His father wouldn't give up the company and his mother was determined to make that happen, so there was no end in sight to the Retirement Wars. And apparently, Bennett was the one who would be paying.

"So I'm just supposed to give her free rein in my house?"

"She has excellent taste."

Yes, she did. Elegant. Understated. But hardly masculine. "It's not my style," he complained uselessly.

"Beige is no one's style, Bennett," his sister said.

"Fine. I'll try Serena."

She laughed again. "Good luck with that. There's not even room for Jack to move in there."

"Jack has that gigantic mansion in Laguna. Why aren't they living there?" Why was no one helping him?

"Because Serena wants to wait until they're married to live together. Trust me, Jack's not happy, either."

"Well, why would she do that?" It didn't make any sense. Now that she and Jack were back together and engaged, Serena was happier than she'd ever been,

"Because she wants Alli to get used to the idea first, and apparently Jack has to build a castle in the backyard."

"A *castle*?"

"Long story," Amanda said, then offered, "Why don't you try Justin?"

One hand clamped tight around the icy cold black iron railing surrounding his deck. Turning his face into the ocean wind, he felt irritation swell inside him. Their youngest brother had pretty much cut himself off from the family the last couple of years. And when he was being generous of mind, Bennett could admit, at least to himself, that he hadn't helped the situation any. But, damn it, Justin should be here. Involved.

At the very least, helping with the parental situation.

"Okay," Amanda allowed, "that was a cheap shot."

"Yeah. It was." He rubbed the spot between his eyebrows, and it did nothing for the ache settled there.

"Fine then, change of subject," Amanda said brightly. "Tell me more about the woman who's doing the job on The Carey."

"From one mess to another? That's a change of subject?" His mutter sounded pissy, even to himself.

"I looked her up," Amanda said, ignoring Bennett's bad mood. "She's got lots of great reviews."

And she looked far better in person than she did on her website. "I saw them."

"And the before and after pictures she's got on her website look fabulous."

"I saw them." He gritted his teeth and reached for patience that seemed, at the moment, elusive.

"What's she like?" Amanda asked. "You saw *her*, too."

"I did." And instantly, her image rose up in his mind.

Sexy pixie, he thought, helplessly. Small, curvy, with bright green eyes and a wry twist to her mouth that intrigued him more than he'd like to admit. It was as if she was always laughing at some private joke. Or at him. When she looked up at him with that challenging stare, he'd felt something stir inside him. Lust, sure.

What man wouldn't have felt a tug, watching her move so efficiently around the room? He could see her making mental notes as she checked out the ravages of the fire. She was professional and sharp. But he couldn't seem to tear his gaze from the way those faded jeans of hers clung to her legs. From the small, firm breasts beneath her Yates Construction T-shirt. And when he caught a gleam in those emerald green eyes? Well, what she did to him was biology. And he was most definitely male.

But there was something more to her, too. Which he didn't want to think about. And that bothered him. No woman had caught his attention as quickly as she had. She was now officially an employee, and Bennett never mixed business with pleasure. But damned if he wasn't tempted anyway.

"So," Amanda said, "tell me about her."

What could he say that wouldn't set his sister off? "She's a smart-ass."

Amanda's whoop of laughter was so loud Bennett yanked his phone from his ear.

"I like her already," Amanda said finally.

"You would," he muttered, then said more loudly, "She seems competent."

"Wow, high praise."

Shaking his head, he gave a resigned chuckle. "Why did I call you again?"

"Because I'm your intelligent, insightful sister whose judgment you trust implicitly."

"Yeah, that's not it."

"A spark of humor from my brother, Mr. Stoic," she said with approval. "Hannah Yates is already a miracle worker."

"We'll see," he said, and watched the waves race toward the rocks beneath his house. Spray shot into the air over the roar of the water. He turned his back on the ocean, walked back into his office and took a seat behind his desk. And what was wrong with it, he wondered. Just like the one at Carey headquarters, it was steel and chrome and glass and did exactly what he needed it to do. But if it were up to his mother, God knew what his office would look like.

"She's only got four weeks to get the job done."

"She'll do it."

"You sound sure."

"Bennett," Amanda said, her tone serious now, "trust me on this. When a woman is in charge in what is essentially a man's territory, she does what she has to, to keep her word and get things done."

"The bonus I offered doesn't hurt, either," he said, though he had to admit, Amanda had a point.

"A hundred thousand?" She laughed again. "For that, I might have tried to pull it off!"

He smiled, in spite of himself. "I'll tell her if she needs help to call you."

"No thanks," she said. "My plate's already full. But Bennett…you're not going to do your hovering thing over the woman, are you?"

"What's that supposed to mean?"

"You know exactly what I mean. It's what you did to Serena when she first joined the company. What you try to do to Justin. What you do to me until I make you stop. You loom over people, making sure they're doing everything the way you want it done."

"How the hell else can I be sure they will?"

"Oh, I don't know, *trust*?"

The very idea of that was laughable. "This job is too important to take chances. I'll be checking in on her a lot."

"Checking *up*, you mean."

"Whatever."

"Good comeback."

"Amanda, if you're not going to help me get Mom off my back, just say so."

"Thought I already did," she quipped, then as if sensing he was going to hang up on her, she added, "Why don't you get her to show you the website she's got up for the Summer Stars program?"

"Why would I do that?" he muttered, raking one hand through his hair.

"Hovering," she said. "Or looming. Whichever. Anyway, the point being, while she's talking about what she's doing with the big contest, she's *not* redecorating your house."

She might be onto something, he told himself. And he should be keeping a closer eye on the Summer Stars program. The only reason he hadn't was that it had turned into his mother's baby, and he and Candace Carey had been spending entirely too much time together lately already.

The Summer Stars was a new and so far, *very* popular contest. Every year, the Carey Center held the Summer Sensation, a series of concerts spread out over three months. Everything from ballet to symphonies and plays was held in the palatial Center, but this year, Serena had come up with an idea to get the local community involved.

The Summer Stars program had been holding live auditions at the Center, recording them, then putting them on a website so people could vote for their favorite performers. Much like a reality TV show, the performer with the most votes would win and the grand prize was a summer performance night at the Carey Center.

Which was why he needed the restaurant up and running in four weeks. The grand prize winner would be there to be introduced to the public, the media and to be celebrated for their victory.

"Hellooo…"

"Yeah," he said, while Amanda's voice echoed in his ear. "I'm here. It's a good idea. I'll distract Mom tonight with talk of the contest."

"And make sure she's doing everything to your satisfaction?"

"Doesn't that go without saying?"

"You're hopeless," Amanda said, then hung up.

Bennett didn't think of himself as hopeless in any way. Instead, he was focused, determined, and right now that focus would be aimed directly at Hannah Yates. He tucked his phone into his pocket and stared out at the ocean again. But he wasn't seeing the blue of the sea or the windswept clouds scuttling across a diamond bright sky.

Instead, he saw the pixie as she laughed up at him. Hannah Yates.

He already felt in his bones that hiring her might have been a mistake.

Four

Hannah was at The Carey first thing in the morning. With the key in hand, she let herself in, hit the lights and paused just a moment to take in the wreckage. It wasn't the first place she'd seen, postfire. And still, she felt a tiny ping of regret that the beautiful old building had suffered such an indignity.

Picking her way through debris, she made her way to the kitchen and mentally made a list of what she wanted her guys working on when they arrived. Her dad was coming by, too, since, as he'd said, *For a hundred thousand dollars, the Careys get the whole Yates family.*

She'd be glad of his help. There was no better carpenter in California. What he couldn't fix or build from scratch hadn't been invented yet. If he had to, she had no doubt he could build a working car out of cedar.

"Hey, boss!" A shout from the front of the building. "You in here?"

"In the kitchen, Nick!" She turned and waited for her master plumber to walk through the door.

"What a mess," he muttered as soon as he did.

Short and barrel-chested, Nick boasted a full handlebar moustache that he swore his wife, Gina, loved more than him. He had a booming voice, a great laugh and magic hands.

"Damn shame," he went on. "I brought Gina here for dinner on her last birthday."

"Well," Hannah told him. "You can bring her back on her next birthday, too."

He nodded absently, then looked around again. "Want me to start the demo?"

"We'll wait for the others to get here." She opened a cabinet to show stacks of skillets and saucepots, and she had no doubt the others were just as full. "We could start emptying everything, though. Get a jump on it."

"Sure. Damn. I've never seen so many pans. Where do you want to stack it all?"

"For now, we'll use a couple of the tables in the main dining room," she said, and made another mental note to get some boxes in here. Or maybe just talk to King Carey. See if they were keeping all the cookware or getting new. A man who threw money around like he did, might not want dirty pans in his spanking new restaurant.

"Works for me. There's plenty of 'em out there." Nick bent down and grabbed a stack of skillets, bundling them up in his arms. He carried them into the other room and Hannah heard him call out a greeting.

"Hey, Mike, go on in there and start grabbing some

of the pots and pans. And watch yourself. The damn things are heavier than they look."

Hannah was grabbing a handful of saucepans when Mike Holley strolled in. Young, seriously built and looked like a surfer. But he would be the first guy she'd call if she needed a roof repaired. Steve Scott, her foreman, came in right behind Mike, and the two of them entertained each other while they worked.

One by one, all of the guys arrived, with her father bringing up the rear, carrying a jug of coffee and a stack of paper cups.

"Found a way to keep me from bugging you about coffee, did you?" she asked.

Hank shrugged. "The boys'll appreciate it."

"Sure. The boys." To her father, even Carol and Tina were *the boys.* Shaking her head, because really, she never had been able to talk her father into anything he didn't want to do, she swept out one arm to encompass the restaurant and asked, "What do you think?"

"I think it's a damn mess," Hank said, turning in a slow circle to take it all in. "And I'm starting to think you're as crazy as the guy who hired you. What makes you think we can get this done in four weeks?"

Frowning, Hannah took another look around and had to admit, that it was going to be tight. Maybe too tight. But she would give it everything she—and her crew—had to make that deadline. "Dad, if you were still running the business, what would you have done with that offer Bennett Carey made?"

He took a deep breath, blew it out, winked and shrugged. "I'd have said yes just as fast as you did."

She grinned. "Thanks for admitting it."

"There's comfort in knowing we're both willing to take on a huge challenge?"

"Absolutely." Hannah leaned in, kissed his cheek and said, "The guys are in the kitchen, clearing everything out so we can start the demo."

"My favorite day on the job." Her father grinned. "As much as I love building things, there's nothing as much fun as demo day." He headed for the other room with a spring in his step.

Still smiling, Hannah turned toward the front door when it opened. All of the guys were here, so she couldn't imagine who—

Bennett Carey stepped into the room and looked like the king she'd named him, standing in a barnyard. Completely out of place and yet, she thought... Somehow right at home, as well. But then, she told herself, men like Bennett Carey were always so confident, so sure of themselves that they seemed to fit in anywhere. Even if they looked—as he did at the moment—as if they'd rather be anywhere else.

Even knowing that, Hannah couldn't stop her heart from giving a hard jolt, or what felt like a buzz of sensation from dancing up and down her spine. Oh, she might be in some serious trouble here.

From the kitchen came the clashing symphony that symbolized a new job starting, and thankfully that was enough to shake her out of whatever state King Carey had put her in. Hammers, laughter, rock music pumping into the air and the shouts of men and women used to working together. Hannah had always loved the sound, but she watched Bennett wince at the noise.

"Sounds like you're wrecking the place not rebuilding," he said.

"You have to tear things down before you can rebuild," she pointed out.

"It wasn't down enough?" he muttered.

She smiled, then took a long moment to just look at him, and Hannah was forced to muffle a sigh of approval as nerves skittered through her. Backlit by a shaft of sunlight, he stood there motionless as if giving her the time to admire him.

So shc did.

The dark blue suit, crisp white shirt and forest green tie he wore fit him as if made specifically for him. And it probably had been. His hair looked perfect, as well, and she took a mental pause, remembering what she looked like. She wore her faded blue jeans, a red Yates Construction T-shirt and her battered and much loved Doc Martens. Nothing she could do about her wardrobe even if she would, Hannah thought. She'd tried to change herself for a rich man once before, and she still regretted it. So Bennett Carey could take her as she was—or, she thought, even better, he could leave her alone to work.

Another crash from the kitchen and a burst of laughter splintered her thoughts. It was just as well. Sighing over a man she couldn't have was just pointless. "So what can I do for you, Mr. Carey?"

"I wanted to stop in and—"

"Check to make sure we were on the job?"

He scowled at her, and Hannah thought there must be something wrong with her because even that downward curl of his lips looked… Sexy.

"All right, yes. You don't have much time and—"

"And we know that," she finished for him. "We're on it. We're going to stay on it. I don't need a keeper."

"That's a shame because you have one," he said

mildly, though the gleam in his eyes as he looked at her told her he wasn't *feeling* mild. "I'll be stopping in to check on your progress, so get used to it."

She shrugged and smiled. "You're not the first fluttery client I've had."

"*Fluttery*? Is that even a word?"

She nearly laughed at the insult stamped on his features, but somehow she managed to hold it back. She'd only said it to get a reaction from King Carey anyway.

"It's my word, so yes, it is. Besides, you know what I mean. The nervous types. Always worried, have to see for themselves."

He tucked the sides of his jacket back and slipped his hands into his slacks pockets.

"I'm not nervous." He looked around at the mess. "Although maybe I should be. What are all these pans and things here?"

"We emptied the kitchen cabinets. Put everything there until we know what you want to do with them."

"I don't want to do a thing with them." He blew out a breath. "I'll get John Henry to make that call."

"Great. That takes care of one problem."

"You're sure of yourself, aren't you?"

"Actually..." she said, glancing around the restaurant. She saw the debris, the destruction. And she knew that, like most of her clients, all Bennett Carey saw was the rubble. But she could see past all of that to what it was going to be. What she and her crew would do with it. They would bring it back from the darkness and let it live again—better than ever. When she looked back to him, she smiled and said, "Yes. I guess I am."

"I hope that confidence is well-placed," he told her. "I've got a lot on the line here."

"Yeah, me, too," she said, but he wasn't finished.

His gaze fixed on her, he said, "I'm taking a chance on you, Ms. Yates. You and your company."

Well, she felt the sting of that statement. Maybe it wasn't an actual insult, but it was damn close. "We do excellent work, and you know it or you wouldn't have hired us in the first place."

"As you pointed out yesterday, my options were limited."

"You arrogant—"

One eyebrow arched as if he were just waiting for her to give him a reason to fire her, and she wasn't going to give it to him. She didn't know what it was about this man, but apparently on very short acquaintance, he had discovered just how to push her buttons.

Holding up one hand, she said, "I'll apologize for that."

"Thank you."

"Even though you deserved it."

His mouth curved so slightly, it almost didn't qualify as movement. "Quite the apology."

"Look, if you're thinking you can insult me into quitting so you can hire someone else—"

"There is no one else, as you've already pointed out."

"There you go." She walked toward him and lifted her gaze to his as she did. "So bottom line, we're all you've got. Luckily enough for you, we're worth every penny you're going to pay us. The Carey is going to be as beautiful as ever when we're finished with it. And just so you know, this job is important to me and my company."

"For the bonus."

A short, sharp laugh shot from her throat. "Damn straight for the bonus. Did you expect me to say the honor of working on The Carey would be enough?" It wasn't the "honor" of doing this job, it's what working for the Careys would do for her reputation. For her future. But she wasn't about to tell him that. "No. This job is important and it will be done to the high standards Yates Construction believes in."

"Good."

"It will be done quicker if you leave."

His lips twitched again, and she thought she even saw a flash of approval in his eyes before it was gone again.

"I'll go," he said, when another crash from the kitchen sounded out. He kept his gaze on hers as he added, "But I'll be back."

"Good movie."

"What?" He frowned, thought about what he'd just said and sighed. "Right. *Terminator.* Yes. Good movie. The statement stands. Get used to having me around, Ms. Yates—"

"Hannah."

He nodded. "Hannah. Get used to it because you'll be seeing a lot of me for the next few weeks."

She stared after him for a long moment after he left. Well, hell. Now she was looking forward to seeing him. And that was just dangerous. Gorgeous. Rich. Annoying.

What woman wouldn't be fascinated?

Damn it.

Bennett took two meetings after his run-in with Hannah Yates and for the first time in his life, had found it hard to concentrate. Which was completely unacceptable.

They had the Summer Sensation concert series nearly ready to begin and the voting on the Summer Stars was being tabulated. In two weeks, they'd announce the winner with a ton of media fanfare, and in four weeks, they'd have the reception and dinner at The Carey.

And there was Hannah Yates back in his mind again.

Absently, he looked around his office, taking in the huge space, with its chrome, steel, glass and black leather. The furnishings were sparse, but sleekly modern. There were abstract paintings on the walls and floor-to-ceiling tinted windows affording him a view of the world outside. His own desk was steel topped by glass with chrome accents. Even the desk phone looked futuristic in its slim silver casing.

As he looked around, he frowned as he suddenly realized that there wasn't a single soft space in the entire room. Why had he never noticed that before? Why was he noticing *now*?

Damn woman was splintering his thoughts about everything. Couldn't concentrate on meetings. Suddenly giving a damn what kind of furniture he had in his office. It had to be her. None of that had bothered him before Hannah Yates had entered his orbit.

He spun his desk chair around to stare out at the sunny skies beyond the glass and let his mind wander to that early morning visit to the restaurant.

She was so damn *tiny*. Yet every inch of her was packed with curves designed to drive a man crazy. Her jeans sculpted her legs and defined a butt that was world-class. Her T-shirt was tight enough to cling to her breasts and skim her narrow waist. That hair of hers. He'd always preferred long, blond hair on a woman, and yet, here he was, wondering how that short, inky black hair would feel in his hands.

Then there were her eyes. A pure, emerald green.

Sharp. Cool. Dismissive and that really bugged him. Hell, women didn't dismiss Bennett Carey. But she did, with an amusement that was both irritating and intriguing.

He didn't hear his office door open, but closed his eyes on a heartfelt sigh when his father spoke up and ruined a perfectly good daydream.

"What's this about you canceling our cleaning contractor?"

Bennett had known this would be coming, and he'd braced for it, though now that the moment was here, irritation crawled through him. Turning around to face his father, Bennett said, "I found someone better."

"Better?" Martin bunched his fists at his sides. "We've had the Parris company for nearly twenty years."

"Yeah." Bennett stood up to face the man. "And they've been getting lazy, Dad. They're so sure of themselves and our contract with them, they've stopped giving us their best. It's been going on for the last two years."

"What has?"

"Slipshod work," Bennett told him. "They're not bothering to clean where they think it won't be noticed."

"You should have talked to them. Hell. To *me*," Martin argued. "We've got a longstanding relationship with those people."

"And they've been taking advantage of it. I've had complaints from some of the staff at the Center. I looked into it."

"Why didn't I hear about it?"

Boggy ground here, Bennett knew. "Because I'm the CEO, Dad."

Martin's features flushed with color, and Bennett

knew the old man wasn't happy about being left out of the decision-making, but then he hadn't expected him to be.

"So it was time to shake things up," Bennett said flatly. "I've already got a top grade company contracted to take over as of this week."

"Who?"

Bennett looked down at his desk, checked the name to be sure, then lifted his gaze to his father. "Top of the Line. They come highly recommended, have a great reputation and they're 10 percent less expensive than Parris."

"So it's about money. You're saving some pennies—"

"Not pennies, Dad," Bennett interrupted. "And I wasn't the one who made the original suggestion to change companies."

"Who was? And why didn't I hear about any of this until the meeting?"

"Don Mackie, head of our in housecleaning staff, told me about the issues a month ago. I looked into it, talked to the head of Parris and, when that didn't change anything, I made the decision."

"Without me."

"Dad," Bennett said as calmly and quietly as he could manage, "I didn't ask for your opinion on this because it was straightforward and a good business decision."

"I don't like it," Martin muttered darkly.

"Change isn't always a bad thing, Dad." He had the distinct feeling his father was fighting retirement because Martin simply could not imagine not coming into the Carey offices every day. In a way, Bennett understood that. Martin didn't want to give up control, and

Bennett was the same way. And that thought didn't bring him any comfort.

"Damn it, Bennett..." Martin pushed one hand through his gray-streaked hair and Bennett recognized the action as one he himself performed several times a day. Just how much like his father was he, anyway?

He loved his parents. But between his father refusing to let go of the reins of the company and his mother refusing to move out of Bennett's house... Well, even the tightest familial ties could get strained to the snapping point. And right now, he felt as taut as a rope strung across a chasm.

"Dad, I'm in charge of this company. From the big decisions to the smallest—like this one—it's up to me to make them."

"I'm not saying different," his father argued, though that's exactly what he'd been saying. "I simply think you should have told me yourself. Discussed it."

"Why?"

"Why?"

Bennett lifted one hand to shove at his hair, then let it drop to his side. "Because you put *me* in charge. These decisions are mine to make now. Besides, it wasn't anything important, Dad. Not important enough to even warrant this conversation."

Martin's face flushed and his eyes snapped. "Is that right? You don't need the old man's opinion anymore, is that it?"

Sighing, Bennet said with a patience he hadn't thought he possessed, "Dad, you put me in charge for a reason. You knew I could do it and you knew it was time. What's changed?"

Scrubbing one hand across his face, Martin whirled

around, took three or four steps away, then spun back. "I never considered what it would be like to be shut out. To *not* be in charge, and I damn well don't like it."

And that was the bottom line. Martin had spent his entire adult life building the Carey Corporation into the immense company it was today. Together with his wife, he'd raised four kids, trained them to take over and continue the Carey traditions. But now that it was time for that changing of the guard to happen, Martin couldn't bring himself to let go.

"Sorry to hear that Dad," Bennett said, and meant it. His father had built this company into a major player. He'd poured blood, sweat and tears into the making of it, and now that it was his turn to step back, he didn't know what to do with himself.

Bennett didn't even want to think about what it would be like when it was *his* turn. At least his father had a family. A wife who loved him enough to walk away from him in an attempt to wake him up.

What did Bennett have?

Instantly, the sexy pixie popped back into his mind and he ruthlessly pushed her aside.

"Your mother doesn't get it," Martin complained. "She thinks I should just walk away from everything I've spent my life building. Just turn my back and somehow magically not care what happens to it anymore."

"Dad, she knows you'll always care." Bennett shook his head. "What she wants to know is that you care just as much—or more—about *her*."

Martin's jaw dropped and his eyes bugged open. "That's ridiculous. Why the hell would she think I don't care about her? We're *married* for God's sake. We've got four grown kids, a granddaughter and nearly forty years together to show for it."

Wow. His father either really was clueless or he was deliberately not seeing the truth. Either way it had to stop. Soon.

"You know I'm not taking sides in this," Bennett said, feeling uncomfortable already. Hell, he'd spent the last several months avoiding getting dragged into the Retirement Wars. He could see his dad's point, but his mom had more on her side. Which was why he'd stayed out of it.

"Yeah, I know." He huffed out a breath. "What are you trying not to say?"

"Fine." Bennett came out from behind his desk, then leaned one hip against the heavy steel-and-glass slab. "I'm trying not to say that Mom's got a point. You promised her a lot when I took over, and you haven't delivered."

"What the hell kind of thing is that for my son to say?"

"You asked me to tell you."

"Well, I didn't want to hear *that*."

"This is why I stayed out of it."

"It was a good plan. Keep to it," Martin said.

"Wish I had," Bennett muttered.

"What was that?"

"Nothing." He took a breath, looked at his father and said, "Dad. Look. Mom's living with me because she's pissed at you."

"You could throw her out," Martin said slyly.

Bennett choked out a laugh. "Yeah, that's going to happen."

Scowling fiercely, the older man muttered, "Well, what should I do then if you won't help me?"

"Jeezz, Dad. You got her to marry you. Figure out what worked back then and do it again."

Martin gave him a long, thoughtful look.

Bennett walked back around his desk and dropped into the chair. "Just please do it somewhere else."

"That's a helluva thing to say to your father," Martin grumbled. "Fine. I'm going. And just so you know, I don't care about the cleaning company."

Bennett threw both hands up. "Then what was this all about?"

"To remind you that I'm not dead yet, Bennett. I'm still a part of this company." He stomped across the office and when he left, he slammed the door behind him hard enough to make one of the paintings on the wall tilt to the left.

Bennett sighed and let his head fall back against his chair. "Believe me, Dad. I know."

Five

By the third day on the job, they were hitting a rhythm.

Hannah was still worried, but feeling better about meeting the impossible deadline.

Tiny and Carol were working on replacing the beams in the attic while Mike was on the roof, pulling out the damaged shingles and roofing paper. Since he'd been able to find replacement shingles of the same style and color, they'd be able to patch the roof without having to replace the whole thing. Another time saver.

"Hannah! Can you come over here for a minute?"

Marco Benzi, late forties with brown eyes and a perpetual three-day growth of beard on his cheeks, waved her over to where he stood beside an open fuse box.

"Is there a problem?"

"Not yet," he said, then tapped one of the old fuses. "This box is practically an antique."

She sighed. “Well, that’s just perfect news.”

“No, the good news is that the wiring in the building is safe.”

“Um…the kitchen wasn’t so safe.”

“A short started that fire.” He shook his head. “A spark was all it took. But the rest of the building checks out. Still. This thing’s got to be replaced. It doesn’t even have an RCD. That’s asking for trouble.”

Residual Current Devices were automatic protection devices in a fuse box. They contained switches that would trip a circuit under dangerous conditions and instantly disconnect the electricity. Preventing fires. Saving lives. If The Carey had had an updated fuse box before the fire, there might not have been one.

“Replace it all,” she said. Hannah wasn’t about to risk another fire in the building she was trying to save.

“On it, boss,” Marco said, and went back to work, whistling under his breath.

One more thing, she thought, and had to admit that as a new problem, it was pretty small. Usually on a job, they found more complications than they’d been hired to fix. Rot under a floor. Water damage under a tub being replaced. All kinds of things could go wrong in a house or a business, and it was their job to fix it all. They were damn good at it.

“What’s going on?”

Of course.

Hannah turned to look at King Carey, standing just inside the door. She should have been annoyed with his daily presence. Instead, she’d found herself watching for him. Waiting for him, a sense of expectancy coiled inside her.

This wasn’t good, she told herself. Being attracted to

the man was one thing, enjoying that attraction so much was something else. But then she'd been repeating that mantra since the moment she'd first met him. It didn't seem to help. All he had to do was walk into a room and she felt that now familiar buzz of a near electrical charge lighting up her body.

Hell. Maybe *she* needed an RCD.

"What's going on is work," she said. "Why aren't you off doing yours?"

"Because I had to stop in here first." He checked his watch, and she wondered absently just how many times a day he did that.

"Well, you're here now, so I'll show you around."

His eyebrows rose high on his forehead. "I wasn't expecting that."

"Well, good," she said. "I hate being predictable." She pointed to where Marco was working. "Starting there. Your fuse box is old and outdated. Not to mention dangerous. We're replacing it."

"Okay, good."

When she turned and waved at him to follow, he moved to do just that, stepping into the kitchen right behind her. In fact he was so close to her, Hannah could have sworn she felt the heat of his body pressing into her back. She closed her eyes briefly, took a breath meant to steady herself and, instead, all she managed was to inhale the scent of him. Sort of high-end woodsy. Like glamping, she thought with an inner smile.

"How do you know what you're doing in all of this?"

She looked around, trying to see it as he was. Cabinets torn out, counters ripped off and stacked neatly to one side. Appliances moved to what they were calling the storage area. Tarps on the old wood floors, gaping hole in the ceiling and smoke stains on drywall that had yet to be replaced.

"Actually, it looks good to me. We're making solid progress." She had to speak up over the clatter of noise the guys engendered. "Mike already checked the roof and the support beams. You're in good shape there. Whoever built this place so long ago was a craftsman."

"Good to know."

"Well, except for the wiring and that wasn't his fault. It was up to code sixty years ago." She shrugged. "Anyway, Mike's found replacement shingles, so we don't have to redo the whole roof."

"Also good news since we just did that two years ago," he told her.

She turned and looked up at him. "Tiny and Carol are working the attic, making sure there are no more scorched beams we haven't found yet."

He nodded and watched the hustle in the kitchen.

"Devin Colier is our flooring guy." Hannah used the toe of her boot to shove the tarp aside a bit. "You've got white oak here and it's solid. It's scraped and scarred from years of use and then the added excitement of the firemen and their tools and boots marking things up."

"They don't look good," he said as she dragged the protective tarp back into place.

"They will." She turned her face up to his and stared into his lake-blue eyes. How could a stern stare from him make her stomach spin and her breathing shallow and fast? Deliberately, she took a long, deep breath—taking the scent of him inside her again. He was really fogging up her mind. "Once the new cabinets are installed, Devin's going to come in and sand the floorboards, here and in the dining area."

"Shouldn't you be doing the floors before the cabinets?"

"Common misconception." Oooh. He didn't like the word *common.* "The subfloor is under the cabinets and that's already been replaced due to water damage from the firefighting. The finish flooring is what you'll see and walk on. And we want the kitchen and dining areas to match, so best we sand and stain all at once."

"Makes sense."

This was going way too smoothly, she thought. Where was the arguing? The demanding? Keeping a wary eye on him, she continued, "When that's done, he'll put a stain on." Tipping her head to one side, she asked, "Do you want a dark stain, like it was before? Or maybe a clear coat to let the grain of the wood shine through?"

One eyebrow lifted. "Judging by the way you said that, I know which choice you'd prefer. The clear coat. Is that your professional judgment?"

She shrugged. "A little, I guess. But more, it would look better, I think. Light floors, dark walls. Take some of the 'cave-like' feel of the restaurant away."

"Cave-like?"

He was insulted. She almost smiled because suddenly, they were back to normal.

Holding up both hands for peace, Hannah smiled. "Okay, I didn't mean to throw metaphorical darts at The Carey. But be honest. This place was built six decades ago, when dark cozy places reminded people of the Rat Pack or something. It probably felt…mysterious. Clandestine, even."

"Where do you get this stuff?" He honestly looked stunned.

Why did she so enjoy befuddling him? Probably because she had the feeling it didn't happen often. He was so in control. So studiously proper. "Doesn't matter. Just, trust me. It worked back then."

"It *still* works," he pointed out.

"Ah," she said, waving a finger at him. Again he looked at her as if he were trying to understand a foreign language. "But could it work even better? Times have changed. Moods have changed. Lightening up the restaurant, even this little bit? Gives it a whole new feel. Might bring in younger clientele, too."

Well, that put the scowl back on his face, and what did it say about her, that she preferred him that way? When he was being all calm and reasonable, she really didn't know what to make of him. Besides, that scowl of his was pretty damn sexy.

When he took the time to look around, both in the kitchen and the dining area, Hannah watched him. She could almost see him measuring, weighing his choices and even drawing what was probably a not very clear mental picture of what the finished restaurant would look like. Hannah could appreciate that. He wasn't only a sharp businessman, but he was open enough, willing enough, to consider something that hadn't been on his radar.

When he turned back to her, he nodded. "Go with the clear coat. You might have a point about the place being too dark."

A slow satisfied smile curved her mouth. "Mr. Carey," she said. "There may be hope for you yet."

"That would depend," he said, "on what you're hoping for."

The flash of interest in his eyes kindled something inside her that she fought to ignore, because if she didn't, she might have to admit to what she was hoping for. And at the moment, that was to taste that scowling mouth of his.

So she laughed to cover what she was thinking, feeling, and said, "You never disappoint. And, I'd like to point out that we just had an actual conversation. No arguments. No sniping."

"The day is young," he retorted, then nodded, turned and walked out of the restaurant.

Hannah hated when he got the last word.

Bennett could not stop thinking about Hannah Yates, and that bothered him on several fronts. She wasn't the type of woman he was usually attracted to at all, yet, she was always at the edges of his mind.

"Bennett!"

He blinked like a man coming out of a dead sleep, and maybe he was. God knew, his mind kept drifting off to Hannah at the most inappropriate times. Like now, for instance. He stared at the man sitting across the desk from him.

Jack Colton, his sister Serena's fiancé and one of Bennett's oldest friends—also the head of the Colton Group, one of the largest hotel chains in the world. Jack's blue eyes were now watching him with amusement.

Well, that was annoying.

"What?"

"Good question," Jack said with a grin. "In the middle of talking about that castle I've got to get built in my backyard for Alli, you zone out. Where'd you go?"

"I'm right here," Bennett said, and sat forward, leaning both elbows on his desk.

"Sure, buddy." Jack leaned back in his chair and set his ankle on his knee. "So who is she?"

"I don't know what you're talking about."

"Right." He sat up straight, looked at the back of the steel and black leather chair. "These things are damned uncomfortable—did you know?"

"How would I know," Bennett said. "I don't sit in them."

"You should try them out," Jack told him as he stood up. "But not for long."

Frowning at the chairs, Bennett said, "They don't have to be comfortable. It's not like I want people to sit in here for hours."

"Then good job. Because I guarantee they won't."

Jack was the first person—beyond his sisters—to complain about his office furniture. And maybe, he admitted silently, Jack had a point. Sighing, Bennett asked, "Was there a reason for your visit today?"

His friend laughed shortly. "Good to see you, too."

Pushing one hand through his hair, Bennett swung his chair to one side and tapped his fingers on his desk. "Fine. You want to talk, we'll talk. What's going on? Serena driving you crazy with wedding plans? Because she and Amanda both are doing that to the rest of us. Seems only fair that you have to pay since you're the one who asked her."

Jack slapped one hand to his chest and grinned. "Damn, Bennett, that was so touching."

"What do you want, Jack?"

"I want names." Jack started walking, doing a circuit of the office, turning his head to look back at Bennett.

"Names?" Bennett repeated. "Why? Is Serena pregnant?"

Jack shook his head. "Not yet, and that's not what I meant. You know I promised Alli a castle in the backyard at my house."

"Yeah…and a puppy, Serena says."

"True. But castle first, puppy after," Jack said, and stopped at the windows to take a long look out at the sun-splashed business park. When he turned to Bennett again, he said, "I've been living in Europe for seven years. I have no idea who to call for this. I thought you might have a couple of names of contractors."

Bennett went very still, then narrowed his gaze on the other man. "This is a setup, right? Serena told you about Hannah Yates."

"Of course she did," Jack said with a laugh. "Doesn't mean my question's not valid. I need a contractor. So, is she any good? Could she do it?"

"Probably. But she's not doing anything but the restaurant for the next three and a half weeks."

"Understood," Jack said. "But she could take a look at the yard, give me some ideas."

"I suppose that'd be all right."

"Damn, Bennett, do you have every minute of her day accounted for?"

"Just for the next three and a half weeks. And I don't want her distracted from the job."

"Don't want her distracted," Jack repeated. "Is work all you think about Bennett?"

"What's that supposed to mean?"

"I think it's pretty clear," Jack said with a shake of his head. "When I look at you, I see me not too long ago and it's not good."

"I don't have time to be analyzed, Jack."

Jack pushed the edges of his jacket back and shoved

his hands into his pockets. Shaking his head, he said, "Bennett, we've been friends for a long time."

"Yeah, so?"

"So, I'm wondering when you're finally going to loosen up."

"Loosen up?"

"Yeah." Jack looked at him. "You're so tied up in the company, you don't have a life any more than I did until I found Serena again."

Insulted, Bennett said, "Says the man who just spent the last seven years rebuilding his family's company. You call that 'loose'?"

"No." Pulling his hands free, Jack walked closer. "You're right. I did spend almost every waking hour working or thinking about the company. Then I noticed work was all I had. And maybe you've noticed that I've done some substantial loosening since I moved back to California."

"I noticed you have the time to stop by my office to insult me."

"See? Exactly. You have to make time for the important stuff."

A short bark of laughter shot unexpectedly from Bennett's throat. "So it's important to insult me. Great. Thanks for that."

"No problem." Jack smiled to soften the words, but still, he said, "Bennett, you spend too much time here. Hell, you're trying to get your dad to walk away, but you're here more than he is."

"This is my job."

"This is your *life*," Jack countered. "And if you're not careful, it's going to be all you've got."

"And suddenly you have the answer to life?" Bennett

snorted. "You're wasting your time in the hotel industry. You should be a therapist."

"Don't have the patience for it," Jack admitted. "Just standing here trying to pound sense into your hard head has pushed me to my edge."

"Then step back," Bennett told him. "I don't have a problem. I have a company that needs me. And I'm trying to get my father out because he retired!"

"And is that how long it's going to take to get you to leave?"

Why was everyone so worried all of a sudden about how tightly wound he was or wasn't? His sisters were on him. His mother. Hell, even Hannah Yates had voiced her opinion. And now his friends were jumping on the bandwagon?

Bennett didn't overwork. He worked just enough. He kept tabs on his employees, on his company, on his family members. He had a home. He didn't sleep in his office, for God's sake. Of course, he was forced to admit, he wasn't home much. Less, now that his mother had set up camp there. But that didn't mean he didn't have a life.

"I *like* my life," he muttered darkly.

"Yeah? Why?"

"Why should I have to define that for you?"

"The question is *can* you define why?"

He shot Jack a hard glare. "Because it's the life I built. The one I want. You don't have to live it so what do you care?"

"You're my friend. Soon to be my brother-in-law."

"And?"

"And, I'd like to see you sometimes without having to come to the office to do it." Jack scrubbed one hand across the back of his neck. "Hell, Serena and I invited you to dinner a few nights ago, and you were *here.* Going over some problem with marketing."

All right, yes, he might spend too much time at the company, but in his defense, "Serena can't cook."

Jack laughed as he was meant to. "I was grilling and you missed a good meal with us and with Alli."

Bennett hated it when he was wrong. Thankfully, he told himself, it didn't happen often. But this time, was one of the rare occasions. He should have gone to dinner at Jack's place in Laguna. Bennett hadn't seen much of his niece, Alli, lately, and he missed her.

"I was like you," Jack said. "Until I came back. Until Serena and I reconnected. Now I can see how little my life mattered before."

Bennett buried his impatience and the small bubble of anger that had begun to form. Jack was his friend, and even if Bennett didn't like what the man was saying, he understood where it was coming from. "I get what you're trying to do, Jack. And I should appreciate the thought anyway. But I'm not interested in getting married. I don't—"

"Have the time?" Jack finished for him.

"Funny." He checked his watch. There were still two hours until his next appointment. Standing up, he buttoned his suit jacket. "I'll tell you what. I'm willing to leave the office right now. I'll take you by The Carey. You can meet Hannah Yates and see if she's the contractor for you."

Jack smiled. "You're willing to take off work in the middle of the day to go by the restaurant, *just* to introduce me to your contractor."

Bennett stared at him. "You have a problem with that?"

"Nope I just find it...interesting."

Interesting. Bennett could live with that; he just hoped that his old friend couldn't see that he was really looking forward to seeing Hannah Yates again. Which he didn't want to think about, either.

Hannah felt a disturbance in the force the instant that Bennett Carey entered the restaurant.

She should have been used to it by then, but she wasn't. His spontaneous visits had caused her to be constantly on edge. Waiting for him to walk through the door. And the minute he did, every nerve in her body went on high alert.

Tossing a glance over her shoulder at the crew behind her, she walked into the main dining room to see Bennett and another man with him. She hardly spared the stranger a quick look before focusing on the man she couldn't stop thinking about.

"You're late," she said when her heart dropped out of her throat.

"What?"

"Well, check that famous watch of yours," Hannah teased. "It will show you that you're at least an hour behind when you usually stop by to check on me."

He frowned and Hannah grinned. Walking up to the other man, she held out one hand. "Hannah Yates."

"Jack Colton," he said, and when he released her hand, he looked around the scene. "I know you're working on it, but right now it's..."

"A mess," she said. "But it won't be for long." Turning to Bennett, she added, "John Henry phoned and told me to donate the kitchen counters and the old skillets and pans. He said he'll be expecting a new supply to go with his new kitchen."

"Of course he did," Bennett mused.

"Well, we donated the counters to Habitat for Humanity and the pans to the Goodwill, then broke down the damaged tables. We're building new ones and I thought you might want to consider a couple of longer tables surrounded by banquettes in the back there." She pointed, and the two men turned to look. "Most of the tables are, as you know, round and sufficient for four to six people. But if The Carey's being remade, I thought you might want to allocate some space here for larger gatherings.

"You know, family celebrations, business meetings..." She smiled when he flicked a look in her direction. "If you okay the idea, my dad and another of our crew will build the tables and then construct the banquettes around them. I'm thinking, cream-colored leather for the booths and chairs. What do you think?"

"Wow." Jack grinned and nodded. "I think you might even beat out Bennett's sister Amanda at how many words you can get out in one long breath."

She smiled at him, then shifted her focus to where it wanted to be. Bennett. The fact that he was watching her made her feel warm from head to toe. She steadied herself and said, "I've learned that if I want something, it's easier if I just lay it all out at once."

"Easier on me?" Bennett asked.

She nodded. "That way you only have to get mad once and we're finished."

Jack laughed again, but she hardly heard him. All she could see was Bennett. His gaze locked with hers, and she swore she could see actual flames in those bright blue eyes. Or maybe, she considered, it was the fire inside her being reflected in his eyes.

"Yeah." Jack looked from one to the other of them, then said, "If you don't mind, I'm just going to walk into the kitchen, see what they're doing…"

She hardly noted when he left. Instead, she kept her gaze on Bennett. "Brought a friend with you to help you keep tabs?"

His mouth curved slightly. "Oh, I don't need help."

"Agreed. You seem pretty good at it."

"Well, I've had a lot of practice."

Now her mouth curved. What was it about him? He hovered. He gave unwanted advice. Pronounced orders with that kingly attitude. And yet… Here she was, wondering what that mouth tasted like. Wondering how his hands would feel on her skin. Wondering—

"It's a mess in there, too," Jack announced as he came back into the room. "But it looks like they all know what they're doing."

"That's what I've been trying to tell Mr. Carey."

"I'll tell him for you."

She threw him a quick smile. "It's appreciated."

"He knows as much about construction as I do," Bennett said. "Which is nothing."

"It hasn't stopped you from telling us what to do and how to do it," she reminded him.

"I know how to motivate people."

"By browbeating them?"

"I haven't touched your brow."

"Metaphorical brows."

"As fascinating as this is," Jack interrupted, "I came here to meet you and to ask if you could build a castle."

Well, that got her attention. "A castle? I suppose we could. If we have about ten years and a lot of stone."

He grinned, glanced at Bennett and said, "I like her." Then to Hannah, he added, "A child-sized castle. In my backyard. For my soon-to-be stepdaughter."

"Oh." Her smile was wide and open. "I love that. What a fun idea. I'd love to talk to you about it—"

"In three and a half weeks," Bennett ground out.

She slid her gaze back to him. "I can talk about other jobs while doing one job."

"Multitasking." Jack nodded. "Serena's always telling me that women are stars at multitasking."

"I'm not paying you to multitask," Bennett reminded her, ignoring Jack.

"You'll get what you paid for, Mr. Carey," she said, then looked at Jack. "And when it's finished, we would love to build a castle for you, Mr. Colton."

"Jack, please."

She smiled and nodded. Then when she looked to Bennett again, she felt the smile slowly slide away. "Now, if you'll excuse me, I'll get back to work before you have to check your gold watch and decide if I'm wasting time or not."

Hannah heard Jack laugh as she left the room, but she *felt* Bennett Carey simmering.

Good. So was she.

Six

Hannah hadn't seen Bennett Carey in three days. Not since he'd stopped by the restaurant with his friend Jack Colton.

And she'd Googled Colton. Head of the Colton Group of hotels. Just as she had hoped, doing this job for the Careys was going to lead Yates Construction into other jobs. Sure, building a backyard castle wasn't exactly a huge assignment, but if Jack Colton liked it, he might use her company on jobs for his hotels. Or his house. Or maybe it would be an introduction to someone else. This was just the first of what she knew would be many jobs to come their way.

The first week working on The Carey had gone fast. So fast that Hannah had stayed up nights making notes, juggling their other jobs and worrying about that four-week deadline. Last night, she'd added in researching castles to get an idea of what Jack Colton might eventually want.

Having Bennett Carey continually "dropping by" the restaurant to check on their progress wasn't helping anything, either. This was the most important job they'd ever had, but it was hard to concentrate on construction when King Carey was constantly popping up and shattering her focus.

How could she consider floor joists or drywall, when her brain kept drifting to Bennett Carey's eyes. Or his big hands. Or how she wanted to nibble on his bottom lip for an hour or two?

She carried her first cup of coffee out of the kitchen to the front porch, where she sat on the cedar glider her father built for her when she bought the tiny house in Long Beach. Two years she'd lived there, and it still wasn't what she wanted it to be. What she knew it could be. She'd done the basic remodel, first on the bathroom that had held the smallest tub she'd ever seen. She'd expanded the room, installed a glorious soaker tub that she enjoyed every night, new lighting, new vanity and an oil-rubbed, bronze vessel sink. Along with the walk-in, hand tiled shower, her bathroom now was like taking a vacation in a five-star spa.

The kitchen, however, still looked as it had in the fifties.

"I'll get around to it," she assured herself, settling against the plump pillows stacked on the glider. There would be time for all of it, and extra money once she'd finished the restaurant job.

Six in the morning, the narrow street was quiet but for a few neighbors firing up their cars for the drive to work. The sun was rising and spreading a soft pink across the sky, and Hannah took a moment to simply *enjoy* this time. Every morning, she sat on this glider and thought about the day ahead, making mental notes for the hours to come.

Since she spent her days with the sounds of power tools and loud men shouting and laughing, she relished this slice of silence that started her mornings. She curled her legs up under her, cradled the mug between her palms and sighed a little.

This house, with its wide front porch had called to her the moment she'd seen it. Small, forgotten, allowed to fall—not apart, but asleep. Hannah was slowly waking it up, making it what it had been when it was first built in the fifties. Actually, making it more. She loved it.

But at the moment, she only wanted to enjoy this time alone. These few minutes every morning gave Hannah the center she needed to handle the job, the crew and any problem that popped up.

"Like for example," she muttered, "*this* one."

A gleaming black BMW parked in front of her house, and even before the driver stepped out, she knew who it was. Who else did she know who could afford a car like that?

"Why is King Carey here to ruin my morning?"

He shut the car door and took a long moment to study her house as he would some ancient archeological dig. As if trying to figure out why anyone would want to live there.

"Perfect." She refused to give up her seat on the glider, so she called out, "Isn't this a little early for you?"

His gaze snapped to her, and Hannah could have sworn she felt a jolt of heat shoot right through her. She swallowed hard, then took another sip of coffee, more to keep busy as he stalked up the stone walkway than because she wanted it.

He wore a black suit, black shirt and a tie the color of blood. If he was headed to a meeting, he was going to scare the crap out of his adversary. He didn't scare her, though. What he did to her was better left undefined.

"What're you doing here?" she asked, then held up a hand before he could answer. "No, how did you find out where I live?"

He leaned one shoulder against the porch post, then thought better of it and pushed away. Brushing one hand over his suit jacket to rid himself of dust—or, Hannah thought, *cooties*—he looked at her.

What was it about him that drew her in, she wondered. All week at the job, whenever he stopped by, she had felt his presence before she actually saw him. It was as if the air charged around him and sent her signals by the zip in her blood and the tingling in every one of her nerve endings. Yes, he was gorgeous. But it wasn't just his looks that pulled at her.

It was that constant scowl, the impatient gleam in his eyes and the oh-so-rare half smile that surprised her every now and then. All she knew was that she thought about him when he wasn't there, dreamed about him at night and really resented the hell out of the fact that another rich man was making her think things she shouldn't.

She'd been down this road before, and she knew it ended badly. So why was she allowing herself to repeat her own history? Internally warning herself to get a grip, she paid attention when he started speaking.

"Finding where you lived was difficult. I employed a private detective named Google."

She grinned. There it was again, that unexpected humor that threw her just a little off-balance. "Wow. Was that a joke?"

"Is it so surprising?"

"Actually, yes." She grinned up at him and wasn't surprised when he shifted his gaze away to look around the porch.

She knew what he was seeing. A long, concrete porch, painted a bright yellow with white trim. She had to guess that it was little to nothing like the palace he no doubt lived in.

"Looking for something?"

"What?" His gaze snapped to her. "No."

Sighing, Hannah scooted back on the glider and patted the sky blue-and-yellow-flowered cushion beside her. "Have a seat."

He glanced at the glider, and she could almost *see* the distaste on his face. Her first instinct was to be offended, but she let that go quickly. She couldn't really blame him. He looked as out of place here as she would in one of his board meetings. Hannah had the feeling he didn't do a lot of front porch sitting. And maybe he needed to.

"It doesn't bite," she offered.

"Can you be sure?"

"More humor. A red-letter day." Why did she find that so enticing? Maybe because she knew it was very nearly a gift, these rare peeks at a man who was ordinarily so stiff and stern and all business? Did he ever unwind? Did he sleep in a suit? Was it his birthday suit? Oh, the images that raced through her mind.

He gingerly sat down beside her and frowned at the glider's movement. "Never saw the appeal in rocking chairs."

"It's a glider," she corrected.

"What's the difference?"

"This glides," she pointed out, giving him a half smile. "Rockers rock."

"Whichever." He looked at her. "Why would you want your chair to move?"

"A question for the ages," she muttered. He looked so stiff. So uncomfortable, she nearly laughed. Then she remembered that he had shattered her morning routine and was now, instead of just showing up at the job site, appearing at her house. At the crack of dawn. Across the street, the Morrison family was up and moving. She could tell because in a blink, nearly every light in the house snapped on. Three houses down from them, the light on Doc Burns's front porch clicked off as the older man carried his golf clubs out to his car.

Morning was creeping in, and families up and down the street were beginning to stir.

And it occurred to her that Bennett Carey really didn't belong in her everyday world. A damn shame because she *really* liked looking at him.

"Back to my original question," she said finally, when she turned to look at the tall gorgeous statue sitting beside her. She took a sip of coffee as he stared at her. "What are you doing here?"

He pushed the sleeve of his jacket back and checked that gold watch of his. Wound seriously too tight. His schedule seemed to rule him rather than the other way around, and Hannah had the urge to snap him out of his well-trod rut. At the moment though, she was trying to ignore the flutter of something fabulous happening inside her. He was so close, she could smell his aftershave and feel the heat lifting off his body.

So close, she could reach out and run her hand through his hair. She cupped her fingers more tightly around her coffee cup.

"I've got an early meeting in Los Angeles," he said, "so I won't be able to stop by the restaurant today."

She clucked her tongue. "How will we get by without you?"

His lips twitched. Another sign of humor, and she had to wonder if he knew just what that slight smile did to her. Probably not. If he did, he wouldn't do it.

"Entertaining," he said, then added, "I figured you would be up this early since you're usually at the restaurant by eight."

Wow. Not only did he have his schedule memorized, but hers, too. "Your stalking is very efficient."

"I'm not stalking you, I'm…keeping tabs on you."

She lifted her coffee cup in a toast. "Interesting definition of hovering."

"Stalking. Now hovering?" He shook his head. "I'm the one paying for this job. I'm the one who needs it done."

"Then maybe you're the one who should give us the space to do it."

He pushed off the glider, sending her into a hard back and forth. She didn't move to stop it, only stared at him over the lip of her mug.

He pushed his jacket aside and shoved his hands into his pockets. How could he look so irritated and so… tempting all at the same time? She knew it was a mistake to indulge herself with private fantasies of what could happen between the two of them. It splintered her focus and at the same time, set her up for disaster if she ever allowed herself to *actually* indulge.

"I took a chance on you and your company."

Okay, that got Hannah to her feet. Setting the coffee cup down on the porch railing, she tipped her head back to glare at him and, not for the first time in her life, wished she were five or six inches taller.

"I run a damn good company and you know it," she said, stabbing her index finger at him for emphasis. "And you didn't give us this job out of some generosity of spirit. You had no choice but to 'take a chance' just like I'm taking a chance on you."

A short bark of laughter shot from his throat. "Some chance. You're being paid very well."

"And you're getting your restaurant back in better shape than it was before the fire and in record time. So I guess we're both happy."

He shook his head, whether in admiration or exasperation, she couldn't be sure. Then he spoke and all questions ended.

"You are the most infuriating woman I've ever known."

"I'm both flattered and annoyed," she said. "And right back at you."

"Me?" He was clearly shocked. "How am I infuriating?"

"Oh, I don't know." She tossed both hands high. "The constant checking up on me for instance? Constantly questioning my competence. Checking your watch every other second? Dropping by the job site at all times of the day."

"My restaurant."

"My job site."

Something simmered in the air between them as it had been for the last week. She was almost getting accustomed to the sizzle and burn inside her. God knew, she actually looked forward to it now. For several long seconds the air felt electrified as they stared at each other.

Then he checked his watch again.

"Oh for heaven's sake. You should get rid of that watch."

He snorted. "Not likely. I've got appointments to keep and I'm never late."

"Never?"

"Never." He threw that last word down like it was a trophy he'd earned for being OCD.

"And do you still have time to make your meeting this morning?"

"Not if I don't get on the damn freeway soon."

She grabbed her coffee and sat down on the glider again, even though she knew that recapturing the peace of her private sunrise was futile. Even after he left, his presence would haunt her. Make her remember the sweep of nerves jangling through her whenever he was close. Didn't seem to matter that he could make her so angry.

Right from the beginning, she'd enjoyed his irritability. More than enjoyed—it almost fed the attraction for Hannah. What fun was any kind of relationship if it was always… Nice?

But all she said was, "Well, fly free. Don't let me keep you."

"Like I said," he muttered. "Infuriating."

She toasted him with her coffee again and thought about how she was glad to sit down, since being that close to King Carey always made her knees weak.

"Look," he said after a long, deep breath, "the main reason I stopped by was to tell you that John Henry is going to stop in to see you today. He has a list of changes he wants made in the kitchen and I wanted you to know that whatever he wants, he gets."

Her eyebrows rose. "He must be important to you."

"One of my best friends. But more than that, he's the best chef in California and I plan on keeping him."

"Well, free rein in a kitchen design should do it for you." She took a sip of her now cold coffee. "But you could have called me with that command."

"Yeah," he admitted, staring across the street when one of the Morrison boys raced out to a van and started an engine that desperately needed a muffler. Looking back at her, he said, "I could have. Should have."

Intrigued, she asked, "Why didn't you?"

It took him a second or two of thoughtful silence before he blurted out, "I decided I wanted to see you. Away from the job site." He didn't look happy about that. "Obviously I'm a secret masochist."

She laughed and felt something stir inside her. Yes, she was definitely intrigued by tall, dark and grumpy. "Obviously. Okay another question."

"Sure, why not?"

"How many suits do you own?"

"What?" He scowled at her. "What does that have to do with anything?"

"It's just a question, Mr. Carey."

"Bennett."

She nodded and swallowed hard against another rising swirl of nerves. "Bennett." Pausing, Hannah studied him and thought about it for a second. "You know, I think that's too stuffy. I'll call you Ben."

He frowned. "No one calls me Ben."

"No one? Not even your family?"

"No one," he repeated.

"Well, that's even better," she said lightly, beginning to enjoy herself immensely. "So how many, Ben? Suits."

Still scowling, he admitted, "I have no idea."

"Uh-huh." She stood up, set her mug down on the railing again and asked, "How many pairs of jeans?"

"Two."

She grinned at his quick response. "This is why you need me to call you Ben. Seriously wound too tight."

"I'm getting very tired of hearing that." His lips thinned and a muscle in his jaw twitched as if he were grinding his teeth to keep whatever else it was he wanted to say from spilling out. Then he blurted out, "Does that engine sound off like that every morning?"

Funny, Hannah thought. She'd stopped hearing the loud roar from the car. As she thought it, the boy drove off in a symphony of thunderous noises, and when it was quiet again, she looked up at him and said, "Yes."

"My God. Why hasn't the neighborhood taken up a collection to buy him something different?"

"Because he's a kid and he loves that van."

"No accounting for taste," he mumbled.

"No," she agreed, "there really isn't. Which leads me to this." It was spur-of-the-moment, completely. Maybe it was thinking of him as Ben rather than Bennett. Made him more… Approachable, though no less dangerous. And still, she couldn't resist one little taste.

She went up on her toes, grabbed his suitcoat lapels and pulled him down to her, then laid her mouth on his for three or four long, lingering seconds. One taste, she reminded herself, though oh, how she wanted more. Heat roared through her. Every nerve ending stood up and applauded. Her stomach did a wild roll and spin, and when she let him go, she grabbed the porch railing just to stay steady.

Then she looked up into his eyes and saw heat flashing in the dark blue. "What was that?" he asked.

"That was a kiss."

"Why?"

"I'm not sure," she admitted, cocking her head to study his features as if she'd never seen him before. "I guess, you looked like you needed to be kissed."

"Is that right?" He moved in closer. "And did you need to be kissed, as well?"

"*Need* is a strong word..." God, what had she been thinking? She'd been down this road before. With an über-rich, handsome man who had so little in common with her it was laughable until it all went to hell. And this time, the very rich man could make or break her company.

"*Need*," he said, "is a very strong word, and it almost captures what's happening right now."

"Yeah," she said, and took a step back. It seemed cowardly, even to her, but somehow she couldn't quite stop herself.

Meanwhile, the sky brightened and birds started singing in the trees. Down the street, another car started its engine and the throaty purr sounded like a heartbeat racing as fast as her own.

"I think you might be onto something," he murmured.

"What are you talking about?"

"It's what *you* were talking about. *Need*," he repeated, and that single word seemed to reverberate throughout her body, like a plucked harp string, vibrating on and on.

"Uh-huh." Hannah took a deep breath, hoping to steady herself, and though it didn't work, she pretended it had. "Well, you should probably get on the freeway or you'll be late."

"Probably, and as I said, I'm never late," he said. "And yet, I'm not ready to leave."

"Why not?"

"Because now it's you who looks as if she needs something."

Oh God. She knew exactly what she needed. Wanted. Was it so easy to read on her face? If it was, she wouldn't address it. Instead, she went for a lighthearted response. "Coffee? A little peace and quiet? Solitude?"

"None of the above."

"Really?"

"Really." He set his hands at her waist and lifted her off her feet to plant a kiss on her that Hannah swore set her hair on fire.

Her brain simply scrambled. Her blood burned and her heartbeat raced so loudly, it sounded like a drumbeat in her own ears. For what felt like forever, his mouth took hers. His lips, tongue, teeth, played and demanded and gave all at once.

Hannah sank into what he was doing to her. So many sensations rushed through her at once Hannah felt as if her head was about to fly off her shoulders and she wouldn't have cared. She'd never experienced anything like this, and that one small kiss she'd given him was like a sparkler next to this wild explosion of taste, scent, touch. Every inch of her body lit up like a Christmas tree, and she dug her hands into his shoulders to hold on and savor every second.

And just when she was considering crawling up his body like scaling a mountain, he let her go and took a step back.

A little dizzy, a lot horny, she could only blink and stare up at the man who had worked her up just to let her go.

"What?"

He shook his head, scrubbed one hand across his jaw. Then he fired a hard glare at her, as if leaving her achy and wanting was *her* fault.

"I have to go."

"Of course you do." Hannah's breath charged in and out of her lungs, but she felt a bit better when she noticed that he wasn't in much better shape than she was. Her knees were wobbly and the fog over her brain had barely lifted. She still felt… *Otherwhere.* And yeah, she knew that wasn't a real word, but it was the only thing she could think of to describe the feelings racing through her.

He checked his watch.

Hannah wanted to rip that gold watch off his wrist and throw it as far as she could. It would be good for him. And great for her.

"I have a meeting," he repeated.

"So you said. Well. Can't be late."

"No."

"Great. Go. Happy trails." Damned if she'd let him see what he'd done to her.

"Fine. We both have jobs to do."

Wow. He looked as if he wasn't sure what to say, so he fell back on his standard grim expression and crabby, kingly manner. How did a man go from insanely hot to cool and calm in seconds? Did he have some internal switch he could flip when he strayed too far off his normal routine?

Hannah grabbed her coffee cup off the porch rail,

walked past him and opened the front door. She gave him a quick look over her shoulder. "Have fun on the freeway. I hope there's traffic."

She shut the door while he was still looking at her and when she was safely inside, felt one small swell of satisfaction. Hannah Yates had nearly crushed King Carey's blasted schedule. And she knew that while he raced to the freeway to make his meeting, his mind would be filled with thoughts of her.

Seven

As promised, John Henry Mitchell showed up on-site about noon, and Hannah liked him right away. He was so tall he made her feel even shorter than usual. But he had a wide smile and an easy manner that was refreshing after dealing with Bennett Carey.

"It's coming along," the man said as she showed him around the kitchen.

She looked up at him and grinned. "I know it doesn't look like much, but we've got most of the stuff you'll never see finished already." She waved one hand at the wall where the fire had started. The drywall had been pulled off to display the two-by-fours that made up the framing and the new wiring. "Our electrician has completely changed out the old wiring so you'll never have to worry about that again."

"Good to hear," John Henry said, stuffing his hands

into the pockets of his black jeans. "That's not something I want to see again in my lifetime."

"Don't blame you." Hannah steered him to one side of the kitchen to the walk-in pantry. "We've added shelves in here, expanding your storage capabilities," she said, waving one hand to encompass the walls inside.

"That's great," he said, smiling down at her. "It was one of the things I wanted to ask for."

Hannah grinned. "Happy to help. I was thinking you might want a few big bins at the back of the pantry. For storage."

"Good idea." He stepped out and looked at the old freezer. "What about the freezer? Anything you can do with that?"

"We're going to add more shelving and lights. It seems a little dark in there."

"Dark enough that I use a flashlight most days."

She laughed. "I could tear it out and install a new one, but if you want my opinion…"

"I do."

Nodding, she continued. "That's a top-of-the-line freezer. Granted it's twenty years old, but it's still in great shape. I could have our plumber come in and check it out, maybe give the motor a tune-up and make sure the flooring is as good as I think it is. Then we'll add more storage, the new lights and leave the rest of it alone."

"Sounds good." He turned to face the main room and ignored the crew hard at work and the sounds of hammers, saws and a radio currently tuned to a country station. "My real concern," he said, "is with the height of the counters."

Hannah grinned up at him. "I can see why that might be an issue." Heck, with a standard height counter or island, John Henry would have to spend his entire shift nearly bent in half just to work.

"Thought you might."

"Hey, Mike, toss me your tape measure," she called out, and snagged the heavy measure when it sailed across the room toward her.

"Nice catch."

"Thanks." She pulled on the tape measure, set one end on the floor and told John Henry, "The standard height for a kitchen counter is thirty-six inches. Hits most of us about at the hips."

"Not me," he said, laughing.

"True." She grinned. "For you, I was thinking we could make the counters about forty inches high and that should help you out a lot."

"It's great for me, but no one else in my crew is as vertically blessed as I am." Smiling, he said, "If you could do one of the prep counters at forty inches and leave the rest the standard, that would work."

She hadn't expected that and gave him a smile of approval. "Well, that's really nice of you to think of everyone else."

"There are a couple of my sous-chefs who might have to drag in a box to stand on if I had all the counters that high."

"I would sure need one," Hannah said, and found herself really relaxing and enjoying herself with the big man.

"You are a small one," he said, then he looked around again. "Another thing that's high on my list? A twelve-burner gas stove a couple inches taller than standard."

"I think we can handle that." In fact, she liked him so

much, Hannah knew she'd turn everything upside down to find one if she had to.

She led him through the kitchen and back into the dining area. Sunlight streamed through the wide windows and construction dust danced in the beams.

"Is there anything else you need in there?"

He looked down at her and shook his head. "Not that I can think of right now. But if something comes to me, I'll let you know."

"Just call me," she said, and dug one of her business cards out of her back pocket. "My cell number's there, too."

"Thanks, I will." He gave another long look around, then said, "When I leave here, I'm charging all-new skillets and saucepans to Bennett. And whatever else I can find." He clapped his hands together and scrubbed his palms eagerly.

"Ben told me you were supposed to get whatever you wanted for the kitchen."

John Henry's eyebrows lifted. "Ben, is it?"

She frowned a little, embarrassed at the slip. "He's just so…stiff."

"Yeah, I suppose he is, mostly. But I run my kitchen my way and not many chefs can claim that, so I cut him some slack."

"Wish he'd let me run my job site my way," she muttered.

"If it helps," he said, glancing around the room again, "I think you're doing a great job. I can see how it's going to look and I'm impressed."

Hannah sighed and smiled. "I appreciate that. And if you wouldn't mind, maybe you could tell Bennett Carey that you think so."

He laughed, a loud, rolling thunder kind of sound that rippled through the work site. “Hell, Bennett knows damn well you’re doing a good job. The man just cannot relax. He’s always been that way. Got to stay on top of everything. Make sure everyone else is doing a job he thinks he could do better.”

Now Hannah laughed because he was absolutely right. “You described King Carey perfectly.”

“King Carey?” he repeated, and laughed again.

“Didn’t mean to say that,” she admitted. “It’s just what I call him in my head.”

“It fits,” he said, nodding. “But Bennett is also the best friend I ever had. He’s a man you can count on. And if he gives you his word, he’ll die before he breaks it.”

Hannah looked up into his deep brown eyes and saw understanding shining there. As if he knew she was having a really hard time dealing with his friend and he was trying to tell her to hang in there. “You really think a lot of him, don’t you?”

“None higher,” he said. “He’s a good guy, Hannah. But I think you already know that.”

Maybe she did, Hannah thought. The problem was, if she let herself believe it, then she might get drawn even deeper into the feelings for him that were already growing. She couldn’t really risk that, given what she’d already lived through once in her life.

Because no matter what John Henry said, the truth was that Bennett Carey lived in a whole different world than she did and nothing good ever happened when worlds collided.

Bennett fought traffic all the way to LA and silently blamed Hannah for cursing him.

Hell, he blamed Hannah for ruining his whole damn day. Nothing had gone right, starting with the traffic. His first meeting had been a disaster—he'd walked out when the opposing CEO had refused to deal. The second one, with a Realtor trying to negotiate for her client on land she owned in Irvine, had fallen apart when Bennett saw the geologist's report.

Thanks to Hannah, his mind hadn't been on anything but her. Even meeting up with Amanda's fiancé, Henry, for lunch hadn't taken the edge off.

In fact, it had gotten worse. Henry and Bennett had once been great friends, until Amanda fell in love with Henry and Bennett had stumbled across the couple right after they'd had sex. What had followed was a short fistfight and a ten-year rivalry that had only ended recently.

"Damn it." Bennett stopped behind a delivery truck and put the BMW into Neutral. With traffic back to Orange County a typical nightmare, Bennett knew he'd be there for a while. He'd even stayed in LA later than he'd had to, hoping to miss most of the rush hour freeway mess. "For all the good that did me," he muttered.

While music pumped out around him, Bennett let his mind wander, and naturally, it went straight to that morning.

Hannah was driving him crazy. Not once in his life had he ever been attracted to a woman more at home in jeans than business wear or elegant dresses. She was tiny, but strong and so damn self-confident they kept butting heads. And damn it, he liked that, too. He'd never known a woman to argue with him like Hannah did. Or to challenge him. Or to call him out for scowling at her.

He shouldn't appreciate her so much, but he did, and now that he'd had a taste of her, he wanted more.

Traffic inched forward, and while he grumbled to himself about having to be in Los Angeles at all, Bennett thought about lunch with Henry.

At a busy, popular Mexican restaurant, Henry took a sip of his beer and said, "Amanda says you're trying to convince your mom to move out of your house."

"Trying and failing," Bennett admitted, and picked up his own beer. "Unless you and my sister are willing to take her in."

"I am, but Mandy says no way. She's convinced your mom will drive her nuts over the wedding planning." Henry shrugged. "I wouldn't mind at all. You know I always liked your mom and dad."

"I know."

"But hell, Bennett, Mandy's making me insane with wedding stuff already. If I had both of them doing it? No, thanks."

Bennett sighed and reluctantly admitted, "I get it." He didn't want to understand, but hell. He was on Henry's side in this, and that was unusual enough since he and his old friend had been at war for the last ten years. He was glad their friendship was finally getting back on track, though.

"How about you get Mandy to work on getting our father to come around?" he asked. "If she can't badger him into actual retirement, nothing can."

"I should complain about you calling my fiancée a nag," Henry mused with a smile, "but since you're her brother and you've known her longer, I'll let it ride."

"Thanks."

"How's the reno on the restaurant coming?"

And just like that, the tension was back and Bennett's

heartbeat spiked. "It's only been a week, but seems to be moving along."

"That's it?" Henry just stared at him. "That's your whole report? Mandy says you're stopping in at The Carey every damn day to ride herd on your contractor, and all I get is 'it's coming along'?"

"Mandy's got a big mouth."

Henry winced. "See, there you go again. I should be giving you a hard time over that one, too. But yeah, she does. So why are you stopping in every day? Don't trust your contractor?"

Trust. *Well, that was a question. He was beginning to think she was as good at her job as she'd claimed to be. But what she was doing to him, he hadn't counted on. And didn't know what the hell to do about it.*

"Ah," Henry said thoughtfully, "so what's she like?"

"What?"

"The contractor. What's she like?"

"Annoying."

Henry laughed.

"Thanks very much. So happy you're amused."

"Oh, come on, Bennett. It's great for me, seeing a woman get under your skin."

"I didn't say that."

"Didn't have to, man. It's clear."

"The only thing that's clear," Bennett said, "is that this conversation is over."

Henry laughed outright, set his beer down and leaned toward him. "Come on. You've got to see my side."

"Your side of what?"

"Hell, Bennett. When Amanda was driving me nuts, can you really tell me you didn't enjoy every damn minute?"

No. He couldn't. He had relished Amanda giving Henry a hard time. But their situation had been different, Bennett assured himself. As much as she hadn't wanted to admit it, Amanda had loved Henry, so naturally, he thought, she'd tortured him.

There was no love between him and Hannah. There was plenty of heat, he could admit to that. And, he thought that maybe sex with her would probably burn out that flame and finally give him some peace of mind. Once he'd had her, he could stop thinking about her. Wondering what she would feel like under him. Over him.

He rubbed his forehead and stifled a groan.

"Yeah," Henry said as he sat back and lifted his beer in a silent toast. "I'm enjoying the hell out of this."

When the car behind him in the chaotic mess of the 405 honked at him, Bennett jerked out of his memories and moved the three feet forward that traffic allowed him.

If he survived this trip, he was going straight to the restaurant. It was time he and Hannah had a long talk.

Hannah loved being alone on the site.

And today she needed it more than ever.

She'd let the crew go at six because they'd all been putting in a lot of overtime and she didn't want to wear them out when they still had so far to go. But as for her, having this time to herself, in the quiet, gave her a chance to unwind at her own pace. And since the kitchen was at the back of the restaurant, far from the street, it was as if she were alone in the world. Considering the day she'd had so far, alone was a very good thing.

She stood back to check out the work done so far. Under the glare of the bare, overhead lightbulbs, the kitchen looked like less of a disaster area and more like a work in progress. Without the crew there, she could concentrate on a few of the touches she thought would give the kitchen just a little extra oomph.

Hannah smiled to herself as she spread wood glue on a pine slat, then crouched to apply it to the end of a new cabinet. The slats were decorative, and when the cabinets were painted, the extra pieces would look as if they'd been carved into the cabinets themselves.

When she had the last slat in place, she reached down for the right-angle wood clamp. She had to clamp the wood overnight to give the glue a chance to set up.

Smiling to herself, Hannah kept her left hand on the slat and swept out to reach the clamp. And couldn't. "Damn it."

"What's wrong?'

She jolted and just managed to swallow a shout of surprise. Looking back over her shoulder, Hannah said, "What are you doing here, Ben?"

"I went by your house. You weren't there. So I came here."

"Because you assumed I had no life?"

"No because I assumed you'd be working overtime to earn that bonus."

"Okay," she allowed with a shrug, "good assumption."

"So I repeat. What's wrong?"

She blew out a breath. "I can't reach the wood clamp."

He walked closer, every step measured, as if he were crossing a minefield. And hell, maybe he was. After the way they'd left things that morning, not surprising that they were both a little… Defensive.

"This?" He bent down, scooped up the tool and held it out to her.

"Yes. And as long as you're here, you can put it on while I hold the slat in place."

"And how do I do that?"

She smiled up at him, surprised he was willing to admit there was something he couldn't do. Why did that make her like him just a little more?

"Open the mouth of the clamp and set it right here, against the corner of the cabinet. That way it holds the slat in place."

Frowning to himself, he concentrated on aligning the tool perfectly and when he had it right, she said, "Now tighten it. You don't have to go nuts, just tight enough to make sure it holds."

She watched him concentrate and realized that she wanted that focus on her. The KISS—she thought of it in capital letters—had haunted her all day. She hadn't wanted it to, but also hadn't been able to stop it. Hannah knew better. Knew she shouldn't be fantasizing about Bennett Carey, but thoughts about him gnawed at the edges of her mind constantly.

For days now, she'd felt a buzz of expectation humming throughout her body, and every night she tossed and turned through dreams where Bennett Carey was the master of all lovers. She really wanted to find out if her dreams were remotely close to reality.

"Is that good?" he asked.

"What?"

"The clamp," he said. "Is that good?"

"Oh. Yeah. Yeah, it's fine." She let go of the wooden slat and when Bennett stood up, she tested the clamp just to make sure.

"Had to check?" he asked.

She looked up at him. "Wouldn't you?"

He smiled. "Yes, I would."

Why did he have to smile? That one small expression, however brief, changed everything about him. His eyes got warmer, the tension dropped out of his shoulders and he became even more tempting than when he scowled at her.

With her head tipped back, she looked into his eyes—those clear lake-blue eyes that were so hard to read and so rarely shone with laughter. He was a mystery to her. A man who seemed so closed down, but who had such fire in those eyes. A man who could spark her temper in a blink and spark desire even faster.

Why was she so intrigued by a man she shouldn't even be looking at?

God, it was so quiet in the kitchen, she could hear her own heartbeat thundering in her ears. How had she gotten to this point? From the first, he'd attracted her. Then, in spite of his crabby attitude, she'd liked him. The heat between them had always been there, and now it burned so fiercely she could hardly remember a time when she *didn't* want Ben with a need that was soul deep.

Was this more than like? Probably. Most likely. Oh, she didn't want to take that last, long tumble into love, because she just couldn't risk it again. Risk loving a rich man only for him to turn on her. She had to find a way to stop the slippery slide toward loving Ben because they would never be together. His world and hers were too far apart.

But that simple truth didn't seem to be enough to keep her from caring, more and more. How could one week change so much without really changing anything?

"So," she asked, when she was sure her voice wouldn't quiver, "why did you come looking for me?"

His gaze locked on hers. "I thought we should…talk about this morning."

"What is there to talk about?" *So much*, she thought.

He moved in closer, and it was only then she noticed that he'd taken his tie off and the collar of his shirt was opened. Hell, that was practically naked for Bennett Carey.

Naked.

She shook her head hoping to clear it but all she accomplished was making herself a little dizzier than she already was. Probably not good.

"You said you kissed me because I needed it."

"And you kissed me back for the same reason?"

"More or less," he admitted, then moved in even closer until she could see the tension in his eyes and feel heat pumping from his body. "So tell me, Hannah. What do I need now?"

Her mouth went dry. His eyes told her exactly what he needed. And in this particular area, they were just alike.

"Look," she said, trying and failing to smooth out the situation, "I just thought we should get that kiss out of the way because it just felt like it was *there*, all the time. You know, building sexual tension and—"

"Uh-huh," he said. "So it wasn't just need. It was clearing the air."

"Exactly!" Pleased, she nodded and gave him a smile that felt a little shaky. Because that kiss hadn't cleared up anything. It had clouded the situation even more than it had been, and right now, she felt as if she were completely blind.

"Right." He was so close now she could see the pulse beat at the base of his throat. It was fast. Like hers.

Hannah realized that by kissing Ben that morning,

she'd started something that couldn't be stopped. The silence in the restaurant was overpowering and in the strained quiet, the only sounds she heard were her own heartbeat and the rush of her own breath.

"Ben," she whispered, her gaze locked on his, "this isn't a good idea."

"No?" He shook his head, never taking his eyes off her. "You're wrong, Hannah. It's the only idea that matters at the moment."

She swallowed hard and waited. For what, she wasn't entirely sure. But in the next moment, Ben cleared that up for her.

"We should probably get something else out of the way, don't you think?" In a finger snap, he snaked his arms out and pulled her in close, then bent to take her mouth with a hunger that matched her own.

Hannah simply dissolved for one long, luscious moment. Her head spun crazily, and everything in her kindled in the fires he was stoking. Her breath was gone and she didn't care if it came back. She clutched at his shoulders to hold herself up. Their tongues tangled in a wild, frenzied dance of lust that clanged in her head like alarm bells. But it was too late for internal warnings. She'd had her chance to keep her distance and instead had allowed herself to feel…too much for a man she shouldn't have allowed into her heart in the first place.

His hands stroked up and down her back with a fierce possessiveness that pulsated inside her. Hannah gave herself up to it, exploring his mouth with the same intensity he gave her. It was as if every moment spent with him, every bit of sexual tension and heat had suddenly burst through a closed and locked door to demand satisfaction.

When he abruptly broke the kiss and looked down at her, Hannah had to blink a few times, just to bring him into focus. Breath raging, heart near to bursting, she looked up into those deep blue eyes as he asked, "So is it out of the way yet?"

A harsh, broken laugh shot from her throat. "You know, I think we still have work to do."

His lips twitched. "I'm your man."

For now, she thought, then stopped thinking entirely. When he kissed her again it was as if he'd slipped a leash that had been holding him back as she had been restraining herself.

The calm, rational Bennett Carey disappeared and Ben—a man with no control, no boundaries stepped in to take over. His hands were everywhere. She felt him as if he were surrounding her. His breath brushed against her skin. His lips trailed up and down her throat, and his hands moved over her, exploring what felt like every inch of her. He touched her face, her throat, skimmed one hand down her shirt, and even through the fabric and her bra, her breast burned when he touched her.

Her head fell back as he held her tighter, tighter. His mouth took hers and then slid from her lips to the length of her throat, licking, tasting, nibbling until she was one raw nerve. Her heart pounded so hard, she was surprised it didn't simply jump right out of her chest. Her whole body felt as if it was on a high burn, and every time he touched her, kissed her, it only increased the heat.

"Oh, Ben..." Words slipped past the knot in her throat, and she caught her breath on the last one.

"No more talking," he muttered. "We don't need words now."

He undid the button and zipper on her jeans and slid

one hand down and under the slender elastic of her panties to touch her. Cup her. His mouth took hers again as she rocked into his touch and groaned aloud at the first stroke of his fingers.

It had been so long since she'd been touched. Since she'd felt a man's need for her. Since she'd shared that need, and Hannah wasn't about to waste a second wondering if they were doing the right thing or not.

He tore his hand free, broke their kiss and looked wild as he stared down at her. His eyes flashed with desire, with need, with the same fires now engulfing Hannah.

"That's it," he muttered. "Now. It's got to be now, so if you're going to change your mind, here's your chance."

Changing her mind wasn't even an option. All Hannah wanted now was to be with him. To take all he offered and give him what they both wanted so badly. Decisions had been made. Steps taken. Everything she had ever done had brought her to this moment, and she didn't want to be anywhere else.

She looked up into those lake-blue eyes with fires kindled deep inside them, and said, "You're wasting time."

Eight

He laughed. A short, sharp bark of amusement that both fed the fire engulfing her and made her grin in response. "I like that about you, Hannah. I never have to guess what you're thinking."

She reached up and cupped his cheek in her palm. Instantly, his smile faded and desire swamped his features again. This Ben Carey was one she hardly recognized. But she liked him. A lot.

In one smooth move, he lifted her off her feet and Hannah instinctively wrapped her legs around his waist. It felt so good to be pressed tightly to him. His arms were like a vise around her and she loved it. His breathing was harsh, strained and she understood. She felt his heartbeat hammering in rhythm to her own. And she wriggled against the hard length of him pressing into her body.

He carried her to the nearest wall and she grinned

when he slammed her back against it and instantly began undoing her jeans and pulling them down. She twisted and writhed in his arms, helping as much as she could without him putting her down. Clearly he had no intention of letting her go. He held her pinned against the wall and reached down to pull off one of her boots and one leg of her jeans.

"Hurry," Hannah whispered on a choked laugh.

"I am," he insisted, and straightened to kiss her again. "The jeans look great on you, but a skirt would have been easier."

"Not to work in," she said, and caught his face in her hands to kiss him with everything she had. He groaned and snapped the band of her black bikini underwear.

Pulling her mouth from his, Hannah laughed wildly, and then she reached for his slacks and in a few seconds, she had him free and curled her fingers around him.

Bennett groaned harder, deeper when she touched him, and she watched him grit his teeth as if he were calling on every ounce of control he possessed. Hannah knew how he felt because she was so desperate for him, so incredibly beyond ready, she felt as if she might explode before they actually got down to doing the deed.

"You should know," she managed to say, "I don't normally do things like this."

"Neither do I. Don't care."

"Yeah, but just wanted you to know."

"Consider me informed," he said, and buried his face in the curve of her neck.

"Ohhh..." she said on a moan, while he ran his tongue over her pulse beat "...you should hurry."

"That's the plan," he muttered against her throat.

And then he was there, driving into her heat, and

Hannah stopped thinking entirely. Nothing mattered but what he was doing to her. What he was making her feel. Hannah held on and moved with him, taking him deeper, higher. At the small of his back, she dug her heels in, pulling him to her, holding him close. Closer.

"Ben! Ben…" Her head fell back against the wall, and she fought for breath as he continued to claim her body with a single-minded concentration that pushed her ever nearer to the edge of a release that threatened to shake her to her soul.

"Damn it, Hannah," he ground out, "just let go. Let go and fall."

She wanted to, and at the same time, she wanted to hold out against a climax and simply revel in the ride. But her body wouldn't allow her to wait. The coils of tension within tightened until it was desperation that drove her.

"Close. So. Close." She lifted her head, looked into his eyes and saw the same desperation she was feeling reflected back at her.

In the next moment, the world tilted, and all she could see were the fireworks shattering behind her eyes. Her body tightened, coiled, then burst with an orgasm that stopped her world. She'd expected, hoped for a "pop" of release because it had been a long time since she'd been with a man. But Ben Carey's skills—even up against a wall—were so incredible that she was trembling and holding on to him just so she wouldn't slide off the face of the Earth. She cried out his name and clutched at his shoulders with a desperate grip as her body rocked on and on.

And moments later, she held him as he fought through that last barrier and claimed what he'd already given her. Her world tilted wildly and then steadied again as her heart thudded in her chest. What swept through her was a warmth she'd never known. A *connection* to this man she'd known for only a week.

She didn't question it because what would have been the point? It had happened. She'd taken that last, tumbling step into love, whether she wanted to or not. Brushing his hair with her fingers, she held his head against her and for just a moment, reveled in what she was feeling.

Dangerous, she told herself, but the warning was too late, and if it had come earlier, she didn't know that she would have listened anyway. His strength wrapped around her. His breath dusted against her skin and his galloping heartbeat slammed in time with her own.

So unexpected. So… Scary. And yet, somehow wonderful.

When they could both breathe again, he lifted his head, looked at her and said, "Hi."

She laughed and held him tighter. She might love him, but she also knew enough to know he wouldn't want to hear that, so she said, "Yeah, hi to you, too. That was…"

"Surprising," he finished for her.

"Yeah. Good word." She didn't want to move but knew she had to. When he shifted to set her on her feet, Hannah braced her back against the wall again, this time for balance.

"Stupid time to bring this up," Ben said as they both rearranged their clothes. And Hannah bent to scoop up her discarded boot and put it back on.

"I wasn't thinking," he blurted out as if he couldn't believe that himself. "And I haven't carried condoms with me since I was eighteen hoping to get lucky."

She looked up at him. "Well, we're covered as long as you're healthy."

"I am." He looked insulted that she would think otherwise.

"Me, too. I'm also on birth control, so not a problem."

He pushed both hands through his hair, walked a few steps away, then swung around and came back to her. "Well, it's a problem for me."

And in a blink, she thought with an inner sigh, Ben was gone and Bennett was back.

"Didn't seem to be an issue for you a minute ago," she pointed out.

"True. But I don't treat women like this. Slamming you up against a wall—"

"It's a good wall. And trust me," she added, "I didn't mind a bit."

He laughed shortly and scrubbed one hand across the back of his neck. "I shouldn't have…"

"*You* didn't do anything. *We* did," she said, "and if you're going to have regrets and start beating yourself up over this, you should know I don't want to hear it." How could she not love him? she asked herself. So ready to berate himself for something she too had clearly wanted.

"You don't have regrets?"

"I try not to," she said. "About anything." Frowning slightly, she muttered, "Doesn't always work."

"Nice if you can do it."

"It takes practice." She looked at him and saw that he was thinking and rethinking what had just happened, and Hannah tried not to take it personally. For Bennett Carey, having a woman against a wall in an empty restaurant was probably so shocking he didn't know what to do next.

Well, she did.

"You know what?" Walking up to him, she laid one hand on his chest and smiled to herself when he lifted one hand to cover hers. "This was a first for me, too."

"Great. That makes me feel better." He was scowling again and for some odd reason, Hannah found it…endearing. He was clearly so far out of his comfort zone, he was off-balance. But then, so was she. It wasn't every day you discovered you were in love with a man you never should have gotten involved with. A contrary man who loved schedules and rarely laughed. A rich man who could, if he wanted to, ruin her. A man she'd known about ten minutes.

But time, it seemed, had nothing to do with what she felt. And she knew that he wouldn't want to hear it. Heck, she wasn't ready to *feel* it.

"If it helps, I feel great."

He laughed and her breath caught. Bennett Carey was gorgeous when he was scowling, but when the man really smiled, it was heart-stopping. Was it any wonder she'd been toast right from the beginning?

Hannah went up on her toes and brushed her lips against his. "I think we could both use a glass of wine and something to eat."

He looked into her eyes and nodded. "Among other things."

She blew out a breath. "You remember where I live, right?"

"I do."

"Then let's lock up and go see what's in my freezer."

When she started walking, Bennett's hand came down on her shoulder and he spun her around to face him. Staring into her eyes, he said, "I don't know what the hell's happening here, Hannah. This wasn't the plan."

"Not everything has to be planned, Ben."

His lips curved briefly, but he shook his head. "In my world, they do."

"You're in my world now," she pointed out with a smile.

"True," he said with a quick glance at the work-in-progress job site surrounding them. "So I guess you should know. I'm not finished with you yet."

"Me, either," she said, and since she did know what was happening—at least with her—she reached up to smooth his hair back from his forehead. "That's why we need the meal."

Bennett waited while she tore open a frozen pizza and watched as she turned the oven on to preheat it. Her kitchen was small. Hell, the whole house could have fit inside his home three or four times. The walls were a lemon yellow and the cabinets were dark green. And even while he noticed, he silently admitted that he didn't give a good damn what color her kitchen was.

Instead, he focused on her. That short, black hair of hers he now knew was as smooth as silk. Her compact, curvy body fit against him as if she were a missing piece, locking into place.

That thought brought him up short. He wasn't looking for missing pieces. He was only trying to get her out of his system, not deeper into it. That's why he was here, he assured himself. To burn out this… Whatever it was between them. Once that was done, things could get back to normal.

She turned her head to look at him, and when she

smiled, everything inside him fisted. He was hard and hot and aching for her and damned if he wanted to wait for a frozen pizza. He pushed off the wall, crossed the small room and picked her up.

Laughing, she asked, "What are you doing?"

"Looking for a bedroom," he muttered past the knot of need in his throat. "Any bedroom."

She hooked her arms around his neck and said, "Down the hall, first door on the left."

It didn't take long to make the trip. And he didn't care. All he could think about now, was the small, strong woman wrapped around him. Her humor, her strength and the way she tasted and smelled, crawled into his system and crowded out every other thought. In her room, he didn't bother to look at the surroundings. All he needed was a horizontal surface, and if she didn't have a bed, the floor would have to do.

"Thank God," he muttered, "a bed."

"Well, of course there's a bed," she said, still laughing.

He'd never known a woman like her. No other woman he'd ever been with would laugh during sex. Always before, sex had been quietly satisfying. Civilized. But Hannah Yates had changed everything. She was changing *him.* He was different with her than he was with anyone else. He knew it. What he *didn't* know was how he felt about that. At the moment though, all he cared about was her. Being with Hannah again. Watching her eyes glaze over with pleasure. Feeling her hands on him.

Bennett dropped her on the bed and tore at his clothes, while he watched her do the same. He couldn't remember a single time in his life when he'd been as eager for anything as he was to be able to indulge himself—and her, as they hadn't taken the time to do at the restaurant. Moonlight pooled in the room and draped across her now naked body like silk. And when she smiled at him, all thoughts vanished from his mind.

He covered her body with his and took the moment to relish the feel of her soft skin against his. She sighed and he felt it deep inside him. Bennett didn't want to think about what that meant, so he shut his mind down and instead focused only on touching her. He couldn't get enough of her. So small, so strong, so soft. She was, at the moment, *everything.*

"I've been wanting this for days," he whispered.

"Me, too," she said, and trailed one finger down the center of his chest, making him shiver.

"It'll be better than the wall."

"I don't know," she said, scraping her fingers along his back. "The wall was pretty impressive."

"I do my best work horizontal."

"Guess you're going to have to prove that," she said, and arched into him.

"I love a challenge," he whispered, and kissed her, diving into her mouth, her breath, her sighs.

Then he drew back, cupped her breasts in his palms and reveled in the way she reacted, tipping her head back, closing her eyes and arching into his touch. She was so expressive, holding nothing back, and that made him want to give her more. Sliding along her body, he swept one hand down the length of her while once again claiming her mouth, that amazing mouth, with his. She threaded her fingers through his hair and parted her lips for him. Their tongues tangled in a breathless dance that pushed them both along a now familiar road to an ending that he already knew would be shattering.

She shifted slightly to run her hands up and down

his back, and her calloused, gentle touch drove him crazy. Minutes that could have been hours passed and he couldn't wait a moment longer. He slipped into her heat in a long, slow slide that had her moaning and his own self-control dissolving.

Her legs came up and around his hips, and when he moved, she moved with him, creating a friction of desire that pushed them both.

"You feel so good, Hannah," he ground out, looking down into her green eyes that seemed to hold the world's secrets.

"Ben…you make me feel…" Her voice broke off on a sigh, and he wished he knew what she was going to say. He wanted all of her and that want was startling to him. He'd wanted to burn her out of his system, and instead, he had the distinct impression now that he was burning her into his very bones.

But that was a worry for another day.

Tonight, there was only now.

She sighed his name as her body tightened around his, and Bennett pushed her harder, drove them both a little crazier with a faster pace that she raced to match. Suddenly, Hannah caught his face in her hands drew his head down to hers and kissed him as her body shook and trembled with an orgasm that was so rich and full, he felt it, as well.

And while she kissed him, he let himself join her in the fall.

"Where is Bennett?" Serena looked around the Carey Center as if half expecting her older brother to pop up from behind a row of seats.

"I don't know," Amanda said. "This is not like Bennett. He's *late*."

Jack Colton and Henry Porter sat behind their fiancés and shared a knowing look.

"Perhaps," Candace Carey said as she lifted Alli onto her lap, "Bennett has finally decided that having a life is more important than sacrificing yourself on the Carey Corporation altar."

"Candy," Martin said, sparing a quick glance at his daughters. "I'm here, aren't I?"

She turned to spear him with a glare. "Being at the last auditions for the Summer Stars program is *not* getting a life. It's a part of our business."

"I can't win with you," he muttered.

"Of course you can," Candace said, giving Alli a hug. "You just don't like what you have to do to win."

Martin slumped back in his chair and glowered silently.

When the next contestant walked across the stage, looking nervous, Serena leaned into Amanda. "Should we call Bennett? Make sure he's okay?"

Henry's muffled laughter had both women turning to look at him. Shaking his head, Henry said, "I saw him earlier today, and if I'm right… Bennett's more than fine and you really don't want to call him."

"Damn it!" Bennett jolted up in bed, and Hannah's head slid off his chest to land on the mattress.

"Hey!" So much for the cozy afterglow. "What's wrong?"

He turned to look at her. "Sorry. Sorry."

She felt her heart do a long, slow and probably inevitable roll. His hair was tousled, his eyes shadowed and oh, that talented mouth of his was, once again, scowling. "What're you doing?"

"I'm supposed to be at the Carey Center right now." He glanced at his watch as if to confirm what he already knew.

Hannah laughed. "Even naked, you check your watch?"

"I'm *late*."

He said those two words as if they were a particularly complicated foreign language. Shaking her head, Hannah sat up, rubbed one hand across his shoulders, because she needed to touch him again, then teased, "But you're *never* late."

He whipped his head around to give her an even deeper scowl, and Hannah laughed harder.

"I'm glad you're enjoying yourself," he muttered. What the hell was happening to him? So wrapped up in a woman he forgot his obligations? First time he'd experienced *that*. But then, everything about Hannah was a new experience, wasn't it?

"Very much," she said, grinning. "So. Your choices are, to get dressed and race to the Center. *Or*, stay here and have a naked pizza picnic in my bed, followed by… *dessert*."

One corner of his mouth tipped up as he stared at her. She was intoxicating. His sexy pixie. The last thing he wanted to do right then was leave. His body was already stirring for her again, and he vaguely wondered if he would *ever* be able to get enough of her. Everything was changing, and he wasn't sure how he felt about it. But now didn't seem the time for self-reflection.

"Well?" she asked, running one hand through that short, spiky hair.

Very deliberately, he undid the clasp on his watch and

tossed it over his shoulder to land on his discarded suit. "It's been a long time since I was on a picnic."

"Oh, I love a good picnic." She held his face in her hands and kissed him until he laid her down on the bed again.

Pizza came much later.

At the Center the following day, Bennett managed to avoid answering questions from his family. Not showing up where he was supposed to be was so out of character for him, it was no wonder they were curious. But he wasn't about to satisfy that curiosity. Hell, he couldn't explain it to himself.

He'd finally left Hannah's house about 2:00 a.m. and, on that long drive back to his place in Dana Point, had a singularly futile argument with himself. Being with Hannah had affected him more than he had thought it would. She was impossibly attractive, amused at all the wrong times and strong enough that when he said he had to leave, she'd kissed him goodbye and watched him go without trying to convince him to stay.

Why hadn't she wanted him to stay?

"Damn woman is confusing the hell out of me." Shutting her out of his mind, he turned to the sheaf of papers on his desk and tried to concentrate on work. If a sexy pixie slipped past those mental barriers now and then, it wasn't because he hadn't tried.

He was grateful when his office door swung open. Until he saw his father. Then he figured an argument with someone besides himself might be more satisfying.

"Hi, Dad. What's up?"

"What's *up*?" Martin stalked across the room and

dropped into one of the visitor chairs opposite Bennett's desk. "Your mother has a lunch date. With a *man*."

"Really?" Surprise colored his tone, and he had to wonder what his mother was up to. She'd moved into his house to bring his father around and that obviously wasn't working. Had she moved on to a more devious plan?

Women really were dangerous.

"Of course really. Why would I say it if I didn't mean it?"

"You wouldn't."

"Exactly." Martin jumped up from the chair as if he were on a spring. Walking in a tight circle, Martin waved both hands in the air. "It's Evan Williams."

Bennett frowned to himself. "You mean the manager for the San Diego chorus?"

Martin jabbed his finger at his son. "That's the one."

"But isn't he around forty?"

His father stopped in a slice of sunlight that worked to define the misery on the man's face and the powerless sheen in his eyes. Martin Carey was worried. About time, too, Bennett told himself.

"Thirty-eight," Martin snapped. "That rat bastard is thirty-eight! What the hell is your mother thinking? A younger man? Why is she doing this?"

Bennett smothered a smile he hadn't expected.

"Hell," Martin continued, "why is *he* doing this?"

"Mom's a beautiful woman," Bennett said thoughtfully.

Martin's gaze snapped to his son, irritation carved into his features. "Well, I know that."

"Have you told her that lately?"

"She has a mirror, doesn't she?"

Bennett's eyes rolled. "Dad—"

"I know, I know." He waved one hand. "Stupid thing to say."

"Or think."

"That, too. But damn it, she's my *wife*. She's moved out of our house. She's got a *date*, for God's sake, with a man young enough to be her son…" He walked over and dropped into the chair again. "And she won't talk to me."

"Because it doesn't do her any good," Bennett said, and realized that something had shifted for him. He'd tried very hard not to get involved in the Retirement Wars, but now, he could see exactly what his mother had been talking about.

Bennett had wanted his father to retire because, by God, *he* was the CEO now. It was his turn to run the family company. To build on it just as Martin had. Now, though, he could see that Martin had spent so many years devoted to the company that he'd actually *forgotten* how to have a life, too.

Last night had brought that home to Bennett. He prided himself on timeliness. On being where he was supposed to be at all times. A schedule kept the world from spinning out of control.

And yet, a night with Hannah had shown him that tossing that schedule aside could open you up to all kinds of interesting possibilities. Maybe keeping a daily list of obligations, responsibilities and duties wasn't the key to happiness. Maybe he didn't actually need to wear his watch every day of his life. Maybe he needed to embrace the kind of freedom Hannah represented.

Even as that thought settled in his mind, he mentally reeled back from it. Was he really trying to rethink his entire world after knowing this woman for little more than a week? Preposterous. He liked his life just as it was. Hannah was an intriguing… Aberration. They didn't have a relationship. What they had was great sex and a business deal.

"Are you listening to me?" his father demanded, drawing Bennett out of his thoughts.

"Not really," he admitted. "Dad, nothing's changed. Mom's going to lunch with a man who wants to spend time with her. I don't blame her."

"Whose side are you on?"

"Mine," Bennett murmured, then louder, he said, "If you want Mom back, then pay attention to her. Stop complaining and take care of it."

"My own son." Martin rose slowly and gave Bennett a hard look. "I come to you for help and this is what I get? Complaining, is it? You think any of this is easy? It's not. Just you wait until you've got a woman tying your guts into knots. Then we'll see how much complaining *you* do."

"Which is why," Bennett said softly as his father stormed from the office, "I will never let a woman tie my guts into knots."

"This is just…delicious." Amanda Carey nudged her sister, Serena, and both women laughed and leaned in closer to Hannah. "He missed an appointment," Amanda said, clearly delighted. "That never happens, Hannah. And, since you are the only new player in Bennett's oh-so-organized world, we figured that you're behind that particular miracle. So we had to come and meet you!"

"Exactly," Serena said, reaching out to give Hannah's hand a pat. "We had to see the woman who's managed to throw Bennett's world out of alignment."

Hannah was still a little stunned by the visit. Ben's

sisters had shown up at the job site and insisted on taking her off for lunch so they could "chat." That had thrown her off completely, but the Carey women would not be told no, and then Hank Yates had stepped in and told Hannah to go.

So here they were at a Mexican restaurant on Pacific Coast Highway, and Hannah could only listen as the sisters talked to and around her. Amanda had shoulder-length blond hair, blue eyes a little paler than Ben's and a square cut sapphire with a circle of diamonds glittering on her left ring finger.

Serena's hair was a little shorter, a little darker blond, and her blue eyes were darker than her sister's but lighter than Ben's. Her left ring finger boasted a gigantic emerald.

"Ben's world is still scheduled tightly. I haven't done anything," Hannah said, and took a sip of her iced tea.

"Ben?" Amanda grinned, and said, "No one has ever called him Ben. But you do. How interesting…"

"It's not—"

"I think he really likes you," Serena said softly. "He's never just blown off an appointment before. Especially not one with the family."

"She's right," Amanda agreed. "He really does like you."

He wanted her—that much Hannah knew. But anything more than that? She didn't think so. Although, she remembered him tossing his watch over his shoulder. Maybe he liked her a little. Which was a pale emotion compared to the love she felt for him. "Oh? Did he tell you that?"

"Oh hell, no," Amanda said with a short laugh. "He'd rather have his tongue cut out."

"Charming, Mandy. Way to scare her off."

"She doesn't look like she scares easy," Amanda said.

"I don't." Hannah looked from one to the other of them. She really didn't know what to make of this meeting. She was an only child and had no idea how to deal with siblings. Anyone's siblings. "Look, I get you're his sisters and you're worried about him."

"No, that's not it at all," Amanda said, smiling. "Bennett can take care of himself. Usually. But not showing up last night? That's huge. That means something."

"We were...busy," Hannah said, and wished the waitress would show up with her tacos so she'd have something to stuff in her mouth.

"Well, that sounds interesting."

"Mandy..." Serena smiled at Hannah. "We really only wanted to meet you. We're not trying to insinuate anything or embarrass you."

"I didn't—" Amanda cut herself off and shrugged. "She's right. I wasn't trying to give you a hard time. It's just that Bennett has always been such a man of routine—even when he was a kid—that we just had to meet the woman who could make him miss an appointment."

Hannah smiled at both of the women. She understood what they meant, and she appreciated it even though she didn't actually know what to do with it. "Look. It's really great of you both to come out to meet me. And I get why you wanted to. But there's nothing between Ben and me." Sadly, the only thing they shared was a night of amazing sex. She wasn't even sure they'd be repeating *that*, let alone share anything else.

Serena shook her head. "None of us believe that, Hannah. Not even you."

She sighed and turned her head to look out the window at the traffic passing on PCH. Laguna Beach was an arts and crafts kind of town, with more art galleries than restaurants. People flocked here for the spectacular scenery, the gorgeous beaches and the tide pools that had captivated generations of children. And right now, she wished she were outside, just one of the pedestrians wandering along the sidewalks.

It would be nice if she could believe Ben's sisters. Believe that he had feelings for her. But she couldn't. Couldn't allow herself to believe it. Because even if he did care for her, what would it change? Yes, she loved him, but was love enough to bridge the differences between them?

"Even if I thought there could be, I wouldn't be interested."

"Well, why the hell not?" Amanda asked. "What's wrong with Ben—Bennett?"

"Nothing." She smiled because she admired loyalty and she loved that Bennett's sisters would come here to meet her, to defend him. "But we're from two different worlds and I've both been there and done that and have zero interest in doing it again."

"You make this sound like *West Side Story*," Serena said. "Or the Montagues and Capulets."

Hannah laughed a little as the waitress finally arrived with their lunches. She waited until the woman was gone again before saying, "Nothing quite so dramatic. But experience is a really good teacher." She took a breath and blew it out before she confessed, "I dated a rich guy once. I was even engaged to him. Briefly"

And never, she admitted silently, felt for him what she felt for Ben. How could she feel so much for him in so little time? Was it possible to love so quickly? And what was she supposed to do about it?

"Names," Amanda said, waving her fork. "I need names."

Hannah smiled and shrugged. What did it matter? "Davis Buckley."

"Oh." Serena's mouth twisted into a show of distaste. "Really, Hannah? Why on earth would you…no. Never mind." She held up a hand, backing off and admitting it was none of her business.

"Please, I'm not afraid to say it," Amanda spoke up. "The man is a toad, Hannah. What on earth did you see in him?"

Now that her tacos were there, she was ignoring her lunch completely. Thinking back, she could see how she'd been romanced into believing Davis's lies. Letting herself be blinded by the beautiful places he took her to, by the gifts he showered on her. By the empty words he offered her, promising to always be there for her. To give her the love she'd always dreamed of. But how to explain that to someone else?

"It was a combination of things, I guess," she finally said, and poked at her rice and beans with the tines of her fork. She could talk about it, though she hated remembering how stupid and trusting she'd been. "I'm embarrassed to say, Davis romanced me with flowers and attention and pretty words. My Dad was sick at the time, and I was lost and overwhelmed with the business, and Davis offered to help me with all of it.

"I believed I could trust him and I was wrong."

"Not surprising. Davis is very good at misrepresenting himself. And don't be embarrassed. We've all made blunders with men."

"Oh, have we ever," Serena murmured.

Hannah really appreciated the solidarity from Ben's

sisters. She'd never had a lot of time in her life to make and keep good female friends. And sitting here across from these two women, Hannah realized how much she had missed by not having friends to talk with.

"Well, when he asked me to marry him, he swore he would help with the construction company because he believed in me." She looked at the other women and felt their sympathy before she added, "Instead of helping me though, he was trying to force me to quit the business and sell out.

"I finally discovered that he'd invested in a construction company that was in direct competition with us. So basically, if he could get me to leave Yates Construction, it was paving the way for his own new start-up."

"Devious man," Serena murmured.

Amanda nodded. "Like I said. A toad."

"Definitely toad-like," Hannah agreed. "When I broke off the engagement, he handed me a list of the money I owed him for his 'investment' in me."

"He hit a new low," Amanda said.

"I've almost paid him off, though it's taken me a long time. But when Ben offered us a bonus for finishing the restaurant in four weeks, I saw it as a gift from the construction gods. I can pay Davis off and get him out of my life forever."

There was a long moment of silence before Serena spoke up and said, "I admire you so much."

"Really, why?" Hannah turned to face the woman.

"Because you've made your own way. You built your company. You made a mistake, sure, but you're digging yourself out of it. That takes strength. I admire that," Serena said.

"So do I," Amanda added. "You didn't let the toad

destroy you. And you're going to finish the restaurant job on time, so you'll have the bonus money to get rid of him forever. You're taking care of business. And that's excellent.

"Plus, you're getting to Bennett and that practically makes you a superhero!"

Hannah smiled, but she didn't know that Amanda was right about that. Oh, they were right about Davis. He was loathsome. But Ben was far wealthier than Davis Buckley, and that made her nervous. If Ben turned out to be as toady as Davis, he could ruin her business—or worse, pick up her debts and take it over. Okay, that sounded a little paranoid even to her. But who could blame her for being nervous after Davis?

She shook her head and took a bite of her taco. Silence stretched out for another minute or two, before Amanda spoke up again.

"It pains me to say this about my brother, who at times makes me want to tear his hair out," she said, "but Bennett is nothing like Davis. *No one* is like Davis."

"True," Serena agreed.

"I get that," Hannah said. "But I don't want you guys to get the wrong idea. Whatever is going on between Ben and I isn't going to last. So there's no point in pretending it will. We're too different."

"You're both very hardheaded," Serena said. "So you have that in common."

"Good point," Amanda said, smiling at her sister.

"Funny." Hannah grinned. This lunch had turned out better than she'd thought it would. She'd enjoyed herself with the two women and had to wonder why they were so different from Bennett. Had he made a deliberate effort to be schedule driven and emotionally cut off?

Why? Because he was the head of the Carey Corporation? Or had he simply gotten into the habit of keeping himself one step removed and only needed someone to push him out of that too-tight rut?

"You know," she mused, "Ben's really lucky to have you both."

Amanda reached out and gave her hand a squeeze. "Oh, be sure to tell him that, will you?"

Nine

Bennett walked into his house and was instantly assailed by an overly sweet, completely overpowering scent. Not surprising, he thought as he walked farther into what his family called the beige house.

Vases of roses were everywhere. Roses in full bloom. Rosebuds. Tiny roses. Even a damn rosebush in a huge clay pot! In every color of the rainbow, they were freaking everywhere. Walking through the foyer into the main room, Bennett looked around, stunned at the madness. On tables, along the hearth, on the floor, on the bay window.

Yet, past the roses, he took a look at his house and maybe for the first time, realized that his sisters and his mother might be right. His house—not a home, just a house—was as beige as his sisters had claimed. The furniture was spare and modern and looked as comfortable as a medieval rack. On the beige walls were white canvases with black spots and swirls that looked, he realized, like someone had turned his little niece loose with a paintbrush.

How had he never noticed this before? Because, he told himself, he was hardly ever here. When he was, he went straight to his bedroom. He didn't spend time in any of these rooms. He'd bought the house because it was a good investment. Because a man should own a house. Because… Hell, did it matter?

Instantly, an image of a tiny, lemon yellow kitchen leaped into his mind, and he quickly pushed it back out. This wasn't about Hannah. Not everything was about Hannah.

"Ah, Bennett!"

He closed his eyes briefly, then nodded. "Hello, Mother. I see Dad's sent you flowers."

She glanced around, then checked her hair in a mirror. "Yes. Another empty gesture."

His eyebrows lifted. "Several hundred roses is quite the gesture."

His mother just looked at him. "If it changes nothing," she said, "it means nothing."

How did he land in the middle of his parents' war?

"Mom," Bennett said quietly, "he's trying."

She looked up at him then, and he felt a swell of love for the woman who'd always been the rock in their family. He hated seeing his parents at odds like this, but there didn't seem to be a damn thing he could do about helping the situation.

"I love your father, Bennett. But until he makes good on his promise, he's not really trying at all." She picked up a black leather bag and slipped it over her shoulder.

"Are you going out?" he asked, and noticed for the first time that she was wearing a cool blue dress and black heels.

"I am. I'm going to dinner. With Evan."

"I thought you had lunch with him." Bennett felt a quick blast of panic and instantly knew how his dad had felt earlier.

"I did. Now we're having dinner." She walked to the door. "He's a lovely man and I enjoy his company."

He thought about jumping in front of the door to block her escape but knew that wouldn't work. "Mom, he's only a few years older than *me*."

"Age doesn't mean anything, honey." She reached up and patted his cheek.

"Sure. And size doesn't matter."

She chuckled and shook her head. "Oh, don't look so horrified. I'm not doing anything wrong."

"You're married to my father and you're going on a date," he pointed out with what he considered remarkable patience.

"You're being silly, Bennett, and I just don't have time to listen right now." She walked to the door and stopped again. "Oh, before I forget. Amanda and Serena met your lady friend and liked her very much. I'm looking forward to meeting her myself."

A sinking sensation opened in his chest. "My what?"

"The woman you're seeing? I'm so happy you listened to me about having a healthy sexual relationship." She cocked her head to one side and studied him. "Honestly, Bennett, sweetheart. You must not have had sex yet because you still seem very tense. Maybe you should call that nice young woman the girls told me about and see if the two of you could have sex tonight."

He opened his mouth to say… *Something.* But nothing came out. What could he possibly say to that?

"Don't. Just…don't." What the hell was happening to his life? Lady friend? Sexual relationship? His *sisters*?

"Oh fine, Bennett. Won't say another word. But you should bring her to dinner." She leaned in and kissed his cheek. "Well, I have to rush. Don't wait up, sweetie."

And she was gone. *Don't wait up?* His mother was on a date. His sisters liked Hannah. *Bring her to dinner.* What the hell.

"No," he said aloud to the empty room. "It stops now."

This had already gotten out of hand. Damned if his family was going to corner him into a relationship—no matter how much he wanted Hannah. She wasn't the kind of woman who would fit into his world, and there was no way he could fit into hers. And hell, that didn't make any sense even to him. Different worlds? Where were they, medieval England? No, it was more than that.

Just look at his parents. More than forty years together and they were at war. Hell, if they couldn't make it work, who the hell could? No, he didn't need that kind of upheaval. He had a life he'd built carefully on hard work and routine. Hannah didn't do routine.

She argued with him, was *amused* at his control and rigid adherence to schedules. She was as devoted to her company as he was to his, so how could they make that work? Always at odds over whose job came first? That sounded terrible.

She was funny and strong and confident, and she hit him on a level no other woman ever had. He wanted her, but that wasn't enough for him to stay involved. So. Better to end it now.

He should have been happy about that decision.

He wasn't.

The second week of the job was over and they were getting much closer to the finish line. *Really impressive*, Hannah thought, *what unlimited overtime and the promise of a bonus could do.* She sat back on her heels and looked around.

The floors had been sanded and covered with a tarp again to protect them until they could be refinished. The new cabinets were in, but the counters were still being made. The framing in the attic was almost complete and the work on the roof had been completed.

And she hadn't seen Ben since the night she'd experienced the best sex of her life. Since the night she'd been forced to admit to herself that she was in love with a man who would have no interest in hearing how she felt.

"Why hasn't he been checking up on me? Does he suddenly trust me?" She snorted at the very thought. "No. He's hiding from me."

Part of her actually enjoyed knowing he was scared, while most of her was just angry. Hard to imagine a grown man *hiding* from a woman because there was a danger to his oh-so-scheduled rut.

"Talking to yourself is never a good sign."

She smiled and looked to the doorway where her father stood, leaning against the doorjamb, watching her.

"I'm the only one who truly understands me," she quipped, knowing it wouldn't placate him.

"Oh, I don't know," he said, pushing off to walk to

her. He sat down on the floor beside her and said, "I think I understand you pretty well."

Hannah sighed. There was no keeping things from Hank Yates. "You do. Always have."

He reached out and tapped her nose with his index finger. "Uh-huh. Which is how I know you're in love with Bennett Carey."

"Don't be silly." She looked away because she couldn't meet those eyes of his and not confess everything.

"You've never lied to me before. Be a shame to start now."

"Oh, Dad," she said, shaking her head. "How could I possibly love a man so rigid? So married to a schedule that he wears his gold watch to *bed*?" She winced a little as she'd pretty much just told her father she'd slept with Bennett Carey. Then she rushed on with more questions and complaints. "He owns a bazillion suits and *two* pairs of jeans. Can you imagine?"

"No, I actually can't."

"Me, either," she agreed with a sharp nod. "He checks up on me—or at least he *did*, every ten seconds, and now all of a sudden, bam, he's gone? What? I suddenly became trustworthy?"

"You don't think so."

"No, I don't. I think he's staying away on purpose and I don't care. Well," she amended, "I shouldn't care. And I don't."

"Okay, good," Hank soothed.

Her head fell back. "How can you fall in love in a *week*? That's ridiculous."

"Time's got nothing to do with it." He looked over at her and smiled. "Took me two years to fall in love with your mother. And look how that turned out."

"Dad…" She laid her hand on his.

"That wasn't a bid for sympathy. I don't regret a thing, Hannah. How could I when I have you?" He smiled again, then added, "My point is, I had to work myself into love. I feel like, if it just drops on you, unexpectedly, that's how you know it's real."

She thought about that for a minute or two and wondered if he was right. But even if he was, what did that mean for her?

"All that said," her father continued, "I don't want to see you in the same kind of mess you were in with Davis."

"This is different, Dad." Wasn't it?

"I don't know. Davis used you. So is Bennett, in his own way."

Well, that caught her attention. "How?"

"By manipulating you into taking this job. By waving his money at you to get you to jump."

"No, that wasn't manipulation." Hannah shook her head. "I knew what I was doing. With that bonus, I can pay off Davis, invest in the company and give a little extra to the guys who work for us."

"I know all that. But I'm asking. Bennett was here every day, checking on the work. On *you*. Now he hasn't been here in a week. Why?"

"I told you, I think he's hiding from me."

"Doesn't say much for the man," he mused.

"I don't know. I guess I could understand why he's avoiding me if I wasn't so mad about it."

"Really?"

"It really doesn't matter anyway, Dad." She shook her head and let go of all the hurt and the anger and the resentment that she'd been holding against Ben. "There's nothing I can do about it. If he wants to ignore me, shouldn't I let him?" Of course she should. "Why should it be up to me to go hunt him down and make him talk to me?"

Hank shrugged, crossed his feet at the ankles and said, "Well, that's a question. I'm not saying I trust the guy, but if you love him, are you willing to let him walk away? If you love him, don't you deserve to have him face you and say whatever it is he's avoiding saying?" He turned his head to meet her eyes. "If you love him, are you willing to settle for less?"

Hannah tipped her head to his shoulder and found the comfort there that she'd always found with her father. "If you don't trust him, why are you saying all of this?"

"Because I trust you." He patted her hand and said softly, "Because I love you and I want you to be happy. If that means this guy…well, if he hurts you, we'll still have words. But I'm on your side, kiddo. Always."

"I know that, Dad," she whispered. "Thanks. I just don't know what I should do."

"Since when?" He laughed a little. "You've always known what you want and I've never seen you back down. Are you really going to start now?"

He was right. But dealing with Ben was different. He was a man she never would have met if not for this job. They lived in two separate worlds, and when worlds collide, things could get ugly.

But did they have to collide? Couldn't they just sort of meet in the middle? Didn't she owe it to herself to find out?

Bennett was getting ready for a meeting when his cell phone rang. He glanced at the screen, then sat down at his desk again to answer. "Justin. Here's a surprise."

His younger brother was the ghost in the Carey family. There, but not present. He skipped more family meetings than he attended. He wasn't involved in the company business at all and made no secret of the fact that he wasn't in the slightest bit interested.

Bennett loved his brother, but with everything going on at the moment, he didn't have much patience for him.

"Yeah, Bennett, I need to talk to you."

"Great," he said, leaning back in his chair and studying the ceiling. "There's a family meeting in a half hour. Why don't you join us?"

"I'm in La Jolla."

A two-hour drive that on the 5 freeway could become a four-hour drive. "Right. Okay, well, I do have to be at the meeting."

"You have a half hour," Justin reminded him. "I only need a few minutes."

"Fine." Bennett waited while his brother went silent, and he didn't like not having his mind constantly occupied. The minute nothing was going on, his brain filled with images of Hannah. A week since he'd seen her. A week since the most amazing night of his life. But it wasn't just the sex that held him captivated, it was the woman herself. He'd never known anyone like her. Strong and funny and impatient. It was a damned intriguing combination. And he missed seeing her. Missed that smile of hers and the way her green eyes lit up when she looked at him. Missed everything about her, and that's why he wasn't going to think about her.

Scowling, he interrupted Justin's musings and demanded, "What is it?"

"Okay," he said, "I know we've got our problems, but I need your help."

Instantly, Bennett's demeanor changed. He sat up and asked, "Are you all right?"

"Yeah, I'm fine. I just..." He blew out a breath. "Hell, Bennett, I need a loan."

"Money? This call's about money?" That frown carved itself into his face. "Damn it, Justin..."

"I know. If I was a part of the company..."

"I wasn't going to say that."

"But you're thinking it," his brother muttered.

Yes, he was. "How much?"

Justin told him and Bennett choked. "Seriously?"

"I know it's a lot. But I need it to seal the deal I've been working on."

"What kind of deal?" Bennett asked the question they'd all been wondering about.

"I can't tell you. Yet," he added quickly. "But it's big, I can tell you that. Look, Bennett, I'll pay the loan back to the company at the end of next month. I've got trust money due then, and it's all yours."

Bennett would lend his brother the money, of course. There wasn't a question of that. They were all Careys. But this time there was going to be a price tag. "Look, I'll give you the money on one condition."

"Damn it, Bennett."

"Hear me out." Hell, Justin needed him, and Bennett didn't want to waste a golden opportunity. "You come to the Summer Stars dinner in two weeks, and the money's yours."

"What? Why?"

"Because you're a Carey, Justin," Bennett told him on a sigh. "Whether or not you want to be involved in the company, you *are* involved in the family. I want you there, so the Careys can present a united front. It's a big night for all of us."

There was a long pause as Justin considered it, though Bennett knew damn well he'd go for it. He needed the money.

"It would mean a lot to Mom."

"That's fighting dirty."

Bennett grinned and wished his brother could see it. "I know. And, one more thing. I want you to convince Mom to move out of my house."

Justin laughed, and Bennett sneered at the phone.

"You realize this is blackmail," Justin finally said.

"What's your point?"

"Okay, fine. It's a deal," Justin said. "I'll be there. Where's the dinner being held?"

"The Carey."

Justin gave a long, low whistle. "The fire damage has been repaired already?"

"It will be." Again, Hannah raced through his mind. He waited a second until his thoughts cleared. "So, you'll be there?"

"I'll be there. I make no promises about Mom, though. She's not going to listen to any of us as long as Dad's not cooperating."

"You're the baby in the family. Use your power wisely."

Laughing, Justin said, "Agreed. You'll transfer the money today?"

"You'll have it this afternoon."

"Thanks, Bennett. I owe you."

"Damn straight you do. Pay me back at the dinner."

When he hung up and his assistant buzzed in, Bennett

muttered a curse. He checked his watch and shrugged. "What is it, David?"

"There's a Hannah Yates here to see you, sir."

His heart gave a hard jolt, and everything inside him twisted into what felt like a giant knot. A week since he'd seen her and it had taken everything in him to stay away from the restaurant. He'd made calls. Checked in. Even had his assistant go in his place once. But he hadn't wanted to see Hannah. Because he couldn't risk her getting even deeper inside him. Because he knew that seeing her again wouldn't be enough. He'd have to touch her. Hold her. And he wasn't entirely sure he'd be able to let her go again.

Though his plan hadn't worked very well because he still saw her every night when he closed his eyes. He heard her laugh. Saw those brilliant green eyes. Caught her scent in his lungs and woke up aching for her. What the hell was that? Lust? No. Couldn't be. If it was just lust, he wouldn't have bothered to distance himself. He'd have been back at her place the day after that one spectacular night.

No, it was more and he didn't want to acknowledge it even to himself. They were too different. Too far apart. She didn't believe in watches. He lived by one. She wore jeans. His world was dominated by suits and elegance. Her laugh was loud and happy and he never found much to laugh at. At least he hadn't, until he'd met her.

He was a different man when he was with Hannah, and Bennett wasn't sure he even *knew* that man. It was unsettling and so, the easiest way to put things back the way they should be, he told himself, was to stay away from the one woman who rocked his world.

Yet now she was here. Why? He wouldn't find out

unless he talked to her, which was just what he'd been avoiding for a week. *So are you going to keep hiding like a coward?* he asked himself.

"Send her in."

He stood up, buttoned his suit jacket and faced the door. When it opened, she stepped inside and Bennett's breath caught in his lungs. A part of him wondered what David had thought of Hannah Yates in her dark blue jeans, work boots and Yates Construction T-shirt. Of course she'd shown up as herself. Hannah didn't play games. Didn't pretend to be something she wasn't. Damned if he didn't like that about her.

Hell, he liked everything about her.

"What is up with you?" She snapped out the question and her green eyes shone like there were flames in the depths.

Yeah. He liked her.

"What do you mean?"

"Oh please." She walked across the room in short, fast strides that brought her to a stop right in front of him.

He caught her scent on his next breath, and for a moment, he wondered if he'd ever truly be free of it. Or if he wanted to be.

"You know damn well why I'm here." She folded her arms beneath her small, yet perfect breasts and hitched one hip higher than the other. "You're not checking up on me anymore."

He laughed shortly. "I thought you hated that."

"Turns out I hate *not* being checked on more." She read his expression correctly because she added, "Yes. Surprised me, too."

God, he'd missed her. He'd known it of course. The last week, he'd done little more than think about her, dream about her, and he'd told himself it was just the desire pumping inside him. But it was more. So much more that he reeled back from the knowledge of it.

There she stood, facing him down, glaring at him with those emerald eyes of hers and it was taking everything he had not to grab her up and take that mouth of hers in a kiss that would sear both of them. And what would be the point? When the job was finished, he wouldn't see her again. The Carey had brought them together, and when it was completed, it would end that connection, as well. Bennett needed to get back to the life he understood with his lists and schedules. Hannah was a disruption to all of that. And Bennett needed that structure. He wasn't sure he knew how to live without it.

But then, he didn't know if he could live without her, either. Or the fire they shared and that he couldn't stop thinking about.

"I've got more to keep track of than the restaurant."

"Uh-huh. That didn't stop you before."

"Hannah, what do you want to hear?"

She tipped her head to one side and fixed her green eyes on his. He couldn't have looked away even if he'd wanted to—and he really didn't want to.

"I want you to admit that you miss me. That it scares the crap out of you how much you miss me," she said, moving closer, keeping her gaze locked with his. "And I want you to admit that you haven't been able to stop thinking about me."

"If I did, what does that accomplish?" he wondered.

"It's honesty, Ben. The least we owe each other is that."

"You want honest?" He moved through the last few inches separating them and took hold of her shoulders.

"Fine. I want you. I want you all the damn time and it's pissing me off."

She grinned and something in his chest simply melted. Was it his heart or just the ice that he'd kept that organ encased in?

"That's a good start," Hannah said.

"I stayed away because I had to. For my own sanity." He pulled her up onto her toes. His insides were jumping, his heart racing and he couldn't deny that seeing her again had suddenly made everything right again. And that made him mad, too. "What's between us is heat, but it's the kind that will burn itself out."

"How do you know?" she asked, her eyes spearing into his.

"That's what happens when a fire burns too hot."

"Not if you keep stoking it," she whispered. "Why don't we see how long it will burn?"

Tempting. Oh, so tempting. But then, everything about her tempted him. Bennett couldn't get enough of her even while telling himself he'd already had too much.

"And if we both get enveloped by the flames?"

Her mouth curved and the want that twisted inside him grew exponentially. This had never happened to him. This pulsing desire that only seemed to get bigger and bigger. Always before, Bennett could have a woman he desired and walk away clean, leaving her in the past, knowing that they'd both been satisfied with what they'd shared. He never lost control with a woman because none of them, he realized, had meant a damn thing to him.

Now though, Hannah Yates had crept into every corner of his mind, his body. He saw her and wanted her. Away from her, he wanted her. And he saw no end in sight. If the fire did burn itself out, wouldn't it be better to at least warm himself with it while it lasted? Could he walk away now, knowing that those flames were still hot enough to scorch them both?

"Being enveloped doesn't sound so bad," she whispered.

"This is a mistake, Hannah."

"And you never make mistakes, Ben?"

He rubbed his hands up and down her arms, feeling the strength in her, loving the hard, sculpted lines of her. Her short black hair against her white skin was alluring, and the gleam in her eyes drew him ever deeper.

"I guess I'm about to," he said softly, then bent his head to catch her mouth with his.

Instantly, she was all in. No coyness. No pretense of shyness. She gave all she was and let him know that they were in this together—wherever it led. Business, meetings, schedules, drained from his mind as he was filled with Hannah. A week, and it was as if it had been a year since he'd touched her.

Sunlight played in the room and the shush of the air conditioner sighed in the background, but all he could focus on was *her.* He couldn't have her here, in his office, as much as he might want to. But that didn't mean he couldn't at least touch her. He swept one hand down the length of her, and when she arched into him, he cupped the center of her and felt her response right down to his bones. Bennett felt her heat against his hand, right through the fabric of her jeans, and that heat ratcheted up what was already simmering inside him.

She held nothing back. Not even here, in his office, with the world right outside that closed door. Rocking her hips against his hand, she whimpered and a moan slid from her throat as he continued to ravage her mouth with his own. His blood was boiling and he couldn't imagine why he had thought staying away from her was a good idea. Nothing was better than this. Being with her. Touching her. Feeling her body coil in expectation.

He kissed her as she came, swallowing the choked whimpers sliding from her throat, and when finally, she went limp against him, he pulled his head back, smiled down into glassy, emerald green eyes and said, "I'll come to your house tonight."

"Yeah," she agreed on a sigh. "Good idea. You can finish what you started."

One corner of his mouth lifted. "Well, you know how I am about wanting jobs completed."

"I love a man with a schedule."

He smiled then and wondered why he hadn't recoiled from the word *love.*

"You should really do that more often," she said, reaching up to cup his face between her palms. "Smile, I mean. I'll see what I can do about that tonight."

"Might take a while," he warned.

"I finish the jobs I start," she said, and headed to the closed door.

Before she could open it and sail out of the office entirely, he spoke up. "Hannah. Come with me. To the awards dinner at the restaurant."

She turned to look at him and he could see the question in her eyes. He didn't know if he was giving her the answer she wanted, but he said, "I want you there. With me."

Hannah watched him for a long moment before finally nodding. "I want to be there. With you."

His assistant buzzed in. "Mr. Carey, they're waiting for you in the conference room."

He hit the answering button. "Tell them I'll be late."

Hannah's eyes went wide, and she gave him the grin that made him think of her as a sexy pixie. His heart rolled over, then thundered in his chest.

"I like you tossing aside the schedule," she admitted.

"You're making it too easy."

"No," she said, turning the doorknob slowly, "it's not just me, Ben. You're enjoying it."

When she was gone, he had to admit it… She was right.

Ten

For the next two weeks, they were together and Hannah told herself that it wouldn't end. Lying with him in her bed every night, making scrambled eggs and toast for dinner, or bringing home Chinese, they sat on her bed and picnicked naked and it was perfect. Her father had been right, she thought, when he'd told her to go after what she wanted, and still, she held back.

She never said the one word she knew might shatter what they had.

Love.

Ben hadn't said it, but she hadn't expected him to. He was the kind of man who looked at everything from every possible angle and tried to find the best way to handle a situation, no matter how long it might take. And she knew that *love* wasn't in his plans or on his schedule. He cared. She knew that. Felt that. But love from him remained elusive.

Yet, the restaurant was finished. The job complete. The bonus awarded and she was finally free of Davis. Her crew had the extra cash she'd promised them, and she'd already purchased some of the new equipment she'd dreamed about.

Now she had to wrestle with the situation she was in with Bennett Carey.

Hannah was impatient. She wanted more from him than just being her lover. She wanted the *L* word. Wanted tomorrow and the next day and the day after that. If that made her greedy or selfish, then she'd just have to live with it. The last two weeks had been everything she'd ever dreamed of having in her life, and she hated the thought that now the job was done what she shared with Ben might be ending.

When he rolled to one side and drew her up close, wrapping one arm around her, she snuggled in and listened to the hard thump of his heartbeat. This was what she wanted. Needed. But did she have the nerve to say so? Even as she thought it, she realized she had called Ben a coward for hiding from her and what he felt for her. But wasn't she doing the same thing now?

She wasn't brave enough to tell him she loved him. She wanted to be—she just wasn't there yet.

"I don't know if I've ever told you, but I like your house," he murmured, fingers running through her short hair.

Unexpected. She knew what kind of place he must be used to, though she'd never seen his home. She tipped her head back to look at him. "Thanks."

He smiled. He did that more often now and still she treasured every one. “Like your bedroom for instance…”

Hannah laughed. “Yeah, I know you like this room.”

He gave her a hard hug. “I like the color. This deep—what is it called?”

“Burgundy.”

“Right. Well, it’s nice. Restful, sort of gives the room a quiet cave-like feel.”

“Oh, that’s nice!”

“You know what I mean. It’s intimate. Cozy, somehow. You should hear my sisters and mother go on about my house. *Beige, Bennett. No one likes beige.*”

“They’re right.” She lifted her head, braced her arm on his chest and took the opportunity to ask, “Why do we never go to your house?”

Moonlight drifted through the gap in the curtains and lay across his face, so she watched his features tighten. “Because, my mother’s living there. She’s punishing my father for not retiring as he promised, and she refuses to leave.”

“And you don’t want to introduce me,” she said, and hoped he didn’t hear the hurt in her voice.

“That’s not exactly it,” he argued. “She drives me crazy, Hannah.”

“You’re lucky,” she said.

“And you don’t know my mother,” he said, trying for lighthearted and failing.

A quick jab of pain because he never took her around his family. It was as if this side of him, this thing they shared, was to be kept secret. Guarded from everyone. Why?

“I’d like to,” she said.

“Hannah…”

"I know." She sat up and looked down at him. "No one knows we're together like this. We don't see my friends or your family. We hide what we are to each other and sneak around like teenagers."

"I don't consider it hiding," he argued. "I consider it private."

"From your family?"

He laughed shortly. "Especially from my family."

"Great." That hurt pooling inside her widened and deepened. *Especially his family.* Pushing off the bed, she switched on a bedside light, and the soft, golden glow of the bulb had Ben tossing one arm across his eyes like a vampire reeling back from a cross.

A moment later, he lowered his arm, then held out one hand to her, silently asking her to join him again. She sat on the edge of the bed and took his hand, but forced herself to ask, "Are you ashamed of me?"

"What?" Pure astonishment colored his tone and etched itself across his features. "Where the hell did that come from?"

"The hiding."

He blew out a breath, and frustration was in his voice when he said, "It's not you, Hannah. It's my mom. If I took you to the house, she'd assume we were..."

"What? Together?" she asked, as the first stirrings of anger began to bubble inside her. "Aren't we?"

He scowled, an expression she was all too familiar with. "Of course we are, but she would think that it was more than it is."

"I see." Her voice sounded cold, even to her. Amazing how quickly pain could turn to outrage. "Why don't you explain to me what *this* is, exactly, Ben?"

He pushed both hands through his hair in a show of

exasperation. And when he spoke, he didn't answer her. "How did we get onto this anyway?"

"I met your sisters," she reminded him, ignoring his question in favor of her own.

"Yeah, I know. They're still talking about you, asking questions."

"And what do you tell them?" This was important. To her. To them. Couldn't he see that?

"Nothing," he admitted. "I don't talk about my private life with them, Hannah."

Disappointment warred with the anger and not surprisingly, anger won the day.

"That's what family is for, Ben. Talking to them about the important things in your life."

"That's not who I am, Hannah. You know that."

"What I know is," she said with a shake of her head, "instead of being impatient with your mother, you should be appreciating having her in your life."

He snorted.

"I mean it. My mother left my dad and me when I was barely old enough to walk." His smile faded and his eyes fixed on hers. "She decided she didn't want to be a wife. A mother. And left to find her own joy. Never saw her again. Do you know what it would mean to me to have a mother who wanted to know what was happening in my life?"

"Hannah..."

"No, it's fine. I'm fine." She got off the bed again because she thought better on her feet. Looking down at him, she drew his features into her brain so that no matter what happened next, she would always be able to see him when she closed her eyes. "The thing is, Ben, you should know that this…thing, between us? It's more than just temporary for me."

She could see the wariness in his gaze even before he said, "Hannah, don't."

Hannah had come too far now, and she wouldn't stop even if she could have. She was through being a coward. She'd gone to his office, hadn't she? Well, she needed that kind of courage now, too. "Too late. I should have said something before. But somehow I was afraid that if I did, it would all end. Now I realize though, if I don't say something, it *will* end, because something in me will die." She took a breath, met his gaze squarely and said, "I love you, Ben. I have almost from the start."

"Damn it, Hannah." Now he pushed off the bed and stood staring at her across the mattress. "You don't mean that."

"Don't tell me what I mean. I said *love* and I meant *love.*" At the look on his face, she muttered, "Though at the moment, I couldn't tell you *why* I love you."

"Exactly. You can't. We have nothing in common, Hannah."

"That's too easy, Ben." She snatched up her short, pale blue robe from a nearby chair and shrugged it on. "If you don't want to feel something for me, have the guts to admit it. Things in common? What does that even mean? No.

"I've done a lot of thinking about this, too. I know you're the rich guy, living in a beige house that you're never in. I'm the contractor living in a brightly colored tiny house that you already admitted you like."

"That's—"

"We both love our families. We're both hard workers. We both have big plans. And what we have here?"

She waved a hand at the bed with the rumpled sheet and duvet. "That's magic, Ben. And you damn well know it. So if you don't want me, just say so, but don't give me those pale reasons for backing away."

"I do want you," he admitted. "Always will. But I don't even know if I'm capable of what you're wanting from me."

"You'll never know if you don't try."

"Maybe I don't want to know."

Nodding, blinking fast to keep the tears gathering in her eyes from falling, Hannah said, "Well. That's honest, anyway. I really think you should go now, Ben."

She'd taken her shot. Told him how she felt, even knowing that it would probably end just as it had. But she wouldn't regret it. Wouldn't second-guess herself for falling in love with Bennett Carey. Love wasn't a decision to make. It just… *Was.*

"I don't want to leave you like this, Hannah."

"But you do want to leave, so you really should." She walked out of her bedroom, headed for the kitchen. He could get dressed and leave on his own. God knew, he'd spent enough time here to be able to find the damn door without her.

"All set for the Summer Stars celebration?" Amanda dropped into one of the visitor chairs in Bennett's office and crossed her legs.

"Of course I'm set," he answered, barely looking at his sister. "Why wouldn't I be set?"

The damn celebration. At the damn restaurant that Hannah had restored not only to its former glory but to something it should always have been. Sure. He'd love to be there. Without her.

"Well, of course," Amanda mused. "I can hear the joy in your voice."

He lifted his gaze and scowled at her.

"Oh please, like the death stare is going to work." Amanda waved one hand at him dismissively. "I'm your sister, Bennett. I've seen your 'go away' stare since you were ten."

"And yet, you remain." Deliberately he lowered his gaze to the papers in front of him and tried to see them as more than black smudges on a white background.

"How's Hannah?"

"Why ask me?"

"Because I have cleverly deduced that you've made a mess of things with her and that's why you've become a human Death Star wandering these illustrious corridors."

"Do you *practice* being annoying?" He tossed his pen down and leaned back in his chair.

"No practice required," she quipped. "It's a gift."

"Return it."

"Oh, a joke. Very exciting." Amanda leaned forward, speared her gaze into his and asked, "What did you do?"

"I didn't do a damn thing."

"That's what they all say."

"Damn it, Amanda, butt out."

"Not going to happen."

"She said she loves me," he blurted, then wished with everything inside him he could call it back.

"Oh, Bennett," she said on a sigh. "That's not news to anyone but you."

"You might've told me." He stood up, walked to the wall of windows and stared out at the sea.

"It wouldn't have helped."

No, it wouldn't have. He could admit that, at least to himself. God, he could still see her, standing beside her bed, wearing nothing but moonlight. Everything in him yearned for her. Probably always would. But he saw his parents now, at war after nearly forty years. Living with someone wasn't easy in the best of times, and he wasn't an easy man at *any* time. How long before he and Hannah made each other miserable? How long before their differences tore them apart?

Wasn't it easier to end it now rather than years from now when there might be kids involved? Hell, his parents had been together forever. It hadn't always been sunshine and roses, either. He remembered arguments. Hard words and cold silences—and the two of them had shared common ground. If it was hard for *them*, how much harder would it be for him and Hannah?

Bennett turned to look at his sister. "I appreciate the concern, but it's done, Mandy. Finished. And we'll just have to deal with it."

"I love you, Bennett, but sometimes, you're so male, I just want to clock you." She stood up, smoothed her skirt and shook her head. "You're making a mistake, you know."

"Funny. I said the same thing to Hannah not so long ago."

"She should have listened," Amanda murmured.

"Yeah," Bennett said when his sister was gone. "She should have."

Hannah took her measurements, then noted them on her tablet. When she had the second set of measurements, she did the same, and then measured everything again just to make sure.

The sun was streaming down on Jack Colton's backyard and the roar of the sea was like a throaty purr in the background. The wind kicked at her, just to make maneuvering her measuring tape more interesting. Looking at the length of the backyard made her smile.

Not only was Yates Construction going to build a real stone castle—kid-sized, of course—but Jack wanted a retaining wall along the property to make sure his new daughter wouldn't go racing off a cliff.

"Good policy," she said to herself.

"I always trust people who talk to themselves."

Hannah whirled around and watched an older woman in a beautiful, pale green jacket and skirt walk across the lawn toward her. She had short, chestnut-colored hair, blue eyes and a soft smile curving her mouth. And Hannah had a very good idea who the woman was.

"You're Ben's mother."

"I am," she said with a broader smile. "How did you know?"

"He has your eyes."

"Isn't that nice of you to say? Please. Call me Candace. And you're Hannah." She tipped her head to one side as if to study her more closely. "I have to confess that I came here specifically to meet you."

Instantly, Hannah wished she were dressed better for the occasion. Her Yates Construction T-shirt, blue jeans and work boots probably weren't making the best of impressions. Yet even as she thought it, she realized it didn't matter. This was who she was. If that wasn't good enough for the Careys, then too damn bad. Besides, Ben wasn't in her life anymore, and that thought brought a sinking sensation to the pit of her stomach.

It had only been two days since he'd walked out of

her house—her life—and it felt like years. She couldn't imagine what surviving the coming years would be like. Empty, emptier, emptiest.

"It's nice to meet you," she finally said when she realized she'd been quiet too long.

"Oh, you don't think so at the moment," the other woman said, reaching out to pat her hand. "But you will. For me, I'm enjoying it."

"Happy to help."

She laughed. "Oh yes. Definitely enjoying it. Please, let's sit down for a second. Jack told me you'd be here, checking the property for Alli's castle."

That's right. "Alli's your granddaughter."

"Yes, and don't encourage me, I have hundreds of photos on my phone and I'll bore you brainless."

Hannah relaxed. It was impossible to remain stiff and uncomfortable around this woman. Ben was stupid to complain about her.

She followed Candace to a low stone bench tucked beneath a shade tree. When she sat down, Candace said, "Oh, Alli is going to love that castle. Do you have a design for it yet?"

"Yeah, actually. The architect is working on the plans now. When he's finished, we'll start. Should have the permits by next week, and then we'll be good to go."

Candace shook her head and the dappled sunlight caught the highlights in her hair. "I'm so impressed by you."

"You are?" That she hadn't expected.

"Oh yes. A woman running a construction company? That's very admirable."

"Well, thank you."

"My daughter Mandy tells me you love my son."

"Quite the segue."

Candace waved a manicured hand absently. "No point in not talking about it, is there?"

"I suppose not." Hannah shifted on the bench to look at the other woman squarely. "It doesn't matter now anyway. I did love him. But I'll get over it."

In twenty or thirty years. She turned her face into the sea breeze and let it ruffle her short, dark hair. Anything to keep from seeing sympathy on Candace's face. She didn't need it or want it.

She didn't get it, either.

"I don't think you should try."

"No offense, Candace," Hannah said quietly, "but you don't get a vote."

She laughed at that and nodded. "True, I don't. But you can't stop me from wishing." She reached out and laid one hand on Hannah's arm. "Bennett is just miserable."

"Yes," she said wryly. "I know."

Another chuckle. "You're perfect for him, I swear."

As much as she liked the sound of that, Hannah said, "No, I'm not. Ask him. He'll tell you."

"Hannah, you are the first woman to ever befuddle my son."

"Befuddle?" Hannah shook her head. "If you asked him, Ben would say I infuriated, frustrated and annoyed him. But I don't think he'd say befuddled."

"That's exactly why you're perfect for him."

"You're not making sense." And she wondered how she could get out of this conversation. Hannah gave a quick look around, but the expansive yard was empty. Not even a damn gardener there to distract Candace. Funny. Suddenly, Hannah understood why Bennett was being driven to distraction by his mother. A hammer, even a velvet-wrapped hammer, could do some damage.

"You don't understand, Hannah." The woman took a breath, looked around the backyard herself, then shifted her gaze until she met Hannah's. "Bennett's always been so stern. So controlled. It was as if he were born wearing an Armani suit—which I can testify he was not."

Hannah smiled.

"It's his nature to be controlling," she continued. "To look after everyone and everything, so that he's never felt he had the right to take something for himself.

"Maybe some of that is our fault," Candace mused. "He is the oldest and so responsible right from the start that we were constantly putting him in charge of his siblings while we were working on the business."

"I don't think that's so unusual," Hannah said.

"Maybe not, but," she added with another smile, "when you're a mother, you'll realize that your full-time hobby becomes looking back and wondering if you did things right. If you should have done them differently and how that might have affected your children." She took a breath and said, "But that's not why I'm here."

"Why are you here?" Hannah asked.

"Because you love my son," Candace said. "And I want that for him. He deserves to be loved and to love in return."

"Yes, well," Hannah said, wishing she were anywhere but there. "I think so, too. But he, unfortunately, doesn't. So while I appreciate the thought, Candace—"

"You wish I would go away."

Hannah opened her mouth, but what could she say? So she closed it again.

Candace chuckled and pushed her windblown hair

back from her face. “You’re a nice woman, Hannah. Too nice to tell me to mind my own business. But I’m going to say what I came here to say. Don’t give up on him. He’s worth the trouble.”

She would love to think that Ben’s mother was right. That all he needed was time to see that they were meant to be together. But how could she believe that when she’d seen for herself how the mere mention of the word *love* had shut him down completely? And there was the “nothing in common” argument, as well.

“You’re coming to the Summer Stars celebration tomorrow night, aren’t you?”

Hannah frowned and shook her head. “I was going to but now I think—”

“Good. I’ll expect you to be there.” Candace stood up and brushed off the seat of her skirt. “It’s as much your celebration as anyone’s, isn’t it? The chance to showcase the work you and your company did. I’ve toured the restaurant and I’m very impressed with your skills and talents.”

“Thank you,” Hannah said as she stood up. “That’s nice to hear but—”

“Hannah,” the older woman said gently. “Do you want him to think you were too afraid to face him?”

“Oh, you’re very clever,” Hannah said after a second or two. “I bet it was impossible for your kids to get anything past you.”

Candace smiled. “Not impossible. But certainly not easy. So. I’ll see you tomorrow night?”

She shouldn’t, of course. She should stay far, far away from Ben Carey. But as she looked at his mother, Hannah knew she wasn’t going to do that. She would go to that party, and she would look so good, he’d eat his heart out.

"I like the gleam in your eye, Hannah," Candace said with a wink. "I think the two of us are going to get along very well together."

The Carey was better than ever.

Bennett stood alone near the bar and watched the crowd move through the restaurant and every last one of them couldn't stop talking about the changes. The improvements.

Even the floors were stunning—the lighter stain lifted the entire atmosphere of the place. Hannah had been right about that. Fresh paint in a soft rose color lightened the walls and made the new, lighter tables look like circles of privacy. Flowers graced every table and the larger, banquette tables along one wall. Hannah had been right about that, too, as she'd been about the cream-colored leather.

The kitchen was a damn masterpiece, he had to admit because John Henry hadn't stopped raving about it since the completion. Hannah had talked to the chef, made suggestions and ended up by moving the workstations around to create an easier flow for the chefs and waiters to navigate.

She'd done everything she said she would. She'd delivered first-class work under a killer deadline. She was right about every suggestion she'd made. He missed her. Hell, just seeing his restaurant made him think of her, and that was a nightmare because he was here all the damn time. So she'd be haunting him for the rest of his life.

Bennett's skin seemed to buzz, as if the air itself was suddenly electrified. His gaze swept the room and he spotted her. Here. In the restaurant. Just inside the door.

Yes, he'd invited her, but after that last night at her house, he hadn't expected to see her tonight. Now that she was here, though, he suddenly felt as if he could breathe again. As if the invisible iron bands around his chest had loosened, he drew one long breath and would have sworn he could smell her, even from a distance. Sense memory brought her scent to him, and Bennet hung on to it even as he indulged in a long, leisurely perusal.

She wore an emerald green, strapless dress that clung to her upper body, then fell into a swirl around her legs, stopping just above her knees. Silver links dangled from her earlobes and as she watched the crowd, she wore a small smile that tugged at everything inside him. She was breathtaking.

Bennett threaded his way through the crowd and around the press taking pictures of the Summer Stars winners. When she spotted him, he noticed her chin come up, and he hated that she instinctively made that defensive move.

"You look amazing," he said, his voice pitched low, in spite of the noise in the room.

"Thanks." She tipped her head back to look up at him, and he noticed that her eyes looked a deeper green tonight. Like a forest in the starlit dark. "So do you."

He wanted to touch her. Hell, he wanted to taste her, sink into the feel of her pressed against him. Instead, he took another long breath and prayed for control. "Everyone's talking about how great the restaurant looks."

"Not everyone," she said, and nodded toward the press gathered around a young man and woman, smiling for photographs.

"Ah. Jacob Foley and his sister Sheila," he said. "They won the competition by a few thousand votes. They do sort of Celtic music. Guitar, violin and Sheila sings. They're pretty amazing actually."

"And now they get to perform at the Carey Center one night this summer?"

"That's right." He looked down at her. "We'll promote the hell out of it, and with any luck they can use that performance as a stepping-stone to a career."

"They're that good?"

"They really are. And, the contest was so popular we're going to do it every year, and I don't want to talk about the Summer Stars anymore." He stared down into her eyes and felt his world right itself. That thought both comforted and horrified him. When did she become so damned important? So essential?

"I'm glad you're here."

"Why?"

He choked out a laugh. "Trust you to ask that. Answer's simple. Because I missed you."

"Good. I missed you, too."

Bennett smiled.

"I got a smile out of you, too."

"Not many can," he admitted. He crooked his arm, then threaded her hand through it. "Let me introduce you around."

For the next half hour, Bennett kept her close to his side and introduced her to dozens of people. They made small talk, as always happened at those sorts of things. And through it all he sensed Hannah pulling further and further away from him in spite of the fact that he had her arm in his. He couldn't figure out what was wrong.

Finally though, he found her a chair at a table and left to get glasses of champagne for both of them, hoping that once they had a chance to talk they could find a way to get back to where they were just days ago. Before the love admission. Before everything had changed.

First, of course, he had to find out what was bothering her and try to fix it.

Hannah watched him go and buried the knot of disappointment lodged in her chest. She'd hoped… Stupid. Hopes were futile when confronted with stark reality. And the reality was, Ben was not the man for her. She watched him, and everything inside her ached for things to be different, but he'd just proven to her that nothing would change.

"So—" a voice brushed her ear "—Bennett Carey, huh?"

A cold, sinking sensation opened up in her chest. Hannah turned her head to meet Davis Buckley's cool stare. *The perfect capper to the evening*, she thought. Of course he would be here. The rich and the famous and the press were all over the restaurant. Davis would never miss an event like this one.

As she looked at him, she remembered that at one time, she'd thought Davis was the one, and yet, looking back now, what she had felt for him was such a pale imitation of what she felt for Bennett. It amazed her now to think that she ever could have thought she was in love with the man. He was so obviously… What was the word Amanda Carey had used? Oh right. Toady.

"What do you want, Davis?" Hannah asked, standing up to face him. The rumble of conversation around them was a counterpoint to their lowered voices. "I paid off your 'loan.' We're even. I don't owe you a thing. Not even a moment of my time."

Davis looked her up and down so dismissively, it was all she could do not to kick him. "Now I see why you dumped me. You were after a richer catch. Nice job, hooking Bennett Carey. Many have tried, no one's succeeded."

Astonished, she asked, "What are you talking about?"

"I saw him slavering over you." Davis snorted his disgust. "Do you think I'm stupid?"

"Among other things," Amanda said. "Go away, Davis. And stay away."

"Happy to," he said, looking past her. "Hello, Bennett. Good to see you."

Hannah felt her stomach simply drop. How long had he been standing there? Had he heard them talking? Had he overheard Davis accusing her of dumping him for a "richer catch"? Slowly, she turned around to face the man who was looking at her as if he'd never seen her before. The answer to her question was written all over his face.

He'd heard every word.

"Bennett, it's not what you think."

Eleven

"Can't wait to hear what it actually is, then," Bennett said. Setting the champagne glasses down on the table, he grabbed her hand and headed for the front door. She didn't try to stop him. She wanted to have this out as much as he did. Maybe more.

Once outside, the sea wind slapped at them, but it didn't seem to cool the tempers spiking in each of them.

"Davis Buckley?" Bennett demanded. "You were involved with that slimeball?"

"Engaged, actually," she corrected, though the words tasted bitter on her tongue. He reeled back from that information and stuffed both hands into his pockets.

The parking lot was crowded—mostly expensive sports cars and SUVs, of course. The valets were running in and out, so Bennett steered her toward the side of the building where they could be private. Out of the corner of her eye, Hannah saw someone start toward them—probably hoping to speak to Bennett, then obviously reading the situation, the man suddenly veered away. She couldn't blame him.

Staring up into his eyes, she noticed that right now, they were the color of a stormy sky. Well, she felt the same way. Still, she told him everything. Explained about Davis and how naive she'd been and why she'd needed the job on The Carey and how the bonus had finally paid off her last loan with Davis. When she was finished, she waited for his reaction and it didn't take long.

"Oh, that's great!" He threw both hands up. "So you were 'in love' with him, too?"

She flinched at the sneer in his tone. "I thought I was, yeah. But it's nothing—"

"Let me guess. Nothing like you feel for me?" He shook his head, turned and walked away only to come right back. "Was he right? Did you use me like you used him?"

"Excuse me?" Hannah had had all she could take. She had been willing to cut him a little slack because Davis Buckley had to have been an ugly surprise. But she wouldn't stand there and let him put this all on her. "Davis was the one who used *me.* Like you have."

He snorted. "You can't be serious."

"Funny. Your sisters saw the truth. Why is it you can't?" She cocked her head, set both hands at her hips and said, "You used my skills and my crew's time to get your restaurant up and running for this self-congratulatory party where the combined wealth of your guest list would equal more than the GDP of some *countries.*"

"I hired you. Didn't use you. And now it's a crime to be rich?"

"Of course not," she snapped, "but it should be a crime to be thoughtless about it."

"Thanks very much."

Did he not see it? she wondered, or did he not *want* to see it?

"Ben, you just spent a half hour dragging me around the restaurant, introducing me to all of your rich friends, but never once," she said tightly, "did you tell them that I'm the contractor who did the work on the restaurant. You didn't want them to know that I'm in charge of a crew of men. That I own a construction business."

Bennett scrubbed one hand across his face and shook his head. "That's not what this is about."

"It's exactly that." She stepped in closer, tapped his chest with her index finger and said, "When I told you I was in love with you, you gave me an argument about having nothing in common. But that's not what's driving you, Ben. It's the fact that you're *embarrassed* by what I do for a living."

"I never said that," he argued.

"You didn't have to," she told him and swallowed the hurt burning inside her. "Tonight, you just made it perfectly clear. I'm sorry I'm not some elegant rich woman who won't turn a doorknob for fear of ruining her manicure."

"You're being ridiculous."

"Am I? I don't think so." She did a slow turn, letting him get a good look at her. "This isn't the real me. Or at least it's not the *only* part of me. I wear work boots. I put up Sheetrock and whatever else needs doing on a job site. I take as much pride in my work as you do in yours. I'm running a family business. Just like you. And

I'm damn good at what I do. What I *won't* do is waste my time on a man who's ashamed of who I am.

"Goodbye, Ben. Enjoy your party."

"Wait."

Hannah stopped and looked over her shoulder at him.

"Why did you come here tonight, Hannah?"

"Because I wanted to prove to myself I could face you again. And I wanted you to see me and eat your heart out."

"Well then. Mission accomplished."

That should have made her feel good. But it didn't.

She left him standing there, and one of the valets called her a cab. While she waited, she looked back over her shoulder and saw that he was still standing in the dark, watching her. Her heart ached, but her spine stiffened.

When the cab arrived, she got in and went home.

Alone.

That night, Bennett didn't sleep.

Every time he closed his eyes, he saw Hannah. Saw the flash of anger and hurt in her eyes. Heard her voice, calling him out. Remembered her telling him about being engaged to Davis Buckley, of all people. Was it *his* fault he'd been so shocked by that news that he'd reacted badly?

Yes.

By 7:00 a.m., he was on edge, exhausted and had a headache pounding behind his eyes. So when he heard live music right outside his house, he accepted it as just another form of torture. Pushing out of bed, he walked to the window, looked down and saw a band, complete with drum kit and amplifiers, playing, of all things "Love Will Keep Us Together."

Bennett's chin hit his chest.

Martin Carey was standing right behind the band, staring up at the house, grinning like a loon, obviously waiting for his wife to appear and be swept off her feet by his romantic gesture. Bennett knew that was his parents' song. It was popular when they were dating and when he was a kid, he'd sometimes caught his parents dancing to the song when they thought they were alone.

At the moment, several of his neighbors had come out of their homes and were now dancing to the music, enjoying the morning's surprise entertainment. It was over-the-top, completely unexpected and Bennett thought, he had to give it to his father. Maybe this would be the thing to finally get Candace to forgive him and move the hell out of Bennett's house.

So a few minutes later, when his mother stepped outside, dressed for work in a black-and-white shirtdress and heels, Bennett damn near held his breath. Would she go for it?

No.

The band stopped playing and with his window open, Bennett actually heard the click of his mother's heels on the stone walk. She moved past the band as if they weren't there and stopped in front of Martin. "You just don't understand anything, do you, Marty? You really think playing our song will convince me to come home when nothing has really changed?"

"Candy, this has gone on long enough," his father complained.

"It certainly has," Candace agreed, then glanced at the band. "I'm ignoring your attempt. Not fun to be ignored, is it?"

With that, she slid into her BMW and drove off, leaving Martin and the band behind. The neighbors called out for more music, so the band started playing again and the party continued. Martin got in his car and left. Bennett closed the window, shutting the music down to a muffled roar.

His parents weren't solving this mess. And Bennett wondered what it was women actually *did* want. His mother wasn't impressed with a big romantic gesture. Hannah kept her relationship with Davis Buckley a secret—or had she? They hadn't talked about their pasts. Maybe she would have told him, but he probably would have reacted just as he had. And his sisters were on her side. Worse, Hannah had accused him of being ashamed of her.

He scowled and caught his own reflection in the mirror across from the bed. *Hard to lie to yourself when the truth is right there staring at you.*

"Damn it," he told the face staring back at him. "She was right. You were being a damn snob. You avoided telling people that *she* restored the restaurant, when in reality, you should have been proud to introduce a stunning woman who is so blasted talented she could build a house from the ground up by herself."

Had he become such an elitist that he couldn't see anyone's worth beyond their financial bottom line? Was a career or a business only worth admiring if it could be done in an expensive suit or elegant dress? That was a damned depressing thought. And humiliating.

As for Davis Buckley. Hell. Hannah had had the good sense to end that engagement—not to mention working her gorgeous ass off to pay back the man's loans so she could be free of him entirely. But had Bennett taken the time to realize that when it counted?

No.

He pushed one hand through his hair and yanked on that hair for good measure. What the hell was wrong with him? He had a beautiful woman tell him she loved him, and he accused her of trying to use him?

Instead of grabbing at his chance for love and happiness, he'd tossed it back in her face and embarrassed her by refusing to appreciate her for the amazing woman she was. Hell, his parents had been married forty years. Even now, with the Retirement Wars going on, there was no talk of divorce. They loved each other so much each was trying to convince the other to see things their way. How could he *not* believe in love with the Careys as an example?

Staring at his reflection, he jabbed one finger at the man in the mirror. "*You* are an idiot."

"You're an idiot, that's what you are," Hannah muttered darkly. She'd allowed herself to love Ben, and as it turned out, he might be even worse than Davis. At least Davis Buckley was up front about the kind of man he was. Ben had fooled her into thinking he was different. Sure, a little closed off and a walking frown, but a good guy.

But at the core of things, he was like every other rich client she'd ever known.

"And that's why you're an idiot," she said.

"What's that, boss?" Tiny pushed his hat back and squinted at her in the bright sunlight.

"Nothing," she assured him. "Just talking to myself."

"Hah, when I do that, my wife says I'm losing it." When she turned a steely stare on him, he quickly added, "I don't think that, of course."

"Right." She stared up at the back of the house they

were working on. They had to cut away the eaves and part of the roof to attach the new front porch roof. This remodel was a good idea, she thought. They'd pour concrete in a day or two, giving the homeowners the kind of porch that had room for a few chairs and a table. The roof would afford protection from sunlight and rain and give their house the kind of character the original builder had decided against.

"Okay, you guys work on breaking up the old porch while I get to work on the eaves." She set the ladder to lean against the roof and started climbing while her crew took care of the demo on the ground.

"Uh, boss…"

"Tiny, just break up the concrete, okay?" She didn't want to talk. Not even to herself anymore. Talk didn't solve anything. Going over and over what had happened between her and Ben didn't solve anything, either.

"Boss, there's someone here to see you…"

She sighed, half turned on the ladder to watch Ben cross the front yard to stand beneath her, looking up. Wearing one of his ever-present suits and very expensive shoes, he looked as out of place as she had felt at the big party at The Carey.

Oh, and it was humiliating to admit that even after everything they'd said to each other, Hannah's heartbeat still jittered when she saw him. Her pulse raced and everything in her wished things were different. But since they weren't, she would just wish he would leave.

"Go away, Ben. I'm working."

Bennett took a breath and scrubbed one hand across his jaw. He'd started his morning off by talking to Hannah's father, and that man had been as *welcoming* as her crew was at the moment. He understood their attitude. Hell, he'd caused it by bringing Hannah pain. What he *couldn't* take was the hurt in her eyes when she looked at him.

"I was wrong," he said, loud enough for everyone to hear over the sound of power tools. And as soon as he spoke, those tools were shut off, apparently so the crew wouldn't miss whatever happened next.

"I agree," she said, and kept climbing. "Now go away."

"Come down so we can talk," he said.

"I have nothing to say," she told him, and used the claw end of her hammer to peel up one of the eave boards. When she had it free, she tossed it to the ground, and he jumped back to avoid being hit.

"Almost got me," he said.

"I'll try harder next time," she told him.

He grinned briefly. Damn, he loved this woman.

"Okay that's it," Bennet muttered and started for the ladder. "If you won't come down, I'll come up."

"Do you have a death wish?" She looked down at him, stunned surprise on her face. "Get down before you upset the balance and kill us both."

"The balance is already upset Hannah," he said, keeping his gaze on her as he climbed. One of his feet slid off a rung and he made a mental note not to wear dress shoes the next time he climbed a ladder.

"Whose fault is that?" she asked.

"Mine," he admitted. It wasn't as difficult as he'd thought it would be, talking to her, telling her what he needed her to hear. All he had to do was go with his gut. "I was wrong. And careless. And shortsighted."

Someone on the crew applauded. Bennett ignored him.

"Damn it, Hannah," he said. "I love you. I'm proud of you and everything you can do. I love who you are.

Your talent. Your pride. Your confidence. Your laugh. All I want is another chance to prove it."

She looked down at him, and he saw something in her eyes that gave him hope.

"I handled this all wrong, Hannah," he admitted, ignoring the cheers and applause from her crew. He knew her father was down there, too, listening, but he wasn't speaking to any of them. Only one person mattered here. "I hurt you and I didn't mean to. I didn't value you, and that will never happen again. I love you, Hannah, and that will never change."

She turned, leaned one hip against a rung of the ladder, and said, "Ben, I think I believe you, but that doesn't change the reality. I don't belong in your world any more than you belong in mine."

He smiled. "That's bull, Hannah, and you know it. We make the worlds the way they are. And, I'd like to point out that I'm in your world right now and the universe didn't explode."

"Yet," she muttered.

Bennett grinned. "Hannah, we can build our own place, the best of both our worlds and screw anyone who tries to tell us differently. Be with me, Hannah. Love me. Make a family with me. I miss you. I miss *us*."

Her gaze locked with his, and he felt her wants and desires as surely as his own. How could he have been so blind as to let her nearly slip away from him?

"I won't stop working, Ben. I want to grow my company until we're the number one contracting company in Southern California."

More cheers from the crew, and who could blame them? "That sounds great to me. You deserve nothing less."

More applause from the crew. "You can start by renovating my house because my whole family says it's boring."

"They're probably right," she said, lips twitching.

"It'll be a challenge," he said, smiling.

"*You're* the real challenge," she retorted.

"Agreed." He stared into her eyes, and said, "I'm as stubborn and single-minded as you are, so that might make for a bumpy road sometimes. But damn it, Hannah, I want to be on that road with you. Only with you. We can build a great life together."

"I want kids," she warned him.

"As many as we want."

"I'll teach them how to use tools," she said.

"Great. You can teach me at the same time."

Grinning now, Hannah looked over at her father. Ben followed her gaze and saw the older man give two thumbs-up. Then she turned her gaze back to Bennett, and when she leaned down to kiss him, he stopped her.

"Can we get down on the ground for the kissing part?"

She laughed, and the sound was like a musical balm to his soul. Once they were on their own two feet again, Bennett swept her into a hard embrace and kissed her until they were both breathless. And while the crew around them laughed and shouted, Bennett dug into his pocket for the ring he'd purchased only that morning.

"Channel set diamonds," she whispered, looking up at him.

He shrugged and slipped it onto her finger. "So nothing will get caught in machinery."

Hannah sighed, lifted one hand to cup his cheek and whispered, "I can't believe you thought of that."

Bennett held her tightly to him and murmured, "I will

always think of you first. I will always love you. Forever and then beyond that."

Hannah smiled up at him and said, "I love you, Ben. Now and always. And to prove it, I promise to attend all of the fancy parties you want me to."

"And I promise not to use power tools unsupervised," he said.

"Thank God," she said, throwing herself at him, wrapping her arms around his neck and holding on.

When he held her tight and swung her in a circle, Bennett whispered, "Thank you. For loving me enough to change my world forever."

She looked down into his eyes and promised, "Forever, King Carey."

* * * * *

HOLIDAY PLAYBOOK

YAHRAH ST. JOHN

To my husband, Freddie Blackman, for encouraging me to continue writing after losing my dad.

One

"Anything new to report, Giana?" Roman Lockett asked during the Atlanta Cougars' managers' meeting the Monday after the long Thanksgiving weekend.

As the chief marketing and branding officer, Giana Lockett oversaw the football team's marketing efforts and business operations and strategies surrounding the team's brand. She hated when her brother called her out like he was the teacher and she was the student, especially since she was the only woman sitting at a table full of men.

"I've begun working with the Lockett Foundation to help spearhead the league's efforts in youth football and community outreach, as well as finalizing a college basketball tournament here at the arena."

"That's great, Giana," her father, Josiah Lockett, chimed in. "And what about endorsements for Curtis?"

Curtis Jackson was a star wide receiver and the Atlanta Cougars' newest recruit.

"We've got Curtis teed up for sneaker, fast food, cell phone and luxury vehicle endorsements."

"And what about sports drinks?" her father pressed.

Giana knew exactly what he was asking about. Her father wanted to work with *LEAN, a* sports drink brand owned by Wynn Starks's company. But the elusive billionaire had kept Giana at arm's length for much of the year. Usually, it was the other way around with companies coming to athletes, but LEAN seemed determined *not* to join forces with the Atlanta Cougars, which was why the deal was especially appealing to her father. He hated being told no.

Giana had gone through the usual channels of making a pitch to Starks's marketing team about what a great partnership they could have. And she'd spoken with his personal assistant in the hopes she'd make headway, but for months Wynn Starks had doggedly given her the slip. Her perseverance had won out and she'd garnered a meeting for today.

"I'm exploring different options," Giana finally replied, keeping her response cagey.

"Excellent. Sounds like you have it under control." Roman gave her a wink. "Let's move on to the injured list as we head into the playoffs."

The meeting finished up shortly after. Her father rushed off for an appointment, leaving Giana blessedly free from another tirade about why she hadn't managed to get the Starks Inc. deal.

"Thanks for the assist, Rome," Giana said after the remaining staff cleared the room.

"I've got your back."

Giana glanced up at her big brother. "Thank you." At six foot two, her brother was several inches taller than her. Today he was in a gray designer suit with a navy tie and looked every bit the general manager he'd become several months ago when their father stepped back from the role. Roman was easy on the eyes, with milk chocolate skin the same as hers and a sculpted beard.

"I knew Dad was about to fire into you on LEAN, and I didn't think you wanted the heat."

"I didn't, but don't worry. I have a meeting scheduled with Wynn Starks today and hope to land the deal."

Roman's bushy eyebrows rose. "Sure you're not overconfident, Gigi? He has been hard to pin down."

"I play to win, Rome," Giana responded. "Same as you."

"Go get 'em, tiger." He laughed when she sashayed out of the room.

Minutes later when she returned to her office, however, her boss lady ego was deflated. "What do you mean, he canceled?" Giana folded her arms across the blazer of her navy blue suit and regarded her assistant, Mara Hall. "I thought this was a done deal."

"It was until his PA called me a few minutes ago and said Mr. Starks is fully booked and didn't have a minute to spare."

Giana rolled her eyes. It was a bald-faced lie. Wynn Starks must have learned she was on his calendar and told his PA to call off their meeting. A meeting she'd booked weeks ago. She couldn't understand why he managed to foil her every time, but she refused to play by the rules any longer. "Mara, can you get me the report Nico Shapiro did on Mr. Starks?"

Nico was the investigator the Atlanta Cougars kept on retainer to handle delicate situations. He was damn good at his job.

"Of course." Mara left her office, and Giana leaned back in her executive chair and fumed.

If Mr. Starks wanted to play hardball, that's exactly what Giana would do. She hadn't grown up around three brothers without learning how to play dirty.

Mara returned several minutes later holding a manila folder. She handed it to her. "Thank you," Giana responded. "Can you close the door, please?"

Once Mara had gone, Giana reviewed the report again.

It stated Wynn frequented a local gym and liked to box. So she came up with a strategy. She would show up where he was until he had no choice but to talk to her.

Wynn Starks was in a foul mood. He'd thought it was going to be a good day. He'd run five miles. The workout had cleared his mind and gotten him into the right head space to run the sports drink company he'd founded a decade ago.

Riding his limited-edition MTT Turbine Streetfighter to the office, he'd felt the wind against his face and felt alive. But that had been the last of the good vibes this morning. The first miss had been when he arrived and his personal assistant, Sam Clark, had informed him he had a meeting scheduled with Giana Lockett.

Sam was an unassuming young fellow with pale skin, floppy brown hair and a warm smile, who preferred Dockers and a polo shirt to a suit and tie.

Wynn's face scrunched into a frown as he finished off the protein shake Sam had waiting for him. "I thought I eighty-sixed that meeting?" He guzzled the shake, and before he could hand it to Sam, his assistant was already taking the container from him.

"Yes, you did, but she rescheduled."

"I'm not interested in meeting a spoiled rich princess who wouldn't know the value of hard work if it hit her in the face."

After Giana Lockett reached out to him the first time, Wynn had done his research. She hailed from the Locketts, who owned the Cougars, Atlanta's football franchise. They were connected and well-known in town and were exactly the kind of people Wynn steered clear of. They reminded him too much of his ex-wife Christine's family. They were all about money, power and privilege which wasn't everything in Wynn's mind. He'd always tried to make sure his money, power and privilege were used to help others and not just make his pockets fatter.

Wynn wasn't a fan of football players. When he'd been in high school, he'd been mercilessly bullied by jocks on the football team. He'd always been lean and trim, but back then he'd been much smaller and they'd taken advantage of him, taking his lunch money or stuffing him in his locker. Because of the experience he'd steered clear of football teams and instead focused his attention on other athletes.

"She's been very persistent," Sam stated, following him into his office.

"Give her the brush-off. I don't care how you do it. Just get rid of her."

Sam left, and Wynn thought the day would improve, but then he'd heard from focus groups that the new drink Starks Inc. planned on debuting wasn't up to par and its release would have to be pushed back. Wynn gritted his teeth. He hated failure.

Starks Inc. specialized in sports drinks, fresh-made juices and smoothies. His initial effort, LEAN, had brand-name recognition and had put Starks Inc. on the map. The investors who'd made him a billionaire several times over at the age of thirty were expecting the next big thing, and Wynn had to deliver.

He was still feeling out of sorts when he showed up to his favorite gym in Buckhead to meet his best friend, Silas Tucker, later that afternoon for one of their regular sparring sessions. Silas was a famous restaurateur in Atlanta and owned several restaurants. He'd made it big after winning a chefs' competition on television.

"Hey, man, it's good to see you," Silas said, giving Wynn a one-armed hug.

Silas and Wynn were about the same height and were both athletic and lean, which was why they matched perfectly in the boxing ring. Their biggest difference? Silas's dark looks always served him well with the ladies who liked chocolate brothers over Wynn's tawny light brown complexion and perpetual five o'clock shadow.

"Give me a minute and I'll be right out." Wynn headed toward the locker room and changed into a tank and shorts. After placing his duffel bag in the locker, he walked back to the gym. He loved the energy here and needed to blow off some steam.

"What's with the frown?" Silas asked when Wynn came toward him. "Bad day at the office?"

When he didn't reply, Silas didn't pry. His friend knew when Wynn was ready to talk, he would. Instead, Silas joined him in a quick warmup of some squats with a kettle ball, shoulder stretches and jump rope. Wynn did his usual one-two bounce on his feet and then left hook, right jab combination.

Once his muscles were sufficiently warmed up, Wynn began wrapping his hands to prevent sprains. He strapped one gloved wrist in place before finishing the other. When he was ready to go, he joined Silas in the ring and put his mouth guard in place and his helmet over his head.

"What's new?" Silas asked as they began sparring.

"The usual work, work and work."

"Life isn't all about work, my friend. You've been going ninety miles an hour for a few years, since before Starks Inc. went public. In case you didn't know it, you've arrived."

Silas paused, which gave Wynn the opportunity to give him a one-two punch. "Hey, no fair. I wasn't ready." Silas rubbed his jaw with his gloved hand.

"Perhaps you should stop talking, then," Wynn replied, stepping back into a boxing stance. "I have some aggression to get rid of." If he couldn't punish himself in the ring, he would go for another run or work out in his home gym.

"The best way to get rid of this tension is with a little female attention, if you get my drift," Silas responded with a quick right-cross hook.

Wynn bobbed to the outside and missed the incoming

attack. "When I'm in need of female company, I know how to find it."

"You could have fooled me. When was your last date?"

Wynn couldn't recall, but it didn't much matter because he wasn't interested in women. He hadn't been since his ex-wife, Christine Davis, had stomped all over his heart and damn near taken his business. Lucky for him, his ironclad prenup had survived the battle. He was congratulating himself when a hush fell across the gym.

"What the hell?" Wynn went to turn around and Silas returned with a quick hook, which brought Wynn to his knees just in time to see the most fabulous set of toned brown legs come into his line of sight. No wonder every man in the gym had gone silent. This intruder had legs for days, and Wynn could only imagine what they might feel like wrapped around him.

Wynn's eyes traveled up the woman's body until he found himself looking into the stormy dark brown eyes of none other than Giana Lockett.

Her expression said it all.

She was angry—livid, in fact. Even without her saying a word, Wynn could feel his body respond to her. It was a twist in the gut, knowing a beautiful woman could have this effect on him when he'd sworn off women for an indefinite period. He swore as he rose to his feet, because he suspected Giana had come to give him a piece of her mind—and despite himself, Wynn was excited at the prospect.

Giana folded her arms across the sports bra top she was wearing along with her high-waisted leggings. She knew her outfit was revealing, but she'd wanted to grab Wynn Starks's attention, maybe even push him a little to finally take notice of her. She hadn't thought about how her outfit might be viewed by the other men working out in the gym.

All she'd known was she had to shake things up, even if it meant coming to his home turf.

She walked toward the ring where Wynn was sparring with another man and got a good look at all six feet three inches of him.

Giana couldn't resist licking her suddenly dry lips. Online and in the pictures in Nico's folder, Wynn Starks had looked sleek and groomed, but right now he looked dangerous. His tank and gym shorts showed off his athletic physique, trim hips and muscled arms. He had closely cropped dark hair, thick eyebrows and deep brown eyes. Shadowy stubble outlined his strong jaw. Her body warmed, but Giana fought off the sentiment. She was here for business, and she wouldn't let Wynn's good looks deter her.

"Mr. Starks. You're a hard man to get in touch with," Giana said when he gave no indication he intended to speak.

She watched him whisper something into his friend's ear and couldn't help but notice the other man's smirk as he exited the ring stage left. Then Wynn was taking off his boxing gloves and lifting the ropes to jump down until he was standing a few feet away from her.

"Did you ever think perhaps I didn't want to be found?"

"We had an appointment."

"Which I canceled, but clearly you didn't take the hint. Tell me, Giana Lockett, do you always make it a habit of stalking people and going places you're *not* wanted?"

"You know who I am?" Giana responded.

"Of course I do." Wynn's fierce eyes met hers. "You're a Lockett. Everyone in this towns knows you."

"Then you know I'm a businesswoman, Mr. Starks, and maybe, just maybe if you'd given me some professional courtesy and kept our previous appointments, I wouldn't have taken the drastic measure of accosting you at the gym." She caught the way Wynn's eyes roamed from her face down to the sports bra she was wearing and lower to her snug-fitting leggings.

"I appreciate what you're wearing, Ms. Lockett, as I'm sure every other man here in the gym does." He quickly surveyed the room. "But that was your intent, right? You wanted to be noticed." He walked past her to some shelving, which held rolled-up towels. He grabbed one and wiped the sweat off his face.

"I want you to stop canceling our appointments and hear me out," she responded hotly.

"I'm afraid your actions have been for naught, Ms. Lockett, because I'm not buying whatever it is you're selling." Wynn had never shared his history of bullying with anyone in interviews, so Giana had no idea he was not a fan of football jocks. He went to walk past her, but Giana reached out and grabbed his arm.

"Wait!" She glared up at him, and his gaze lingered on her. For a few brief seconds, Giana saw a shift in Wynn, because he'd felt it, too—a jolt of electricity zinged up her arm and Giana felt a rush of sexual awareness. Immediately, she pulled back her hand and cradled it close to her body, as if she'd been burned.

She didn't want to jeopardize their business with any pesky feelings. And Wynn's expression quickly changed back to hostility, as if she'd imagined the moment of connection.

"Won't you at least give me a chance?" She had to get him to see she was more than a pretty face. "The Atlanta Cougars and our players can be a great resource to help build Starks Inc.'s recognition in the marketplace."

"I don't need you or anyone else coming in here telling me how to run my company. I've done quite well on my own thus far," Wynn stated. "Go home, Ms. Lockett."

Wynn left her standing in the middle of the gym.

Scorned.

Of all the pigheaded men Giana had ever dealt with,

Wynn Starks was the worst. For some reason, he held a very low opinion of her, and she couldn't fathom why. She'd never met him, but Wynn Starks certainly had a block where she was concerned, and for the life of her, Giana couldn't figure out how to break through it.

Two

"You ready for that drink?" Silas asked once Wynn came out of the shower room with a towel wrapped around his waist. Silas was already dressed in blue jeans, a button-down shirt and sneakers.

"Hell yeah!" Wynn said. "Give me a few minutes."

"No problem. I'll wait for you outside. Then you can tell me why you gave Giana Lockett the brush-off."

Once Silas had gone, Wynn dried off. He couldn't explain why he'd been rude to Giana—only thing he knew was as soon as he'd seen her jet-black hair in a sleek ponytail and her skimpy outfit clinging to those perfect round breasts and curved hips, he'd lost his mind.

Giana had been wearing sexy clothes to tease him. To get a rise out of him. And she had. In more ways than one. When she'd touched his arm, a current of electricity had shot straight to the lower half of his body, reminding Wynn it had been a long time since he'd been with a woman.

Was that why he'd felt the frisson of electricity spark between them?

Wynn didn't care what it was, because he didn't want to do business with the Locketts. Josiah Lockett had a reputation for being a hard-ass, although he had taken a back seat recently to allow his son Roman to take over as general manager. Nonetheless, Wynn wasn't a big fan of football after his bullying experience in high school and preferred working with other athletes to represent his brands.

After he changed back into his jeans and T-shirt, he met Silas outside where he was leaning against his Ferrari 812. "Ready to head to the bar? We can get that drink. I can bring you back for your bike."

Wynn slid inside, and once they were on the road, Silas got right to the point. "So, what's up with you and Giana Lockett?"

Wynn frowned. "There's nothing between us. I hardly know her."

Silas chuckled and glanced at Wynn. "You could have fooled me. The vibes you two were giving off were definitely of the sexual variety."

Wynn rolled his eyes and stared out the window as Silas took them to one of their favorite bars a few miles away. "Well, you got it wrong."

"If you say so, but I think you're protesting a little too much."

"Why are you so quick to talk about my love life anyway? Up until a couple of months ago, you and Janelle were on opposite sides of the world." Silas and his supermodel wife, Janelle, had been estranged and living apart for years. They'd only recently reunited.

"Which is why I know bachelorhood is not for me," Silas returned. "I missed my wife, and I can tell you we are making up for lost time."

Wynn laughed heartily. "Good for you, but marriage isn't for everyone."

"C'mon, you were happy at some point with Christine, right?"

"Initially, things did go well, and I enjoyed the sense of belonging to another person, but then Christine showed her true colors. I'm telling you, marriage and relationships are off the table for me."

"I thought time was supposed to heal wounds?"

"I'm living proof it's a damn lie," Wynn responded with a snort.

Silas pulled his Ferrari into a parking space outside. The place was busy with the happy hour crowd, but he and Silas managed to squeeze in at the bar. Wynn ordered a bourbon while Silas ordered a whiskey.

"So why is Giana sweating you anyway? What does she want?"

Wynn sipped his bourbon before answering. "My guess is she wants an endorsement deal for one of her players."

"And would that be such a bad thing?" Silas inquired. "The Atlanta Cougars are having an amazing season now that they have Curtis Jackson. There's even talk they could go to the championship."

"Yeah, but have you forgotten what happened to me in high school? The terrible bullying I received at the hands of those football jocks? Because I haven't."

"Of course not, but you can't blame every football player for the actions of some bad apples. Don't limit yourself. Having a player as popular as Curtis Jackson with his clean-cut image would be great for *LEAN*."

Wynn frowned. LEAN was his baby. He wouldn't turn that over to just anyone. "I hear you."

"Do you? And what about Giana Lockett? If you ask me, you should be trying to get to know the lady better. She's a beautiful woman, and if you don't want her, someone else will."

"From what I've learned, Giana is currently single."

"You interested in her?"

"No, I'm not." But even as Wynn said the words, he knew they were a lie. The air between them had been charged with sexual tension. He'd had a visceral reaction to Giana the moment he'd seen her from the boxing ring.

But he would have to forget her beautiful bone structure, smooth mocha complexion, almond-shaped eyes and sensual mouth that promised sin. Wynn couldn't afford a dalliance with another rich girl and reminded himself Giana Lockett was off-limits.

Giana wasn't happy with how the afternoon had gone. She'd thought going to one of Wynn's favorite places and talking to him in person would produce a different result. It hadn't. Instead, he seemed more determined than ever to thwart her at every turn.

Dejected, Giana walked to the main house of her parents' estate in Tuxedo Park to raid the freezer for her favorite moose tracks ice cream.

When Roman had married and bought a house in Buckhead with his new wife, Shantel, Giana had used the opportunity to move into the guesthouse and finally get out from under her mother's discerning eye. She could have moved out sooner, but her mother liked having her children near and as the only girl in the family, Giana had acquiesced.

But Giana was terrible at shopping for herself. There wasn't much in her fridge other than a bottle of champagne and a leftover charcuterie plate from one of her charity events. And she desperately needed a sugar fix to drown her disappointment. She knew she'd find what she was looking for at her parents' house.

Giana was grateful when she opened the stainless steel freezer and found their butler, Gerard, had stocked it with her favorite ice cream. Gerard had been with the family for as long as she remembered and always spoiled her.

Since she was little, she'd always been given anything she ever asked for, be it a pony when she was eight, a brand-new

Porsche when she turned sixteen or an expensive debutante dress, because she had been a daddy's girl. However, when it came time for her to step out of the shadows and be her own person, her father had been surprised to learn she had a mind of her own. Giana didn't want to be the conventional rich man's wife. She wanted a career, and she'd fought tooth and nail for her success. Wynn Starks would not stop her. Her father wanted the account and pleasing him had always been of utmost importance to her. She supposed it had to do with proving she was as good at business as Roman.

She sank her spoon into the sweet, creamy mixture and sighed in bliss as the sweetness hit her taste buds.

"That good, huh?" her brother Xavier said from behind her. She swiveled around on the bar stool. Xavier stood well over six feet and had a deep brown complexion, eyes the color of cognac and short, curly hair cropped close to his head. With his beard, broad nose and full lips, the ladies had gone wild over him during his quarterback days.

She grinned. "Yeah, it is." She ate another spoonful. "What are you doing here?"

"I was hoping you might be interested in catching dinner, but I see you're having dessert instead."

"My afternoon was an epic failure, so I figured why not death by chocolate."

"Surely it can't be that bad," Xavier said, walking to the cabinets across from her and pulling another spoon from the drawer. He joined her at the oversize quartz island and dipped his spoon in the container for a heaping portion. After tasting it, he too let out a sigh.

"See—" Giana pointed her finger at him "—it's good. And the reason I'm annoyed is because I've failed yet again to get Wynn Starks on board with letting the Atlanta Cougars represent his brands."

She didn't like failure of any kind, and neither did her father. He was a hard taskmaster, and he would accept nothing less than success. She wanted to show her father there wasn't anything she couldn't do and she was just as good as Roman when it came to business.

Xavier shrugged. "Then move on. There are tons of other endorsements out there for someone as popular as Curtis. I remember when I was a quarterback…" He stopped mid-sentence and didn't finish.

Giana understood. Xavier didn't like talking about the period when he'd been the Atlanta Cougars' star quarterback. After winning a Heisman trophy in college, he'd gone pro and had been the best in the business. His future had been bright until the terrible game when he'd injured his knee. It had ended his playing career and caused him to walk with a slight limp to this day. Ever since he was a little boy, Xavier had always had a football in his hand. It had been his life's blood. It had been hard losing that, but he'd finally moved on and was doing well as a commentator for a sports network.

"I know I should find an alternate company," Giana responded, "but Daddy seems focused on Starks Inc. I'm not sure why. Maybe it's because Wynn refuses to give us an audience. I mean, today, I went to a lot of trouble to get his attention, and still nada."

Xavier frowned and set aside his spoon. "What did you do?"

"I showed up at the gym where he works out to confront him."

"You did what?" His voice grew loud.

Giana rolled her eyes. "Oh, don't give me that no-she-didn't look. I'm not someone who takes no for an answer."

"And I take it you were turned away and came home with your tail between your legs?" Xavier said with a laugh. He grabbed his spoon to continue eating.

"Maybe."

Wynn might have dismissed her, but he didn't dislike her. He liked her moxie even though he tried to hide it. There'd been a flicker of interest lurking in those dark brown depths, and truth be told, she'd felt the sizzle, too, but she wasn't going to exploit it. This wasn't personal. She would try one more time to get him to listen and see what a great partnership Starks Inc. and the Cougars could have. If he didn't, she would go with another company.

"So, what next?"

"I'm not giving up, if that's what you mean."

"Of course not. It's not in your DNA." Xavier laughed. "I doubt the poor bastard knows what he's got into for refusing you."

Giana smiled. She was used to fighting to get what she wanted. Her father had been dead set against her going to college and being away from the family. He'd seen Giana in a traditional role of wife and mother and going to a finishing school like her mother had, but Giana had had other ideas. She deserved the same Ivy League education as her older brothers Roman and Julian, and she'd persevered.

Wynn Starks would be no different.

He had a weakness, and she would find it.

Three

A solution came the following day when Giana and Mara were sifting through her invitations. There were a lot to choose from; her social calendar was usually filled with work engagements or charity commitments on behalf of the Lockett Foundation.

Her mother had started the organization a decade ago in the hopes the Atlanta Cougars' platform could bring support and financial assistance to local community groups. As the charity grew, so had its commitments to the Salvation Army, as well as to nonprofits helping with multiple sclerosis, breast cancer, Alzheimer's and autism. Giana was proud of her work, but it left little time for a social life.

She finally found what she was looking for: an invitation to a gala for Wynn Starks's favorite charity, the Boys & Girls Clubs of America, coming up this weekend. In one of his rare interviews, he'd mentioned how he'd used their services in his youth. If they could connect on something close to his heart, it could be a real game changer.

Which was why on Saturday night she found herself seated in the back of a limousine wearing a new gown that had cost a fortune in the hopes of garnering a few minutes of his time. It was a long shot, but she had to try.

In her opinion she looked like a sparkly disco ball, but her stylist had insisted the silver metallic gown with a high halter neckline and major thigh-high slit was a showstopper. The back of the floor-length dress plunged into a deep V right above her waistline. The stylist had paired it with large silver and diamond earrings and metallic silver strappy Jimmy Choo sandals.

It was certainly dramatic and might even raise a few eyebrows, but the rest of her look couldn't be touched. Her hair had been styled into textured waves tucked behind one ear with a deep side part, and her makeup was perfection, with a sculpted brow, smoky eye and rosy nude lip.

A small group of paparazzi was on hand when she exited the vehicle. Giana waved and stopped for photos before making her way inside the downtown hotel. Since it was shortly after Thanksgiving, the hotel had already put an enormous Christmas tree in the lobby covered with white and gold ornaments, poinsettias and garland.

Giana took the elevator to the mezzanine level and upon her arrival was greeted by many acquaintances she knew from her charity events. But she was only interested in one person, and she quickly scanned the room.

She found Wynn talking to the mayor and his wife. He was very animated and smiling, which was something he hadn't done when he'd been around her. He had a great smile, and nothing could distract from his sex appeal. He was imposingly masculine, with powerful shoulders and a broad, strong chest in a custom black tuxedo with hand-stitched shoes.

It took all Giana's willpower to look away from such physical perfection. Her cheeks burned because she'd been riveted to the spot by him. She focused on the conversation she was having with one of the Boys & Girls Clubs directors. When the time was right, she would approach him and let the chips fall where they may.

Damn minx!

Wynn couldn't believe Giana Lockett had shown up to *his* charity event. Although he couldn't say it was his, entirely; it was open to all the elite movers and shakers in town. He shouldn't be surprised to see her, because her family was well-known in Atlanta for their charitable efforts, but he still was.

He'd noticed her almost immediately when she'd sashayed that cute little bottom of hers into the room. *How could he not?* Her metallic dress shined like a diamond.

He wasn't supposed to be having feelings like this. He'd already had a go-round with a rich prima donna. He refused to do it again, but his libido had other ideas. He wanted to confront Giana, but as MC for the evening, his services were required.

Wynn went onstage and performed his duties to the best of his ability. He spotlighted the great work the Boys & Girls Clubs had done and encouraged the guests to donate to the worthy cause. He expressed how much the organization had helped him during his youth. Because of the club, Wynn had a big brother to turn to who had helped him out during a difficult time. Unfortunately, Les Moore had died from prostate cancer a few years ago, but he'd had a profound impact on Wynn's life.

After his speech, Wynn settled in at his table, but he could feel Giana's eyes boring a hole in the back of his head from where she was seated, directly behind him. Soon he would have to squash any hopes she had once and for all.

Giana was having a lovely conversation with Mavis Bradley, an elderly widow who'd inherited the lion's share of her husband's estate after he passed. Mavis was a wealthy benefactor of several charities, and Giana was telling her about the Lockett Foundation's next event when she felt an ominous presence behind her.

She turned and found Wynn glaring at her.

She swallowed and forced herself to breathe. Remembering her manners, she turned to Mavis. "Mavis, I'd like you to meet Wynn Starks. He runs Starks Inc., a health and sports drink company."

"Mr. Starks, you gave a great speech earlier," Mrs. Bradley said. "I was moved."

"Thank you, ma'am." He inclined his head. "Would you mind terribly if I stole Giana away? I've been waiting all night for a chance to dance with her."

"Oh, of course not. You young folks go right ahead." She waved them off.

Giana did the best she could to maintain her composure as he guided her toward the dance floor. She could feel his hot palm on her bare back as if he were branding her. Once there, he pulled her toward him, taking her hand in his and sliding his arm around her waist. Then she made the mistake of glancing up at Wynn.

Everything about him was strong. The determined set of his clean-shaven jaw—though she'd preferred the five o'clock shadow from yesterday. The eyes as dark as midnight fringed by thick, ink-black lashes. The muscular, fit body, which showed he wasn't afraid of a little sweat. She'd read his bio and knew once he set a goal, he did everything in his power to achieve it. To be a self-made billionaire at thirty was quite impressive.

She hazarded him another glance, but shouldn't have, because once she did, she was tethered to his gaze. She couldn't look away even if she tried. He was mesmerizing. Enthralling. Magnetic. She dragged her eyes downward and instead found herself staring at his incredible sumptuous mouth and wondering what it would be like to have that mouth on hers.

Oh God, she was in trouble.

"What's wrong, Giana?" Wynn asked, peering down at her. "Get more than you bargained for?"

She didn't cower easily; instead, she smiled sweetly up at him. "Of course not. I know exactly what I'm doing—trying to get an audience with an elusive billionaire who's playing hard to get."

"Is that right?" he whispered so only she could hear him. His lips were centimeters from her ear. "I wonder if we should test that theory, hmm…?"

"Test away." The moment she uttered the taunt, Giana wished she could take it back, because Wynn pulled her even closer. And when his hips brushed hers, Giana felt the unmistakable imprint of his arousal. The room disappeared, and it felt as if they were the only two people in the whole world. She followed his lead and smiled wide as Wynn easily spun her around the dance floor.

When the familiar song ended, Giana looked up and met Wynn's gaze. Their eyes locked on each other, and Wynn thrust his fingers into her hair. Giana knew if he kissed her, he would possess her tonight. And so, with as much dignity as she could muster, she spun out of his grasp and rushed out of the room.

Wynn watched Giana flee like her dress was on fire. He understood, because he hadn't expected to *want* to kiss her after that incendiary dance. However, once he'd seen her from across the room looking divine in a dress that had been made for her body, he'd been entranced, even if he didn't want to admit it to himself. She'd given true meaning to the word *radiant*.

Despite the fact that he'd shunned her on multiple occasions, he liked that Giana held her head high and shoulders straight and showed grit and determination. She was a force to be reckoned with. And as far as the gown and tantalizing heels, all he could think about was taking it all off her.

When they danced, he'd been unable to hide how aware of her he was. When he'd finally touched her, the buttery-soft smoothness of her milk chocolate skin had blood and heat rushing through his body. If she hadn't run away, he most certainly would have kissed her. As a matter of fact, he still wanted to.

And why should he deny himself?

It was time to end his self-imposed celibacy and get back to the land of the living—and there was a chocolate siren calling to him. Rich and spoiled, she was exactly the kind of woman he steered clear of, but she revved him up like no other woman ever had. He liked her fire and her fighting spirit.

Before he knew it, Wynn was chasing after Giana. He caught sight of her at the end of the hall as she waited for the elevator. With long strides he nearly caught up. He saw her deer-in-the-headlights reaction when she realized she'd poked the tiger. Then she was stepping into the elevator. He had seconds to catch her or the spell would be broken.

Wynn reached out and blocked the elevator doors from closing. It beeped loudly as he stood in the entrance regarding her. She recoiled back against the wall, because she knew she'd been caught and there was nowhere to hide.

He stepped in and the elevator doors closed, sealing them inside.

Four

Giana straightened her spine. She, Giana Lockett, who'd never run away from a fight, had fled once she'd come into full contact with Wynn Starks. "What do you want?" Her voice cracked, and she hoped he didn't catch the breathiness.

"Giana." The way he said it felt like a caress against her skin. "We both know why I'm here."

"Do we?" she countered.

"Are you really going to hide behind bravado rather than acknowledge what's happening?" His dark brown gaze bored into hers. "All right, I'll play along."

"Nothing is happening here. I assumed you came after me to take me to task for showing up at your precious charity event."

He chuckled. "Oh, no doubt. I was angry."

Was, meaning past tense? So, he wasn't upset anymore? Why did Giana suspect that didn't bode well for her? She didn't like the heated look in his eyes, as if he was imagining her without any clothes on. But hadn't she imagined him in the same way? She needed to get out of here before…

Clonk.

The elevator skidded to an abrupt halt, and the lights went out, plunging them into darkness. Rather than panic, Giana reached inside her purse and produced her iPhone and turned on the flashlight. She shined it on Wynn. "What the hell is going on?"

"We must be stuck," he said with a shrug. "It happens." He reached for the box on the elevator panel containing the emergency phone and dialed out. Giana heard his side of the conversation as he spoke to the person on the other end. "Yes, there's myself and another occupant. All right. We'll be here."

Once he'd hung up and closed the box, Giana asked, "What did they say? How long are we going to be stuck in here?"

"Not long. The elevator company has been called and they'll be here soon. Are you claustrophobic?"

Giana shook her head. She didn't relish the idea of being locked up for an indefinite length of time with a man she was inappropriately attracted to. She should be focused on business, not those thick lips of his and what they could do to her.

Good Lord, get a hold of yourself, Giana! She smoothed her hair back, and when she glanced up, she found Wynn was staring at her again.

"Shall we pick up where we left off in the conversation?"

"Must we? We could be here for a while given that it's—" Giana glanced down at her Cartier watch "—after ten on a Saturday night. I doubt elevator technicians are going to be rushing to our rescue."

"Is there something else you'd rather be doing, Giana?" He smiled at her from the other side of the cab. "Because I can think of a few things off the top of my head."

Giana knew where he was heading, but an idea sparked

in her mind. "Since you're a captive audience, I can tell you why the Atlanta Cougars are the right team to handle endorsements of your sports drink."

"And *that's* how you would like to spend your time alone with me?" He quirked a brow. "Hmm… I beg to differ."

"What else would there be?"

"Perhaps I should show rather than tell you." Within the span of seconds, Wynn went from leaning against the wall to moving toward her. All Giana could do was step backward, so that she was up against the elevator wall. Wynn cupped either side of her face, tilting her face upward. Her phone slid out of her hands to the floor with a thud. "Tell me you want this as much as I do."

Giana nodded. "Yes."

Wynn stared at her lips for what seemed like an eternity before he leaned in to brush his mouth across hers. The kiss was featherlight considering the rampant tension between them, so Giana leaned closer for more. Their lips met again, and this time the kiss turned incendiary, causing adrenaline to surge through her veins.

Giana's lips parted in an unspoken invitation, allowing Wynn inside. His tongue slid between her lips, tangling with hers, and Giana moaned. The kiss obliterated rational thought, and Giana forgot time and space. Instead, she exulted in his drugging kisses and craved the satisfaction his mouth could give. Wynn understood, because instinctively, he deepened the kiss. Giana clasped her hands around the back of his head for a better fit.

What was it that made Wynn's kiss different from other men's? It wasn't just a matter of technique, although Wynn knew exactly how to use his mouth, tongue and teeth. It was the passion, the all-consuming hunger, and Giana couldn't do anything but grip his bulging biceps and hang on for the ride.

Wynn stirred her to a fever pitch, making Giana ache. When his knee nudged her legs apart so he could settle himself between them, her sluggish brain allowed it. That's when she felt the press of his arousal against her, and her belly clenched in response. He moved his hands upward to cup the weight of her breasts in his palms. He gently squeezed the flesh, making her nipples tighten and causing a tumult of sensations to rush through her.

Giana was panting by the time Wynn wrenched his mouth away. His eyes blazed down at her as he brushed some wayward strands of her hair from her forehead. "I want you, Giana." His voice had a sexy rasp that made her heart flutter.

"I want you too."

That's when his hands left her breasts and began moving downward while his lips trailed kisses down her ear to her neck. That's where he stayed, causing Giana to clasp his lapels. Then she felt cool air against her legs. Wynn was lifting her dress and caressing her legs, steadily moving his fingers upward toward the soft flesh of her thighs.

"Part your legs for me, Giana," Wynn whispered in her ear.

Giana closed her eyes. She couldn't believe she was making out with Wynn in the elevator, but she did as he asked and shuddered when his hands slipped between her legs. "I—we—shouldn't..."

"Oh, this tells me we should," he murmured as he parted her folds and found her drenched. His mouth returned to hers while his hand continued with the most devastating intimate exploration Giana ever endured. She tried to fight the feelings, but it was a futile effort. Wynn's touch was skillful, and her whole body stiffened as a powerful climax overtook her.

"Wynn!" she cried out as she came and convulsed against his hand.

When the shudders finally subsided, he murmured, "You're incredible, Giana. I have a room upstairs because

I didn't want to drink and drive. When we get there, I can make love to you properly."

Giana felt as if he'd poured a bucket of ice water over her head as she came down from her high and realized the mistake she'd made.

She was thankful the elevator lurched downward then, and the lights flickered on, because it allowed her a few precious seconds to smooth down her dress and hair before the elevator doors pinged open. A technician was there, but Giana didn't even look at him as she rushed out of the car, through the lobby and out into the night air.

She jumped in the first taxi she saw. "Go. Go. Go!" she yelled. She had to get away from the scene of the crime as soon as possible.

Wynn swished the two fingers of bourbon in his glass back and forth and took a long gulp as he stared out of the hotel window. He'd commandeered the top-floor suite, which came with an impressive view. He was trying to understand what had gotten into him tonight. *Was he frustrated?* Had he gone too long without a woman? The latter could be true. All he knew was he'd been unable to walk away from Giana tonight.

On the dance floor, the look that passed between them had been pure lust, and it had overwhelmed him more than anything he'd ever experienced. His arousal had been almost unbearable. He'd been caught in the grip of something *elemental,* and he'd felt powerless to stop it. That was why he'd gone after her into the elevator, paving the way for their first kiss.

And the kiss had been epic!

He could still remember the way she tasted. The way she felt in his arms. The sounds she made when she came. He doubted he could forget her sweet moans when his fingers had been buried deep inside her. He'd nearly come from feeling her flesh spasming around his fingers. He had little control left, and Wynn knew if the elevator hadn't started working again, he would have taken her right there up against the wall.

Wynn downed the remainder of his drink and headed for the shower. Once inside, he turned the taps as cold as he could take them. After Christine, his mantra was that all women were shallow and conniving and untrustworthy. So why, after the cold shower, was he still having trouble forgetting Giana Lockett?

Why? Because he'd gotten a taste of her, and now that he had, he wouldn't be satisfied until he had the entire meal.

Five

"Giana, I'm surprised to see you," her brother Julian said when she stopped by his new home the following afternoon. Julian had just married Elyse Robinson, the daughter of their father's former business partner. They'd returned from their honeymoon last week.

"Can't a sister drop by?" she asked, glancing at him and noticing his shirt was unbuttoned.

"Of course you can," Julian said, fussing with his shirt as she walked into the foyer. "But you usually call first."

Giana glanced around the living room and saw it was set up for a romantic indoor picnic, complete with candles and flowers. Her hand flew to her mouth. "Oh my God, Julian. I'm sorry. How dense can I be? You are newlyweds, and I interrupted a private moment. I'm going." She started toward the door.

Julian grasped her arm. "It's okay. You're here now. C'mon in." He motioned her to the leather sofa and sat down next to her.

"No, it's not. I have to remember you're not my single brother anymore. I can't just drop by when the mood strikes," Giana replied, turning to face him. "In the future, I will be sure to phone ahead. Please give Elyse my apologies."

"You can give them to her yourself," Julian said when Elyse came down the stairs dressed in a silk loungewear set that suited her slender figure. It was hard to believe she was in her second trimester.

"Elyse, I'm so sorry," Giana began, but her sister-in-law interrupted her.

"Like Julian said, you are family, and you can always stop by." Elyse leaned over the couch and gave Giana a quick kiss on the cheek. The new Mrs. Lockett looked radiant; her light fawn-colored skin positively glowed with health. Marriage and pregnancy agreed with her.

"Thank you. I need to talk to Julian." Giana was at a loss for words. "Would you mind giving us a minute?"

"Not at all," Elyse said. "Make yourself at home. I'll be upstairs if you need me."

Once she'd gone upstairs, Giana finally shifted toward Julian. "I'm truly sorry for stopping by unannounced, but I've made a horrible mistake, and I know you've been in my shoes."

Julian threw back his head and laughed. "You mean because I'm the screwup?"

His laughter was infectious, and Giana couldn't resist laughing, too. "Well, sort of."

"Don't sugarcoat it, sis. I've always been the troublemaker in the family, but you and Roman, you could do no wrong. What's going on?"

"I made out with Wynn Starks in an elevator," Giana blurted.

"Oh, really? I'm intrigued. Tell me more," Julian said, leaning back on the couch.

"We got stuck in an elevator and, well, one thing led to another."

"You slept with him?"

She heard the shock in her brother's voice and understood because it was completely out of character for her. Julian was the one who'd been a ladies' man before marrying Elyse.

Giana shook her head. Although she might have wanted to, and Lord knew her body craved it last night. "No. Once the elevator started working again, I made my escape." She must have looked a sight when the doors opened, with her hair in disarray and her lips devoid of lipstick. Wynn was probably wearing it, but she hadn't stayed to find out.

"What's the problem?" Julian said. "You had a little fun in the dark. And when the lights came on, the party was over."

"Julian!" Giana slapped his arm. "C'mon, be serious here. I'm supposed to be trying to convince Wynn to bring his business to the Cougars."

"You can still do that, but the waters are a bit muddied."

"What do you suggest I do?"

"Talk to him. And you'll either come to a decision on the business deal or you'll end up in bed together."

"I'm only interested in one of those options," Giana replied.

Julian cocked his head to look at her. "C'mon, Gigi. It's me you're talking to. You can be honest, which is why you came here."

Giana exhaled. He was right. She knew Julian wouldn't judge her and she could speak her mind. "I'm attracted to him. Could I see myself jumping his bones? Absolutely, but I also want to show Daddy what I can do."

"Gigi, you have to stop trying to please the old man and do what's right for you, even if means you're a little selfish and spend some alone time with Wynn." Julian winked, and Giana rolled her eyes. "I've seen you work hard for years, and does our father really see you? I know he didn't see me because I wasn't the heir apparent or the star quarterback like Roman and Xavier."

"Our relationship is different."

Julian grinned. "You're his favorite, no doubt."

"That's not true."

"It is, and I don't begrudge you," Julian replied. "But you also have to do what's right for you. So what if you don't get Wynn's business? It is not the end of the world. Starks Inc. isn't the only fish in the sea. You've brought Curtis and all the Cougar players great deals. You do remarkable work. You can't lose sight of what's important."

Giana smiled. "Thank you, Julian. It's exactly what I needed to hear."

Julian bowed. "Glad to be of service. Now—" he glanced toward the stairs "—if you don't mind…"

Giana could take a hint. The newlyweds wanted to be alone. "Thank you for listening. You're a good big brother." She leaned toward him for a hug.

"I'm the best one, right?" Julian asked.

"Don't push your luck," she said with a laugh and quickly exited. Once inside her Mercedes-Benz Maybach, Giana considered Julian's advice. She wasn't sure she could let go of her desire to please their father. It was part of who she was, and she doubted it would change anytime soon. But she also couldn't deny spending time with Wynn held a certain appeal.

Perhaps she should take a different approach. She'd been doing the chasing, constantly trying to get Wynn to consider a partnership with the Atlanta Cougars. It was time she let Wynn come to her.

Come Monday morning, Wynn knew what he had to do. Over the weekend, he'd been unable to stop thinking about Giana and how good she'd felt in his arms. Although he'd tried his best to ignore the attraction, his mind and body were not in agreement.

He'd already run his usual five miles and spent time in the sauna, but his mind wasn't clear. After a couple of hours, Wynn called Sam into his office.

"Yes, Mr. Starks?"

"Get me Giana Lockett on the line."

"Pardon?" Sam's expression showed he was confused, since Wynn's directive was to give the lovely marketer the cold shoulder.

"You heard me. I'd like to speak with her."

"Of course, I'll get right on it," Sam said and exited his office.

Wynn turned to stare out at the Atlanta skyline. It had taken a lot to get to this fortieth-floor corner office. Starks Inc. was now among the top one hundred companies in Atlanta, but his life hadn't always been this good.

His mind wandered back to a time when he'd had a happy family, a mother and a father. A wonderful life, a big home, but it had all been a lie. His mother had cheated and left his father, Jeffrey Starks, and Wynn for another man. She'd never looked back. It broke his father, and he'd struggled to recover not only emotionally, but financially as well.

During the divorce, his mother hadn't wanted custody of Wynn. Instead, she'd sued for half of everything, arguing she was entitled to it after twelve years of marriage. And she'd won. The end result left Wynn and his father moving into a small one-bedroom apartment. Wynn would never forget those times or the look of abject misery he'd sometimes witness on his father's face, though Jeffrey did his best to cover it up.

He'd never forgiven his mother for destroying their family, leaving them with nothing. That anger fueled Wynn to start Starks Inc. Many people, including his main competitor, Blaine Smith, thought he was crazy to attempt a start-up company on his own. He and Blaine had worked at Coca-Cola together right after college. When Wynn had discussed starting his own business one day focusing on sports drinks, Blaine had called it a pipe dream. But Wynn had goals and a vision.

"Ms. Lockett is on line one," Sam's voice rang out, interrupting Wynn's thoughts.

"Thank you, Sam."

Inhaling deeply, Wynn picked up the receiver. "Giana."

"Mr. Starks."

Wynn's jaw tightened. "After everything we shared in the elevator, Giana, are we really using surnames?"

"Don't you think it's best?"

"No, I don't. I think we should explore what's between us, which is why I called. I'd like to take you to dinner." He wanted to fully discover every part of the chocolate beauty's body and refused to be dissuaded from his purpose. This was about scratching an itch, and once he did, he would move on.

"Like a date?"

Wynn laughed. "That's usually what two people do who are attracted to each other."

The other end of the line was silent. He didn't know what he'd expected. That she would jump because he said he wanted to go out with her? If she wasn't going to come to him willingly, he would have to dangle some bait. "Perhaps we could talk about the Atlanta Cougars and Starks Inc. working together."

He heard her audible intake of breath. "You don't play fair, Wynn. You're no more interested in doing business with me than you were a few days ago. This is all about your ego taking a hit. The answer is no."

"Giana, I know you felt it. How perfectly we fit together. And you know how I know? Because you came apart in my arms in the elevator."

"Stop it, Wynn."

"You don't strike me as a coward. If anything, you're like a fearless Amazon, as good as any man in battle."

"I am," she stated emphatically. "Because I've had to be."

"Then we have something in common," Wynn said. "Dine with me tonight at my place." When she began to speak, he interrupted. "Don't say no. Think about it. Think about how good you felt in the elevator. I promise you, Giana, it will be ten times better tonight." Wynn hung up before she could turn him down again. His heart was beating wildly in his chest.

He wanted her to say yes. To answer the call they'd both felt in those stolen moments in the dark. *Was she woman enough to accept the gauntlet he'd thrown down?*

He thought so, but only time would tell.

Giana placed the phone back in the cradle. She *wanted* to go to dinner with Wynn, the man, but it wouldn't get her anywhere with Wynn, the business owner. She couldn't fathom why he refused to work with her.

Nico had given her a full dossier on Wynn, but Giana had only been interested in the parts related to Starks Inc. Perhaps she was going about this the wrong way. Perhaps she needed to delve deeper to understand what lay at the root of his continued avoidance of her and the Atlanta Cougars as a business partner.

She unlocked the drawer at her desk and withdrew Nico's file on Wynn. This time she read it through and was surprised by what she found. She had already known about his parents' divorce and his father losing everything, because Wynn had spoken about it during a rare interview. It's what caused Wynn to pull himself up by his bootstraps and become a success.

It was also of interest that Wynn had been married before to Christine Davis, a wealthy socialite. Giana knew of her because they traveled in the same circles, but they hadn't formally met. According to the report, she and Wynn had an acrimonious divorce. She'd sued him for half of Starks Inc., even though he'd started the company prior to their marriage and they had a prenup. The judge had ruled in Wynn's favor due to the ironclad prenup. But the whole thing had been particularly traumatic because Wynn had been in the process of taking his company public when Christine sued him.

Was Wynn's aversion to Gianna because of Christine? Because they both came from wealthy backgrounds, while his family had lost everything? The clues certainly pointed in that direction. At least, now she knew and could be armed going into battle. All she had to do was figure out a plan to show Wynn she wasn't like Christine.

Did that mean she was going to the dinner tonight?

Absolutely.

She was ready to play.

Wynn walked down the hall to the kitchen and was pleased with the inviting ambience. The lighting was low, and soft music echoed through the surround speakers. It was the mood he wanted for the evening. Wynn wanted Giana's guard down so they could get to know each other.

He'd donned a small apron and was even cooking for her himself. He'd given Sam a very specific grocery list and now found all the ingredients laid out on the large granite kitchen island. He planned on feeding Giana a sumptuous grilled marinated steak with his famous lyonnaise potatoes and asparagus. He would pair it with a cabernet and also serve a spring salad with a blood orange vinaigrette.

Once, he'd enjoyed cooking for Christine. It had been nothing for him to whip something up for dinner, but that had been a long time ago. Now he rarely occupied the kitchen except to make a quick smoothie, eat the takeout he'd brought home or heat up a plate left by a private chef he sometimes used. He'd thought about using him tonight but decided against it.

He was looking forward to showing off his culinary skills, and he had all the best at his fingertips with a stainless steel Sub-Zero refrigerator and gas range.

He poured himself a bourbon and set about getting everything prepared. He was done with prep when the doorbell rang.

Giana.

After washing his hands, he rushed to the front door and opened it. Giana was on the opposite side, looking gorgeous in a flowing black-and-fuchsia-print dress with puffed sleeves and a shawl wrapped around her shoulders. She looked elegant and sexy, but Wynn was thinking of all the ways he planned to get her out of the outfit.

He must have been staring, because she asked, "Can I come in? It's cold out."

"Of course." He motioned her inside and closed the door. Did she know she was entering the lion's den? Because before the night was over, he intended to devour every delectable inch of her.

Six

"I love your home," Giana said as she entered. It had been a relatively short drive since Wynn lived only a few miles from her parents in Tuxedo Park. She'd expected a grandiose old-school mansion. But when she'd pulled her Mercedes-Maybach into the driveway and punched in the code he'd given her, the wrought-iron gates swung open to reveal a modern masterpiece.

"Thank you." Wynn was dressed in jeans and a T-shirt. The casual look suited him, even though he filled out a tuxedo quite nicely.

"I brought you this." She held out a bottle of expensive wine her butler had assured her would pair well with any meal.

"That wasn't necessary, but thank you. Come. I'll give you the five-second tour."

Giana looked around the grand foyer with its vast ceiling and followed Wynn into the great room.

The home had a flowing floor plan with the great room

leading to the family room and a massive kitchen. Everything was light and bright, exactly what Giana would like. She loved the floor-to-ceiling cabinets, waterfall countertops and dark, rich custom wood cabinetry. Wynn had shown attention to detail, because the home had elegant moldings, a stone fireplace and large glass panel doors that were open to reveal an outdoor living area and lagoon-style pool and spa.

"Quite impressive," Giana said when they returned to the kitchen from the terrace.

"I liked the open concept," Wynn said and headed to the grill on the stove.

"What are you cooking tonight?" she asked, crossing to peek over his shoulder. When she did, she got a tantalizing whiff of soap and a hint of spice. He turned around so quickly that Giana lost her footing, but Wynn caught her. Their eyes connected, and Giana was captivated.

"Uh, thanks." She didn't step away. Instead she allowed Wynn to hold her tighter. When he wrapped his hands around her waist to hold her close, she reciprocated.

She lifted her face to his and they both leaned in at the exact same moment for a kiss. His mouth grazed hers, weaving magic. Her lips opened under his, and he accepted the invitation, his tongue quickly seeking entry and fusing them closer together. Giana's breathing became shallow, her breaths mingling with his, but just as quickly as it began, it was over and Wynn was releasing her.

"You shouldn't have done that." Her voice was shaky as she retreated to a safe distance on the other side of the island.

"I would have liked to do a whole lot more, but I promised you dinner and to hear your pitch. And I'm nothing if not a man of my word." He reached for the bottle of wine she'd brought. "Would you like a glass?"

Giana nodded. She needed something to help relax her, because she was as tight as a bow. Kissing Wynn was a mistake. She'd told herself she would keep dinner tonight professional, but after only a few minutes in his company they were lip-locked. It didn't bode well for her plan to pitch him a deal with the Cougars. Would he even be willing to listen? Or was this just an elaborate ploy to get her into his bed?

Wynn opened the bottle with ease and then reached for two glasses on the island and poured wine into each one. "For the lady." He offered her the wine and raised his glass. "*Salut!*"

"*Salut!*" She greedily accepted and took a long luxurious sip. Taking a deep breath, she reminded herself, as she'd done on the drive over, she wouldn't let him seduce her. "You never answered my question. What are you making?" She hadn't seen what was on the stove because she'd been too caught up in his scent. "Or did you have a chef whip something up?"

Wynn smiled when he looked at her. "Although I have a private chef at my disposal, I wanted to make you dinner myself tonight. We're having a grilled steak with my special blend of seasonings accompanied by lyonnaise potatoes and asparagus with hollandaise."

"The potatoes and asparagus sound great, but I'm going to have to pass on the steak."

Wynn frowned. "What do you mean?"

"I'm a pescatarian."

"Pescatarian?" On Wynn's lips, the word sounded like a filthy curse.

"I won't apologize for not eating meat," Giana stated with a frown. "Perhaps you should have done your homework and found out what I like. Or how about this? Asked me."

His dark eyes glittered from across the room, but Giana wasn't backing down. "Let me see what's in the fridge," he said. "I can probably whip up some scallops for you."

Giana offered a smile. "That would be lovely. Thank you."

An hour later, Giana was stuffed. They'd sat in the dining room, where Wynn served dish after dish. First was a delicious salad with a vinaigrette dressing, followed by seared scallops, potatoes and asparagus with hollandaise for her. Wynn wolfed down an enormous steak along with the potatoes and a heaping mound of asparagus. She wondered where he put it all.

He'd created a romantic setting complete with candles, crystal flutes and a bouquet of red roses, but Wynn needn't have bothered. Giana didn't intend on going to bed with him.

"My hat's off to the chef. When did you learn to cook?"

"After my mom walked out on my father and me," Wynn stated matter-of-factly. "My father was a terrible cook, and I figured if I didn't want to starve, I was going to have to learn to fend for myself."

"Sounds like you're still upset with your mother," Giana replied, watching him as the candlelight played over his features. "Do you talk to her?"

"No."

His one-word answer told Giana that he wasn't going to brook further discussion on the topic. "And your father? He must be very proud of everything you've accomplished."

"He is. Jeffrey Starks is one of the reasons I've worked so hard. I want to give him back half of what he gave me."

Giana smiled. "I feel the same way about my dad. I know everyone sees his tough exterior, but he's not that way with me. He's got a soft spot."

"Because you're a daddy's girl."

"Through and through." She smiled unabashedly. "I don't deny it. But it has made me have to work harder."

"How so?"

"Daddy puts me on a pedestal. I think he wants me to be more like my mother, but I'm not. I'm more like him. It killed him when I told him I wasn't interested in a finishing school but wanted to go to college for a business degree like my oldest brother, Roman."

"He wanted you to be a wife and mother?"

Giana nodded. "I was an excellent student and with my

scores easily got into Princeton, but my father wanted me to be a stay at home wife and mother. And when I got back from college, it was even harder. There aren't a lot of women working for professional football teams like the Cougars."

"But you've persevered?"

"Yes. I've had to prove myself to men who think I have no place at the table, but their skepticism only makes me work harder. Though I must say seeing my brothers get married this year has made think about a family someday. What about you?"

"What about me?"

"Don't act dense, Wynn. Do you want a family?"

"Maybe." Wynn shrugged. "I was married once, and it ended badly. So, it's kind of turned me sour on marriage. But I did want children."

"Past tense?"

"If the right woman came along, I could want them again."

"Did you love her?" Giana asked. At Wynn's frown, she added, "Your ex-wife?"

"I thought I did, but I realized later it was lust, nothing more. I didn't really know her, and we certainly didn't share core values. And that's important."

"I agree. Core values are what distinguish the Atlanta Cougars from a lot of other franchises."

Wynn leaned back in his chair and grinned at her. "I should have known you weren't going to give up on work, Giana." He rose from his chair and took their empty plates into the kitchen.

"And you wouldn't expect anything less," Giana said, following him inside with both empty wineglasses. "So how about this." She placed the glasses on the counter. "I saw a pool table in your bonus room down the hall, so I'll offer you this challenge. If I win the best of three games, you'll give me your business after you hear me out tonight."

"And if I win?"

Giana shrugged. "I don't know. What do you want?"

"If I win, you acknowledge the chemistry between us, even if it means we become better acquainted."

Giana wondered if it wasn't a fair trade, because in her opinion she won both ways. On the one hand, she would finally garner Wynn's business, which had eluded her for the past year. And on the other, she would find out if Wynn made love as well as he kissed.

"You're on." She shook his hand.

Giana has no idea what she's gotten herself into, Wynn thought as he racked the balls into a triangle in the middle of table. Once the table was set, he walked over to the pool cues, but Giana was already grabbing hers and chalking the top.

"You play?" he inquired. He'd been looking forward to leaning over her round derriere and showing her how to put her hand on the table and make the cue pass through her index finger.

"Of course, or I wouldn't have suggested it," she responded flippantly.

He stopped chalking his cue stick to regard her. "Feisty much?"

"You've no idea. Are we flipping a coin on who goes first?"

"No need. You go."

"Okay, I'll break." Giana sashayed right in front of him and bent over the table, giving him a delectable view of her pert behind. With a quick tap, she distributed the balls across the billiard table. "Seven striped. Center pocket."

She took the first shot easily, knocking it into the first pocket. The second one soon followed. It was only on her fourth shot that she missed.

"You're good."

"Did you imagine otherwise? I grew up in a family surrounded by men. I had to learn. When my brothers were outside playing football, I went out there with them, because I didn't want to be stuck in the kitchen with my mother. She hated it because her daughter kept coming back inside with scrapes and bruises."

Wynn took his turn. "But they only made you stronger. Tougher."

"That's right. I know some people think I got my position because of nepotism, but you don't know my father. He brought me to the table as head of marketing because he'd seen my success with branding the team."

"Red ball. Left pocket." Wynn leaned over and executed a perfect move. He missed the third shot, leaving Giana to take another run for it.

"So, you see, I've learned the business from the ground up and can tell you that the Atlanta Cougars' core values are based on family, teamwork, commitment, dedication and service." Giana hit a ball into the right pocket. "My family and the players stand behind those principles. You'll find many give back to the community, as does my family. It's why we created the Lockett Foundation."

"You sound like an infomercial." Wynn's comment made Giana lose focus, and she missed her shot.

The hurt expression on her face made Wynn realize he'd offended her. She was placing her cue stick on the pool table like she was about to quit. "Giana, I—I'm sorry."

"I can see I was deluding myself. You're never going to give my family a break, because you think all of us rich folks are alike, which is the pot calling the kettle black. I mean, look at this place." She made a sweeping gesture with her arm, indicating the expensively furnished room. "I'm here to tell you, we are not all the same. We're not. Some of us care about other people. It's not all about the money." Giana rushed from the room and was nearly to the great room, but Wynn caught her in the hallway and clasped his hand around her arm.

"Giana, please wait."

"Why?" she asked, jerking her arm away. "So you can ridicule me and my family some more? No, thank you."

"So I can apologize. I was rude and completely insensitive. I'm sorry. Please don't go."

She stared at him for several long beats. Wynn silently willed her to stay. He enjoyed her company and didn't want the night to end. Not like this. Had he gone so long without dating that he didn't know how to talk? "Let's finish our game. You do want the chance to convince me to do an endorsement deal with Curtis, right?"

That brought a smile to her face, and Wynn had never felt more relieved. He hadn't fumbled the ball.

They returned to the game room and Giana easily won the first game, but Wynn took the second round. He was revved up when they began the third and final game. As they played, Giana quickly explained how Curtis would be a great athlete for Wynn's endorsement. She was getting ahead of herself since the pitch was supposed to come after the game was over, but she had Wynn's attention and for the first time, he listened.

"Most players have their own agents, who of course help them get their endorsement deals, but since the Cougars are one of the most popular and recognizable brands, we've started going after endorsements on behalf of our players."

"What makes my company any different?" Wynn took his shot, landing another ball in the center pocket.

Giana's heart sank. Her chance was slipping away.

"Simply put, Tim Jackson. Curtis's father is his agent and holds a lot of sway over his son. Mr. Jackson likes what he's seen in you—a young man from a single father who has pushed himself to achieve great success, same as his son. He really identifies with you."

After missing his next shot, Wynn turned to her. "Why have you never said this before?"

This was Giana's chance. She took a tough shot but missed it. *Damn!* "Because you've never given me the opportunity, Wynn."

"I was wrong. Curtis might be the right man to represent LEAN. I'd like to meet him. I'm sorry for not realizing that sooner." He put his cue stick down. "Seems as if all I've done is apologize to you tonight."

"I appreciate you finally hearing me out." She glanced down at her watch. "And it's late. I should really head home."

"Not so fast. I think there's one ball left to play." They both glanced at the table; indeed, one colored ball was on the table, and it was Wynn's turn. He leaned over and with a smooth motion executed the shot, sending it sinking in the left pocket. "I do believe I'm the winner."

Giana frowned and folded her arms across her chest. "If you were a gentleman, you would have let me leave."

Wynn tossed thc cue stick on the table and stalked toward her. "I'm no gentleman."

Suddenly Giana was in his arms and he was kissing her so hungrily, she gasped. "Yes, Wynn, yes." One last stab of reason coursed through her, telling her to stop before it was too late, but she simply couldn't ignore the passion between them anymore.

She wanted him too badly.

She coiled her arms greedily around his neck, and Wynn took that as an invitation, wrapping her legs around his waist and carrying her down the hall to his bedroom.

Seven

Wynn laid Giana down on his bed and kissed her the way he'd wanted to do all night. His teeth nipped at her bottom lip until she opened her mouth. She moaned when he slid his tongue against hers. He loved how open and responsive Giana was, because it fed his own desire. He couldn't resist sweeping his hands down her body to her breasts, which swelled in his palms. He used the hard pads of his fingertips to brush the sensitive flesh back and forth until they pebbled beneath the dress—a dress he wanted off.

He reached for her dress and quickly dispensed with it. Then he returned to her side, taking her in his arms again. He used his mouth to explore the curves of her throat, and then his tongue found the vulnerable area behind her ear and teased it until she trembled against him. And he would have continued, but it appeared that Giana no longer wanted to be on the receiving end, because she was pushing him down so she could slide on top of him and take off his shirt.

"Do you think you're the only one who can be in charge?"

she asked as her hair fell around him like a curtain. Wynn lifted his shoulders so Giana could remove his T-shirt and toss it aside.

"You can take off my clothes any day," he teased, but talking stopped when her wet tongue brushed over one of his nipples. Wynn couldn't help but release an involuntary groan. He wanted to touch her, too, but she pushed his hands aside and moved to the waistband of his jeans. He heard her unsteady intake of breath as she eased down the straining zipper. He shifted uncomfortably on the bed and watched as Giana peeled his jeans along with his boxers down his legs until they too joined the shirt on the floor.

When he was completely naked, Giana boldly reached for him, taking his hot, hard length in her hand. She squeezed him firmly and then began working him up and down with her hand. She was a master, as evidenced by his choppy breathing. Wynn tried to grab her hand to stop her and take back control, but she had him in a death grip. So he just gave in, especially when she leaned over and began to stroke and tease him with her mouth. His thighs went rigid and his hands ran through her hair, mussing it up as she pressed her mouth to him. "Giana…"

Wynn was powerless to stop the rising passion she stirred in him or the feverish movement of his hips. He was close. *So close.* Giana gripped him firmer and faster, signaling she wouldn't stop until she'd tasted him, *all of him*. He tried to hold on, but a hoarse cry escaped him. His pelvis pistoned and his fingers knotted in her hair as he gave her everything.

Giana licked her lips as she looked up at Wynn. She was gratified knowing she could give him such a powerful release. She was no stranger to sex. She knew it could be fun and had always enjoyed it, but sex with Wynn was like a whole other high.

And she suspected she was going to have to pay a hefty price for working him into a lather, because Wynn had her flat on her back in seconds and was unclasping her bra and sliding her panties down her legs. Then his hands and mouth began roving the length of her, both worshipping and arousing.

His hands found her breasts and toyed with her nipples, and then his lips were brushing across them. Giana loved the way Wynn suckled them deep into his mouth and she rocked up to him, but it wasn't enough. She was frantic with desire, having nearly come from having had him inside her mouth. She appreciated he'd been willing to give up control, but now desire was swirling around her. There was an insistent pulse between her legs that needed to be answered. So, when Wynn's hands and mouth leisurely traced a path to her quivering belly and the source of her need, Giana wanted to cry out with joy.

His tongue parted her folds, and Giana held her breath in anticipation. She cried out when he focused on the center of her—sucking, licking and going deep to show proof of his attraction to her. Unbearable heat flooded through her, and her head fell backward and then she screamed. But Wynn wasn't finished; she watched him move from the bed to produce a condom from his jeans, don protection and slither up the bed to cover her with his body.

Even though she was coming off the high of her climax, Giana felt Wynn's swollen length against her belly. He gently and slowly kissed her lips before making his way along her jawline, down to the slender column of her throat. She tilted her head back and groaned. Only then did he ease her thighs a little wider to accommodate him. Finding her warm and moist, Wynn easily slid inside her. Once he was settled deep, he withdrew and then plunged deep again. Giana shrieked with delight.

"You like that, do you?" he murmured.

"Yes, Wynn," she moaned. "I want more."

With her fingers clutching his muscular back and her nipples pressed firmly against his rock-hard chest, Wynn began to move faster with firm, measured strokes. She followed his steady rhythm by locking her legs around his waist and writhed helplessly, grinding her hips against his.

If she had her way, she would burrow closer, have him touch her everywhere, because his lovemaking both drugged her and ignited her desire with equal measure. She loved the way his tongue teased, the way he nipped at her ear and his sure strokes.

Giana could feel herself on the brink.

"Let go, Giana," he urged.

And she responded instinctively. She cried out as sensation after sensation overtook her body. She let the throaty sighs come through as she absorbed each of his thrusts and abandoned herself to pleasure.

He did the same and buried his face in her neck. Wynn shuddered violently and she squeezed him hard with her inner muscles so she could make the intense moment last, but eventually her mind went blank and she descended into sleep completely satisfied.

When Giana finally awoke sometime later with Wynn as her pillow, she caught the smug expression on his face. "Don't give me that look," she murmured. "This wasn't a foregone conclusion."

His brows rose. "Wasn't it? You were always going to end up in my bed tonight, Giana."

Was he right?

Maybe.

She had been consumed by lust and needy for the satisfaction Wynn could give, but she hadn't been the only one. He'd wanted her just as much, and to prove it, she pushed him down and rolled on top, kneeling astride him. Then their mouths fastened onto each other, tongues searching. There was no doubt as to what they both wanted and would have. After he'd eased on another condom, Giana lifted her bottom and sank down onto him. Wynn accepted her and took her tight nipples into his hot mouth. Giana lost it and began rocking her hips back and forth.

"Yes, that's it," he murmured. "Take what you want, Giana. The night is young."

They kissed and touched like they were starved for sensation only the other person could give. She felt Wynn reach between them, his fingers teasing, swirling and stroking the sensitive nub of her clitoris. He exploited it, drawing out her sobs as she rode him up and down. When she began to tire, his fingers dug into the flesh at her hips and he held her there while the lower half of his body pumped into her with sure deep movements. He curled strands of her hair around his finger and tugged her downward, kissing her long and deep. He pushed Giana to the limit, and she gave him what he'd been seeking—total surrender. He lasted until she climaxed, and then their bodies shuddered as one.

Giana climbed off Wynn in a fog and collapsed back on to the bed, unable to move or speak. Then she heard the sound of Wynn's even breathing. He was fast asleep.

At first, Giana didn't move, because she was afraid of disturbing him. But she was the one who was disturbed by what had transpired between them. She felt dazed and disoriented. The sex had been phenomenal. And she was no novice. She'd had other partners, some of whom left her satisfied, but any other man she'd ever been with paled in comparison to sex with Wynn. Giana felt free and liberated to be the sexual creature she'd known was underneath. Wynn matched her enthusiasm, and it was both thrilling and scary. She could get addicted to this feeling.

She needed some space to gather herself and get herself back under control. The rational part of her brain told her to take tonight for what it was—two consenting adults enjoying each other. But she also couldn't ignore the risk that bringing intimacy into their relationship could jeopardize Wynn's doing business with the Cougars. Did he think she'd slept with him for the deal? She hadn't. She wanted him as much as he wanted her. If her family found out about their relationship, she doubted they'd approve. And what if they had a falling out and he reneged on their deal? So she rose as quietly as she could, collected her dress, lingerie and shoes, and crept to the bathroom. She dressed and then looked in the mirror. She was quite a sight, with her lipstick clean gone, her mascara smudged and her hair going in every direction. She looked as if she'd been thoroughly tumbled in bed.

And hadn't she?

Wynn had been the most exceptional lover she'd ever had. But she couldn't face him in the morning light, and… what? Have an awkward conversation about what came next? *No, thank you.* Her flight instinct was best. She opened his bedroom door and stole a glance at the massive bed. Wynn was still sprawled out, completely satiated. And so, after one final look at his sleeping face, she retrieved her purse from the great room and left.

It was after 2:00 a.m. when Giana made her way into her parents' kitchen. After the aerobic adventures of the evening, she was starved and in the mood for a late-night snack. The stove's overhead light was on. She would quietly make herself a snack and head back to the guesthouse. She was closing the fridge after gathering all her ingredients when the back door suddenly opened and a hooded figured crept inside.

"Xavier!" she whispered, dropping her items on the counter. "You nearly scared me half to death!"

He jumped as if he'd been caught with his hand in the cookie jar. "Giana! What on earth are you doing up? And here at the main house, no less?"

"I could ask you the same thing. I'm not the only one creeping at this ungodly hour," Giana said, getting a plate from the cabinet and returning to her fixings.

He grinned unabashedly. "That's my business."

"Yet you want to know mine?" Giana asked. She cut a large bagel and topped it with cream cheese and smoked salmon. "What's up with you, Xavier? You've been very secretive lately."

"I'm sorry, sis." Xavier sat down at the island. "I've been going through some stuff."

"Care to elaborate?" Giana asked, cutting the bagel down the middle. She picked up half and took a large bite.

"Only if you'll share." Xavier eyed the other half of her bagel.

Giana rolled her eyes. "Fine." She inclined her head and watched as Xavier greedily began devouring it. "I'm waiting."

"I can't tell you much right now as I don't want to compromise my lady, but I've sort of been seeing someone."

Giana's eyes surveyed his. "You are?" She hadn't heard a thing from anyone in the family.

"Yeah, I'm keeping it on the down low for right now, because she's kind of a celebrity," Xavier said after he'd devoured the bagel in a few minutes. "And you know how the family gets."

"I sure do. I can imagine you're not looking for a repeat of Roman's and Julian's experiences."

Their father had wanted Roman to get Shantel to sign a prenup. Roman had refused and nearly left the family and his job at the Cougars. In the end, Josiah had backed down and even stepped down as general manager so Roman could take over.

Elyse hadn't fared much better at first. When their father discovered she was his former business partner's daughter and might be holding a grudge, he'd interfered. Julian and Elyse almost called it quits. Luckily, love won out.

Xavier shook his head. "Affirmative."

"So that leaves you creeping in at all hours of the night?"

"For now, I'm respecting her wishes to keep this quiet. And you?"

Giana straightened. "What about me?" She was eager to change the subject.

"You don't get to call me out without revealing what you've been up to, not that I can't tell. I'm not mad if you want to get your swerve on, big sis."

Giana felt herself flush. She couldn't believe her baby brother was talking about her sex life. "Xavier!"

"What?" He shrugged. "Don't act like you don't have needs, Gigi. I know you put up this front to everyone that you've got everything under control and you don't need a man, but it's okay if you want one."

Giana shook her head. "I'm not having this conversation with you."

"Better me than having Mom or Dad come in here and find you creeping in the middle of the night."

"Point taken."

"Listen, I'm glad we had this talk," Xavier said, rising to his six-foot-four height. "And I'll be sure to keep this little tête-à-tête to ourselves. You have a good night now!" He waved as he headed out of the kitchen.

Xavier was right. If their parents caught Xavier sneaking in, it would have been no big deal, just a man sowing his wild oats. But if they'd found Giana? It would have been the end of the world. Her mother would have talked to Giana about maintaining her reputation while her father would have given her the disapproving look usually reserved for Julian.

Giana wasn't ashamed of going to bed with Wynn, but she wouldn't be made to feel as if she'd done something wrong, either. It was just sex, after all. And good sex. She would hold her head up high and act like men did. It was a one-night stand.

Yet, her heart told her, the evening had meant so much more.

Eight

Wynn awoke to sunlight coming through the window and the realization he was in bed *alone.* The sheets beside him were cold, which meant he had been that way for some time. "Giana?"

No answer.

He jumped out of the bed and rushed to the bathroom. No Giana. Slowly, he walked back to the master suite and glanced around. Her clothes, which had been strewn across the floor, were gone.

Why had Giana sneaked out like a thief in the night? The least she could have done was wake him up. Allowed him to walk her out. Or make her breakfast in bed. Of course, they probably would have ended up right back in bed, forget breakfast.

Being with other women, Christine included, didn't compare to being with Giana. She had bewitched him last night, because she'd been as eager as he was. Every touch, every taste, every look had led them here…to mind-blowing sex. It's why he was now awake with a stiff erection.

He went back into the bathroom and stepped into the shower, hoping the punishing cold spray would help rid him of his desire so he could go back to normal. He'd tasted Giana and scratched an itch; it would have to be enough. However, once he turned off the water and dried himself, Wynn realized it was a lie. He couldn't forget the mocha beauty, and he would have to find some way of seeing her again. And he knew exactly how.

"You wanted to see me, Roman?" Giana inquired, walking into his office and making herself comfortable on his sofa. After not getting much sleep the night before, it had been a long morning, and no amount of coffee had been able to keep her alert. She hadn't been in a business mood, so she'd shrugged into a casual mango-colored wrap dress and swirled her hair into a twist along with some heeled sandals.

"Giana. I would ask you to come in, but you're already here." As usual, Roman was annoyed because she hadn't waited for his assistant to announce her. She never had and never would.

"You're my brother. Why stand on ceremony?"

"Why indeed." Roman walked over to her. Fortunately for her, he seemed to be in a relaxed mood, having removed his suit jacket, which was hanging over his chair. "As you know, I have a monthly call with Mr. Jackson on his son's career, and he inquired about Curtis's endorsement of LEAN. I wanted to check in with you to see if you'd made any progress."

"Yes, I did." Giana barely managed to stifle a yawn.

Roman's brow rose. "Long night?"

Giana smiled. "You have no idea."

"Really? What has my little sister been up to these days?"

"Nothing I care to share with my big brother," she responded. "And as for Starks Inc., inroads have been made.

Wynn will be a lot more amenable to having Curtis sponsor his products."

Her brother cocked his head to the side. "Wynn? You're on a first-name basis?"

Giana smoothed imaginary wrinkles in her dress and avoided the question. "Our objective was to get Curtis on an account his father approves of. LEAN is a perfect fit, and let's just say I'm confident it's going to happen."

"I'm impressed. I know how much you wanted this deal. You fought for it. And won."

"Thank you. I hope Daddy will agree."

"Agree about what?" Their father's voice boomed from the doorway.

"Does anyone knock around here?" Roman asked in an exasperated tone.

"I own the building," Josiah replied and then turned his dark gaze on Giana. "So what do you hope I agree about?"

"Giana has convinced me LEAN would be in good hands with Curtis Jackson representing us," Wynn said from the doorway.

"For Christ's sake." Roman threw up his hands in defeat over yet another unannounced guest.

Giana felt a whoosh, as if she'd been knocked down on her butt. Wynn looked like a dream, his handmade suit and silk tie perfectly complementing his tawny coloring and searing brown eyes. Her mouth felt suddenly dry as his eyes held hers from across the room.

"Is that right?" Her father looked at Wynn and then at Giana.

Giana swallowed and then rose to her feet. "Yes, it is. It was so good of you to stop by, Mr. Starks." She walked toward him and Wynn managed to keep his expression neutral, though Giana could feel his eyes devouring her with each step she took. When she made it within a few inches of him, she stopped. "I was telling my family Starks Inc. is entertaining the idea of having Curtis as a celebrity endorsement."

"Fantastic news, Gigi," her father said. "I'm glad you're seeing the partnership Starks Inc. and the Atlanta Cougars can have together, Mr. Starks."

Wynn looked at Giana. "Oh, I see lots of potential. But a big sticking point for me is exclusivity—so that Curtis and the Atlanta Cougars won't deal with any sports drink company other than Starks Inc."

"I'm sure that can be arranged," Giana said. "Can't it, Roman?" She looked at her brother.

"Not so fast, Starks," Roman replied. "You're welcome to speak with Curtis about an exclusive contract with him, but we can't limit our players' options for other endorsements."

"That wasn't what I was hoping for." Giana felt the heat fizz inside her veins when Wynn stared in her direction. "Can we talk about this in further detail at lunch, Giana?"

"Of course." Her father ushered her toward Wynn. "She would love to, wouldn't you, Gigi?"

To her annoyance, Wynn placed his hand on the small of her back. "I'll take good care of her, Mr. Lockett. Roman." He nodded at her brother, and soon he was ushering Giana down the hall and toward the elevator bank.

"Exactly what do you think you're doing?" Giana whispered. She smiled at several colleagues as they walked past. As soon as they arrived at the elevators, the doors to one swished open and Wynn eased her inside.

"Finishing what we started," he answered. When they were in between floors, he pushed the stop button. He stepped forward and, in a single fluid movement, slid his fingers through her hair. "Just one kiss."

As annoyed as she was by his high-handedness, Wynn didn't need to coax her mouth open. Giana met him halfway and closed her eyes just as his lips moved over hers.

She tasted like honey, warm and sweet, and Wynn hungered for her. When he'd seen her sitting in her brother's office with her legs crossed, all he could think about was having those very same brown legs wrapped around him as she rode him *hard*.

Giana gave a tiny sigh deep in her throat and then parted her lips so he could taste her. His tongue glided into her mouth, deepening the kiss, and her lips clung to his as if she was as frantic and as desperate as he was to quench the fire deep within. Her hands took on a life of their own and slid around his neck, and then she was leaning into him. Wynn hauled her closer until she was splayed across his body.

Finally, he broke the kiss to stare into her desire-filled eyes. "What are you doing to me, woman?"

"Nothing," Giana said, easing herself away from him and trying to repair her hair, which had come free of the knot. "This is just the usual guy-girl chemistry."

He took a step forward, back into her personal space. He placed a finger under her chin and tipped it upward to stare into her eyes. "You should know chemistry can lead to some explosive reactions."

"Don't..."

Wynn brushed a thumb across her lips. "Don't what? Acknowledge what's between us? If that kiss showed you anything, it's that we can't ignore it."

"And what are you suggesting, we give in to it?" Giana asked, reaching past him to push the button and jolt the elevator back into action.

"Why not?"

"Because we'll be in business together. I don't want to feel like this is a quid pro quo."

"It's not like that," Wynn said. "I agreed with you before we went to bed together, and vice versa. Or are you saying you had sex with me as incentive for me changing my mind?"

Giana eyes flew to his. "Of course not!"

"Then it's settled. Business is business. And personal is personal."

The elevator chimed, and the doors opened. Once again,

Wynn placed his hand on Giana's back to lead her through the lobby to his limousine waiting outside the arena.

"Where are we going?" Giana asked when he helped her into the limo.

"Lunch." He climbed in beside her.

"Is that all it is? Lunch?"

Wynn grinned. "Yes, unless you would like to go back to my place, and we can pick up where we unceremoniously left off this morning when I woke up to find my bed empty."

He was still smarting over her rebuff, and now was as good a time as any to speak his mind.

As the car pulled away from the arena, Giana shifted away from Wynn. His thigh was nudged a little too close to hers, and she needed to create some physical distance between them. The close quarters weren't good for her heart rate. "Was your visit today about Starks Inc. or your enormous ego?"

"My ego is fine," Wynn responded. "I was merely stating you ran away like a scared schoolgirl."

Giana turned to face the window. "I wasn't scared. I merely had a lot on my plate today." All of which got pushed aside when Wynn walked into the room. She would need to call Mara and rearrange her afternoon. She turned to face him. "Everything isn't all about you."

"True, but can't you admit last night shook you, too?"

Too? She'd certainly thought about him all morning and had been beating herself up over whether she should have slept with him, but at the end of the day, she didn't regret it. She was confident in her sexuality and understood the laws of attraction, but that didn't stop her from wanting more from this man. "What do you mean?"

"I was as floored as you were by the intensity of our night together, Giana, but unlike you, I didn't run away. When I woke up this morning, I was ready to pull you into my arms, have a repeat performance and leisurely make breakfast for you."

"Oh yeah, and what would you have made?"

"I'd have made you a mean spinach and mushroom omelet, poured you a glass of fresh-squeezed orange juice and a cup of coffee, and brought it all on a tray to serve you in bed."

Giana smiled. Perhaps she had been too eager to leave. She'd have thought like most men, he wanted her to go without the pesky emotions or recriminations over the night before. "Do you treat all your ladies like this or am I special?"

"There are no 'all my ladies,'" Wynn responded, and Giana could have sworn she saw something flicker in his eyes. Was it hurt? "When I date a woman, I date one at a time."

"Of course, I didn't mean to insinuate otherwise."

"Good. Then you won't mind us picking up where we left off this evening."

Giana glared at him. "Your arrogance knows no bounds. Do you really think I'm going to fall into bed with you again?" At his smirk, she held a palm up. "Wait, don't answer that."

He frowned. "Why are you playing so hard to get, Giana?"

He sucked in a deep breath while he waited for her answer. Her hesitancy gave him a chance to look his fill. She was stunning in a mango-colored wrap dress. Giana was proportionally built, with round hips and small yet perfectly formed breasts. Breasts he'd held in his hands while his mouth played havoc with her nipples.

When he glanced up, he found her watching him. "You want to bring your eyes back here." She motioned upward to her face.

He grinned sheepishly at being caught openly ogling, but he was a man after all. And he was with a beautiful woman with her hair done up in some clever arrangement. His hands fisted at his sides as he remembered what it felt like to drag his fingers through the soft, curly masses. "I want you to agree to go out with me."

Giana shook her head. "That isn't what you said. You said you want to pick up where we left off—which was the bedroom."

"Semantics. So, let me be clear, Giana. I want to spend time with you, in and out of bed. Exclusively."

"Exclusively?"

"I don't like to share. Will you agree to my terms?"

"Why don't you try persuading me over lunch?" Giana replied, surprising him with her response.

They arrived at Chops Lobster Bar in Buckhead a short while later. With its dark wood paneling and white tablecloths, it was the perfect meeting spot. Wynn put his hand on her back and steered her toward the maître d', who led them to a table situated in the corner away from the crowd.

"I hope this is acceptable, Mr. Starks?"

"Yes, thank you," Wynn said, helping Giana into her seat then taking his own. He accepted the menu from the maître d' and placed it on the table. He wasn't interested in the food.

Giana was peering at her menu as if it held the secrets of the universe.

"Are you seeing someone, Giana?"

Her eyes popped up from the menu to peer at him. "You sure know how to get down to business."

"I see no reason not to be direct. I thought you would appreciate it."

"I do. And no, I'm not seeing anyone. Quite frankly, I haven't had the time. My career takes up much of my time."

"Really? A beautiful and accomplished woman such as yourself is single? I would have thought you would have a gaggle of men lining up around the block to date you."

"Afraid not." She shook her head.

"What about serious relationships?"

"One. Martin and I were both in business school and getting serious. I was thinking of introducing him to my family, but then Martin started hinting about marriage and babies."

"And you lost interest?"

"He assumed I would give up my dreams and fall in line like a Girl Scout. Needless to say, the relationship didn't last. And since then, well, I've found success is a deterrent to having a relationship."

The waiter returned to take their order. Giana opted for salmon with curry lobster sauce and a sesame sushi rice cake, while Wynn went for the lobster BLT with a side salad. Once the waiter had gone, Giana moved from the topic of her love life straight to business to find out what campaigns Wynn might have in mind for Curtis. They also discussed Wynn's need for exclusivity.

"I have to look out for Starks Inc.'s interest," Wynn explained. "My main competitor, Blaine Smith, is always sniffing around, trying to take a bite out of our market share. I'm just ensuring the snake is kept at bay."

"I've met Blaine," Giana said. "I'm not a fan, but it sounds like you have some history."

"We do," Wynn responded. "Blaine and I worked together back in the day. I was fine-tuning LEAN after work and mentioned starting my own sports drink business, but with his family's money, Blaine got there first. LEAN is very popular with the sports fanatics and constantly outranks Smith International's concoction. I feel like Blaine is always looking for a leg up on me and although I don't mind healthy competition, this is personal, ya know? I feel like he stole my idea. I'm hoping the Atlanta Cougars won't get in bed with him."

Giana held out a hand to shake. "Now I really don't like him. I can't speak for Roman, but as chief marketing and branding officer, I can promise you I won't actively seek out Blaine to do business. How's that?"

"I guess it will have to be enough."

They talked shop for the remainder of the lunch, and Wynn was surprised to find an hour had passed. He appreciated Giana's sharp mind. They would make a great team.

"When can I meet the illustrious Curtis Jackson?" Wynn asked. "You know LEAN is my baby, and I'm very protective."

"I will discuss it with Curtis and have my assistant get back to yours with some times." She rose to her feet.

Wynn took it to mean their lunch date was over and pushed back his chair. He didn't like being dismissed, but he had Giana in his crosshairs. "Of course, I'll drop you back at your office."

"Oh, there's no need. My assistant, Mara, is waiting for me outside," she said, walking in front of him.

"When did you have time to call her?" He caught a sly smile on Giana's face. Then he remembered how she'd made a pit stop in the ladies' room earlier. *Was she afraid of being alone with him again?* "Of course, I wouldn't want to keep you from any pressing Atlanta Cougars business. I'll walk you to the car."

He followed her out of the restaurant, watching the sway of her hips as she walked. Once they were outside, a dark sedan was indeed waiting for her at the curb, and Giana went to rush toward it, but he put a hand on her arm to stop her.

She turned around, and their eyes met. "Enjoy the rest of your day, Giana." He brushed his fingertips down her cheek.

He walked away, leaving Giana with her mouth agape over his touch.

Nine

"You secured Wynn Starks?" Julian said as he strolled into Giana's office later in the afternoon. "Congratulations." He clapped as he came forward to her desk and took a seat across from her.

Giana smiled. "Was there ever any doubt?"

"Not in my mind," Julian stated. "So how did you sell Wynn on the Cougars? Wynn Starks wouldn't even take your call a month ago," Julian continued. "Now he's coming to your place of work to tell you in person Curtis will be the face of Starks Inc. What gives?"

"Fine, Julian, I'll admit Wynn and I may have hooked up, but it was a one-time thing."

"Ha." Julian laughed and leaned back in his seat. "Kid yourself if you want to, but you have the man's nose wide open."

Giana chuckled at her brother's turn of phrase. "Just because he might want more doesn't mean I do."

"No?" Julian raised a brow.

"No," Giana stated more firmly. But it was more to convince herself than her brother. She couldn't get involved with Wynn any more than she already had. If she were to get seriously involved with Wynn or any man, they had to offer more than being an exclusive bedmate. And in Wynn's case, mixing business with pleasure was a bad idea. It had taken more than a year to get a meeting with him and convince him to do a partnership with the Cougars. A relationship between, whether purely physical or not would bring a host of complications she didn't need. There would be scrutiny by her family, not to mention the business implications if they ended the relationship and either wanted out of the deal. Both companies' reputations would take a hit along with their pocketbooks.

Though she had to admit the invitation was tempting. Wynn was an incredible lover and they'd shared an amazing night, but one time was all it should ever be. He was dangerous to her self-control. When she was around him, she seemed to have none, as evidenced by her making out with him in elevators.

Julian shrugged. "I don't think Wynn got the memo. And given everything I've heard about him, once he set his eyes on something, he'll stop at nothing to achieve it."

"What do you mean, given everything you've heard? Did you have him investigated?" She pushed to her feet.

"Didn't need to," Julian replied, standing as well. "Nico told me you had a dossier on Wynn. So I read it."

"Why?"

"When my baby sister tells me she's become intimately involved with a man we intend to do business with, I want to know more."

Giana spun away from him to face the window. She didn't need her brother getting in her business. "I don't need your protection, Julian. I can handle myself."

"I'm sure you can, Gigi," Julian said. Seconds later, Giana felt his hands on her shoulder as he turned her back around to face him. "But I would be remiss if I didn't check the man out. Make sure he didn't have any skeletons in his closet."

Giana let out a sigh. "All right."

Julian stroked her cheek with his palm. "You're not mad at me?"

"You know I have never been able to stay mad at you for long." She offered him a smile.

"Good. I have to go. I have some players to tend to in the rehab clinic."

After he'd gone, Giana thought about Wynn. Was Julian right? Was Wynn going to keep chipping at her defenses until she agreed to date him? Because if he did, Giana wasn't sure she had the willpower to say no. Whenever he touched her, her brain short-circuited and she lost control. Giana didn't like the feeling. She was used to her life being nice, neat and orderly, and Wynn Starks flipped the script every single time.

She would have to keep it strictly business between them and hope he stayed in his lane.

Wynn was feeling thwarted, and he didn't like it one bit. He'd tried unsuccessfully for the last two days to reach Giana. Sure, they had a meeting on the books on Friday for Wynn to discuss the LEAN endorsement with Curtis and Tim Jackson, but as for the two of them? Nada. Every time he called her office, her assistant told him she was busy. He knew it to be a lie. She was avoiding him.

Was this how she felt when he'd ignored her calls and canceled meetings? Was this retribution? If so, Wynn supposed he had it coming, but it didn't mean he had to like it. Now that he'd been with Giana, he wanted more than one night with her. He had to convince her she couldn't turn her back on the kind of passion they shared. They were well suited to one another.

She made him feel alive, and Wynn hadn't felt this way in a long time. It was exciting and scary all at once.

Instead of worrying about it, Wynn decided to take his mind off himself and help others, so he'd come to the local Boys & Girls Club he volunteered at to meet with his little brother after working until midafternoon. Donnell Evans was being raised by a single mother who worked two jobs to keep food on the table. He was a good kid, and Wynn was happy to supply a much-needed male influence in his life.

He found Donnell on the basketball court along with Silas and his mentee Eric late Thursday afternoon. "Hey, guys," Wynn said, running toward them. "Can I get in on the action?" Before he'd left the office, he'd changed into a T-shirt and basketball shorts.

"Yeah, man." Silas gave him a one-armed hug, and Wynn gave Donnell a fist bump.

"What's up, young man?" Wynn said, giving the twelve-year-old the once-over. The dark-skinned youth was sporting short twists and looked as if he'd grown another inch or so since the last time he'd seen him.

"I'm good, Mr. Starks," Donnell said.

"I told you, you can call me Wynn."

"I know, but my mama would kill me if she heard me, so if it's all the same to you, I'll call you Mr. Starks," Donnell responded.

"A game of two against two?" Silas offered.

"Let's do it," Wynn replied.

Wynn and Donnell faced off against Silas and Eric. Wynn had Silas on skill, but Silas had him on speed. Somehow, Wynn and Donnell managed to beat their opponents, but only by one point.

When the game was over, Wynn suggested burgers, and the young men eagerly nodded their heads in unison. "C'mon, get your things and we'll meet you outside."

While the boys went to get their book bags, Silas glanced at Wynn. "You were on fire out there."

"Was I?" He headed to the vending machines outside the basketball court and bought four bottled waters. He tossed one to Silas and then chugged his. When he was finished, he wiped his mouth with the back of his hand.

"Yeah, you were," Silas said. "And it makes me wonder if it has something to do with Giana Lockett."

"Nah, we're not doing this here," Wynn said, glancing at the locker room to see if the boys were coming.

"We don't have to talk about it, but my intuition tells me something went down between you and her."

Wynn didn't get a chance to answer, because the boys came back. "I'll drive," Wynn said. He'd taken his BMW X6 to work. He'd needed to be in control of the wheel since he didn't have any control over his love life at the moment. "C'mon."

Once they were buckled up, Wynn drove them to a nearby restaurant known for their burgers, fries and milkshakes. After placing their order, Donnell and Eric headed over to the arcade games, leaving Wynn and Silas alone again.

"You ready to tell me what happened?" Silas asked.

"You're not going to leave this alone, are you?"

Silas shook his head. "Nope. So, you might as well tell me."

"All right." He glanced at the boys. "Giana and I hooked up."

Silas's eyes grew wide. "Really? At least your self-imposed celibacy is over. How was it?"

"It was damn good, but now she won't give me the time of day."

"What did you do?"

Wynn frowned. "Why do you think I did something?" Silas cocked his head to the side, so Wynn continued, "I didn't do anything wrong. She's the one who snuck out of my bed in the middle of the night. And when I confronted her about it, she told me it was a onetime thing."

"And what did you say?"

"I told her I wanted more."

"A relationship?"

Wynn shook his head. "No, of course not. I told you, those days are over. But I told her I would commit to exclusively seeing her."

"As bed buddies? C'mon, Wynn, even to me you sound like a jerk."

"I can't offer more than that."

Silas shrugged. "And you wonder why she's not rushing to take you up on your offer?"

Wynn was cut off from responding because the waitress returned with a tray loaded with their food. Wynn called the boys. "Donnell, Eric, come on over. Let's eat."

Wynn enjoyed his double cheeseburger, fries and chocolate milkshake, but he couldn't get Silas's words out of his mind. Was that why Giana wasn't interested? Did she want more than an exclusive sexual relationship? If so, Wynn wasn't sure he was capable of more, because he didn't think there was a woman out there worth committing himself to.

Giana was certainly special, but Wynn wasn't sure he was ready to take the risk. In the meantime, he had to convince her they shouldn't deny themselves the pleasure of each other's company—each other's bodies—while they figured it out. He just hoped she would agree.

"Curtis, Mr. Jackson, I'm so glad you could make it," Giana said, shaking both men's hands as they came into the Atlanta Cougars' conference room at the arena on Friday. Tall with dark brown eyes, skin the color of tree bark and short curly hair, Curtis was a striking young man.

"Thank you for having us, Ms. Lockett," Tim Jackson replied. The elder Jackson was over six feet, not quite his son's height, but his presence was always felt. Today, he'd come dressed for business in a sports coat, button-down shirt and jeans, while Curtis was dressed in a track suit, because he had practice after the meeting.

"It's my pleasure," Giana said. "I'm happy to finally report Mr. Starks has agreed to have Curtis represent Starks Inc."

"Wonderful," Tim said. "What changed his mind?"

"You did," Wynn said, strolling into the conference room as if he owned the place with a man Giana assumed was his attorney. Wynn was wearing a slate-gray suit with a light blue shirt, both clearly custom-made and tailored to his frame. Once again, Giana was caught off guard by Wynn's presence. She had a hard time looking away from him, but she forced herself.

"Mr. Jackson, meet Wynn Starks. Wynn, this is Curtis and his father, Tim Jackson," Giana said, making the introductions.

Wynn offered his hand to Tim. "Pleasure to meet you, sir. And you—" He turned to Curtis. "I look forward to having you represent LEAN."

"I will do you proud, Mr. Starks," Curtis responded. "I've always loved your sports drinks, but LEAN is my favorite."

Wynn beamed with pride. "Why, thank you. It's my baby, so it means a lot to have someone of your good character representing the product."

"We knew Curtis would be a perfect fit. It's why I wanted my son to do this endorsement, Mr. Starks," Tim said.

"Call me Wynn."

"Wynn it is." Tim smiled. "Your story is impressive. It reminded me of me and Curtis. You faced long odds coming from a single-parent home raised by your father, and now look what you've made of yourself." He motioned toward Wynn's appearance.

"I wouldn't be where I am without my father, as I'm sure your son will agree."

"Absolutely," Curtis stated with a large grin. "My dad—" he patted his father's shoulders lovingly "—is my hero."

"We need more Black fathers like yourself in the community, Mr. Jackson," Wynn said. "I thought maybe we could somehow spotlight Black fathers in our first promotion."

He flicked a glance at Giana, and despite the tension coiled in her stomach, she felt a smile form on her lips.

"Of course. Let's get down to business," Giana said, motioning everyone to the table.

An hour later, after all terms were agreed to, including Wynn's exclusivity clause, and after seeing the Jacksons out, Giana finally released a long-held sigh. Nearly a year's effort had finally come to fruition. She'd inked the endorsement deal with Wynn. She returned to the conference room and found Wynn alone.

"Where's your attorney?" Giana asked, going to the settee and opening a bottle of sparkling water. She poured some into a glass and walked over to the table to sit across from him. Wynn wore a smug smile on his face, as if he'd engineered this deal when *she'd* been the one championing it.

"His work is done. He's gone."

"As you should be," she responded, sipping her water.

Wynn placed his forearms on the table and leaned forward. "We have unfinished business."

She raised a brow. "Do we?"

"I'm not leaving here until you agree to meet for drinks later."

"And why would I do that, Wynn? I believe I told you *this*—" she motioned back and forth between them "—was going nowhere."

"What are you so afraid of, Giana?"

"I'm not afraid."

"I beg to differ. So, I'm challenging you to meet me for drinks. The same way you challenged me." He rattled off a favorite haunt frequented by celebrities. "If you come, I'll know you're ready to see where this will go. If you don't, I'll leave you alone."

Giana sat up straight. "You will?" She hadn't realized

how much she was enjoying Wynn having to fight for time with her after she'd chased him for nearly a year.

He nodded and rose to his feet, buttoning his suit jacket as he went. "I'll honor your wishes and keep my distance if that's what you really want."

"What if I don't show?"

"I'm willing to wager when push comes to shove, you'll come. See you soon, Giana."

He left her with a stunned expression and wondering if she was as adventurous as he seemed to think she was.

Ten

Wynn fidgeted in his seat and glanced at his watch. It was after 6:30 p.m., and Giana was nowhere in sight. Had he really gotten it wrong? Was she afraid of exploring their mutual attraction? He hadn't taken Giana for a coward.

In today's meeting, he'd seen her sharp wit and knew the collaboration between Starks Inc. and the Atlanta Cougars would be a good one. But it was water under the bridge. Whether she came tonight or not, they would be in business together for the duration of the endorsement deal.

Wynn downed the rest of his bourbon in two seconds and was about to get up to leave when he heard a beautiful feminine voice say from behind him, "Is this seat taken?"

He released the deep breath he'd been holding and spun around to face Giana. "You came."

She had changed into a leather jacket and a black jumpsuit with a wide leg. It not only flattered her figure but made her look sleek and sexy. She'd also loosened her hair from the updo, and it hung in luxurious waves down her back.

"Did you doubt I would?" She grinned, and he could see a dimple in her right cheek that he hadn't noticed before.

Wynn glanced at his watch. "It's nearly seven."

"Yeah, well." She shrugged as she slid onto the bar stool beside him. "I ran into a bit of traffic on the way here. An accident on I-85. I would have been here sooner."

He gave her a sideways glance. "I'm glad I was right." He motioned the bartender over. "What would you like to drink?"

"I'll have whatever he's drinking," Giana said to the bartender, nodding toward his glass of bourbon.

"Coming right up," the tattooed blond bartender said. He reached for a tumbler, poured two thumbs of the high-end bourbon into it and then slid it her way. Then he topped off Wynn's before heading over to another couple down the bar.

"Cheers." Wynn held up his glass.

"Cheers." Giana clinked her glass with his and surprisingly threw back her head and killed the entire drink while he merely took a sip.

"Giana! You were supposed to sip that," Wynn laughed.

"It's been a long year courting you, Wynn. I deserve this drink and much more."

Wynn chuckled. "Was I that difficult?"

Giana snorted. "You know you were, but it's behind us." She spun around to look him dead in the eye. "Although the intensity of the other night shocked the hell out of me, I'm here because I'm no coward."

"I'm glad you're not."

"I'd like to explore the dynamic between us and see where it goes, but understand this, Wynn, it won't be on your terms."

He frowned. He didn't like where this was going. "What do you mean?"

"I won't be just your bedmate."

"No? What do you want?"

"If you want me to go out on the limb with you, then you have to be willing to give something in return."

"Like what?"

"I admit I'm not exactly comfortable being with someone with whom I have a working relationship," Giana started, "but I'm willing to go there. Just get one thing straight—I won't be your booty call, Wynn. Exclusive or not. You have to be willing to explore the possibility we could be more."

Silas had been right. She wanted a relationship, which was one of Wynn's hard limits. After Christine, he'd steered clear of them. Wynn wasn't aiming to repeat past mistakes. "Giana—"

"No, Wynn," she interrupted him. "This is nonnegotiable. If you want to be with me, you have to be willing to put your heart on the table, the same as me. Those are my terms."

"And if I don't accept?"

Giana folded her arms across her chest. "I leave and go home and curl up with a good book."

Staring into her eyes, Wynn knew she wasn't joking. Giana had a stubborn streak. If he said no, she would walk away and never look back. His gut told him if he didn't accept her terms, he ran the risk of missing out on something spectacular, because Giana Lockett was a phenomenal woman. But on the other hand, Wynn hadn't seriously dated anyone since Christine.

"I've been burned in the past," he offered up after a short silence.

"I know."

His eyes immediately darted upward to connect with hers. There wasn't pity in her gaze, merely resolve.

"I only read what was in my investigator's file on you. I don't know the whole story. You can tell me one day," she added, "when you're ready."

Wynn glanced down at the bourbon still in his hand. He picked up the drink and downed it fast, just as Giana had. "I accept your terms."

Giana couldn't believe he'd said yes. Strong, sexy, arrogant Wynn had agreed to her conditions. She'd assumed based on how acrimonious Wynn's divorce had been that he'd turn her down flat and she would be off the hook. As she'd told her father, she wasn't looking for a relationship and wanted to focus on her career. Yet, somehow, by calling Wynn's bluff with one of her own, she'd inadvertently walked her way into a possible relationship.

How had that happened?

She should never have risked it. Now not only her career but her heart was on the line, because Giana feared Wynn had the power to hurt her. Whenever he was around, her defenses and control were gone, and she was vulnerable to his special brand of charm.

"You ready to get out of here?" Wynn asked as he placed several bills on the bar.

"Where are we going?" She was sure the answer was back to his place. He probably wanted her on her back as soon as possible, but Wynn surprised her with his answer.

"It's Friday night. I thought we'd go dancing."

"Dancing?" She couldn't remember the last time she'd done that. Probably when she'd been in college and hanging out with her friends. Since joining the Atlanta Cougars, her life had revolved around becoming the best executive she could be. She wanted to be Roman's right hand as he'd been for their father. She was determined to show she was the best woman for the job. She hadn't had time for dancing.

"C'mon." Wynn took hold of her hand and wove their fingers together. "Let's go." He led her toward the exit. Once outside, she was shocked when he headed toward a motorcycle. He disengaged their hands long enough to hand her a helmet.

"What's this for?"

"Duh? To put on," Wynn stated. "Safety first." He placed the helmet on her head.

Giana pushed up the visor to glare at him. "I'm not getting on that death trap."

"Have you ever been on one?"

"No, but—"

"Then you don't know what you're missing," Wynn said, and before she could object, his big hands circled around her hips and he placed her on top of the bike.

"Wynn! I'm not comfortable with this."

"Trust me, okay? I've got you." Then he was hauling one leg over the bike and turning on the engine. "Wrap your arms around my waist."

Giana did as he instructed and was rewarded with feeling Wynn's rock-hard abs. Seconds later, the motorbike took off.

At first, she was scared out of her wits, but the more Wynn maneuvered the bike in and out of traffic, the more relaxed she became. Giana had never done anything this reckless before. Wynn brought out a youthfulness Giana hadn't felt since she was in college. Eventually, she began leaning into the turns. She loved having her thighs so close to Wynn's. She loved how he handled the bike with ease, and before she knew it, they were pulling into the parking lot of the popular nightclub Latitudes.

Once they stopped, she took off the helmet and shook out her hair, running her fingers through the strands to fluff them out. Giana hated to think about how she must look. When she'd decided to wear her hair down, she'd had no idea she'd get helmet head.

"Stop." Wynn grabbed her hand. "You look beautiful!"

Giana laughed. "If you say so." She followed him toward the entrance, where a big, beefy guy stood manning the door. Wynn walked up to the VIP rope, and the guy immediately opened the rope to allow them to pass.

"Do you come here often?"

Wynn shook his head. "Naw, I know the owner. He used to be one of my kids I mentored at the Boys & Girls Club. I have a standing table if I ever want it."

The club was filled to the rafters with men and women dancing underneath the strobe lights to a pounding mix of R&B and hip-hop. Some of the women were in slinky dresses barely covering their bottoms. Giana felt overdressed in her jumpsuit.

The hostess knew Wynn and gave him a hug and then led them to a roped-off VIP area complete with leather couches and low end tables. "Thanks, Asia," Wynn said.

"Of course. I'll let Alex know you're here. In the meantime, I'll get you a bottle of bourbon." She glanced at Giana. "Can I get you anything?"

"No, thanks. I'll stick to the bourbon," Giana replied and joined Wynn, who was already making himself comfortable on one of the sofas. "You continue to surprise me, Wynn. Considering how the press calls you a recluse, I wouldn't think you'd frequent a place like this." She removed her leather jacket.

"I admit I like to keep to myself," he said, helping her out of it. "But every now and then, I do like to go out and have fun."

"I have a feeling I haven't even skimmed the surface in knowing who you really are."

But as the evening progressed, Giana got a close-up look at this man. She met one of his former mentees who owned the club, and Wynn introduced her as his girlfriend. Then they partied like rock stars, sipping on cocktails and grooving on the dance floor. Afterward, they tucked into some fried shrimp, hush puppies and mozzarella sticks. He'd thought Giana was too bourgeois for such fare, but she'd quickly reminded him it was football food and her family owned a football franchise.

They washed the fried treats down with ice-cold beer and eased back onto the sofa to people watch. They made up stories about the lively group of young women they suspected were having a girls' night and the couple dirty dancing on the floor once the music changed to slow jams.

"I don't think they know what they're doing," Wynn said, rising to his feet and holding out his hand. "I think we should show them how it's done."

Once in the midst of the crowd, Wynn drew Giana into his arms, and they began swaying to the music. When she looked up at him, his eyes glittered with desire, so it was no surprise when he dropped his head and crushed his lips to hers. He kissed her with a fierce possession as if she truly was his lady.

A flicker of passion stirred in the pit of her stomach at the urgency of Wynn's deepening kiss, and Giana curled her arms around his neck. Wynn's tongue expertly dueled with hers, and Giana once again was reminded of the mastery of his kiss. Her mind told her they were making out in the middle of a club like randy teenagers, but her body was in control and she wanted him with a ferocity that shocked her.

When he lifted his head, she wanted to protest. "Let's get out of here," he murmured. "I want you naked underneath me."

"Can't wait."

After grabbing their coats, they started for his bike outside. "My place or yours?" Wynn asked.

"Yours." Giana didn't relish trying to explain why there was a motorcycle outside her parents' guesthouse the next morning.

The ride back to Wynn's place was smooth, and after he punched in the code, the gates opened, allowing them in and closing everyone else out. And that's exactly what Giana wanted, because this time she intended to stay the whole night—and maybe the next morning, too.

Eleven

Wynn had to put a lot on the line to get Giana back to his home, but as he lay on the bed and watched her undress, it was all worth it. Any worries he had about venturing into a new relationship flew out the window when Giana eased the side zipper of the jumpsuit down, allowing it to fall in a silken puddle at her feet, leaving her in a bra and thong.

"Come here," he growled. He wanted to do the honors and remove them himself.

She smiled mischievously as she sauntered toward him and climbed on the bed to straddle him. "You have too many clothes on." She pushed at his shirt. Her fingers worked the buttons slowly but deliberately, undoing the top two before she got frustrated, lifted the tails from his jeans and tore the shirt open, sending buttons flying everywhere.

"I like your eagerness," Wynn commented as her fingertips explored the muscular ridges of his abdomen. Her hands eased upward until she reached his nipples and circled them with her nails. Wynn let out a guttural oath when she lowered her head and tongued them with her hot, wet mouth.

It was as if a dam had broken. He quickly shifted so that she was underneath him and he could kiss her again. She moaned when his hands began hungrily roaming her body. He needed her in a way that made no sense. Without breaking the connection, he reached behind her to unhook her bra and release her gorgeous breasts from their restraints.

A heady rush of achievement flooded his body. He cupped her breasts possessively and teased her nipples, making her back arch. Giana moaned.

"Soon," he promised. Then he lowered his head to take one turgid peak into his mouth and tongued it with wet lashes of his tongue before giving the other breast the same attention. While he made love to her with his mouth, his hands went lower, and she understood his intent, because Giana lifted her hips, allowing him to drag her thong down her shapely legs until she was completely naked.

The sight of her was intoxicating, and Wynn felt like he was high on a drug he hadn't known he was craving. His arousal was straining hard in his jeans, and he couldn't wait to be rid of them. He pushed himself up to a standing position so he could dispense with his clothing. As soon as he got his boxers and jeans off in one movement, his erection sprang forward.

Her mouth dropped open, but she welcomed him by opening her arms. He joined her on the bed and kissed her again. Meanwhile, his fingers trailed down her inner thighs to probe the slick folds at her core. Giana bucked under him, choking out a sob.

"You're so wet," he groaned, drawing his hand away. "I can't wait to be inside you."

"I want that, too, but if you keep doing that, I'll come."

"Babe, that's the point." He continued stroking her, stoking the flame until she cried out.

Wynn loved the way Giana responded to him. His hard-on was getting bigger and bigger by the second. "Give me a moment."

He fumbled in the drawer beside his bed. When he found the foil condom packet, he ripped it open with his teeth and seconds later rejoined her. "Where were we?"

She angled her body, and Wynn settled between her legs. His shaft probed for a moment before thrusting slowly but surely inside her.

Giana gasped. "You feel so good."

He grinned, then dug his fingers into her hips, holding her in place so he could begin to move in and out. Each thrust brought him closer to direct contact with her sensitive nub. "Look at me," he growled into her ear.

She glanced up, her eyes glassy with passion, but she didn't look away as he began slamming into her harder and faster, deeper and deeper until pleasure crashed over them, taking them both in the tidal wave. Giana reached the peak first and shook as her orgasm struck. Wynn was right behind her, shouting as they shattered into a million pieces.

Giana awoke feeling sore in the all the right places. During the night, Wynn had made love to her multiple times, as if he was making up for lost time. Her blood was still fizzing from the amazing orgasm he'd given her before going downstairs to make breakfast. Giana lost track of time, having fallen asleep on and off through the night as Wynn took her to new heights.

He returned to the bed wearing boxer shorts and carrying a tray. She would never tire of looking at him: the broad, well-muscled shoulders, defined abs, lean waist and tightest butt she'd ever encountered. He was irresistible.

She sat up on the bed, pushing the pillows back and not caring that she was completely bare-chested. "What have you got there?" she inquired as he placed the tray on her lap.

"Exactly what I promised if you had stayed a week ago," Wynn stated. "Enjoy." He brushed his lips across hers.

"Looks delicious." Giana grabbed a fork and took a sliver of what she imagined to be a veggie omelet. The flavors exploded in her mouth. "Mmm," she moaned. "This *is* delicious. You really are a good cook."

"Thank you. I need you to keep your strength up if you're going to keep up with me."

Giana laughed. "I've never had someone with so much… er…stamina."

Wynn laughed. "Probably because I've been celibate for a few years."

"You have? Why?" She was stunned by his admission. She'd known he was a recluse, but not *that much of one.*

He shrugged. "After my divorce, I was very ambivalent about the opposite sex. I thought it was better if I focused on building my company. Plus, I was in the middle of taking Starks Inc. public, and it seemed a better use of my energy."

"That explains your enthusiasm in the bedroom now," Giana said, spearing another forkful of omelet.

"Are you worrying if you can keep up with me?"

"Why do you always doubt me?" Giana said. "I assure you, Mr. Starks, I can keep up with the likes of you."

"Care to prove it?" Wynn asked with a smirk.

Giana placed her tray on the nightstand and then pushed Wynn down onto the bed and straddled him. "Allow me to show you."

Giana rushed up from the guesthouse to the Lockett mansion for their weekly Sunday dinner. She'd had to rush out of bed with Wynn to the shower. She'd told him she wouldn't be available for the evening because of their family dinner. He'd been surprised families still did that sort of thing, but he understood. They promised to get together tomorrow after work.

Giana was in an actual relationship, dating exclusively. Wynn had once again brought up the word *exclusive* in bed yesterday afternoon after their marathon lovemaking session. He seemed obsessed with the word, from making sure the Atlanta Cougars only did Starks Inc. sports drink endorsements to making it clear he wouldn't share Giana with another man.

She'd explained she wasn't seeing anyone, but she did plan on keeping her status to herself at dinner. She loved her family, but they could be busybodies.

"Greetings!" she yelled as she walked into the family room and saw the entire Lockett clan gathered around the fireplace. It was a chilly day, and she'd wrapped the wide, faux fur lapels of her wool coat tight around her as she walked up from the guesthouse.

"Darling! There you are." Her mother, Angelique, came toward her. She'd recently cut her shoulder-length jet-black hair into a bob, but it was still perfectly styled, as was the trouser and sweater set with pearls she wore. Her peanut butter complexion was flawless with minimal makeup.

"Hi, Mom." Giana accepted her kiss and hug. "Sorry I'm late."

"It's not like you, Gigi," Julian said with a knowing smirk from behind their mother.

"Time slipped away from me," Giana responded, glaring at him. She walked over to her father by the fireplace and stood on her tippy toes to brush a kiss across his cheek. "Daddy."

"Baby girl." He smiled down at her. "You're looking radiant."

"I wonder why." Julian snickered.

"Do you know something we don't, boy?" Their father's voice boomed over at his middle son.

"Of course not." Julian ignored the curious look on Josiah's face and went to sit next to his wife.

"I, for one, think we should be celebrating Gigi's accomplishment this week," Josiah stated.

"I agree," Roman said, trying to keep Ethan from running around the room. "Shows what hard work and true grit can do. Let me get you a drink. What will you have?" he asked, glancing in Giana's direction.

"I'll have a bourbon neat."

"Since when do you drink bourbon?" her mother asked. "Isn't that a man's drink?"

"Women drink it, too," Giana defended herself. She was starting to like the liquor since it was Wynn's favorite.

"Bourbon coming right up." Roman headed to the bar and began making her drink.

Giana desperately wanted the heat off her and headed toward her nephew, who was sitting on her sister-in-law Shantel's lap. "Hey, sis." She gave her a kiss on the cheek. "How's Ethan?"

"As big as ever," Shantel responded. When Giana went to pull the baby into her arms and take a seat beside her, Shantel whispered in her ear, "You might want to cover the love mark on your neck."

Giana flushed with embarrassment. "Really?"

Shantel nodded, and Giana immediately pulled up the turtleneck she was wearing. She was going to kill Wynn!

"Here you are, Gigi." Roman came forward and handed her a bourbon, which his son thought was for him. "Not for you, little man." Roman placed the tumbler on the cocktail table. "I'll set this aside for when you're ready."

"Does everyone have a drink?" Josiah asked. "A toast to Gigi."

The entire Lockett family lifted their glasses.

"Thank you, everyone. You didn't need to, but I appreciate the shout-out," Giana said.

"I'm surprised Starks held out for as long as he did," Roman replied. "You're like a dog with a bone when you want something. You won't let go."

"Rome!" his mother quickly chastised him. "Your sister is not a dog."

Roman rolled his eyes. "Not what I meant. Only that she's tenacious."

"It's how I raised her to be." Her father's chest was puffed up with pride.

"You'll never find a husband that way, Giana," her mother responded. "Sometimes a man wants a soft place to land."

"Oh, for Christ's sake, Angie. Let Gigi have the win."

Her mother only allowed their father to call her Angie. To everyone else, it was Angelique. "Fine. I want the best for my only daughter, and now the boys are settled, I'd like to see Giana start thinking about marriage and having a family."

"One day, Mama. One day," Giana replied. She handed her nephew back to Shantel, picked up her glass and headed to the French doors, where Xavier had parked himself away from the fray.

Giana sipped her bourbon. "Why are you hiding out over here? Calling your girl?"

Xavier gave her the evil eye. "I told you I was keeping that on the down low. Just like I'm keeping your little secret."

Giana frowned. "What secret?"

Xavier chuckled, and she watched him swipe his iPhone screen several times before showing it to her. Giana gasped. In living color, for the entire world to see, was a picture of her and Wynn at Latitudes in a lip lock.

"Who else has seen this?" she whispered.

"Just me," Xavier replied with a grin. "But it won't stay a secret for long. You're a Lockett, Gigi."

"Damn!" she muttered underneath her breath.

"What are you two conspiring over here about?" Julian asked, coming into their tight circle.

"Nothing," Xavier said, deadpan.

"You're a terrible liar, X," Julian stated and looked at Giana. "Is this about WS?" He used Wynn's initials.

"You know about him and Gigi?" Xavier inquired.

"Uh, yeah. I'm her big brother and confidant," Julian responded.

"Excuse me," Giana said. "I'm standing right here, and I don't appreciate being talked about as if I'm not. Julian, to answer your question, Wynn and I went out the other night, and it appears we were captured on camera."

Xavier handed Julian the phone. "Oh!" Julian exclaimed.

"What?" She glared at him. "I'm a grown woman."

"Clearly," Julian stated, handing the phone back to Xavier. "But this will get out, you know."

"Understood, and I'll handle it in my own way. But for now can we enjoy a quiet family dinner?"

"Sure, sis." Xavier put the phone away. "Tonight is about your victory."

However, the victory was hollow for Giana, because she knew the real world would quickly impede on the little bubble she and Wynn had created for themselves over the weekend. The two of them would be a big scoop, and everyone in town would want to know how reclusive billionaire Wynn Starks had snagged Atlanta's football princess.

Giana would have to put on her thinking cap and figure out how she could spin this in their favor.

Twelve

Giana couldn't believe how easily she'd gone from career-minded single girl to lust-starved female in a week, but she had, and it was all because of Wynn. He brought out the sensual side of her nature and her competitive spirit. This morning after she'd woken up in bed alone, she'd found him downstairs in his gym pounding a punching bag. She'd greedily drunk in his naked torso and clearly defined muscles.

Then she'd joined Wynn. He'd picked up a couple of punch pads and allowed Giana to give it a go. She surprised him by launching a few jabs she'd learned from her brothers, but Wynn was fast and ducked quickly. That only spurred Giana on until eventually she landed a right uppercut on Wynn's jaw, making him stumble backward. She smiled when she thought about Wynn reaching for her in retribution until she landed on the mat underneath him. Her clothes quickly evaporated, and the rest, as they say, was history.

"Care to walk with me to get some coffee?" Roman asked

from the doorway of her office as he interrupted Giana's sexual rewind several days later.

"Sure," Giana said, joining him in a walk to the cafeteria in high-heeled stilettos, tailored slacks and a silk blouse. "What's going on?"

"Not here." Roman shook his head as they passed several executives on their way.

Giana glanced at him, not liking his authoritative tone. Once they were alone again and nearly to the cafeteria, she grabbed her brother's arm and pulled him aside. "Roman, what's going on?"

"Maybe you can tell me," he said, pulling out his phone to show her a picture of her and Wynn kissing on Friday night.

Giana sucked in a breath. "So, you know. So what?"

"So what?" Roman's voice rose. "How long has this been going on, Gigi?"

"That's none of your business."

"Like hell it isn't," he hissed quietly. "Is this why Starks gave us his business? Please tell me you didn't—"

"Don't you dare finish the rest of the sentence, Roman Lockett. The partnership between Starks Inc. and the Atlanta Cougars is a good one. This had nothing to do with our private relationship."

Roman lowered his head. "Of course. I'm sorry. I shouldn't have implied otherwise. It's just…" He paused. "When I saw the photo, I wanted to punch the guy for messing with my baby sister. I know how hard you lobbied for his business, and if he took advantage of you in any way…"

"I'll tell you what I told Julian and Xavier. I'm a grown woman and I can fight my own battles."

Roman's eyes grew wide with concern. "Are you telling me *they* knew about this before me?"

Giana rolled her eyes and folded her arms across her chest. "It's not a competition, Roman. But yes, I confided in Julian. And Xavier, he saw me coming in late."

"If he saw you, then that means…"

Giana smiled. "He was creeping, too."

"Does everyone in this family have secrets?" Roman wondered aloud. "Now that I'm married with a baby, I seem to be out of the loop."

"You're not, Rome," Giana said, tucking one arm through his as they walked. "But you are in a different phase in your life. And it's okay. I'm glad you're happy with Shantel and Ethan."

Roman grinned, showing off his naturally straight teeth. Giana had always been jealous; she'd needed to get braces when she was twelve to achieve her pearly whites. "Thank you, Gigi. So, what are you going to do?"

"What do you mean? Wynn and I are dating. Or at least we started to, and we'll take it from there."

"Is that what you're going to tell Mom and Dad?"

"I haven't exactly gotten that far. This is a very new development. Can't I have a second to enjoy it before I have to figure it all out?"

"Of course. I want you to be aware Mama is going to hear wedding bells."

"She can hear them all she wants, but right now this is totally casual." Or at least that's what Giana was telling herself, even though her belly flip-flopped and her heart skipped a beat every time she saw Wynn.

I mean, really, when all is said and done, how long will it really last?

"How would you like to respond to a request for interviews about your relationship with Ms. Lockett?" Sam asked Wynn later that afternoon.

"My relationship?"

"Yes, several local newspapers caught wind of your outing on Friday night."

"They did?" Wynn asked, coming toward Sam, who was nervously holding his iPad.

"Oh, I forgot, you hate social media," Sam said. "Which

is why I keep track of yours. You and Ms. Lockett were caught in a rather compromising position at Latitudes, and it's been tweeted several times. Here, look." Sam handed Wynn the iPad.

There it was in color, for all the world to see: Giana and him wrapped up in each other's arms as if they couldn't get close enough. Wynn scanned a few lines of one of the articles, which was all speculation on how *he* as a reclusive bachelor was ready to let loose with Atlanta's favorite daughter.

He thrust the iPad back at Sam. "You can respond with no comment. I'm not going to discuss my love life with the media."

"You realize that's only going to fan the flames."

"Maybe, but I'll need to speak with Giana first. Can you give me some privacy?"

"Of course," Sam said, leaving the office. Once the door closed, Wynn reached inside his jeans pocket and pulled out his iPhone. Over the weekend, he'd made sure Giana put her personal number in his phone so he had direct access to her and vice versa, whenever the mood struck.

She answered on the second ring. "Hey, you."

"Hey, yourself," Wynn said. "How's your day going?"

"Well, it could be better if I wasn't dodging questions about the nature of our relationship. How long we've been seeing each other and the like. How about you?"

"Same. It's why I called. I thought we should sync up on our stories."

"There is no story but the truth," Giana replied evenly. "We're newly dating."

"Do you really think the media will take that at face value?" Wynn inquired. He'd known some salacious tabloids to make up fodder just to sell newspapers.

"If you want, we can tell our side of the story. You know, make it official. I've got the annual Christmas event coming up on Saturday night, and I'm in need of a date. Care to join me?"

"Of course. Will I see you later?"

"Afraid not. I have a 6:00 p.m. meeting with one of my players and their agent."

Wynn glanced at his watch. It was only three o'clock. "No problem. I'll wait for you."

Seven hours later, Wynn was starting to get anxious. He'd known Giana was going to be late, but he hadn't anticipated she'd be occupied the entire night. He'd already run five miles, made dinner and watched *Jeopardy!*, his favorite guilty pleasure, before falling off to sleep. He hadn't realized how late it was until the ten o'clock news came on and Giana hadn't arrived.

Despite telling himself their relationship was casual, Wynn had gone through the trouble of lighting some candles and chilling a bottle of champagne, but now the candles were burned to the wick and the ice in the champagne bucket had melted. He was surprised when his doorbell rang.

Wynn glanced down at his watch. It was ten fifteen. He slowly walked to the door and looked through the window, making out a feminine form.

Giana.

He swung open the door. "Do you have any idea—"

The words died on his lips when he saw what Giana was wearing: a trench coat open to reveal the most delicious lace bustier and G-string getup. The jet-black creation was trimmed in red and tied together at the waist. It flattered every curve from the lace cups showing her ample cleavage to her round hips, which gave way to slender thighs encased in a pair of sheer thigh-high stockings attached to garters.

Wynn licked his lips.

"I'm sorry I'm late," Giana began with a sexy pout on her scarlet-red lips, "but I was hoping this might make up for it?"

"Come here, woman." He hauled her to him, lifting her

off her feet and carrying her inside the house. He brought his mouth down hard on hers, his hand tightening in her hair, which she'd blessedly left hanging in soft curls down her shoulders. He kissed her fiercely, instantly lost in the heat and softness of her lips. When he deepened the kiss, her fingers curled around him, gripping, tugging and tearing at his shirt. Once he was bare-chested, she ran her fingers over his skin, touching his stomach, and his body became taut.

"I need you now, Giana." His voice was thick with desire.

"I need you, too."

Wynn didn't think he was going to make it to his bedroom, and he didn't even try, because she was already tugging at his belt, then the button and zipper on his jeans, finally dragging them down his legs. He stepped out of them only to return and kiss her anywhere he could find purchase: her face, her throat, her collarbone. And when he came to her breasts, he cupped them before bending down to lick the tips through the fabric of her bustier. They hardened beneath his tongue, so he took one nipple in his mouth and sucked hard through the fabric.

"Wynn..."

He heard the pleading in her voice and answered by wrapping one of her legs around his waist and snatching the flimsy G-string fabric away, ripping it into shreds. He would have to get her a new one. In the meantime, he reveled in the way Giana melted against his fingertips, rocking against his hand. He felt her tighten around his fingers.

"Don't stop," she gasped. "Don't stop—"

Her muscles tensed and she gasped, arching her back as she completely unraveled around him.

Giana felt dazed and disoriented. She watched Wynn reach for a condom in his jeans pocket while simultaneously holding her upright. He tore it open with his teeth and smoothed it on his steel length. Then he was shifting upward and driving inside her.

"Wynn—"

He kissed her through her moan, swallowing her words as pure animal instinct took over. She tilted her hips, welcoming the sweet intrusion of having his length fill her. Then he began thrusting hard and fast, giving her exactly what she needed. Her nails sank into Wynn's shoulders as she surrendered to the moment, and soon, Giana found herself tipping closer toward the edge.

Wynn growled low in his throat as he found a steady rhythm and pounded into her. When he reached the pinnacle, he called out her name, and she called out his when yet another orgasm rocked through her. Their voices were a harmony of pleasure and need. Afterward, Giana's legs gave way, and she might have fallen to the floor, but Wynn held her up with his strong hands and thighs.

"I've got you," he murmured.

And he did. In one swift movement, he was swinging her into his arms and kicking his clothes out of the way as he strode toward his bedroom.

Thirteen

"Tell me again why I agreed to do this," Wynn said when he and Giana were on their way to her Christmas charity event the next Saturday. He looked especially handsome in a black tuxedo with satin lapels and a black shirt.

"Because you agreed to my terms." Giana smoothed her hair, which she wore in an elegant side-swept style that went well with her one-shouldered tulle gown by Elie Saab. Giana adored the dress's glittering gold and burgundy colors. Intricate beading ran across the bodice and down one side, while the other side was slightly sheer and had a flower pattern. "We can't just stay at your place. We have to go out sometime."

Over the last week, when she wasn't at work or overseeing one of the numerous charities funded by the Lockett Foundation, she had been with Wynn. After Monday night, when she'd arrived at his place in a trench coat and lingerie, their relationship had settled into an easy rhythm. A few nights Wynn cooked, which Giana was happy about, because she hadn't inherited her mother's natural penchant for domesticity.

Wynn, meanwhile, loved to show his culinary skills. And now that he knew she was a pescatarian, he'd cooked several new dishes that had turned out to be quite delicious.

"We went out last night," Wynn said, fidgeting with the bow tie she'd insisted he wear because it matched the colors of her dress. She knew their being matchy-matchy might make a statement that they were a couple, but they'd both agreed they would make their relationship status official tonight. Not only with the media, but also her family.

Her parents would be on hand for tonight's event, and as general manager of the Atlanta Cougars, Roman was sure to attend with Shantel. When she'd asked Julian if he was going to make it for moral support, he'd told her Elyse was feeling under the weather, so Giana gave him a pass to stay home with his ill wife. That left Xavier to accompany her as her backup plan, but her younger sibling had been MIA the last few days, so Giana was on her own.

"Don't get me wrong. I appreciated last night," Giana responded. They'd met up with Silas and Janelle, who was in town for a photo shoot. They'd all gone to the blues club where Roman had taken Tim and Curtis Jackson when he was trying to convince Curtis to sign with the Atlanta Cougars. Even though it wasn't the sort of place Giana would normally frequent, she'd enjoyed herself tremendously. However, every time she'd looked over at Silas and Janelle, she could tell they were so in love, it had made Giana envious. Would she and Wynn be that way one day?

"But?" Wynn prompted.

Giana turned to him. "But tonight is a big deal. Aren't you nervous?"

"Not at all. I already know your father and Roman. I'm sure I can charm your mother."

Giana chuckled. She loved Wynn's arrogance and confidence. "Yes, but you met Josiah and Roman in a business capacity, not as the man sleeping with their daughter or sister."

"True," Wynn said, "but I can't sweat the small stuff. I am who I am. They can either take me or leave me."

And that second possibility was exactly what Giana was afraid of.

Exiting the limo, Giana and Wynn were greeted by flashing lights and a crowd of reporters. She caught a couple of "who are you wearing tonight" questions, but the majority were "how long have you and Wynn been a couple?" and "when did you start dating?"

"No comment." Wynn politely waved aside the questions, then took her hand.

Their plan was to give an exclusive to one of the more reputable magazines, but first they had to get through tonight. Giana was pleased when the event coordinator came forward and told her everything was going smoothly. "Thank you, Clarissa. The place looks marvelous. It has just the right amount of Christmas spirit."

There were wreaths on the walls and garlands decorated with twigs, winterberry and silvery pine cones swathing the doors. Red and white paper bells hung down from the ceiling, and an enormous Christmas tree held a cascade of colorful ornaments.

"Are my parents here yet?" Giana asked.

"They're with the Whitmores," Clarissa responded. "I believe your mother is trying to get her to increase her donation."

"If anyone can, it's my mother. Thank you." Giana touched the older woman's shoulder and glanced up at Wynn. "Are you ready?"

"No time like the present." He took her hand and they walked over to her parents as Doug and Malorie Whitmore were leaving.

"Good evening." Giana smiled as she approached her

parents. She caught the surprised look in her father's eye at her choice of companion. "Daddy, I believe you know Wynn, but Mama, you haven't met. Allow me to introduce you to Wynn Starks."

"Wynn Starks of Starks Inc.?" her mother inquired with a raised brow.

"One and the same, ma'am," Wynn replied.

"Well, well." Her mother smiled from ear to ear. "Wonders never cease. Come, young man." She circled her arm through Wynn's. "Tell me more about yourself."

Wynn glanced at Giana, and she shrugged. He would either sink or swim, but Giana was certain he would swim.

Once they'd gone, her father turned to her. "Starks, huh? I didn't know you were so well acquainted."

"We are. Care for a drink, Daddy?"

"I'll have some of the bourbon you've been prone to drinking lately."

Giana smiled and signaled to a waiter. "C'mon, Daddy. I know you have something to say."

"Damn right," he said, grabbing her arm and pulling her aside so they couldn't be overheard. "How long have you been in bed with Starks?"

"Daddy!" Giana flushed.

"I didn't mean literally, but clearly I'm on to something."

"I'm not going to dignify that with a response."

"You don't have to." Her father glanced over at Wynn, who appeared to be regaling her mother with a story, because Giana could hear her laughter all the way across the room. Wynn really could charm the socks off any woman when he wanted to.

"I thought you wanted to focus on your career and not get bogged down," her father continued.

"We're dating, Daddy."

His thick, bushy eyebrows rose in question. "I don't think so, baby girl. That man—" he inclined his head "—is the kind of man you marry. He's going to want a house full of children and you flat on your back."

"Good lord, Daddy. What am I going to do with you? Are you stuck in the '50s?"

"I'm not, but I know a man's man when I see one, and Wynn is not used to two chiefs."

"That may be so, but I can hold my own against any man, Wynn included. No one is going to stop me from reaching my goals."

"All right, Gigi, no need to try and convince me. At least not yet. But a time will come when you might have to choose which you want more—a good man or your career."

Her father left Giana to rejoin his wife, at which point Wynn excused himself. As the new man in her life came striding toward her, full of swagger, Giana wondered if her father was right.

Would she have to choose?

Wynn had nearly reached Giana when a familiar figure clad in a silver lamé gown, with café au lait skin and a long, sleek ponytail, came into his line of vision. He didn't need to be a rocket scientist to figure out who she was. He would know—or rather *smell*—her anywhere.

His ex.

Christine Davis.

She wore a scent that used to drive him crazy but now was an annoyance. He'd made it his duty in life to ensure their paths never crossed. Wynn supposed it was why the media had dubbed him a recluse, and that was fine with him. He liked his alone time. But Christine had always had a way of getting under his skin. He prayed tonight, in front of Giana and her family, wasn't one of those nights.

"Wynn, what a surprise to see you here," Christine purred out of fire engine–red lips. She was overly made up from her lips to the outrageous lashes she wore.

"Christine." Wynn stepped away from her, but she moved

in front of him to block his path. He sighed. If she didn't want to play nice, neither would he. "What do you want?"

"Want? For starters, I'd like more of the green stuff you swindled me out of in the prenuptial agreement, but I'll have to make do with what I have."

"You were generously compensated for the two—" he held up two fingers "—years of our marriage. You were entitled to nothing more and nothing less."

Her eyes narrowed into thin slits. "I *should* have been given much more for putting up with the likes of you, especially since you were such a bore in bed."

He knew she was trying to goad him and quickly fired back, "I don't think my lady minds." Wynn hated himself the moment he stooped to his ex's level.

Christine's head immediately swung around so she could regard Giana, who was standing across the room. She was head and shoulders above the rest of the women here, and she knew it. When he'd arrived to pick her up at the Lockett mansion in Tuxedo Park, he'd been blown away by her beauty.

"Oh, she will," Christine said, spinning back around to face him. "Just as I was. She's using you to get her jollies, or even to make a statement to her parents, but at the end of the day, a woman like her isn't interested in a man like you for the long term. You're not even in the same class as her. Mark my words—you have a short shelf life, Wynn."

"Go to hell!" Wynn's voice was raised, and several people looked over at him to see what had precipitated such an outburst. Meanwhile Christine was smiling like a cat that got the cream. She'd provoked him, as she'd intended, but he wasn't going to give her any more fodder. Instead, he headed straight for the open bar. Once there, he ordered a double of the finest bourbon they had available.

"Wynn."

He turned to see Roman Lockett at his side. "Roman. What can I do for you?"

"One, you can try not embarrassing my family any further, and two, you can make sure that you don't hurt my sister."

Wynn regarded him. He appreciated the big brother routine, but he wasn't in the mood. He sipped his bourbon. "Why would you think either of those two things would happen?"

"That little outburst a moment ago," Roman whispered, "was in poor taste. Perhaps you should keep your past where it belongs."

Wynn wanted to punch Roman. He really did, but the man was right. He shouldn't have let Christine rile him up. But at the same time, he wouldn't be pushed around by Christine or Roman. Hell, by anyone.

"You have nothing to fear from me." Wynn downed the rest of his bourbon. "And for the record, I'm a grown-ass man, Roman. I've got this." He placed his glass on the bar and stepped away to find his lady.

Why was everyone trying to get in their way? Giana hadn't been lying when she said becoming official tonight would have its challenges. He'd charmed her mother well enough, but then Christine and now Roman had put up roadblocks. *Was it any wonder he was on edge?*

Stalking away from Roman, he scanned the crowd for Giana. She'd moved from her last location, but he found her near the doorway of the ballroom. When he approached, she smiled and held out her hand to welcome him, lacing their fingers together. The small gesture was exactly what he needed.

A soft place to land.

Fourteen

"Do you want to talk about what happened tonight?" Giana asked on the ride back to the Lockett mansion. She'd told Wynn she wanted to go home because she planned to do some Christmas shopping tomorrow with her sisters-in-law, Shantel and Elyse. That was true, but she also wanted a night alone to herself, because she felt different.

Wynn wasn't her run-of-the-mill relationship. The other men she'd been with had lacked the maturity and thoughtfulness she'd found with Wynn. And talk about intense—the sex between them was so intimate. He wanted all of her, and it made her feel helpless and a bit off balance. Giana had never shown up to another man's house wearing lingerie. She wouldn't have dared. She was Giana Lockett, chief marketing and branding officer of the Atlanta Cougars, but Wynn made her feel carefree, as if anything were possible.

"Not really," Wynn responded, and Giana blinked several times to remind herself of what she'd asked. Oh yes, if he wanted to talk about yelling at his ex-wife.

Giana had caught the exchange between them earlier. Afterward, Wynn had been reserved when he joined her. Her family might not have noticed the change, because his expression had been serene, but Giana was beginning to be able to read his moods by the angle of his jaw or the glitter in his eye.

The rest of her family had seen his public face because he refused to let on he was upset, but Giana knew otherwise.

"You don't have to lie to me, Wynn. I thought you agreed to a relationship at least in theory, and part of that means sharing your feelings."

"If you recall, I opted for sex, exclusive sex," Wynn said with a grin, sliding closer to her on the seat.

"Oh no, you don't." Giana held up a hand against his chest. "Don't try to thwart my questions by seduction." Though he wouldn't have to try very hard. A shiver raced through her at feeling his hard chest against her palm.

"Damn." Wynn sighed and leaned back against the seat. He faced the windows for several moments, and Giana wondered if he was going to ignore her. But then he said, "I shouldn't have let Christine get to me. I'm sorry if I embarrassed you or your family."

"You didn't do any such thing," Giana stated fiercely. "*She* approached you. It wasn't the other way around."

"Yeah, but I rose to the occasion."

The limo slowly came to a halt, and Giana thought that was the end of their conversation and their night. But instead, when the chauffeur opened her door, Wynn got out and walked with her to the guesthouse. She was hoping he wouldn't leave and they could pick up where they left off. Once she'd unlocked the door, she turned on several lamps, flooding the living room with light.

"This is an awfully nice guesthouse," Wynn said, looking around and running his hand along the marble fireplace.

Giana saw the large living space through his eyes. It was open and airy and, in the morning, sunlight flooded the room from the myriad of windows. She loved to sit in the bay window seat with her morning cup of coffee and soak up the rays.

"It is, but I don't really want to talk about decor, Wynn, and I think you know that. I want to know why tonight upset you."

Wynn turned around to face her, and Giana could see he was warring with himself over his answer, but in the end he said, "Because… Christine and I have been divorced for over three years. I thought I'd safely put her in a box where she couldn't get to me. I guess I was wrong."

"No, you're human, Wynn," Giana replied. "Although it's long over, she once meant something to you."

"I refuse to give her that kind of power over me. She doesn't deserve it. She's a liar and a cheat!"

"Okay, now we're getting somewhere, because you're telling me how you really feel."

"You really want to hear the ugly truth, Giana? I'll tell you. Christine was looking for a sucker and she found one in me, the lonely boy who'd never felt loved by his mother. She said all the right things to make me believe she wanted a husband and a family, but she didn't. I think I was some sort of social experiment for her. A project, if you will. A way to rebel against the man her parents wanted her to marry. The man she ended up cheating on me with."

"Oh my God!" Giana's hand flew to her mouth. "I had no idea."

"Because I keep my private life private, Giana." Wynn rubbed his palm across his closely cropped hair. "I kept that out of the divorce proceedings because I didn't want them to get any uglier than they already were. Just like my mother left my father, Christine left me for another man, and just like my mother she tried to take me to the cleaner's."

"I thought you had a prenup?"

"We did. And I'm glad that despite how besotted I was, I insisted on one before we married," Wynn explained. "However, while we were separated, Christine got wind of my plans to take Starks Inc. public, and she tried to delay the proceedings. But in the end, we divorced before the IPO."

"Is that why she's so incensed?"

Wynn shrugged. "Partly. And because I didn't beg to take her back. She took me for such a dope that she thought I would, but I didn't. She's been furious ever since."

"Thank you for telling me, Wynn."

"You said you wanted me *all in*? Well, I am in, Giana. Are you sure you're ready to take me with all my baggage?" Wynn asked. "Because it's not too late to bail and go back to just sex."

He said it with a crooked grin, but Giana knew he was trying to make light of having spoken his truth. "Not at all." She reached behind her and began to unzip her dress. "In fact, I would say I want to go forward." She inclined her head toward the bedroom as her dress dropped to the floor, leaving her in a thong and nothing more.

Naked hunger was etched across Wynn's face. Seconds later, his lips were crushing hers in a kiss designed to taste, torment, dominate and give. Giana wrapped her arms around his neck and her legs around his waist as Wynn swiftly carried her to the bedroom.

"Good morning," Giana cheerily said when she walked into the kitchen of the main house the next morning. After they shared a shower, a car had come to pick up Wynn and take him back home, leaving Giana to face the music alone. She found her father and mother already sitting at the breakfast table surrounded by platters heaping with bacon, eggs and pastries.

"Good morning." Her mother regarded her as Giana took a seat across from her. "You're very chipper."

"I feel great." And she did, despite having stayed up half the night offering herself as a balm to Wynn's wounds. He'd taken her again and again, her name constantly on his lips as an incantation or a prayer—Giana couldn't be sure which, because it had been mingled with her own fervent cries of pleasure. Eventually, they'd both fallen into a deep sleep. Giana felt as if she'd truly come home. She'd never had this feeling before with any other man, not even Martin. That had been child's play. When it came to how deeply Wynn touched her, she found herself starting to believe in happily-ever-after.

Giana thanked Gerard when he came and filled her mug with steaming-hot coffee. She quickly took a sip.

"That's good, darling," her mother said. "I was so happy to meet that new young man of yours, Wynn Starks. He's very intense, but charming."

She felt herself smile. "Thanks, Mama."

"It got me to thinking."

"Oh Lord, woman," her father replied, rolling his eyes upward. "What have you got cooking in that mind of yours?" He put down his coffee cup.

"Nothing bad." She reached across the table and patted his hand. Then she turned to Giana. "With Christmas right around the corner, I was thinking you should ask Wynn to join us at the cabin in Gatlinburg. He could spend the holiday with the family."

"Really?" Giana was floored. Usually, her mother only wanted family around. "Are you sure?"

"Of course. I can see how taken you are with him and vice versa. Seems only fitting we should get to know him better. I mean, who knows, he could be a part of this family someday."

"Hush, your mouth, woman," her father tsked. "She's just dating Starks."

Her mother shrugged. "I know what I saw, Josiah."

"And what did you see?" Giana inquired. She was curious if she'd given off any sort of vibe of her growing feelings for Wynn.

"I saw two people falling in love."

Giana's stomach plummeted. *Love. Her mother thought they were in love.* She'd barely been able to get Wynn to commit to the idea of a relationship, let alone the word *love.* She was still struggling with how to describe her feelings for Wynn, but love? "Look at the time." Giana glanced down at her watch. "I have to get going."

"So soon?" her mother asked. "You've only had coffee."

Giana reached across the table to grab a croissant off the platter heaped with pastries. "I'm meeting Shantel and Elyse for some last-minute Christmas shopping. I'll take this to go. Have a great day." She quickly kissed both her parents and made a hasty exit.

Once she was in the corridor, Giana leaned against the wall and inhaled deeply. Her mother had it wrong. Or did she? Giana felt different than she had with Martin. She wanted to spend all her free time with Wynn, in and out of bed. She laughed at his silly jokes, watched the old martial arts movies he liked even though she didn't understand a thing, had even started running with him. And their physical connection was off the charts. Did that mean she was in love? Giana wasn't scared that she might fall in love. She was scared Wynn might never allow himself to.

"Dad, it's so good to hear from you," Wynn said when his father called him that afternoon. "How are you enjoying the cruise?"

Now that he'd *made it,* Wynn had told his father to quit his day job, because if he had anything to say about it, Jeffrey Starks would never have to work again. Wynn hadn't forgotten how his father scrimped and saved so there was always a roof over his head and food on the table. And growing up, Wynn had had a bottomless pit for a stomach. He definitely understood his mentees at the Boys & Girls Club always being hungry.

"It's been the best time of my life," Jeffrey said. "Now I know how the other half lives."

"I'm glad," Wynn responded.

"I've even met someone."

"You have?"

"Yes, she's a widow. Her husband left her with a large sum, so she'll never have to worry about money, and she's traveling the world."

"And you would like to join her?" Wynn asked the question his dad was beating around the bush getting to.

"I think so. It's been so long since I've felt this way, son."

"I know, Dad." It had been hard on his father to lose the love of his life to another man. After the divorce, his father became withdrawn. Although he'd tried to be there for Wynn, a light went out in his eyes. Wynn would give anything to see his father happy again.

"But Christmas is in a few days," his father said on the other end of the line. "I wouldn't want to leave you alone."

"I'm not a child."

"I know, but it's always been me and you. It's our tradition."

"And we'll still have it," Wynn responded. "But I want you to be happy, and if exploring this new relationship will do that, then you should go."

"But I can't possibly afford—"

"I told you not to worry about finances," Wynn interrupted. "I have you covered. Whatever you need, whatever you want. I'll add a sizable amount to your account, that way you can take as much or as little as you need."

"Son, it's so extravagant."

"You deserve it." *And a whole lot more*, Wynn thought.

"What will you do for Christmas?"

"Work."

"Work isn't everything, son. You have to make room in your life for more."

Wynn's mind wandered to Giana. There was so much more he intended to do with her. And it surprised him how excited he was at the prospect. After Christine, he hadn't thought he was capable of loving anyone, but if anyone made him want to be a believer again, it was Giana.

"Don't you worry about me, Dad. I'll be fine."

They ended the call with promises of reconnecting in the new year. Afterward, Wynn wondered what he was going to do with his time. Now that the holidays were approaching, he usually gave his staff time off to spend time with their families. But with his dad out of town, Wynn was going to have find something or *someone* to occupy *his* time.

Fifteen

"Tell us what's really going on between you and Wynn Starks," Shantel said while she, Giana and Elyse shopped at the Lennox Mall.

"Yeah, I'm dying to know, too." Elyse's eyes were lit up with merriment. "But if you don't mind, I'd like to take a seat." They'd been at it for a few hours, racking up toys for Ethan and Elyse's baby girl due next year, as well as gifts for Roman and Julian.

Giana struggled with what if anything to get Wynn. In the end, because he loved to cook, she'd settled for a grill and spice set along with a chef's hat and coat. But picking his gift wasn't the only thing on Giana's mind; her mother had thrown her for a loop when she'd said they looked like two people falling in love. Giana hadn't been able to get the thought out of her head all day.

"How about we stop here for a snack?" Giana asked. They were near the food court, and Elyse had been eyeing the Auntie Anne's pretzels.

"Did you catch that?" Shantel asked Elyse, giving Giana the side eye. "The way she changed the subject? But we're on to you."

"What?" Giana asked. "Elyse is eating for two."

Elyse laughed. "You're so thoughtful, Giana. And while, yes, I would love to eat an entire batch of those mini pretzel hot dogs drenched in sweet mustard, I want to hear more about you and Wynn."

"We're dating," Giana answered honestly. "I'm not sure what my brothers might have told you, but there's not much more."

"No?" Shantel asked. "You seem awfully cagey."

"C'mon, Shantel. That's not fair. You shouldn't psychoanalyze family," Giana said.

Shantel shrugged. "I'm not, but I can tell when someone is holding something back. Don't know if it's a curse or a gift. Do you want to give us the non-pat answer?"

"She can," Elyse said, rubbing her small belly, "after you get me those pretzel bites."

"See, I knew you were hungry," Giana teased. "I'll go get them." She needed the opportunity to collect her thoughts. Shantel was used to getting people to talk, and Giana wasn't sure she could keep her sister-in-law's curiosity at bay. After obtaining Elyse's sweet and savory snack, she headed back to the duo sitting at one of the café tables.

"Here you are, my dear." Giana handed the box to Elyse along with a lemonade.

"Thank you." Elyse immediately dug into the pretzel bites.

"Now back to me." Shantel used her index and middle fingers to motion for Giana to look into her eyes. "You were going to give us the real deal?"

Giana sighed and then told the truth. "Wynn and I started out as a one-night stand. I was content with that, but then he showed up to my work and said he wanted more than one night."

"How did you feel?" Shantel inquired.

"It surprised me. And I was nervous about mixing business with pleasure. I'm used to keeping my worlds very separate and mixing the two could potentially have disastrous consequences for both companies. Plus, I wasn't looking for anything serious, and he was telling me he wanted to see me exclusively. But everything was on *his* terms. I told him I would only agree if we were in a relationship. Honestly, considering his history of being a recluse, I assumed he would say no. He surprised me when he agreed to my demand."

Elyse laughed as she stuffed more pretzel bites into her mouth. "He called your bluff?"

"Yes, and I couldn't very well take it back, now could I?" And Giana wasn't sure she'd wanted to.

"And now?" Shantel asked quietly. "How do you feel about Wynn?"

"I've grown to care about him," Giana answered honestly. "It wasn't something I was looking for. I mean, my focus is my career. Becoming involved with Wynn is a recipe for drama. What if the attraction fades? Then where are we? I didn't think I had any time for..." She stopped herself before she said the four-letter word, but Shantel picked up on it.

"Love? Well, let me tell you, Giana, you can't predict it or stop it when it happens. You have to allow yourself to feel. And from the looks of it, and this is strictly from the outside looking in, you're trying to block the emotion."

"I agree," Elyse jumped in, brushing crumbs off her face now that she'd demolished the entire snack. "When I realized I was falling for Julian, I thought I could stop it. I mean, I was initially on a revenge mission because I blamed Josiah for my father losing everything. Julian was the enemy. But I can tell you, love is a powerful force and it won't be denied."

"What do I do?" Giana asked, glancing back and forth between the two women.

"Embrace it." Shantel smiled. "I'm not saying it's not scary, but I promise you, Giana, the reward is so worth it."

"Well, I don't know if I'm there yet," Giana said, and she noticed her sisters-in-law exchange a skeptical look. "I'm not."

But she could be, and that scared Giana most of all. Because what if she fell in love with Wynn and he didn't feel the same? What would she do with all these feelings? Giana didn't know if she could box them back up once she'd allowed them to escape. Perhaps spending Christmas with Wynn would give her the clarity she needed to figure out if love was worth it or if she should walk away.

"You want me to spend Christmas with your family?" Wynn asked when Giana came over to his place late Monday evening. If he was honest, he'd missed her yesterday. After discussing his failed marriage following the charity gala, he'd felt closer to Giana. And if he'd had his druthers, they would have spent the entire day in bed yesterday. When she said she had plans with her sisters-in-law and her weekly family dinner, he'd put on his best face not to show his disappointment.

"Yes, would that be such a bad thing?" Giana asked, a frown marring her mocha features.

"No, of course not," Wynn responded, "and I'm sorry if you thought otherwise. I'm surprised. Christmas is usually reserved for family."

"My mother thought since you and I are dating you might..." Her voice faltered, and for the first time Wynn saw the uncertainty in Giana's eyes. He hated himself for making her doubt herself.

"Of course I'll come." Giana gave an audible sigh of relief. "Come here." He patted the sofa beside him. "Let me reassure you how happy I am."

He pulled her toward him. Initially, he felt her reluctance, but with a gentle tug she fell forward into his lap, and Wynn's hand circled to her nape to pull her into a kiss.

When they finally broke apart, they were both breathing hard, but it was Giana's stomach growling that made him ask, "What do you say we think about dinner?"

"Actually, I was thinking I could cook for you."

"Cook for me?" Since they'd started seeing each other, he'd done the majority of the cooking.

Giana punched him on the shoulder. "Don't act so surprised. I may not be as talented as you are in the kitchen, but I can make several good dishes, some of which are strictly vegetarian."

"Of course you can." Wynn laughed. "And I can't wait to try them."

He watched as she eased off the sofa and headed to the kitchen. He didn't know why her suggestion had been a shock, but then again, much of what Giana did wasn't what Wynn expected. She had more depth and character than he'd ever imagined. It made Wynn realize he'd judged her harshly based on his cynical view of the world. It wasn't easy breaking bad habits, but he was going to do his best to try.

He followed her into the kitchen and watched her search through his fridge for ingredients: eggplant, arugula, onions, garlic, fresh spinach, ricotta and eggs, followed by some store-bought marinara sauce and lasagna noodles from the cupboard. Meanwhile, he retrieved a bottle of red wine and poured them two glasses.

"Thank you," she said, taking a sip.

"Okay, I'm intrigued," Wynn said, drinking his wine as he watched her get a chopping board and start slicing and dicing vegetables. "What are you making?"

"Eggplant lasagna. Eggplant is a good substitute for protein. You won't be able to tell the difference." He doubted it. He was a meat and potatoes kind of guy, but he sensed how important it was for Giana to show him a different side of herself.

A spoiled princess wouldn't know her way around a kitchen, but Giana was comfortable roasting the eggplant and sautéing the onion, garlic and spinach. When she was done, she started on a ricotta mixture, which included egg, basil and salt and pepper. Afterward, she began layering a greased baking dish with all her ingredients.

Wynn was impressed. Christine would never have been caught dead getting her hands dirty like this. Although he knew he shouldn't compare the two of them, he didn't get close to a lot of women and didn't have much of a frame of reference. And Giana was so different. He was seeing that more and more each day. There were many facets to her. She was a strong and confident businesswoman, a loving daughter, a proud sister. If you'd asked him a month ago if he'd consider dating, he would have said no, but Giana made Wynn hopeful there were truly some good women left.

When he snapped out of his thoughts, he found Giana putting arugula, pine nuts, basil, garlic and olive oil in a food processor and squeezing a lemon into the mixture. "I guess I should have asked this first, but are you allergic to nuts?" Her hand was on the power button.

"No allergies."

She smiled. "Good." She hit the button. "You'll like this pesto over the lasagna. It gives a bright and peppery finish." When she was done, she turned off the food processor and set aside the arugula pesto. "We've got a bit of time before it's ready." Picking up her glass, she moved and walked in between his legs to peer at him. "So, what do you think?"

"I think I was wrong to doubt your culinary skills."

"Don't judge a book by its cover, Wynn. There's more to me than what you see."

"I know that."

"Do you?"

He nodded. "I do." He wrapped his arms around her

waist. "And I'm thankful you haven't given me the boot after all my preconceived notions."

"No, I think I'll keep you." Her grin was genuine, and it struck a chord deep in Wynn's belly. But he'd been down this road before, falling too hard and too quick. He and Giana were mixing business and pleasure, and that was a slippery slope. One wrong move and they could both fall headlong into disaster, which could severely damage Starks Inc. So why couldn't he walk away from Giana when self-preservation advised him it was the best course of action?

Because if any woman was worth taking a risk on, it was Giana.

Giana was nervous as she and Wynn made the approximately four-hour drive to her parents' mountain-view mansion in Gatlinburg on Wednesday morning. The drive was pleasant enough. They'd left Atlanta early to get a jump on traffic. According to the GPS, they would arrive by early afternoon. Her parents had gone up the night before, and the rest of the family was driving up this morning.

Giana had never invited a man she was dating to participate in a family event, and certainly not one as important as Christmas. Her mother went all out when it came to the holiday. The six-bedroom, seven-and-a-half-bath vacation home would be bursting with holiday decor.

"You're nervous," Wynn said, glancing over at Giana as she drummed her fingers against her jeans. Since it was going to be significantly colder in the mountains, she'd dressed for the occasion in a thick fringe sweater, knee-high boots and her favorite jeans that made her butt look like a million bucks. For his part, Wynn looked delectable in a turtleneck, faded jeans, his favorite leather jacket and boots.

"I'm not."

"Liar." But he didn't say anything more, leaving her to her own thoughts. She didn't know how the weekend would go—all she knew was that it was an important stepping-stone in their relationship. They were establishing themselves as a couple. *Did Wynn understand the significance?*

Giana did.

Her parents would see them as a couple, and it would be a lot harder convincing her mother not to hear marriage bells in their future. But what could she do? If she'd declined the invitation on his behalf, her parents might think negatively of him. And so here they were, driving up the paved driveway past hundreds of trees to the mansion at the top of the hill.

Giana did love the mansion. It was a retreat in the middle of the forest surrounded by nothing but mountains and trees in every direction. When the car came to a stop, Giana took a deep breath and exited the vehicle.

It was certainly chilly out, and she hugged her wool jacket with the faux fur lapels a little bit tighter to her chest.

"Why don't you go ahead inside and get warm," Wynn said as he came around to the trunk. "I'll bring our bags in."

"Sounds like a plan."

She climbed the oversize front steps and opened the front door. "Hello?"

Her mother appeared several seconds later. "Giana!" She rushed toward her, enveloping her in a hug. "Good to see you, sweetheart, but where is Wynn?" She looked behind Giana.

"He's getting the luggage."

"Come in by the fire." Her mother led her into the living room, where her father was already set up in his favorite recliner reading a book.

"Daddy!"

"Baby girl." He rose to greet her with a hug and a kiss. "How was the drive up?"

"Not bad. Minimal traffic."

"Glad to hear it."

Giana looked toward the front door and rushed over to

help Wynn with her bags. She'd overpacked for a four-day weekend and had two suitcases and a carry-on bag.

"Giana, how many clothes do you need?" her mother asked as she approached Wynn. "How are you, my dear?" She kissed his cheek.

"Well, Mrs. Lockett. Thank you so much for inviting me."

"You're absolutely welcome. And I'm afraid you're going to have to take those bags up yourself. We only brought minimal staff—Gerard, and our cook to help me with the meals."

"Not a problem at all," Wynn replied. "Show me where."

"Follow me." Giana grabbed her carry-on while Wynn waddled up the stairs with two large suitcases. "Just down the hall." She motioned for him to go ahead to the last door at the end of the corridor. Since they'd arrived early, they had first choice of bedrooms, and she wouldn't be sandwiched between her brothers.

"This is great, Giana," Wynn said once he opened the door and saw the four-poster bed, the rustic antiques, oriental rugs and separate living room with a fireplace.

"Mom updated it several years ago." She pointed to the white paneled walls and wood beams. "She wanted a farmhouse feel in the middle of the forest, but she kept this original fireplace." Giana fingered the stacked stone.

"It's a nice place to spend Christmas," Wynn said, placing the bags on a luggage rack near the closet.

"Take off your coat and let's go downstairs and have a hot toddy."

"A hot toddy?" Wynn laughed. "I'm certainly not in Kansas anymore."

He wasn't. Neither was she. They were both in new territory here. She'd never really brought a man to meet her family so Wynn's being here was significant. Giana suspected by the end of the weekend, she'd know exactly where they stood and that scared her most of all.

Sixteen

Wynn was moved. Seeing the Locketts in all their glory was a sight to behold. After he and Giana went downstairs, they'd joined her parents for hot toddies in the living room. The drink consisted of his favorite bourbon, honey, lemon juice, a cinnamon stick and four cloves. He wasn't sure if he would like it, but Giana's mother insisted, and he'd rather enjoyed it.

A couple of toddies later, Wynn felt mellow. He supposed that was why he enjoyed the ruckus of the Lockett brood when they arrived. Giana's brothers and their families brought a whole lot of commotion, and they made a big fuss over Roman and Shantel's toddler with their arrival.

Mrs. Lockett went into full nana mode with her grandson. Meanwhile, Giana morphed in front of Wynn's eyes, roughhousing with her brothers, Roman, Julian and late arrival Xavier. She gave as good as she got and didn't mind giving them a hard time, either. Josiah's attempts to corral the bunch were worthless.

They even included Wynn when it was time to decorate the Christmas tree, which had been freshly cut that morning. Apparently, it was a tradition for them to decorate it on the first night of their stay. And Mrs. Lockett had gone all out, bringing out bin after bin of ornaments and decorations. Two hours later, the nine-foot-tall tree was bedecked in white and gold, bearing all the Lockett family trinkets and ornaments.

While the Locketts laughed and talked, Wynn quietly slipped out of the room, drink in hand. He went to the front porch and sank into one of the half dozen Adirondack chairs set out there.

The Locketts' joy and happiness made Wynn sad. Once upon a time, his family had been like the Locketts, but his mother had turned her back on him and his father. And they'd lost everything. Everything Wynn had cherished and taken for granted. Family. Stability. Love. In the snap of a finger, all those things were gone, and he and his father had been left to pick up the pieces.

"Wynn?"

He turned and glanced up to find Giana standing in front of him with a blanket wrapped around her shoulders. "I was looking for you everywhere."

"I'm sorry. I needed some fresh air." He sipped his drink.

"I'm sure having all my family in one room can be overwhelming." Giana sat beside him.

He shook his head. "It wasn't that. It was just…"

Giana reached across to him and slid her delicate hand into his. "Just what?"

Wynn brought her hand to his mouth and kissed the back of it. "It's nothing. You should go back inside. I don't want to keep you from your family."

"You're not. Tell me, Wynn. What's bothering you?"

"It sounds bad, but I'm jealous."

"Of what?"

"Of your family," he responded. "Of your closeness. Of

the bond between you." Giana looked at him, but Wynn couldn't return her gaze. He was too caught up in his own feelings. "You don't realize how lucky you are to have each other."

"We are, and I wouldn't trade them for anything in the world. My family means everything to me."

"As they should."

He sensed Giana rise from her chair and felt her above him. She was holding out her hand to him. "C'mon, allow me to share my crazy family with you."

"With my melancholy mood, I should stay out here."

"I'm not letting you sulk, Starks. Get your butt up and come join the fun."

He grinned up at her. He kind of liked it when Giana bossed him around. "All right."

After he got out of his own head, the rest of the evening turned out better than Wynn could have hoped for. Mrs. Lockett and her cook made a hearty vegetable soup teamed with fresh bread. Then after dinner, he joined the Locketts in a rousing game of charades, which included having Giana on the floor attempting to do the worm dance so they could guess the word *bookworm*.

Wynn was in stitches and couldn't remember the last time he'd laughed so hard.

"What's so funny?" Giana asked when they finally retired to bed and began to undress.

"Seeing you on the floor attempting the worm was the highlight of my evening." Wynn chuckled as he shrugged out of his own clothes until he was naked.

"Hey." She swatted his arm and unclipped her bra, causing it to fall to the floor. "Don't laugh at me. You figured it out."

"After your horrible dance move attempt," Wynn replied with a smile, "we sure did."

"Don't be smug," Giana scolded and slid her bikini panties down her legs. "Because tomorrow is another day, and when we play flag football, you'll see who's boss."

"Oh, you can boss me anytime you want," Wynn said, hauling Giana forward until she fell naked on top of him. He pulled her up and astride him, settling her so he could feel the molten heat of her. Then he cupped her cheeks and pulled her head toward his. "Matter of fact, why don't you start now."

Their mouths fused in a kiss that made the ache inside Giana's body rise to a fever pitch. He clutched the back of her head with one hand while running his fingers through her hair. Giana had never felt as close to another man as she felt to Wynn. He was slowly starting to let her in, which meant a lot. His past with his family and ex-wife scared him, but Giana felt deep down that Wynn could overcome it if he only let himself.

And she was going to take Shantel's advice and let herself feel her feelings, too.

She would hold nothing back tonight, and if she meant anything to Wynn, he would feel it. He would know she'd fallen in love with him from the time she'd seen him standing in that boxing ring glowering down at her.

"Giana?" He glanced her way, and she realized she'd gotten lost for a moment in her thoughts. "Are you with me?"

She nodded, but he looked as if he didn't believe her. Then he lowered his head to close his lips over one of her nipples. He tugged, licked and teased until Giana felt heat and dampness between her legs. Then his hand was there, right where she needed him to be. She placed her hands over his just as his fingers began moving inside her, filling her, stretching her. She arched against his hand as need and tension gathered in the pit of her stomach.

"Wynn..." His name was a gasp of pleasure.

"You want more?"

"Yes!" she groaned.

"Good, because I have to taste you." And his mouth replaced his hand between her legs. His tongue dipped inside to tease her, and he lavished attention on the sensitive bundle of nerves, tasting her slowly and deeply. She rose and cried out as a powerful orgasm shot through her, rolling over her in unending waves.

The orgasm was great, but she wanted more. Wynn understood and rolled a condom that appeared out of nowhere onto his straining erection. "I thought I was boss," Giana said, and before he could react, pushed him backward. She spread her hands over the hard muscles of his broad chest and lowered herself onto him, taking all of him in, inch by delicious inch. And it felt right, like he fit perfectly inside her.

When their bodies were finally connected, Giana began to move, and they quickly found their rhythm. When she looked down at Wynn, he was watching her. He grasped her hips and thrust in unison with her, slowly at first and then faster and faster as they both raced toward their peak.

Giana couldn't imagine how she'd thought she could make love to this man night after night and not fall in love, because she had indeed lost her heart to Wynn Starks.

The next morning, Christmas Eve, Giana awoke to find herself alone in bed. She touched the sheets, and they were cool, which meant Wynn had been gone awhile. Had he seen something in her eyes last night that scared him away? She'd tried to mask her expression while they'd made love, but she'd never been in love before. Had he figured it out?

Giana threw back the covers and went straight to the en suite. After showering and dressing in distressed jeans and a tunic sweater, she descended the stairs to find she was the only one who'd slept in.

Most of her family were already seated at the large breakfast table that easily sat twelve. It was piled high with platters of bacon, eggs, grits and biscuits.

"There you are, darling," her mother said while she poured her father some coffee from a carafe. "I thought we were going to have to send Wynn up to get you."

Giana glanced around and saw Wynn coming from the kitchen carrying a large bowl. He was dressed in jeans and thick sweater. "What have you got there?" she asked.

"Gravy to go with the biscuits," Wynn said with a smile. When he walked past her, he brushed his lips across hers before placing the bowl on the table.

She followed Wynn as he headed back into the kitchen. "How long have you been up?"

Wynn shrugged. "I don't know. A while. I came down for coffee, and your mother was already up. When I offered to help and she found out I can cook, she recruited me to help out, because your chef was feeling under the weather."

Giana laughed. "You shouldn't have told her that. Now you'll be in the kitchen all weekend."

"I don't mind. It's nice to be included."

"C'mon, let's get something to eat," Giana said.

As they passed through the doorway, Elyse yelled out, "Stop."

Giana frowned. "Why?"

"Look up." Elyse motioned above them, and Giana realized they were underneath the mistletoe. "Kiss. Kiss. Kiss," she chanted. Shantel joined in, and the next thing Giana knew, Wynn was dipping her backward into a whirlwind kiss in front of her entire family.

When he set her upright, his eyes were glittering with passion, and Giana was slightly dazed. "Time to eat," he whispered in her ear, tugging her into her chair.

Giana followed him to an empty seat and sank into it. Beside her, Xavier said, "You okay?"

"Yes, why?"

"You seem a little shook."

"I'm fine." Giana put her napkin into her lap. "Just ready for some breakfast."

As the family passed around the breakfast platters, Giana went through the motions, but she worried that now that she'd acknowledged to herself she was in love with Wynn, she wouldn't be able to keep the feelings bottled up inside much longer.

"What do you think about going shooting with us, Wynn?" Josiah asked once the breakfast dishes were cleared and they were all sitting around the table chatting.

"Shooting?"

"Yeah, usually we go out hunting in the early morning, but we all slept in," Roman explained from across the table.

"The ladies are going shopping in town, so we menfolk can go have some fun," Josiah crowed.

"Giana?" Wynn glanced at her. "What do you think?"

"You should go. It'll be fun."

"You don't mind?"

"Of course she doesn't mind," Josiah responded sharply. "You aren't tied at the hip." He rose from his chair. "C'mon, let's saddle up."

Wynn chuckled. He would ignore her father's brusqueness because he knew that Josiah was used to ordering his family around. Although Wynn wasn't one of them, he wanted to stay on Josiah's good side for Giana's sake. He leaned down and kissed her. "I'll see you soon."

An hour later, after donning a heavier coat on loan from Roman, Wynn joined the Lockett men on a short drive to a sportsman's shooting club near their mountain retreat.

Wynn didn't know much about guns, but Giana's brothers were good teachers. They'd brought an assortment of rifles and handguns so they could shoot at the one-hundred-and two-hundred-yard rifle ranges and do some skeet shooting.

"We'll start you off with a small handgun," Roman said, handing Wynn a Glock. Then he showed him how to load the magazine. "Now position yourself like this." He advised

Wynn on how to take off the safety and line up the target. “All right, you see the target in front of you, now shoot.”

Wynn pulled the trigger and hit the mark, but missed the bull’s-eye.

“So, tell us about you and my sister,” Julian said while he loaded his Sig Sauer with bullets.

Wynn put the handgun down and turned to Julian. “What would you like to know?”

“What your intentions are. Gigi is our little sister and I can tell you, me and my brothers—” he inclined his head to Roman and Xavier standing nearby “—are worried.”

“Why?”

“Because you’re the first man Giana has brought home,” Roman responded.

Wynn wasn’t surprised to hear that; Giana was career-minded and that was her main focus. “Am I being penalized because of it?”

“Of course not,” Roman said, “but it does make us protective of her. We don’t want her to get her heart broken.”

“And you think I’ll do that?”

“Honestly?” Roman quirked a brow.

Wynn folded his arms across his chest. “Please.”

Josiah placed a hand on Roman’s shoulder and pushed him aside. “You don’t have a good track record, son. I read your file. Your divorce was acrimonious, and you haven’t dated since then.”

Wynn seethed inwardly. His private life was his business and no one else’s. However, he wasn’t about to get into an argument with Giana’s father, not when he understood where the concern came from. A place of love.

Her father and brothers only wanted the best for Giana. Wynn couldn’t say for certain that was him. He’d gone into this thinking of Giana as a dalliance and nothing more, but somewhere along the way, it had changed. This was turning into the relationship Giana had asked Wynn to be open to. And he was doing that.

"You're right, Josiah. I have been selective about the people I spend my time with."

"I understand you have needs, Wynn. All men do. But my daughter deserves to be something more than a bed warmer."

"I never said otherwise," Wynn said sharply. "Giana is an incredible woman, and I'm lucky to spend time with her."

"Yes, you are," Josiah stated, poking his finger in Wynn's chest. "So you had better treat her right."

"Of course. My intentions are honorable."

"Meaning you would marry my daughter?" Josiah pushed.

Marriage.

After Christine, Wynn had vowed he'd never marry again. The betrayal and heartache he'd endured had been too much. Wynn wasn't sure he was prepared to put himself out there again, because he didn't want to end up like his father.

"Well?" Xavier said. "Are you going to answer?"

Wynn let out a sigh. "Yes. If I can speak freely?"

"Of course." Josiah nodded.

"The answer is I don't know," Wynn stated. "I don't take marriage lightly, not after a failed one. Giana and I are getting to know each other, and whether that will lead to marriage or not, no one knows. But I'm open to it. I'm not seeing anyone else. We are exclusive, and Giana is my sole focus. She makes me happy, and I hope I've brought her some happiness as well."

Josiah nodded. "I appreciate your honesty, son." He placed his large hand on Wynn's shoulders. "Happiness is all I have ever wanted for my daughter—hell, for all my children. But aren't you concerned with the pitfalls of mixing business with pleasure?"

"I admit it's not an easy road to navigate, Mr. Lockett, but Giana and I are adults and we're committed to doing what's in the best interest for the Atlanta Cougars and Starks Inc."

"Wise words, but not always easy to stand by. But my daughter's a tough cookie, so I hope you're right. I just want the best for everyone." He glanced at Roman, Julian and Xavier. "Even the youngest, who seeks to hide from us the fact he's seeing someone."

Wynn turned to see a deer-in-the-headlights expression on Xavier's face.

"How did I get dragged into this discussion?" Xavier asked.

"Because you've been creeping at all hours of the night," Josiah replied, "and don't think your mother and I haven't noticed."

While Josiah gave his youngest son the third degree, Wynn stepped away for a breather. He was happy to be off the hot seat. The conversation had taken a serious turn after the fun and games of shooting, but Wynn knew it wasn't over. He had a lot of thinking to do about where he wanted his relationship with Giana to go.

He wasn't about to bare his heart to her family—not when he hadn't made sense of the emotions himself.

Last night, once again, he'd opened up to Giana, sharing more of himself. He was peeling back layers, layers he hadn't shown to anyone, and it scared him.

He hadn't lied to her family when he'd said Giana made him happy, because she did. When they'd made love and their eyes locked, they'd been connected by pleasure. And when he'd spilled himself deep inside her, his entire body trembling, Giana had held him like no woman ever had. Afterward they'd lain there, entwined and breathing together.

Wynn felt lost. When he'd woken up this morning and Giana was still sleeping, he'd been relieved to have time to make sense of the night before. He'd headed downstairs, grateful for the distraction of cooking with her mother rather than having to face facts.

He was falling for Giana. Hard.

Seventeen

"You and Wynn are cozy," her mother said as she and Giana browsed the produce section of the local supermarket. Elyse and Shantel had gone to the baby store next door, leaving Giana alone to face her mother's interrogation.

"Things are going well," Giana replied, picking up a piece of honeydew melon and smelling it.

Her mother was choosing sweet potatoes from a bin. "I can tell. I've never seen you look happier."

"Really?" Giana put down the piece of fruit.

"Of course. I'm your mother. I know you." Her mother placed a dozen sweet potatoes in plastic bags. "I know you think you and your father are more alike, but I bore you. I pay attention to what you don't say."

"And what is it that you think you know?"

Her mother walked over and grabbed both her hands. "You're in love with Wynn."

Giana shook her head. "You can't—you can't know that."

"Why? Because you're trying to act like you're not? What are you so afraid of, Giana?"

"That he won't love me back, Mama." The words were out of her mouth before Giana could take them back.

"Doesn't it feel better to say them out loud?"

Giana shook her head. "No, not really."

Her mother squeezed one of her hands. "You can't hold it all inside, Giana. You have to let it out and tell Wynn how you really feel."

"And what if he doesn't feel the same way? What then?"

"Then you'll know. And you can move on and not be in limbo. But something tells me you have nothing to worry about."

"Why? Has he said something?"

"No, it's a mother's intuition. And I trust my gut. It's never led me wrong."

"I wish I was as sure as you, Mama, but I'm not. I'm conflicted. I wasn't looking for love. I thought I didn't need it."

"But it found you anyway. It was like that with your father and me. Sometimes when loves strikes, you have to answer the call, even if doesn't fit in the perfect box you'd envisioned. Now, come on, I have a few more things to get for Christmas dinner." Her mother headed to the next aisle while Giana trailed behind her.

On the ride back from shopping, Giana couldn't stop thinking about what her mother had said about revealing her feelings to Wynn. She was afraid. She had no idea how he would react if she told him. What if Giana said those three words and he didn't say them back? She would be devastated. If their relationship ended on a sour note, how would it affect Starks Inc.'s relationship with the Cougars? All of her efforts to land the account for herself as well as to prove to her father she had business chops like Roman would be called into question. Plus, Giana would still have to deal with Wynn on Curtis's marketing campaign. She could delegate to another member of her team, but the Starks Inc. account was her baby. This was so *complicated.* Those were her thoughts as they arrived at the mountain mansion and found the men had returned from their shooting excursion.

Giana pulled Wynn aside to join her upstairs on the conservation deck, which had a 360-degree view of the mountains. With the sun setting, the view would be phenomenal. "Come with me." She took Wynn's hand and grabbed her jacket on the way out.

Giana went to the very edge of the deck and looked at the sun setting over the horizon. Wynn came behind her and, placing his hands on either side, closed her in.

"The view is great up here," he said, "but I like another one better." He nuzzled her neck, and Giana sighed, leaning her head back against his shoulder. Wynn swept his lips across the nape of her neck once, then twice, before Giana spun around in his arms.

"I missed you," Wynn said and then kissed her deeply. His tongue slid inside her mouth while his body pressed closer, crushing her breasts and making Giana's heart pound madly.

When Wynn finally lifted his head, she asked the question she was dying to know the answer to. "How did everything go?"

"As well as can be expected."

Giana stared into his dark brown eyes and frowned. "Did something happen?"

His hold on her loosened, but he didn't let go. "If you count your brothers and father asking my intentions toward you, then yes."

"And what did you say?"

"I told them the truth. That I don't know."

Giana wasn't sure what answer she'd hoped for, but that wasn't it. Although she wasn't looking for a declaration of love, the nonchalance was a little more than she was ready for, given her newly minted feelings for Wynn.

"We should go downstairs and get ready for dinner."

Giana pulled away from his embrace. "My mother is a stickler for promptness."

"Giana, wait!" Wynn called out, but Giana was already descending the steps. She didn't want him to see the tears steadily falling down her cheeks. She would keep her feelings to herself, because Wynn *wouldn't* or *couldn't* receive her love.

Wynn stared at Giana's retreating figure. He didn't need to be a genius to know he'd said the wrong thing. She'd wanted to know if he was open to *more* between them. Instead of telling her what he'd told her father and brothers, which was he was open to the idea of love and marriage, he'd taken the easy way out.

Hadn't he promised he wouldn't hurt her? Or at the very least, he would do his best not to? But when met with her eager face looking up at him, in the tough moment, he'd backed down.

Wynn wanted to go after Giana, to tell her he was falling for her, but he'd only just admitted it to himself. He was trying to understand how he'd fallen so hard and so quickly for the beautiful executive when all he'd wanted was a quick romp in the hay. But from the moment he'd had a taste of her, he'd wanted no one but Giana. She made him feel more like the man he could be if he wasn't so damaged by his past. Wynn wasn't sure he deserved someone like Giana, and that was the scariest part of all.

After the sky turned dark and a chill came to the air, Wynn returned downstairs and headed for the bedroom, but Giana wasn't there. There was a note stating dinner would be ready soon and then it would be time for the annual Lockett Christmas Eve pajama jam. She'd mentioned the night before how everyone got in their pajamas to watch Christmas movies, but he hadn't thought she was serious. Wynn was glad he'd decided to pack some pajamas, because he typically liked to sleep in the nude.

Wynn went ahead and put on the black T-shirt and pajama bottoms he'd brought and headed downstairs. He found Giana in the kitchen with her mother, getting dinner ready.

"Hey, ladies. Anything I can do?" Wynn looked at Giana, but she didn't say a word.

"I appreciated the assist this morning, but you're a guest," Mrs. Lockett replied. "Relax with the others."

"All right." He leaned over to brush his lips across Giana's cheek. Her eyes fluttered closed, but she remained mum, so Wynn went to join everyone in the family room. He didn't like the tension between them, but he couldn't very well make it any better if Giana refused to engage with him. He would have to bide his time, and when the time was right, he would make his move.

Giana did her best to keep up a happy face as the entire family gathered to enjoy her mother's famous Christmas Eve dinner of glazed ham, mac and cheese, and sautéed green beans. But she was confused. She'd thought Wynn was feeling as she did, but maybe she was blinded by good sex, mistaking it for love. Her mother seemed to think otherwise, but it was probably wishful thinking.

Giana focused on the positive. Her family was gathered in the family room with Christmas movies playing in the background. Giana loved *This Christmas* with Loretta Devine, Idris Elba and Chris Brown because the family in the movie was messy and complicated, much like hers, but at the end of the day they loved each other and came together at Christmas.

Once the popcorn was popped, she joined Wynn on the floor, where he was sprawled next to her nephew and playing with blocks.

"Hey, you." Wynn smiled when Giana sat cross-legged next to him.

"Hey." Before she could stop him, Wynn pulled her

closer. Giana had no choice but to let him, because she didn't want anyone to know what was going on between them.

When the movie was over, Giana immediately jumped up and headed to the kitchen. Wynn didn't join her, but Julian did.

"What's going on with you and Wynn?" he asked, getting right to the point.

"What do you mean?"

He gave her a "really?" look, so she said, "Nothing's wrong."

"You could have fooled me," Julian replied. "I know what it's like when your significant other is giving you the cold shoulder."

"It's none of your business, Julian. Damn, can't I have some privacy?"

Julian was stunned by her outburst, and his light brown eyes clouded with disbelief. She'd never yelled at him before.

"Julian, I'm, I'm—" But she didn't get to finish, because her brother was already backing up out of the room with his hands up.

"You can have all the privacy you need, Gigi. I was just trying to help." Seconds later, Giana was alone.

She hit the counter with her fist. She couldn't do anything right today. First, she'd pushed Wynn to say something he clearly didn't feel, and now she'd offended Julian, who was only being supportive. It was better if she took herself to bed and hoped for a better day tomorrow. She went back out into the family room and wished everyone a good night.

She'd showered, brushed her teeth and climbed into bed when she heard Wynn enter the room. She wasn't ready to face him. She wouldn't make a fool out of herself again, so she feigned sleep instead until she eventually drifted off.

Wynn awoke before daybreak on Christmas Day, wishing he could go back in time and change his response to

Giana's question. He wanted to tell her that whether their relationship led to marriage or not, he was *open* to it.

It was still dark outside. Wynn glanced at the clock; it was 4:00 a.m. He didn't want another evening like last night, with Giana at odds with him. It had caused a stone to lodge in his gut. He had to fix this.

There was one way he knew he could get through to her. He turned to his side. Giana looked so beautiful. Her eyes were closed, and the hair surrounding her on the pillow looked like a halo.

He leaned over and brushed a featherlight kiss across her closed eyelids and then her lips. Giana's eyes fluttered open. "Wynn? What, what time is it?"

"Time for this." He kissed her again, deeply, and Giana responded. Their mouths locked and their tongues did an intimate little dance. With a groan, Wynn pulled her closer to him so she could feel the throb of his need.

He tore himself away long enough to say, "I'm sorry, Giana. Let me make it up to you."

"Wynn, you don't—"

"Lift up your arms," he said, his voice unsteady. Giana raised her arms, allowing him to skim off the nightie, leaving her in nothing but minuscule panties.

His fingers tiptoed over her breasts, teasing the puckered nipples. Then his lips were on them until Giana moaned softly. He slid down her body, kissing his way as he went. When he came to her belly button, he dipped his tongue into the crevice, eager to savor every bit of her sweet skin, until he came to her hips. He gripped them and drew her toward his mouth. Once her thighs were spread wide, he pushed her panties aside and pressed his lips to the center of her need. A cry escaped her lips.

"Giana, you have to be quiet or you'll wake the entire house," Wynn said, lifting his head.

And then he returned to tasting her with his tongue. He lapped at her and swirled his tongue against the tight nub until her breaths came in increasingly desperate pants. Giana clutched at the sheets as his tongue thrust farther inside her, but he didn't stop. He sucked on that sensitive spot while simultaneously pushing one thick finger inside her. Giana's entire body trembled when he added two fingers. Then three.

"Wynn..."

Her body shook as he drove his fingers harder, higher and faster until she broke apart and quietly reached for a pillow to sob into it.

Wynn slowly moved up her body and wrapped Giana in his arms. She was still trembling from the powerful orgasm. "It's okay, I've got you," he whispered. He didn't need anything for himself. This had been for Giana and Giana alone. Giving her pleasure made him happy. Those were the last thoughts Wynn remembered as he drifted back to sleep.

Giana awoke with a start to find herself partially nude and wrapped in Wynn's arms. Had she imagined waking up this morning to Wynn between her legs taking her to new heights? Or had it been a dream? It had to be real, because Giana had gone to bed wearing a nightie, and now she was just in her panties.

And she felt achy in her core, which meant Wynn had made love to her but not taken any satisfaction for himself. Then she remembered. He'd apologized. Said he was sorry. For what? For not loving her? For not wanting more? She couldn't blame him if she was the fool for wanting their relationship to grow and develop.

She tried to slide out of bed, but when she did, Wynn reached out to hold her in place. "Where do you think you're going?"

"To the shower."

"Uh-uh. Why don't we start again," he said, opening his eyes to peer directly into hers. "Merry Christmas, Giana."

He grasped both sides of her face and brought her lips to his. It was a slow and leisurely kiss, which she didn't resist.

When they parted, she said, "Merry Christmas."

"I want to clear the air, Giana."

"Please." She shook her head and this time successfully managed to escape his grasp. "Please don't." She hopped out of bed, found her robe and wrapped it around her nearly naked body.

"I want to," Wynn insisted, rising to a sitting position. "I want to clear the air. I didn't tell you everything I told your family, and if you don't believe me, you can ask them."

She sat on the edge of the bed. "Fine. Go ahead."

"As I said yesterday, I told them we were getting to know each other, but your father refused to accept my pat answer."

"That doesn't surprise me."

"He pressed me on whether marriage was on the table. And I told him truthfully I didn't know for certain, but I was open to the idea."

Giana frowned in confusion. "I thought after your divorce you would never consider marrying again." She rose and began pacing the floor. "You've said so in every interview."

Wynn threw back the covers and approached her. "I know what I said. I'm allowed to change my mind, aren't I? Especially when a certain chocolate beauty has me wrapped around her little finger."

That brought a smile to Giana's lips. "Don't play with me, Wynn. I can't take it."

He reached for Giana, and this time she didn't resist his embrace. "I'm not playing with you, Giana. I meant what I said. I ran scared yesterday when you asked me point-blank. And I won't tell you it'll be easy to crack the shell around my heart, but I'm willing to try. I trust you, Giana. And believe me when I tell you this, when it comes to women, trust is hard for me."

Giana nodded. "I understand, and you can trust me."

Wynn smiled. "I do believe I can."

* * *

The rest of Christmas couldn't have gone better. She and Wynn joined the Locketts for another large breakfast, followed by a game of flag football, which went swimmingly—if she didn't count the fact that Xavier chose to sit it out. No one could convince her baby brother to pick up a football again. He hadn't since his accident, and no amount of cajoling changed his mind.

Instead, Giana, Wynn and Julian were on one team while Roman, her father and Shantel played on the other. With Elyse's condition, she was sitting it out. Meanwhile, Giana's mother was knee-deep in Christmas dinner preparations.

While they were playing, Giana got the chance to apologize to Julian for biting his head off. Thankfully, her brother wasn't one for holding grudges and instantly put her in a headlock to show his appreciation, but after she gave him an affectionate punch in the stomach, he thought better of his actions and released her. In the end, her father's team kicked their butts. She and Julian were no athletes, and bless his heart, Wynn couldn't hold it down all by himself.

Dinner was a grand affair, complete with a large turkey with all the fixings: corn-bread dressing, cranberry sauce, mac and cheese, collard greens, green bean casserole, sweet potato pie, banana pudding and her mom's famous caramel cake. Afterward, everyone was so full, they retired to the living room, where the men watched football and the ladies played Scrabble.

When they finally went up to bed, Giana and Wynn were exhausted, but it didn't stop them from finding pleasure in each other's arms until the sun rose.

In Giana's opinion, it had been the perfect day.

Eighteen

Wynn enjoyed the long weekend with Giana's family and told them so two days later when everyone was packing up their cars for the four-hour trek back to Atlanta.

"I want to thank you for the hospitality, Mr. and Mrs. Lockett," Wynn said to Giana's parents. "I can't remember the last time I enjoyed the holidays so much."

"You're absolutely welcome." Mrs. Lockett gathered him into a warm hug, which he returned. Giana's mother was warm and caring, like a mom should be. "We enjoyed having you. Don't be a stranger."

Wynn glanced over at Giana, who was talking to her sisters-in-law, and smiled. "I won't be."

Mrs. Lockett practically beamed. "I'm so pleased."

After he shook Josiah's hand and everyone said their goodbyes, Wynn and Giana got on the road. They were both contemplative on the drive back to Atlanta. A lot had happened during their weekend in Tennessee. Although their relationship started off as a bet, he and Giana had laid their cards on the table and agreed they wanted a relationship that might lead to forever. The thought terrified Wynn, and he wanted an ear to listen to his troubles.

Luckily, Giana had a few errands to run upon their return to Atlanta, so after dropping her off at the Lockett guesthouse in Tuxedo Park, Wynn headed over to Silas's penthouse.

"Welcome back." Silas gave him a fist bump and led Wynn inside. "Janelle isn't here. She's off at a photo shoot."

"Okay, cool. And thanks for letting me drop by."

"You're my boy—you can drop by anytime," Silas said with a grin. "How was Christmas with Giana and the Locketts?"

"It was good." When they reached the kitchen, Silas grabbed two Bud Lights from the fridge. He cracked one open and handed it to Wynn, who took a generous pull.

Silas chuckled. "You must have needed that."

"Yeah, I did." Wynn winced. "This weekend was eye-opening, to say the least."

"How so?"

"Giana and I took our relationship to another level."

Silas's shocked expression said it all. "Oh yeah? Things are heating up?"

"They've already been heated," Wynn said with a smirk. "And I'm not talking about sex. We discussed where our relationship was headed."

"And who brought up this topic?" Silas asked, drinking some of his beer.

"It wasn't Giana, if that's what you're thinking. It was her brothers and father. I went out shooting with them, and they wanted to know my intentions."

"As they should. And you answered?"

"I answered as honestly as I could. I told them I wasn't sure, but I was open to making a commitment to Giana."

"Were you telling the truth?"

Wynn rolled his eyes at Silas. "Of course I was."

"But now that you said it, you want to take it back?"

"A little. I wasn't lying to them." Wynn paced the floor and then glanced at Silas. "If I could have a future with anyone, it's Giana. She's an incredible lady."

"But?"

Wynn took another long pull on his beer and set it on the counter. "Why does there have to be a 'but'?"

"Because you left a supposedly great weekend and high-tailed it over here, so, yeah, I would say something is up," Silas responded.

"I don't know. There was something in Giana's eyes when we spoke. I wonder if she's already there, ya know?"

"Meaning you think she's in love with you?"

"Maybe."

"Would that be a bad thing?"

"I don't want to hurt her, Silas, especially if I'm not quite there yet," Wynn replied.

"Are you sure?" Silas asked. "Because you haven't dated anyone in years. Yet you agreed to a relationship with Giana. You spent the last few weeks with her nonstop, as well as Christmas. Admit it. You're drawn to her like a moth to a flame."

Silas was right. From the start, when he'd seen Giana standing in a sports bra and leggings at the gym, he'd been angry and aroused at the same time. "I was attracted to her."

"Well, now you're a lot more than just attracted to her."

"True, but as you've said, I haven't been with a woman for a long time. Maybe I'm making too much of this. Perhaps after such a prolonged celibacy, my brain is primed to mate with the first female who comes along."

Silas cocked his head and stared at him. "Do you really believe that's true, Wynn? Because you would be selling yourself and Giana short. You're both smart people. No matter how good the sex is, I doubt you'd be so easily misled."

"Are you saying you believe it could be real?"

"Doesn't matter what I believe. It's about what you believe, my friend. But I encourage you to not be afraid to pursue this, because if you push Giana away, you might never find another woman like her."

"When did you become so wise?"

"Meeting Janelle changed by life, but I nearly lost her because I was pigheaded and set in my ways. I was so afraid of losing her that I pushed her away. I'm just glad that we're back on the same page. She's the one for me, Wynn. And I'm telling you the same thing could happen to you."

Was Silas right? Was it as easy as giving in to his feelings for Giana? Wynn wasn't sure he could do it; he'd been burned too badly by his last relationship. He would like to take it slow until he was absolutely certain and there were no surprises, but his heart was rushing full steam ahead.

"Daddy, what are you doing here?" Giana asked when she walked into her office Monday morning and found her father standing at the window. Most of their employees were off. It was mainly workaholics like her and Roman who worked during the short holiday week. "Did we have an appointment I forgot about?"

Her father spun around. "Not at all. I wanted to talk to you without your mother present."

That sounded ominous.

"What's going on?" Giana asked, walking toward her executive chair and taking a seat.

"I wanted to talk to you about this Wynn fellow."

"I don't like your tone, Daddy," Giana responded, narrowing her eyes at her father. "I thought you liked him."

"I do, but I also want to caution you about falling too fast, too soon."

"What are you talking—"

"It's obvious you've fallen for the young man, Gigi," her father interrupted, "and I want you to be happy, I truly do. But Wynn has a lot of baggage. His ex-wife did a number on him. I don't want you to get hurt if he's not able to return your affection."

"Daddy, I don't want to talk about this with you."

"Maybe not." He came toward her to sit on the edge of her desk. "But we're in a business relationship with him. What if it goes south and he pulls the contract with us?"

Giana's head flicked upward. "Our contract is airtight. I helped draft it myself." She had taken several law courses in college to ensure she understood contracts.

"Yes, but the exclusive contract is only with Curtis. I think it would be a good idea to have another sports drink company in our back pocket, so I've arranged a meeting with Blaine Smith."

"Daddy, Smith International is one of Starks Inc.'s biggest competitors. I would prefer not to go into business with him. Wynn made it very clear that the contract would be exclusive with his company."

"We aren't agreeing to anything and it can't hurt to take a meeting."

"No." Giana shook her head. "Absolutely not. I won't do it." And she meant it. It was the first time she had gone against her father's wishes, but she was adamant on this point.

"Where's your killer spirit, Giana? I thought your career was of utmost importance to you?"

"It still is," Giana replied, "but it would mean a lot to Wynn if we didn't pursue a deal with Smith International."

"Very well." Her father held up his hands in mock surrender. "If that's how you want to go about this. But it shows me how deeply you're invested in Wynn."

"I am." Saying it out loud only reinforced it.

Her father nodded and left her office. Giana stared at the door for a long time after he was gone. She couldn't believe Josiah had sprung this on her, not after the amazing Christmas weekend she and Wynn had shared. Other than the one evening they hadn't been on the same page, it had been bliss.

That's how it was with Wynn—he drenched her days with laughter, passion and adventure. If they could only hold on to the special moment they'd shared in Gatlinburg, it would be perfect. But they were back in Atlanta. Could the magic they'd found in Tennessee last, or would the real world threaten it?

Later, when they were in bed watching the news, Giana brought up a topic she'd been thinking about. "Have you thought about New Year's Eve?" It was only a few days away.

"Thought about it?" Wynn asked. "No, why?"

"Holidays are a big thing with my family. The Atlanta Cougars host an annual New Year's Eve bash. Did you receive your invitation?"

"Yes, I did."

"Well, I was hoping you would be my date."

Wynn smiled. "Were you worried otherwise?"

She shrugged. "No, but you hadn't exactly brought up the pending holiday."

"I'm sorry about that," Wynn replied. "It's been a long time since I've had to think about someone other than myself, but I promise I'll get better at it."

"You don't have to come if you don't want to," Giana said. "No pressure." Even though she desperately wanted him to say he would ring in the new year with her. It would symbolize he was ready and willing to get serious about their relationship.

Wynn cupped her cheeks in his hands. "Yes, I want to, Giana. There's no place I would rather be."

Giana broke out in a smile. "That's wonderful."

"Now let's go to bed," he growled and tossed the covers over their heads. Giana knew this New Year's was going to be the best one yet, because she was with the man she loved.

"You don't have to come, Giana," Wynn said when she insisted on joining him at the Boys & Girls Club to meet with his mentee Donnell.

"Yes, I do," Giana responded. "I want to get to know you, *all* of you, and that means seeing all facets of you, including the young man who once needed the services of this organization and who now comes to give back."

"Don't make me out to be some sort of hero, Giana," Wynn replied. "Because I'm not. I'm doing the right thing. There are many boys out there who need guidance, who need someone to care. And although I knew my father loved me, there were times I would have been lost growing up if it hadn't been for Les in the Boys & Girls Club. Who knows what direction I might have gone?"

"But you are a hero, at least to me."

"Come on." He grabbed her hand once they were out of the Alfa Romeo 4C Spider. "I want you to meet Donnell Evans."

A short while later, Giana was bowled over at seeing Wynn with his mentee. He had a way with the young man, who clearly looked up to Wynn.

"Donnell, I'd like you to meet my girlfriend, Giana Lockett," Wynn said.

"Girlfriend?" Donnell's eyes grew wide as saucers.

Giana's heart fluttered in her chest, because Wynn hadn't hesitated when he used the word. *Girlfriend.* He'd said it loud and clear.

Giana waved. "Hi, Donnell. It's a pleasure to meet you."

"I came to bring you your Christmas gift," Wynn said, producing a box from behind his back and giving it to Donnell. "Sorry I'm late, but I went with Giana's family to the mountains."

"Sounds cool, Mr. Starks, and it's no problem at all. I know you always come through." Donnell accepted the package.

And come through Wynn did. Donnell was shocked to unwrap the gift and find a brand-new PlayStation 5.

"This is awesome, Mr. Starks." Donnell rushed toward

Wynn and wrapped his arms around his middle. "Thank you so much. I can't wait to play it."

"You can't without games," Giana said, handing him a bag she'd been hiding behind her back. It contained several games for the PlayStation.

"Oh man, everyone is going to be so jealous," Donnell said, smiling from ear to ear. "Can I go show Eric?"

"Of course," Wynn said. "I'll be right here."

They both watched the young man rush out of the room and seconds later heard squeals of delight over his new Christmas gift.

"Do you think it was too extravagant?" Wynn asked, glancing in her direction.

Giana's eyes misted, and she shook her head. "Not at all."

Wynn appreciated that Giana was making the effort to get to know him and his passion for helping others. She was truly a remarkable woman. It surprised him to realize that he could see a future with Giana, just the two of them and a bunch of milk chocolate babies with her dimples. God help him, but he was in love with the woman.

Nineteen

"Roman, do you have any idea what this meeting is about?" Giana asked when they were both summoned to Tuxedo Park's country club on Wednesday for lunch with their father.

Roman had graciously agreed to drive, and on the way over, they'd talked about the Christmas weekend and Wynn.

"No, I don't, but on another topic, I'd like to admit, Giana, I was wrong about Wynn," Roman said.

Giana turned to him. "How so?"

"I thought perhaps you were using him for business, but I can see what you two share is the real thing and he really cares about you."

Giana felt a warm glow suffuse her cheeks, and she couldn't resist smiling. "Thank you. I think Wynn and I both thought we were compatible in the bedroom, but we've discovered we can laugh, talk and have fun together. He brings out a freedom in me I hadn't expected."

"I thought after the incident at the gala, Wynn was not ready for love, but I'm happy to see I was wrong."

Giana thought back to how she'd felt seeing Wynn with his ex-wife. She'd felt jealous and wanted to rip her eyes out, but instead she'd held her head up high. In the end, Giana was victorious, because she had Wynn, while Christine was left to sulk about what could have been.

They pulled into the country club parking lot, and Roman gave the valet the keys to his Maserati Levante. Together they walked to the host stand of the club's restaurant and were greeted by the maître d'. "Mr. and Ms. Lockett, pleasure to see you both again. If you'll follow me, your father is already seated."

"Lead the way." Roman allowed Giana to precede him to the table.

However, as they approached, Giana recognized the other occupant sitting next to her father. It was none other than Blaine Smith. Giana was furious. She'd told her father in no uncertain terms she wouldn't speak to Blaine, let alone entertain a meeting with him, yet he'd gone behind her back and arranged this.

"Gigi!" Her father wore a large, gregarious grin, and she wanted to wipe it off his smug face. Now she understood why Roman and Julian had complained that he could be manipulative.

"Father." Giana only used the word when she was angry with him, and his raised brow acknowledged that he knew it. "Blaine."

Blaine was tall and lanky with short, dark blond hair and blue eyes. He wore a custom-made slate-gray Italian suit with a blue-striped tie. "It's so good to see you, Giana. You're looking well," he said, rising to greet her and shake her hand.

"Thank you." She'd met Blaine a few years ago.

"Roman." Blaine nodded at her brother, who stood like a statue by her side. Roman understood what her father was doing: making a power play when as general manager Roman made all the decisions.

"Join us," their father said, indicating for them to sit down.

Giana glanced at Roman, and she understood what his raised eyebrow meant. If she wanted to walk, he would support her. But she was a consummate professional, so she sat down at the table.

"Your father was telling me how well the Cougars are doing now that you've acquired Curtis."

"Curtis is not an acquisition like the fancy Ferrari you drive, Blaine," Roman retorted, and Giana appreciated her brother's fervor. "He's a human being."

Blaine smiled wanly. "Of course. I merely meant he's been a great addition to the team. Your winning record has improved."

Her father jumped in. "Yes, it has. And it's put us in the position to only accept the best offers for our players."

Giana gave her father a warning glance, but he didn't heed it.

"I've always wanted to partner with the Cougars, Josiah, but the team and I—" Blaine glanced at Giana and then Roman "—have never been able to come to a deal."

That's because Giana thought Blaine was a slimy rat. She hadn't liked the way he'd treated some of the other athletes who'd endorsed his products, and she certainly wasn't going to foster a relationship with a man she didn't trust. Her opinion of him hadn't changed.

Why had her father done this? He had to have known she would never agree to this. Was he purposely trying to sabotage her relationship with Wynn? Because if Wynn saw her with Blaine, he would view this as a betrayal. She was ending this meeting, and she prayed he would never find out about it.

"I appreciate you meeting me, Silas," Wynn said as they sat down at their table at the Tuxedo Park country club restaurant that afternoon.

"Of course, what's going on?"

"When I was at the Boys & Girls Club with Giana yesterday, the director pulled me aside and told me, despite the charity event, they are still a little short for the next year. I was thinking you and I could subsidize the rest. I think it's important for the kids in the community to have someplace to go."

Silas nodded. "I couldn't agree with you more. And I'll give however much you think we need."

Wynn reached across the table and shook his hand. "You're a good man."

"You knew I was going to agree," Silas said. "Was that the only reason you called?"

Wynn shrugged. "Primarily, but I wanted to talk to you about a realization I've come to."

Silas grinned. "I think I know what you're about to say."

"The speed of my and Giana's relationship has been a bit jarring. Christine really messed me up, man. She made it hard to trust myself and my judgment. But I think I could be in love, Silas."

For Giana, he wanted to be that man. He wanted to be a man she could count on for the long haul. He believed in love again, and it was all thanks to her. He was no longer hardened by the pain of his ex-wife's betrayal. Wynn felt as if a burden had been lifted and he could finally breathe again.

"That's wonderful, Wynn. I know you're unsure of yourself, but it's okay," Silas responded. "It's part of the process, but I've seen the change in you. You look happier. Content. Satisfied."

Wynn grinned. "I am."

"Then the best is yet to come," Silas replied.

"I couldn't agree with you more." Wynn grinned from ear to ear. "Let's toast. To a good thing."

They held up their drinks and toasted to the future. They

enjoyed a lively lunch talking about Silas and Janelle's upcoming vow renewal and Wynn's new sports drink, which had finally received the seal of approval from the focus group. When they were done with their meal, they started toward the exit. Wynn was feeling really good about his relationship with Giana, and she was very much on his mind. So much so that when he looked over and saw Giana at a table, he almost thought he was imagining things. But it was her.

And she wasn't alone. Roman was sitting beside her, and Wynn heard Josiah's bold laugh. But at first he couldn't make out the man beside him until he turned to the side to say something to Josiah.

It was Blaine.

Blaine Smith.

Wynn stopped dead in his tracks and stared.

He understood why Blaine would be cozying up to the Locketts, but why would Giana be meeting with him? He'd told her about the animosity between them. Although he'd asked for exclusivity in the Cougars deal, Roman hadn't promised it. But Giana had told him she wouldn't actively pursue doing business with Blaine. She couldn't be thinking of going back on her word, could she?

"Wynn..." He heard Silas calling his name, but Wynn couldn't stop himself from walking toward the Locketts' table. When he arrived, Giana glanced up at him, and the guilty look she gave him was telling. He'd trusted her, and she'd betrayed him.

"What's going on here?" Giana heard Wynn's question, but she couldn't answer. Her stomach plummeted the moment she saw him standing behind her father.

What was he doing here?

Never in a million years would she have imagined seeing him here; in fact, she'd never seen him at the country club before.

Blaine turned around with a smug smile that Giana wanted to wipe off his face. "Wynn, what brings you to this neck of the woods? I thought you preferred your motorbike and wings to eating in polite society," he said, taking in Wynn's usual attire of motorcycle jacket, jeans and T-shirt.

Giana glared across the table at Blaine, but Wynn took the insult on the chin. "I thought I saw someone I knew," Wynn stated, "but clearly I was wrong."

His words hit their mark, because Giana shot to her feet. "Wynn, can I speak with you, please?"

His dark eyes bored into hers. "No need. It looks like you're real busy here, so I'll take my leave."

"I would appreciate that," Blaine responded. "I was in the middle of making a deal with the Locketts on having one of their boys endorse my drinks."

"Is that right? Good for you," Wynn replied. "Roman. Josiah." He inclined his head and turned on his heel to leave, but Giana rushed after him, in the process knocking her chair to the floor with a loud thud.

"Wynn, please wait!" Giana cried. She trotted to keep up with him, finally reaching him in the lobby, where he was pacing the floor back and forth with his head hung low. "Wynn…"

He looked at her, and Giana saw hurt and betrayal lurking in the depths of those brown eyes. "What is it that you want, Giana? You got your deal. Starks Inc. is tied into a contract with Curtis for years and it would take a whole lot of lawyers to untangle the unholy mess, so what? What more do you want from me?"

"Don't." She shook her head. "Don't do that. Don't act as if the only thing between us is business and we mean nothing to each other."

"I thought we meant more, but instead you go behind my back and take a meeting with Blaine Smith of all people? I told you my feelings about my rival and you promised you wouldn't actively seek him out, yet here you are breaking bread with the man. How am I supposed to not feel betrayed? So why don't you go back in there—" Wynn's voice rose so he was almost yelling "—and enjoy your meal."

"Is it really that easy for you to let me go?" Giana asked.

"What do you expect? I see you with my sworn nemesis and I'm supposed to be believe you were just having tea?" Wynn asked sarcastically. "What I believe—" he pointed his finger at her "—is that you're an ambitious, power-hungry woman desperate to prove to her daddy she has the business chops to do whatever it takes to be like one of the boys. Well, guess what, Giana. You have it." He clapped his hands in applause. "You can stab a man in the back just as good as any man."

"That's not true. I haven't betrayed you, Wynn."

Wynn began laughing uncontrollably. "Are you really going to stand there and lie to my face after I caught you red-handed?"

"I'm asking you to hear me out," Giana pleaded. "To give me the benefit of the doubt. I know this looks bad, but given how close we've grown these last few weeks, don't I deserve that much?"

"You deserve nothing but my back as I leave." He turned to go, but Giana yelled after him.

"You're a coward, Wynn Starks."

He spun around, and his eyes were glittering with rage. Giana took a step backward. She'd never seen him this angry, this hurt. "How dare you call me a coward after what you've done?"

"I didn't do anything, Wynn. I didn't set up this meeting, my father did. I told him I wasn't interested in meeting Blaine, but he went behind my back and arranged it anyway. When I showed up and found him here, I was blindsided."

"Are you seriously going to blame your father for your ambition, Giana? For God's sake, at least own what you've done."

"I won't!" Giana folded her arms across her chest. "Not when I've done nothing wrong. Wynn, you have to believe me."

"I have to believe nothing. I don't know why I ever thought I could trust you. No, you're not a spoiled, pampered princess, but you're as bad as Christine. You used me to get what you want, and as soon as you had it, you're on the next business deal. I don't know why I keep falling for a pretty face and expecting a different result. It's all about money, power and prestige with your type."

"Why would I ask you to spend the holidays with me and my family if I was using you?"

"Because I amuse you, Giana. It's like Christine said, a woman like you was never going to get serious about a guy like me. You need a guy who comes from the right family and has the right pedigree. I'll leave you to go find him."

He started to leave again, but Giana stamped her foot. "Damn it, Wynn. Don't leave like this. Stay. Please fight for me. Fight for us."

He cocked his head. "Us? There is no us. There never was."

Wynn was claiming that she'd buried a dagger in his back, but the dagger was really lodged in her heart. Giana watched as Wynn strode out the door, hopped onto his MTT Turbine Streetfighter and roared away. Giana rushed out the front door and down the steps to see his retreating figure.

Then the reality of the situation hit her.

She'd lost the man she loved, and she'd never be whole again. Giana wanted to crumple to the floor, but instead she went back inside the country club and told Blaine the

Locketts would *not* be doing business with him. She turned to Roman, and he rose to his feet, indicating he supported her. Seeing both his children turn against him, Giana got no further argument from her father.

It was only when Giana was in Roman's Maserati and it was just the two of them that her face fell into her hands and she allowed herself to cry.

Twenty

"He hates me," Giana sobbed into her pillow as Xavier rubbed her back and handed her a Kleenex. All she could see was the devastated look in Wynn's eyes, and it gutted her.

Roman had been a rock. They hadn't gone back to the office. Instead, he'd called Julian and Xavier and her brothers had rallied around her, even offering to go beat Wynn to a bloody pulp for hurting their sister. It had been Giana's desperate plea that they leave it be that made them relent and promise her they wouldn't retaliate. Roman and Julian stayed as long as they could, then they'd gone home to their wives, promising to call and check on her later. But Xavier stayed so she wouldn't be alone.

Didn't Wynn know she would never do anything to hurt him? Couldn't he see how much she loved him? If he couldn't, he was blind, because Giana felt as if she was wearing her heart on her sleeve. Instead, he'd railed at her, called her an opportunist. He thought she'd gone to bed with him, become his lover, all so she could get ahead.

How could he think so little of her? She had ethics and a moral code that would never allow her to do such a thing. But how well did they know each other? It had only been a few weeks since they'd struck up this affair. Yet she'd fallen so spectacularly in love with him in such a short time.

"He doesn't hate you," Xavier said. "But he's having a tantrum and acting like a complete jerk. Perhaps it's for the best, Giana. If he thinks so little of you, then clearly he's not the one for you."

Giana turned over to face her brother. "I don't want to hear that, Xavier, not right now."

"I'm sorry, Gigi, but Wynn hurt you after he promised us he wouldn't."

"Because he thinks I betrayed him." Giana sniffed into the Kleenex.

"Are you defending him?"

Giana shook her head. "I'm so confused. I thought he believed in me and we were building a foundation for…" Her voice trailed off.

"Marriage?" Xavier offered.

Giana shrugged. "Maybe, but certainly a future. But I can see I was fooling myself. I'm not cut out for this love stuff, Xavier. I should stick to business, because at least it's cut-and-dried and I know what to expect."

"Don't do that, Gigi. Any man would be lucky to have you in his life, and Wynn Starks is a fool if he doesn't see he's throwing away a good woman like you."

A smile spread across her lips. "And you're not the least bit partial?"

Xavier grinned. "Just a little."

"Listen, you can go. I heard your phone vibrating several times. Your girl must be eager to get in touch with you. New Year's Eve is tomorrow."

"She can wait," Xavier responded. "You need me more."

"You're a good baby brother, but I'm okay."

"C'mon, at two hundred and seventy-five pounds, I'm far from a baby."

"No matter how old you get, you'll always be my baby brother," Giana said, stroking his cheek. "But I appreciate you staying by my side."

Giana was lucky, because she had an entire family to support her through this crisis. But Wynn? Who did he have? Silas? He and his estranged wife were getting reacquainted, which wouldn't leave much time for Wynn. And his father? Well, Jeffrey Starks was off on an extended cruise, having a romance with a woman he'd met onboard the ship. So Wynn was alone. Giana lowered her head. What was wrong with her? She was still worrying about a man who obviously thought so little of her, who thought she'd betrayed him. Why, oh why hadn't she just walked away when she'd seen Blaine at the table with her father?

All this could have been avoided if she'd taken a stand. Instead, she'd tried to do the professional thing—and tried to please her father. And she'd lost Wynn as a result.

Giana had never felt this way about another man before Wynn. It wasn't just lust. She'd known after the first night they'd made love that being with him had intrinsically felt different. New. Special. For the first time, she'd thought about the future, marriage and having a family with Wynn.

And now, all Giana could envision was an image of herself alone. It broke her heart she hadn't been able to hold on to Wynn and that dream just a little while longer. *Was she ever going to find someone who loved her as much as she loved him?*

Wynn was still in disbelief as he lay out on the chaise on his terrace later that night. The bottle of bourbon on the table next to him was nearly empty. He was ignoring Silas's calls because his friend had witnessed his downfall and Wynn was embarrassed.

How could he have gotten it so spectacularly wrong *again*? He'd believed Giana. Thought she was different than Christine. And she was—she was ambitious with a capital *A*. She wasn't going to let anyone best her, including him. She'd been conning him the entire time, making him think she truly cared for him, maybe even loved him. He'd thought of how she'd responded to him in bed. The sounds she made when she came apart in his arms. He'd been bamboozled because she was good in bed.

Wynn took a long sip of his bourbon. He was tying one on so he could block out the memory of Giana from his mind. Why had she included him in her family celebrations? That meant something to him—that their relationship was growing and developing into something more.

What a fool he was for believing in love again!

Was Giana laughing with her family about what a sucker he'd been? Was he so desperate for love and affection he would take it from anywhere he could get it? If he was, he blamed his mother for making him feel this way. She'd struck a match to their family and burned down their house of cards.

Wynn's cell vibrated next to him. He was about to silence it when he noticed it was his father. He hadn't heard from him in over a week, even at Christmas, but he hadn't expected his dad to have great cell service while out to sea.

Wynn swept his thumb across the phone. "Dad?"

"Wynn, is that you?"

"Yeah."

"You don't sound like yourself. Is everything okay?"

"No, Dad," Wynn responded. "Everything's all wrong."

"Wynn, what's happened?"

Wynn shook his head as if his father could see him. "It doesn't matter."

"Yes, it does. Are you hurt?"

"Not physically."

"Emotionally?" his father asked. "Is a woman involved?"

"Why would you ask?"

"Because the fairer sex always has a way of getting to us like no one else can," his father replied. "Talk to me. Tell me what happened."

"Your son is a fool. I was a duped by a woman I thought cared for me, but instead she was using me to gain my business."

"I doubt it's that simple. Why don't you explain it to me."

Wynn told his father about his initial refusal to meet with Giana, of her relentless pursuit of him and how the script was flipped on him when they were stuck in the elevator.

"Sounds like the attraction was mutual."

"Or convenient," Wynn replied, "helping ensure Giana got exactly what she wanted."

"You think she planned it?"

"No, I wouldn't go that far, but she took advantage of the situation." Wynn went on to tell his father of the bet and how enamored he became with Giana after they became intimate. "Once we had sex, it was like I was addicted."

"And your relationship progressed from there?"

"Yes. We've been pretty much inseparable since then, but the thing is, I wanted an entirely physical relationship. She was the one who pressed for more."

"Do you think perhaps she was sincere about wanting to get to know you?"

"If she were, she wouldn't stab me in the back by going to one of my competitors. Giana knew how I felt about Blaine Smith, but she didn't give a damn. She wanted to prove to her father she has the killer spirit like he does, and she proved it. She's willing to step over anyone, including me."

"I can see how that hurts, son, but did you ever think you could be wrong about her? Perhaps you're jumping to conclusions."

"I don't think I am."

"Your judgment is skewed. Ever since your mother left us, you've been mistrustful of women. Your marriage to

Christine made it even worse, because she betrayed you, solidifying in your mind the idea that no woman could be trusted. But it's not true, Wynn. There are some good women out there."

"I thought Giana was one of them, Dad, but I was wrong."

"Why are you rushing to see the worst in her? I haven't met Giana," his father said, "but I would like to, given what you've just told me. She could be someone you could believe in, love even. Because I want that for you, son. I don't want you to be like me, going through life in a haze. And I can see now it was my fault. I wasn't able to be the father I should have been after your mother left us."

"Don't blame yourself, Dad, not after what she did."

"It takes two for a marriage to fail," his father replied. "That's not to say her infidelity is excusable, it's not, but I wasn't the perfect husband, either. I've made my peace with it, Wynn, and you should, too. The failure of our marriage wasn't solely your mother's fault. You can't keep holding on to the hurt like a shield against love."

"That's not what I'm doing!" Wynn raised his voice.

"Aren't you? You're using what you perceive to be a betrayal by Giana to push her away because you're afraid. Don't give up on love. If you do, you're missing out on a blessing."

"Dad, I know you mean well, but why would she have been with Blaine if not to betray me?"

"Did you give her time to explain?"

Wynn remembered Giana mentioning something about her father setting her up, but he'd thought she was blowing smoke to cover her tracks. "She tried."

"But you didn't let her," his father responded. "Do you want to end up alone with only your business to comfort you? Because I promise if you continue down this path, that's all you'll be left with."

"What do you expect me to do?"

"I expect you to listen, son. Not just with your ears, but with your heart. Deep down, you know the truth."

Wynn sighed. "I appreciate your sage advice."

His father chuckled. "I don't know about sage, but years of experience have shown me how fragile love is. You have to nurture it."

After the call, Wynn thought about his father's advice and put the cap on the bourbon bottle. Had he judged Giana too harshly? Was she telling the truth that her father had set up the meeting without her knowledge? If she was, he had just blown their relationship to smithereens, and he wasn't sure if it could be put back together again.

Wynn woke up the next morning with a pounding headache. Over the course of last night, he'd come to realize his father was right. Maybe the situation was exactly what Giana said it was: Josiah had ambushed her by inviting Blaine Smith to the lunch.

Wynn recalled what Giana had told him about her father, how he'd interfered in Roman and Shantel's relationship by forcing the issue of a prenup. And then there was Julian. Josiah had had Elyse investigated, which revealed she was the daughter of his old business partner, who held a grudge against him. Was it possible Josiah was now trying to cause a rift between him and Giana? But why? He had what he wanted: Starks Inc.'s business.

In the cold light of day and with time to think, Wynn realized he'd overreacted. Betrayal was a big trigger for him. At the first opportunity, he'd condemned Giana, like his father had said. He owed it to himself and Giana to talk to her again and listen like his father suggested.

Listen with his heart.

Deep down, Wynn already knew the truth. But would she listen to him after what he'd done? Thinking she'd hurt him, he'd lashed out at her like a snake trying to get the first strike. He would have to do a lot of groveling to get her to hear him out and accept his declaration of love. And no doubt, he would have to run the gauntlet of Lockett men to get to Giana.

Wynn heard a knock. At first, he thought the pounding was in his head, but now he realized someone was at his front door. He padded barefoot to the foyer, and when he swung the door open, he saw a fist coming at him seconds before he was flattened to the ground.

"That's for my sister," Xavier said, standing above him as Wynn held his throbbing jaw. "I should be beating you to a bloody pulp, but I promised my sister I wouldn't lay hands on you. I couldn't quite keep that promise, so consider this a warning. Stay away from Giana."

"I'm afraid I can't do that, Xavier."

Xavier punched his hand with his other fist. "Do you want another one of these?"

"Not particularly," Wynn said, slowly rising to his feet but keeping his distance. Although Wynn was spry, as a former quarterback, Xavier Lockett was formidable, and Wynn didn't want to tussle with the man.

"Then what? You already made a fool of yourself by throwing away someone as good as my sister."

"You're right."

"Excuse me?"

"I said you're right," Wynn yelled. "I was wrong. I should have never assumed the worst of Giana, but I did because I have a lot of baggage that I haven't done a particularly good job of dealing with."

Xavier frowned. "And what do you want now, a gold medal? You hurt Gigi."

"I know, which is why I have to make things right. To tell her I made a mistake."

"You don't deserve her."

"Probably not, but I love her nonetheless."

"Did you say love?" Xavier sounded skeptical, and Wynn couldn't blame him. Over the past twenty-four hours, he hadn't shown that love. He'd tossed it away because of fear and mistrust. But now Wynn was hoping there was a chance Giana would forgive him and give him a chance to turn the page.

"Yes. I love Giana, and it took realizing I could lose her to make me see it," Wynn said. "I want her back, Xavier, and I'm going to do everything I can to show her how much I love her. And I have an idea."

"You do?" Xavier still sounded skeptical.

"Yeah." Wynn rubbed his beard. "Care to help me out?"

"I don't know, man," Xavier said. "You're in the doghouse, and I don't want to join you."

"Understood, but if what I think is true, which is that Giana loves me as much as I love her, then I'm willing to take the risk."

"Mighty big words."

"It's going to take big actions to back them up," Wynn said. "You with me?" He held out his hand for Xavier to shake.

Xavier smiled. "God help me, but I'm in." He pumped Wynn's hand.

Wynn prayed this would work. And if it did, he would be starting the new year with the woman he loved.

"There you are," Giana's mother said when she finally emerged after twenty-four hours confined to the guesthouse to come to the kitchen in the main house. "Are you all right, darling? You didn't come up for breakfast, and Xavier said you were under the weather."

"I'm fine," Giana said, reaching across the island to grab a homemade cookie from the jar. She closed her eyes and savored the chocolaty goodness.

"I doubt it," her mother replied. "Your father told me about yesterday. Said he overstepped his bounds on a business deal and now Wynn's upset with you."

Giana glanced up. "That's about the long and short of it."

"Care to tell me more?"

Giana shook her head. "Not really." She'd thought incessantly about Wynn for an entire day, and she was plumb exhausted. It was New Year's Eve, and she refused to mope, because in less than twenty-four hours, this year would be over. She would put her relationship with Wynn in the past until eventually he became a footnote in her life. Giana had a great marketing team and could assign one of them to work with Starks Inc., leaving her to run things from behind the scenes. It was possible she could have very little interaction with the man if she planned it right.

"Maybe I could help. Surely it's not as bad as you think?"

"Then Daddy didn't tell you everything," Giana replied, "like the fact that he butted in after I told him I wasn't interested in meeting Wynn's competitor. But did he listen? No."

"Your father is bullheaded, same as you, but he didn't mean any harm."

"He never does, Mama, yet it causes his children pain. First Roman, then Julian and now me. Xavier had better run before Daddy gets him next."

"Gigi." Her mother walked toward her. "It's not like you to talk about your father this way. I expect it from Julian, maybe even Roman, but you've always been your father's favorite."

"Which is why this feels so bad," Giana replied. "I loved Wynn, Mama. I love him still, and Daddy interfered. He may have said it was business, but maybe he can't stand to see us happy."

"I do want you to be happy." Her father's deep baritone voice resonated from behind her, but Giana didn't immediately turn around. "I know I fail sometimes at being a father. No one gave me a playbook."

Giana spun around. "Is that an excuse for your bad behavior?"

"I didn't intentionally set out to come between you and Starks, Gigi. I thought having a second company to work with as a backup for our other players was a good thing for the franchise. As Roman mentioned when Wynn first brought up an exclusive contract with the Atlanta Cougars, it wasn't a smart idea to tie our hands. Curtis is our star, yes, but we have an obligation to help other players find endorsements. It's not fair to put all of our eggs in one basket."

"I told you how Wynn felt about this and *I* wanted to respect his wishes, but you set up the meeting anyway. Why? Because you don't respect me. You don't see me as your equal. You've always groomed Roman to be your successor. Well, guess what, Daddy? I've been right there beside him every step of the way. Like him, I want to run the Atlanta Cougars or at least have more of a role beyond marketing and charity work." She glanced across the island. "No offense, Mama. The foundation does important work for some worthy causes."

"None taken," her mother stated.

"I do respect you, Giana, not because you're my daughter, but because you've earned it. Every time I've told you no or blocked your path, you went around me and showed me you were as smart as your brothers. And I admit at times, I underestimated you. But you are a valuable part of the franchise."

Giana was shocked. Her father had never said any of this to her. "Why is this the first time I'm hearing this?"

Her father shrugged. "It's not easy for a man like me to admit when he's wrong. To admit his daughter showed him up, but you have. You have great instincts and business acumen, Giana. I'm extremely proud of all your accomplishments."

Tears welled in Giana's eyes. "Thank you, Daddy." She hadn't realized she needed to hear it until he said those words of validation. They were like a salve to her wounds.

"What can I do?" her father asked, coming to her and placing his hands on her shoulders. "Do you need me to go to Starks and tell him I arranged the meeting? I'll make it clear that you knew nothing about it and I was the sole mastermind because I wanted to keep the Atlanta Cougars' options open. I'll admit I was trying to take charge of the situation like I always do because I'm a control freak. I'll do it for you, baby girl."

Giana shook her head. "No, you don't have to do that. Wynn honestly believes I betrayed him even after everything we shared, so it's pointless. He doesn't love me the way I love him."

Her father lifted her chin with his finger and gazed into her eyes. "So, you admit you've lost your heart to Starks?"

"I may have lost it, but clearing the air with you, Daddy, I'm slowly gaining it back." Her father pulled Giana into his warm embrace, and she sank into it, allowing herself the comfort only a father's love could provide.

Twenty-One

"This is unexpected," Silas said when he met up with Wynn in a secret location midmorning on New Year's Eve. Wynn had sent Silas a cryptic text message telling him when and where to meet him but hadn't told him why. Silas would figure it out when he arrived.

"Yes, well, I realized I made a big mistake accusing Giana of betraying me when that was far from the case."

"What made you change your mind? Did you speak with her?"

Wynn shook his head. "I haven't seen or spoken to her since we saw her at the country club yesterday. But when I woke up this morning with the mother of all headaches, I realized I knew the truth. Giana would never take a meeting with my archenemy. She has too much integrity, and I was an idiot to accuse her."

Silas let out a long sigh. "I'm so happy to hear you've come to that conclusion all on your own. I was worried about you, man. When you saw her at the table, I was scared.

Scared of the effect something like this might have on your psyche. But I'm glad my fear was in vain and you've seen the error of your ways."

"I have," Wynn said. "Once I was clearheaded enough and spoke to my dad about it last night, I was able to see the situation for what it was. Josiah Lockett was trying to pull a boss move and act like he's still in charge of the Atlanta Cougars. Meeting Blaine wasn't Giana's doing, and I can't wait to tell her."

"How do you think she'll respond?"

"I haven't the foggiest idea," Wynn replied. "But I'm going to talk to her about my past and how it's colored my view of the world and hope I can win her over. I'm going to tell her I love her."

Silas shook his hand. "I'm rooting for you, brother, and after she sees that—" he pointed to the ring box in Wynn's hand "—I think she'll know how serious you are."

Wynn wanted to do something grand to show Giana exactly how he felt and how much she meant to him. He'd even recruited Xavier to ensure his name was on the guest list to get into the Locketts' New Year's Eve party so there were no hiccups. Wynn hoped it wasn't too late to repair the damage he'd done to their relationship.

The annual Lockett New Year's Eve bash at the Fox Theatre was a dazzling affair. The crowded ballroom was filled with white and gold balloons, metallic pom-poms, streamers and towers of champagne flutes on sequined tablecloths. But none of it could get Giana into the party spirit. Even after she'd donned a gold Versace gown with a plunging neckline and chain-link detailing from her wrists all the way down to her ankles, strapped her feet into a pair of four-inch sandals, and put her hair up in a sleek ponytail, Giana still felt like an impostor.

Everyone around her was filled with the holiday spirit, but all Giana wanted to do was curl up under a rock and wait for the clock to strike midnight. Her parents were shining bright near the entrance, greeting guests as they came in. Roman and Shantel were laughing and dancing on a night out away from Ethan. Meanwhile, Julian and Elyse were living it up, because next year they'd have a little one of their own.

Giana would like to get lost herself, but her mother relied on her to help host the splashy party.

"Hey, Gigi, you all right?" Xavier asked, sidling up beside her. He looked debonair in a black tuxedo and crisp white shirt and no tie.

"Yes, I'm fine. Don't I look fine?" She'd done her best to repair the damage a day of crying had done to her eyes and face.

"You look beautiful," he replied. "But all these people—" he tilted his head, indicating the crowd around the room "—don't know you like I do. And they certainly have no idea what went down the other day."

"I don't want to think, much less talk about it."

"That won't make it any less real."

"Maybe not, but putting it out of my mind might make this night a little more palatable." Even though her thoughts kept wandering to what her evening would have been like if Wynn was with her tonight.

And just as if she'd conjured him up, Wynn was walking toward her from across the ballroom. Giana blinked several times, because she was wondering if she was dreaming. But when she opened her eyes and he winked at her, she knew she wasn't.

Wynn was immaculately dressed in a black tuxedo with a red tie. His hair appeared freshly cut and his beard freshly groomed. He looked mouthwatering.

"What are you doing here?" Giana asked.

"Can we talk?" Wynn asked.

"Talk?" Giana snorted. "I think you said enough yesterday, don't you think?"

"Giana, please…"

"What's going on over here?" Out the corner of her eye, Giana saw Julian charging toward Wynn, with Roman close on her brother's heels. But before they could get close enough to cause Wynn bodily harm, Xavier stepped in their path.

Giana was shocked. *What was going on?* She looked at Xavier, who was as cool as a cucumber. Wasn't he as angry with Wynn as the rest of her brothers?

"Step aside, Xavier," Julian said.

"No can do." Xavier shook his head. "Giana and Wynn need to talk."

"Says who?" Roman asked, taking a dangerous step toward Wynn. But Wynn didn't move. He seemed determined to accept whatever was coming his way, as if it were his due.

"I say." Xavier's voice boomed out.

Julian and Roman stared at each another in confusion.

"Listen, after Wynn and Giana speak, if she still wants him to go, I'll be more than happy to throw him out." Xavier glanced at Wynn. "Sorry, but bros come first."

"Understood," Wynn stated. Then he turned to Giana. "Can we talk in private?"

Giana glanced at Xavier, Julian and Roman, then back to Wynn. The pleading look in his eyes won her over. "All right. There's a room in the back. Let's go." She took off, not looking behind her to see if he followed.

Once they were inside the empty room, she spun around to face him. "So, what do you want, Wynn? To take more potshots at me? To demean my character further? Because you already did a bang-up job."

Wynn shook his head. "I don't want to do that, Giana. I came here to apologize."

"Apologize?" Giana croaked.

"Yes." Wynn moved toward her, but Giana swiftly took a few steps back. She hadn't been prepared for this.

"Why?"

"I misjudged you. I treated you unfairly. I believed the worst when you never gave me any reason to doubt your affection for me. And I'm terribly sorry, Giana." His eyes brimmed with tenderness and passion.

"You hurt me, Wynn."

"I know. And I deserve your scorn. But if you will hear me out, I'd like to explain."

Giana folded her arms across her chest. "Very well."

"I've talked to you about my divorce from Christine, but I didn't tell you what my mistrust really stems from."

"Go on."

"Having my mother walk out on me when I was young affected me. She left me and my dad for another man to live her life without us, without me. Do you have any idea how that made me feel?" Giana shook her head. "I'll tell you. I felt unloved and unwanted."

"But you had your dad."

"My father was a broken man. Losing my mother devastated him. He wasn't able to recover from a failed marriage and losing the house he'd bought for her and all the hopes and dreams that came with it. He checked out on me, Giana. It's why I turned to the Boys & Girls Club, because I was desperate for someone to care. And I found that person in my mentor, Les. I wish you could have met him. He was a fantastic guy. Anyway, as the years went by, I hardened my heart and became angrier and angrier at my mother for her betrayal. At one time, I didn't think any woman could be trusted, and then I met Christine."

"And you fell in love." She didn't need to hear him wax lyrical about another woman.

"In lust was more like it," Wynn said. "Looking back, I realize we didn't share the same values or want the same things out of life. I was enamored with a pretty face and so when she too left me for another man, it only proved my theory that all women were evil. And so, like my father, I shut down, closing myself off from the rest of the world for years. I didn't date other women. I focused on my work and became more determined than ever to become a success so no one could take my joy again."

"Wynn, that's a lonely existence."

Wynn nodded. "I didn't even want to acknowledge that side of myself, because I was afraid. Afraid of allowing someone in. But then you came along, pushing through the barriers I'd erected around myself. You were relentless, never taking no for an answer, and when I met you, I was blown away by your beauty and your fierce spirit, too. It's why I didn't want to let you go."

"I thought it was just about sex."

"Oh, the sex has been off the charts, but Giana, for the first time, I was laughing and talking and sharing my life with someone—with you. You were like a breath of fresh air I didn't know I needed. And I fell for you. I fell hard."

"No." A tear slid down her cheek. "Don't say that, because you don't really mean it."

"It's true, baby," Wynn said, moving closer until he was just inches away and could cup her cheeks in his large palms. "It's why it hurt so much when I thought you betrayed me."

"How could you believe that when I've always been on your side? Team Wynn all the way."

"I know, and I'm sorry, Giana. I was a fool," Wynn said. "I meant it when I told your father and brothers that I would never want to hurt you. I love you, Giana. I think I have from the moment I saw you at the boxing ring, and I've been falling deeper and deeper in love with you each day."

Giana lowered her head as tears streamed down her face.

"I know I don't have the right to ask you this, but I'm going to. Forgive me, please. Give me another chance to be the man you want, the man you deserve." Wynn lowered himself to one knee and, reaching inside his tuxedo jacket, produced a ring box. "Be my wife, Giana."

Wynn looked up into Giana's beautiful brown eyes and prayed she would give them a chance to have their happily-ever-after.

Giana was sobbing, so he asked, "Did you hear me?"

She nodded. "I love you, too, Wynn. I think I knew after the first time we made love. I was so overwhelmed by the intensity of my feelings for you. It frightened me and I had to leave."

"I assumed you were running scared because you'd crossed a professional line."

"That, too," Giana said. "I'd never been as intimate with another man like I was with you. I laid it all on the line, Wynn—sharing my hopes, fears and my family with you, and that was scary for me, because I had my life planned out, with my career coming first. But meeting you changed that. Changed me." She stepped away from him. "But sometimes love isn't enough. It's about trust, Wynn. And I'm not sure you trust me. Or that I can trust you with my heart."

"I do trust you, Giana," Wynn said, rising to his feet. "I admit I was momentarily blindsided because of my fear. I've always thought I wasn't good enough or worthy of love because every woman I've loved or thought I loved left me."

"You are worthy, Wynn. And I would never leave you."

He smiled. "I've let my fear of being unwanted and unloved rule me for too long, but no more." Wynn was not going to let his past determine his future. He wanted a life with Giana, and he was going to fight for it. "Tell me it's not too late, Giana. Can you find it in your heart to forgive me?"

Giana was quiet for several beats, and Wynn thought that it was over, that he'd ruined the best thing that had ever happened to him. But then she surprised him. "I can and I do forgive you, Wynn." She smiled through her tears.

"You do?" Wynn furiously kissed her nose and wet

cheeks and placed his forehead on hers. "Your capacity for forgiveness humbles me, Giana."

"That's because you haven't known the kind of love in your life that I've known in mine," Giana responded, reaching upward to stroke his cheek. "But I want that for you, Wynn. For us. I want a life with you. I want marriage and babies. I want the whole thing!"

Wynn whooped loudly and picked Giana up, twirling her in his arms before eventually setting her back on her feet and placing the six-carat cushion-cut halo diamond ring on her finger. "But we don't have to start a family right away. Whenever you're ready and you feel like you've accomplished all your goals, Giana, only then."

Seconds later, he heard the crowd in the ballroom counting down. "Ten, nine, eight, seven…"

Giana circled her arms around Wynn's neck and pulled him into a searing kiss just as the clock struck midnight. "Don't you get it, silly? I've accomplished the greatest thing in my life, and that was finding true love with you."

Epilogue

Two months later

"I can't believe Xavier got *the* Porscha Childs to sing at our engagement party," Giana gushed to Wynn after the popular R&B songstress belted out one of Giana's favorite love songs. The entire family was gathered in the great room at the Lockett mansion, where a small stage had been erected for Porscha.

"Neither can I," Wynn said. "She's amazing. As are you, my love." He swept his lips over hers.

Giana still couldn't believe she was engaged to be married. When they'd come out into the ballroom on New Year's Eve, all smiles, with Giana sporting a huge rock, her family had cheered with delight. And her mother had whispered in Giana's ear, "I told you so."

Her mother's only request had been for Giana to have a long enough engagement so she could plan a proper wedding, since she claimed she'd been thwarted by her older sons' swift marriages. Giana and Wynn had agreed. The extra time would allow Giana to become familiar with her new position as CEO of the Atlanta Cougars. She'd been thrilled when Roman chose her as his second in command.

Meanwhile, Wynn's new sports drink would be coming out in the summer. The first ad would feature Curtis and his dad and other single fathers with their sons. Giana was proud of Wynn, but even more so because he'd gone into therapy to deal with his trust and abandonment issues. Eventually, she hoped he would make peace with his mother, but in the meantime, he was taking steps to heal old wounds.

"So, what did you guys think of Porscha?" Xavier asked with a big grin as he walked toward them.

"You did good, Xavier," Wynn said, shaking his hand.

"Anything for my big sis." He leaned in to give Giana a bear hug. "Now, if you'll excuse me, I'm going to go see if I can get an autograph." And then her wayward brother was rushing off toward the stage.

Giana watched him and Porscha. It might not be discernible to most, but they seemed awfully familiar with one another. She glanced up at Wynn. "Do you..." She paused. "Do you think Porscha is the girl Xavier's been secretly dating?"

Wynn shrugged. "Anything's possible. I mean, look at us. You were a career woman who wasn't looking for love and marriage, and I'd vowed never to commit again. Yet here we are."

"We were struck by Cupid's arrow," Giana said with a smile, turning to her fiancé. Her heart was full of love and joy. "I hope one day Xavier meets the woman who will make him believe in happily-ever-after like I do." She brushed her lips across Wynn's.

"And I want to thank you for taking a chance on me, Giana. I love you."

"And I love you." Giana stood on her tippy toes to bring Wynn's head down to hers in a kiss for the ages. "I'm so glad we got locked in that elevator, because that one kiss in the dark changed my life forever."

* * * * *

COMING SOON!

We really hope you enjoyed reading this book. If you're looking for more romance, be sure to head to the shops when new books are available on

Thursday 1st December

To see which titles are coming soon, please visit

millsandboon.co.uk/nextmonth

MILLS & BOON

MILLS & BOON

THE HEART OF ROMANCE

A ROMANCE FOR EVERY READER

MODERN Prepare to be swept off your feet by sophisticated, sexy and seductive heroes, in some of the world's most glamourous and romantic locations, where power and passion collide.

HISTORICAL Escape with historical heroes from time gone by. Whether your passion is for wicked Regency Rakes, muscled Vikings or rugged Highlanders, awak the romance of the past.

MEDICAL Set your pulse racing with dedicated, delectable doctors in the high-pressure world of medicine, where emotions run high and passion, comfort an love are the best medicine.

True Love Celebrate true love with tender stories of heartfelt romance, from the rush of falling in love to the joy a new baby can bring, and a focus on the emotional heart of a relationship.

Desire Indulge in secrets and scandal, intense drama and plenty of sizzling hot action with powerful and passionate heroes who have it all: wealth, status, good looks…everything but the right woman.

HEROES Experience all the excitement of a gripping thriller, with an intense romance at its heart. Resourceful, true-to-life women and strong, fearless me face danger and desire - a killer combination!

To see which titles are coming soon, please visit

millsandboon.co.uk/nextmonth

Unlimited access to all your favourite Mills & Boon romances!

Start your free trial now

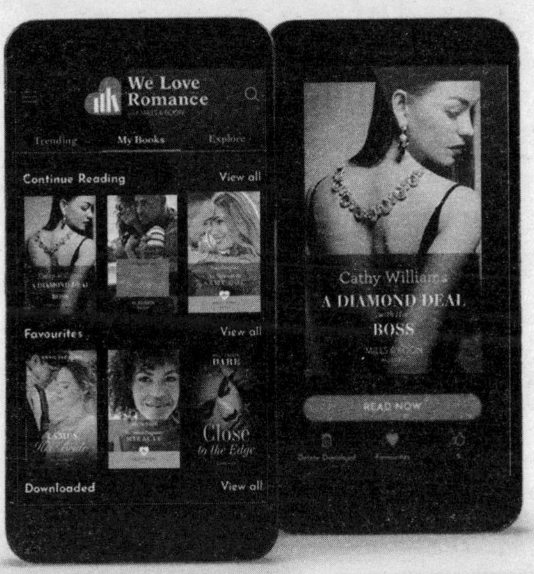

Available at

weloveromance.com

LET'S TALK

Romance

For exclusive extracts, competitions and special offers, find us online:

facebook.com/millsandboon

@MillsandBoon

@MillsandBoonUK

Get in touch on 01413 063232

For all the latest titles coming soon, visit

millsandboon.co.uk/nextmonth

MILLS & BOON
A ROMANCE FOR EVERY READER

- **FREE** delivery direct to your door
- **EXCLUSIVE** offers every month
- **SAVE** up to 25% on pre-paid subscriptions

SUBSCRIBE AND SAVE

millsandboon.co.uk/Subscribe

WANT EVEN MORE

ROMANCE?

SUBSCRIBE AND SAVE TODAY!

'Mills & Boon books, the perfect way to escape for an hour or so.'

MISS W. DYER

'Excellent service, promptly delivered and very good subscription choices.'

MISS A. PEARSON

'You get fantastic special offers and the chance to get books before they hit the shops.'

MRS V. HALL

Visit millsandboon.co.uk/Subscribe and save on brand new books.

JOIN THE MILLS & BOON BOOKCLUB

- **FREE** delivery direct to your door
- **EXCLUSIVE** offers every month
- **EXCITING** rewards programme

Join today at

Millsandboon.co.uk/Bookclub

JOIN US ON SOCIAL MEDIA!

Stay up to date with our latest releases, author news and gossip, special offers and discounts, and all the behind-the-scenes action from Mills & Boon...

millsandboon

millsandboonuk

millsandboon

It might just be true love...

GET YOUR ROMANCE FIX!

MILLS & BOON
— *blog* —

Get the latest romance news, exclusive author interviews, story extracts and much more!

blog.millsandboon.co.uk

MILLS & BOON

Desire

Indulge in secrets and scandal, intense drama and plenty of sizzling hot action with powerful and passionate heroes who have it all: wealth, status, good looks…everything but the right woman.

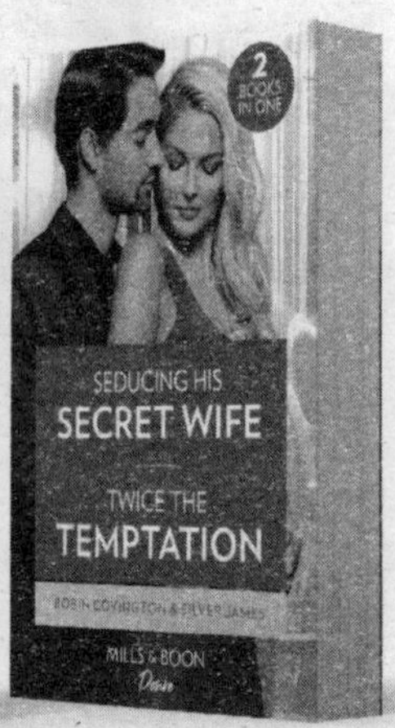

Four Desire stories published every month, find them all at:

millsandboon.co.uk

MILLS & BOON

MODERN

Power and Passion

Prepare to be swept off your feet by sophisticated, sexy and seductive heroes, in some of the world's most glamourous and romantic locations, where power and passion collide.

ight Modern stories published every month, find them all at:

millsandboon.co.uk/Modern

MILLS & BOON
MEDICAL
Pulse-Racing Passion

Set your pulse racing with dedicated, delectable doctors in the high-pressure world of medicine, where emotions run high and passion, comfort and love are the best medicine.

Eight Medical stories published every month, find them all at

millsandboon.co.uk

MILLS & BOON

True Love

Romance from the Heart

Celebrate true love with tender stories of heartfelt romance, from the rush of falling in love to the joy a new baby can bring, and a focus on the emotional heart of a relationship.

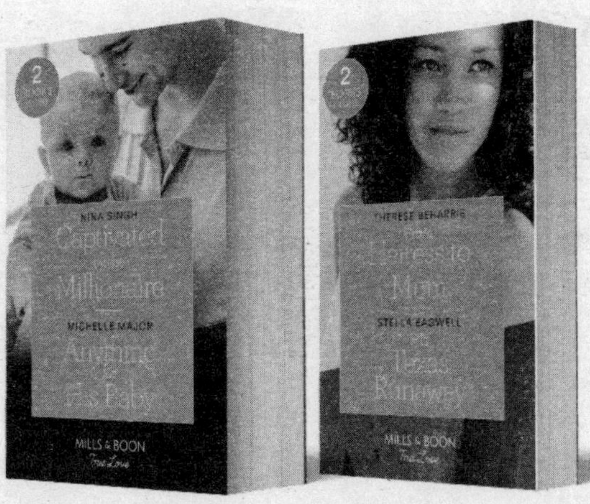

Four True Love stories published every month, find them all at:

millsandboon.co.uk/TrueLove